Anonymous

The Housekeeper's Companion

A Practical Receipt Book and Household Physician

Anonymous

The Housekeeper's Companion
A Practical Receipt Book and Household Physician

ISBN/EAN: 9783337404505

Printed in Europe, USA, Canada, Australia, Japan

Cover: Foto ©Andreas Hilbeck / pixelio.de

More available books at **www.hansebooks.com**

THE HOUSEHOLD PET.

THE

Housekeeper's Companion.

A

PRACTICAL RECEIPT BOOK

AND

HOUSEHOLD PHYSICIAN,

WITH MUCH OTHER VALUABLE INFORMATION.

The whole forming a complete Hand-Book of Reference for Housewives and Mothers.

————

CONTENTS.

INDEX.

INDEX.

INDEX.

INDEX.

INDEX.

INDEX.

INDEX

INDEX.

INDEX.

COASTING.

ETIQUETTE.

Outdoor Etiquette.—When three ladies are walking together, it is better for one to keep a little in advance of the other two, than for all three to persist in maintaining one unbroken line. They cannot all join in conversation without talking across each other—a thing that in-doors or out-of-doors, is awkward, inconvenient, ungenteel, and should always be avoided. Also, three ladies walking abreast occupy too much of the pavement, and, therefore, incommode the other passengers. If you meet a lady with whom you have become but slightly acquainted, and had merely a little conversation (for instance, at a party or a morning visit), and who moves in a circle somewhat higher or more fashionable than your own, it is proper to wait till she recognizes you. Let her not see in you a disposition to obtrude yourself on her notice.

It is not expected that all intimacies formed at watering-places should continue after the parties have returned to their homes. A mutual bow when meeting in the street is sufficient; but there is no interchanging of visits unless ladies have, before parting, testified a desire to continue the acquaintance. In this case the lady who is the senior, or palpably highest in station, makes the first call. It is not customary for a young lady to make the first visit to a married lady.

When meeting them in the street, always speak first to your milliner, mantua-maker, seamstress, or to any one you have been in the habit of employing. To pass without notice servants whom you know is rude and unfeeling, and they will attribute it to pride, not presuming to speak to you themselves unless in reply. There are persons who, having accepted, when in the country, much kindness from the country people, are

2

ashamed to recognize them when they come to town on account of their rustic or unfashionable attire. This is vulgar
and contemptible, and is always seen through and despised.
Those to be avoided are such as wear tawdry finery, paint
their faces and leer, looking graceless, even if they are not dis-
reputable in reality. When meeting a gentleman whom a lady
has no objection to numbering among her acquaintances, she
denotes it by bowing first. If she has any reason to dissap-
prove of his character or habits, she is perfectly justified in
"cutting" him, as it is termed. Let her bow very coldly the
first time, and, after that, not at all. When a lady is walking
between two gentlemen she should divide her conversation as
euqally as practicable, or address most of it to the greater
stranger to her. He to whom she is least on ceremony will
excuse her. If you stop a few minutes in the street to talk to
an acquaintance, draw to one side of the pavement, near the
wall, so as not to impede the passengers, or you may turn and
walk with her as far as the next corner. And never stop to
talk in the middle of a crossing. To speak loudly in the street
is unladylike, and to call across the way to an acquaintance is
in execrable taste. It is best to hasten over and speak to her
if you have anything of importance to say.

When a stranger offers to assist you over a puddle, or something of the kind, do not hesitate or decline as if you thought
he was taking an unwarrantable liberty. He means nothing
but civility; so accept it frankly, and thank him for it.

On being escorted home by a gentleman, a lady expects he
will not leave her till he has rung the bell, and waited until she
is actually in the house, although it has been thought sufficient,
by men who know no better, to walk with her to the foot of
the steps, and then take their departure, leaving her to get in
as she can.

Places of Amusement.—To secure a good seat at any place
of amusement go early. It is better to sit an hour before the
performance begins than to arrive after it has commenced.
The time of waiting will soon pass away in conversation with
the friends whom you have accompanied. When practicable,
leave hats and cloaks in the apartment set apart for them.

When invited to join a party begin to prepare in ample

time, so as not to keep them waiting for you. When a large party is going to a place of amusement (for instance, the theatre or opera) it is better that each family should go thither from their own home (being provided with their own tickets), than that they should all rendezvous at the house of one of the company, at the risk of keeping the whole party waiting perhaps for the very youngest members of it. When a box has been taken, let the tickets be sent to all the persons who are to have seats in it, and not retained by the taker of the box till the whole party have assembled at the door of the theatre. If the tickets are thus distributed, the persons from each house can go when they please without compelling any of the party to wait for them.

To make an entrance after the performance has begun is (or ought to be) very embarrasing to ladies. It excites the attention of all around, diverting attention from the performance; and there is always, when the house is full and the hour late, some delay and difficulty in reaching the seats even when they have been engaged.

If it is a concert, where places cannot be previously secured, there are of course additional reasons for going in due time, and the most sensible and best behaved part of the audience always endeavor to do so. But if you are unavoidably late, be satisfied to pay the penalty by quietly taking back seats, if no others are vacant. Young ladies arriving after the performance had commenced, have been seen walking boldly up to the front benches and standing there, looking steadfastly in the faces of gentlemen who, with their parties, had earned good seats by coming soon after the doors were opened. The ladies persevered in this determined stare till they succeeded in disloging these unfortunate gentlemen, and compelling them to quit their seats, to leave the ladies of their party, and stand for the remainder of the evening in a distant part of the room.

To laugh deridingly or to whisper unfavorable remarks, during the performance of a concert or a play is a rudeness of which no lady is guilty. Occasionally are seen some of that few who, much to the annoyance of those persons near them who really wish to enjoy what they came for, talk audibly in ridicule of the performers, the performers being, in all probability, near enough to hear these vexatious remarks, and to be disconcerted by them. It is also a gross breach of good breeding to anticipate the "good things," or destroy the interest of others in the plot of the piece, by stating what you may know of either, to those near you.

At Church.—Ladies should endeavor always to be in their pews before the service begins, and when the benediction is finished take their departure quietly, without any hurry or bustle. If you go into a church where you are a stranger, wait in the vestibule until you see the sexton, and then request him to show you a vacant seat. This is better than to wander about the aisles alone, or to intrude yourself into a pew where you may cause inconvenience to its owners. If you see that a pew is full you know of course that you cannot obtain a seat in it without dislodging somebody. If a family invites you to go to church with them or to come thither, and to have a seat in their pew, do not take the liberty of asking a friend of your own to accompany you; and, above all, do not bring a child with you. Should you (having a pew of your own) ask another lady to go with you, call for her in due time, and she ought to be quite ready. Place her in a corner seat (it being the most comfortable), and see that she is accommodated with a footstool; and be assiduous in finding the places for her in the prayer book or hymn book.

In visiting a church of a different denomination from your own, comply as far as you can with all the ceremonies observed by the congregation, particularly if you are in a foreign country. Even if some of the observances are not the least in conformity with your own opinions and feelings, remember that you are there as a guest and have no right to offend or displease your hosts by evincing a marked disapprobation of their mode of worship. If you find it very irksome to refrain (which it should not be) you need not go a second time.

Young ladies who, on their way to church, laugh and talk loudly with their escort, are, to say the least, guilty of a serious indiscretion. It is too probable that their escort will occupy a large share of their thoughts during the hours of worship. Nay, there are some so irreverent and so regardless of the sanctity of the place as to indulge in frequent whispers to those near them, or to their friends in adjoining pews.

Visiting.—A lady is said to have the *entree* of her friend's room when she is allowed or assumes the privilege of entering it familiarly at all times, and without any previous intimation— a privilege too often abused. In many cases the visited person has never really granted the privilege (and after growing wise by experience she rarely will), but the visitor, assuming that she herself must under all circumstances be welcome, carries her sociability so far as to become troublesome and inconvenient.

There are few occasions on which it is proper, on entering a house, to run directly to the chamber of your friend, and to enter the room without knocking, or the very instant after knocking, before she has time to desire you to enter or to make the slightest arrangement for your reception. You may find her washing or dressing, or even engaged in repairing clothes —or the room may be in great disorder, or the chambermaid in the act of cleaning it. No one likes unseasonable interruptions, even from a very dear friend.

A familiar visit will always begin more pleasantly if the visitor inquires of the servant at the door if the lady she wishes to see is at home, and then goes into the parlor and stays there until she has sent her name, and ascertained that she can be received upstairs. Then, and not till then, let her go to her friend's room, taking care to knock before entering.

It is extremely rude, on being admitted to a private apartment, to look curiously about as if taking an inventory of all that is to be seen. We have known ladies whose eyes were all the time gazing round, and even slily peering under tables, sofas, &c., turning their heads to look after every person who chanced to move about the room, and giving particular attention to whatever seemed to be in disorder or out of place.

Make no remark upon the work in which you find your friend engaged. If she lays it aside, desire her not to leave it because of your presence, but propound no questions concerning it. Do not look over her books, and ask to borrow them. In short, meddle with nothing.

If you are perfectly certain that you really have the *entree* of your friend's room, you have no right to extend that privilege to any other person who may chance to be with you when you go to see her. It is taking an unjustifiable liberty to in-trude a stranger upon the privacy of her chamber. If another lady is with you waive the privilege of *entrее* for that time, take your companion into the parlor, and send up the names of both.

There are certain unoccupied ladies so over-friendly as to take the *entrее* of the whole house. These are generally ultra-neighborly neighbors, who run in at all hours of the day and. evening; ferret out the ladies of the family wherever they may be; watch their proceedings when engaged, like good house-wives, in inspecting the attics, the store rooms, the cellars, or the kitchen. Never for a moment do they seem to suppose that their hourly visits may perhaps be inconvenient or unsea-sonable; or too selfish to abate their frequency even when they suspect them to be so these inveterate sociablists make their in-cursions at all avenues. They are quite domesticated in your house. They see all, hear all, know all your concerns. Their talk to you is chiefly gossip, and, therefore, their talk about you is chiefly the same. They are *au fait* of everything con-cerning your table. They find out everybody that comes to your house; know all your plans for going to this place or that; are well acquainted with every article you wear; are present at the visits of all your friends, and hear all their conversation. Their own is usually "an infinite deal of nothing."

To avoid the danger of being overwhelmed by the sociabil-ity of an idle neighbor, discourage the first indications of undue intimacy by making your own visits rather few and far be-tween. A young lady of good sense and of proper self-respect will never be too lavish of her society; and, if she has pleasant neighbors, will visit them always in moderation.

To friends or very intimate acquaintance visits may be left to create their own etiquette, as, in fact, they are left, whatever rules may be laid down. Not to go too frequently to the same house; not to stay too long when you do go; to let no intimacy overstep the bounds of courtesy, are obvious hints. Half an hour amply suffices for a visit of ceremony. The lady may not remove any article of her attire, even if politely requested to do so by the mistress of the house. If, however, your visit is to a particular friend, the case is different; even then, it is best to wait till you are invited to do so.

Favorite dogs are never welcome visitors in a drawing room. Many people have even a dislike to such animals; they require watching lest they should leap upon a chair or sofa, or place themselves on a lady's dress, and attentions of the kind are much out of place. Neither ought a mother, when paying a ceremonial visit, to be accompanied by young children. It is frequently difficult to amuse them, and, if not particularly well trained at home, they naturally seize hold of books or those elegant ornaments with which it is fashionable to decorate the drawing-room. In some families evening calls are allowed. Should you chance to visit such a family, and find that they have a party, present yourself and converse for a few minutes with an unembarrassed air, after which you may retire, unless urged to remain. A slight invitation given for the sake of courtesy ought not to be accepted. Make no apology for your unintentional intrusion; but let it be known, in the course of a few days, that you were not aware that your friends had company.

Morning visits are usually paid between the hours of two and four p. m. in winter, and two and five in summer. The object in view in observing this rule is to avoid intruding before the luncheon is removed, and leave in sufficient time to allow the lady of the house leisure for her dinner toilet.

Should the lady you desire to call upon be from home, leave your card; no message is requisite. If your visit is intended for two persons, leave two cards. Do not turn down the corner of your card; that fashion has now exploded.

When introduced to strangers, bow slightly and enter at once into conversation with them; to bow and take no further notice of them, but to continue your conversation with the lady on whom you are calling, is a great want of good breeding. Visits of congratulation should be short, and must always be made before dinner.

Visits of condolence are to be paid with as little delay as possible after the occurrence that calls them forth. Unless you are very intimate, it is an evidence of better taste to leave a card than to intrude upon private sorrow. Should you be so nearly related as to render a personal visit necessary, take care to appear in a quiet dress, and, if the occasion be the death of a person even slightly related to you, go in mourning—deep or otherwise, according to the degree of relationship. It is considered in good taste for ladies to make their calls in black silk or plain colored apparel. It denotes that they sympathize with the afflictions of the family, and such attentions are always pleasing.

Cards must be left on all occasions of a formal character. A lady leaves her own, and two of her husband's—one is intended for the gentleman of the house, and one for the lady. The names of the lady's daughters are often printed on the same card with the name of their mother, and when such a card is left, it implies that mother and daughters have called.

When you arrive in town it is proper to call and leave your card, as an intimation that you are in the neighborhood, thus acting the reverse of what is considered polite when in the country, where the rule is that the stranger wait until called upon.

If the cards are left preparatory to leaving town, the initials P. P. C. (*pour prendre congé*) should be written in pencil on the corner of them.

Cards sent during the illness of a member of a family should be accompanied by verbal inquiries as to the patient's state. Upon the birth of a child, cards may be sent twice or thrice a week for two weeks. Cards may be left or sent the day after a ball. After a dinner party, cards should be left within a week.

A lady's card should be thin and not glazed. Some people omit the prefix "Miss" to their names on the card. This is an affectation of simplicity which takes away all appearance of that quality. It is a thing unknown in English society; though the fashion on the Continent, for a lady to have only her Christian name and her surname on the card.

THE VISITED.—Having invited a friend to pass a few days or weeks at your house, and expecting her at a certain time, meet her on arrival, or, if that be impracticable, send a servant to secure a conveyance and attend to her luggage. It is to be supposed that before her arrival you have inspected the chamber of your guest, to see that none of the articles that are in all genteel and well-furnished houses are wanting—that there are two ewers of fresh water on the stand, and three towels on the rail (two fine and one coarse), a foot-bath, and other requisites. On the mantel-piece a candle or lamp, with a box of lucifer matches beside it—the candle to be replaced by a new one every morning when the chamber-maid arranges the room, or the lamp to be trimmed daily; so that the visitor may have a light at hand whenever she pleases, without ringing the bell and waiting till a servant brings one up.

The room should have an easy chair with a foot cushion before it; a low chair also, to sit on when shoes and stockings are to be changed, &c.

Let the centre table be furnished with a writing-desk, well supplied with all that is necessary; also some books, such as you think your friend would like. Let her find, at least, one bureau vacant, all the drawers empty, so that she may be able to unpack her muslins, &c., and arrange them at once.

Arriving at your house, have your guest's baggage taken at once to the apartment prepared for her, and, when she goes upstairs, send a servant with her to unstrap her trunks. Then let her be left alone to arrange her dress.

Every morning after the chamber-maid has done her duty (the room of the visitor is the first to be put in order), the hostess should go in to see that all is right. This done, no further inspection is necessary. It is very kind and considerate to inquire of your guest if there is any dish or article of food that she particularly likes, so that you may have it on the table while she stays, and, also, if there is anything peculiarly disagreeable to her, so that you may refrain from having it during her visit.

For such deficiencies as may be avoided or remedied, refrain from making the absurd apology that you consider her "no stranger," and that you regard her "just as one of the family." If you invite her at all, it is your duty for your own sake as well as hers to treat her well in everything.

If she desires to assist you in sewing, and has brought no work of her own, you may avail yourself of the offer, and employ her in moderation—but let it be in moderation only, and when sitting in the family circle. When alone in her own room she, of course, would much rather read, write, or occupy herself in some way for her own benefit or amusement.

Let the children be strictly forbidden to run into the apartments of visitors; interdict them from going thither unless sent with a message, and then let them be made to understand that they are always to knock at the door, and not go in until desired to do so. Also that they are not to play and make a noise in the neighborhood of her room. And when she comes into the parlor, that they are not to jump on her lap, put their hands into her pockets, or rummage her work-basket, or rumple and soil her dress by clinging to it with their hands. Neither should they be permitted to amuse themselves by rattling on the lower keys when she is playing on the piano, or interrupt her by teasing her all the time to play "for them to dance." To permit children to ask visitors for pennies or sixpences is mean and contemptible. And if money is given them by a guest, they should be made to return it immediately.

Inquire on the first evening if your visitor is accustomed to taking any refreshment before she retires for the night. If she is, have something sent up to her room every night, unless your own family are in the same habit. These little repasts are very pleasant, especially at the close of a long winter evening, and after coming home from a place of public amusement.

To "welcome the coming—speed the parting guest"—is a good maxim. So, when your visitor is about to leave you, make all smooth and ready for her departure. Let her be called up at an early hour, if she is to set out in the morning. Send a servant up to strap and bring down her trunks, as soon as she has announced that 'they are ready; and see that an early breakfast is prepared for her, and some of the family up and dressed to share it with her. Have a cab or carriage at the door in due time, and let some male member of the family accompany her to the starting place, and see her off, attending to her baggage and procuring tickets.

VISITORS.—When you have invited a friend to take tea with you endeavor to render her visit as agreeable as you can; and try by all means to make her comfortable.

The servant who attends the door should be instructed to show the guest upstairs as soon as she arrives, conducting her to an unoccupied apartment, where she may take off her bonnet and arrange her hair, or any part of her dress that may require change and improvement. The lady should then be left to herself. Nothing is polite that can possibly incommode or embarrass—therefore it is a mistaken civility for the hostess, or some female member of the family, to follow the visitor upstairs, and remain with her all the time she is preparing for her appearance in the parlor. Over officiousness is not politeness, and nothing troublesome and inconvenient is ever agreeable.

The toilet-table should be always well furnished with a clean hair brush and a nice comb; a hand-mirror of sufficient size to afford a glimpse of the back of the head and neck. A small work-box, properly furnished with needles, scissors, thimble and thread, ought to find a place on the dressing table, in case the visitor may have occasion to repair any accident that may have happened to her dress.

The hostess should be in the parlor prepared to receive her visitor, and to give her at once a seat in the corner of a sofa, or on a fauteuil, or large comfortable chair; if a rocking-chair, a footstool is an indispensable appendage. But rocking-chairs are now seldom seen in a parlor; handsome, stuffed easy chairs that are moved on castors are substituted.

If in consequence of dining very late you are in the habit of also taking tea at a late hour—or making but slight preparations for that repast—waive that custom when you expect a friend whom you know to be in the practice of dining early, and who, perhaps, has walked far enough to feel fatigued and to acquire an appetite. For her accommodation order the tea earlier than usual, and let it be what may be called a substantial tea. If there is ample room at table, do not have the tea carried round, particularly if you have but one servant to hand the whole. It is tedious, inconvenient, and unsatisfactory. The absurd practice of eating in gloves has been wisely abolished among genteel people.

Do not, in sitting down to table, inform your guest that "you make no stranger of her," or that you fear she will not be able to enjoy your "plain fare." These apologies are ungenteel and foolish. If your circumstances will not allow you on any consideration to make a little improvement in your usual family fare, your friend is, in all probability, aware of the fact, and will not wish or expect you to incur any inconvenient expense on her account. But, if you are known to possess the means of living well, you ought to do so; and to consider a good though not an extravagantly luxurious table as a necessary part of your expenditure. There is a vast difference between laudable economy and mean economy; the latter (whether it shows itself in bad food, bad fires, bad lights, bad servants) is never excused in persons who dress extravagantly and live surrounded by costly furniture, and who are known to be wealthy and able to afford comfort as well as show.

If you invite a friend to tea in whose own family there is no gentleman or no man-servant, it is your dnty previously to ascertain that you can provide her on that evening with an escort home. If you keep a carriage, it will be most kind to send her home in it.

In inviting a few friends, which means a small, select company, endeavor to bring together people who have community of tastes, feelings and ideas. If you mix the dull and stupid with the bright and animated, the cold and formal with the frank and lively, the professedly serious with the gay and cheerful, the light with the heavy, and, above all, those who pride themselves on their birth with those who boast of "belonging to the people;" none of these "few friends" will enjoy each other's society—the evening will not go off agreeably, and you, and the other members of your family, will have the worst of it. The pleasantest people in the room will naturally congregate together, and the task of entertaining the unentertainable will devolve on yourself and your own people.

If a friend makes an afternoon call, and you wish her to stay and take tea, invite her to do so at once, as soon as she has sat down, and do not wait until she has risen to depart. Should chance visitors come in before the family have gone to tea, let them at once be invited to partake of that repast, which they will, of course, decline, if they have had tea already. In a well-provided house there can be no difficulty in adding something to the family tea table, which, in genteel life, should never be discreditably parsimonious. It is a very mean practice for the members of the family to slip out of the parlor one by one at a time and steal into an adjoining room to avoid in-

viting their visitor to accompany them. How much better to
meet the inconvenience by conducting your accidental guest to
the table, unless she says she has already taken tea, and will
amuse herself with a book while the family are at theirs.

Casual evening visitors should avoid staying too late. Ten
o'clock is the usual time to depart, or at least to prepare for
doing so. If the visit is unduly prolonged, there may be evi-
dent signs of irrepressible drowsiness in the heads of the family, which, when perceived, will annoy the guest, who must then
feel that she has stayed too long.

If you are engaged to take tea with an intimate friend, who
assures you that you will see none but the family, and you
afterwards receive an invitation to join a party to a place of
amusement, which you have long been desirous of, visiting, you
may retract your first engagement, provided you send an apology in due time, telling the exact truth, and telling it in polite
terms. Your intimate friend will take no offence, considering
it perfectly natural that you should prefer the concert, the play,
or the exhibition, to a quiet evening passed at her house with
no other guests. But take care to let her know as early as possible. And be careful not to disappoint her again in a similar
manner.

Obligations to Gentlemen.—In her intercourse with gentlemen a lady should take care to avoid all pecuniary obligation.
The civility which a gentleman conventionally owes to a lady
is a sufficient tax—more she has no right to expect or accept.
A man of good sense and of true politeness will not be offended
at her unwillingness to become his debtor. On the contrary,
he will respect her delicacy and approve her dignity, and consent at once to her becoming her own banker on all occasions
where expense is to be incurred.

When invited to join a party to a place of amusement, let
her consent, if she wishes; but let her state expressly that it is
only on condition of being permitted to pay for her own ticket.
If she steadily adheres to this custom it will soon be understood that such is always her commendable practice; and she
can then, with perfect propriety, at any time, ask for a seat
among friends who intend going. To this accommodation she
could not invite herself if in the continual habit of visiting pub-

lic places at the expense of others. The best time for a lady to pay for herself is to put her money into the hand of the gentleman previous to their departure for the place of performance. He will not be so rude as to refuse it. If he does refuse, she should evince her resentment by going with him no more.

We disapprove of ladies going to charity fairs in the evening, when they require a male escort, and when that escort is likely to be drawn into paying exorbitant prices for gifts to his fair companion—particularly if induced to do so from the fear of appearing mean or of being thought wanting in benevolence. In the evening the young ladies who "have tables" are apt to become especially importunate in urging the sale of their goods, and appear to great disadvantage as amateur shop-keepers, exhibiting a boldness in teasing that no real shop-woman would presume to display. Then the crowd is generally great; the squeezing and pushing very uncomfortable; and most of the company far from genteel. Ladies who are ladies should only visit fancy fairs in the day time, when they can go without gentlemen, none of whom take much pleasure in this mode of raising money, or rather of levying contributions for special purposes.

If you have occasion to send by a gentleman a parcel to a carrier's or railway office give him, along with it, the money to pay for its carriage. If you borrow change, return it to him punctually. He ought to take it as a thing of course, without any comment. When you commission him to buy anything for you, if you know the price, give him the money beforehand; otherwise, pay it as soon as he brings the article.

When visiting a fancy shop with a gentleman, refrain from excessively admiring any handsome or expensive article you may chance to see there; above all, express no wish that you were able to buy it, and to regret that you cannot, lest he should construe these extreme tokens of admiration into hints that you wish him to buy it for you. To allow him to do so would, on your part, be very mean and indelicate, and on his very foolish.

It ought to be a very painful office for young ladies to go round soliciting from gentlemen subscriptions for charitable purposes. Still it is done. Subscription papers should only be offered by persons somewhat advanced in life and of undoubted respectability; and then the application should be made exclusively to those whose circumstances are known to be affluent. When you ask money for a charitable purpose, do so only when quite alone with the person to whom you apply. It is taking an undue advantage to make the request in the presence of others, particularly if there is not wealth as well as benevolence. There is a time for all things, and young ladies are deservedly unpopular when, even in the cause of charity, they seize every opportunity to levy contributions on the purses of gentlemen.

It is wrong to trouble gentlemen with commissions that may cause them inconvenience and expense. We repeat that a lady cannot be too particular in placing herself under obligations to a gentleman. She should scrupulously avoid it in every little thing that may involve him in expense on her account; and he will respect her the more.

Presents.—Having accepted a present, it is your duty, and ought to be your pleasure, to let the giver see that you make use of it, as intended, and that it is not thrown away upon you. If it is an article of dress or of personal decoration, take occasion, on the first suitable opportunity, to wear it in presence of the giver. If an ornament for the centre table or the mantelpiece, place it there. If a book, do not delay reading it. Afterwards, speak of it to her as favorably as you can. If of fruit or flowers, refer to them the next time you see her.

In all cases when a gift is sent to you return a note of thanks, or at least a verbal message to that effect.

Never inquire of the giver what was the price of her gift, or where she bought it. To do so is considered extremely rude.

When an article is presented to you for a specified purpose, it is your duty to use it for that purpose and for no other, according to the wish of the donor. It is mean and dishonorable to give away a present—at least without obtaining permission from the original giver. You have no right to be liberal and generous at the expense of another, or to accept a gift with a secret determination to bestow it yourself on somebody else. If it is an article that you do not want—that you possess already, or that you cannot use for yourself, it is best to say so candidly, at once expressing your thanks for the offer, and requesting your friend to keep it for some other person to whom it will be advantageous.

It is fit that the purchaser of the gift should have the pleasure of doing a kindness with her own hand, and eliciting the gratitude of one whom she knows herself.

Making a valuable present to a rich person is, in most cases, a work of supererogation, unless the gift is of something rare or unique, which cannot be purchased, and which may be seen and used to more advantage at the house of your friend than while in your possession. But to give an expensive article of dress, jewelery, or furniture, to one whose means of buying such things are quite equal (if not superior) to your own, is an absurdity, though not a very uncommon one, as society is now constituted.

There are persons who, believing that presents are generally made with some mercenary view, and being unwilling themselves to receive favors or incur obligations, make a point of repaying them as soon as possible by a gift of something equivalent. This at once implies that they suspect the motive. If sincere in her friendship, the donor of the first present will feel hurt at being directly paid for it, and consider that she has been treated rudely and unjustly. On the other hand, if compensation was secretly desired and really expected, she will be disappointed at receiving nothing in return. Therefore, among persons who can conveniently provide themselves with whatever they may desire, the bestowal of presents is generally a most unthankful business. If you are in opulent circumstances it is best to limit your generosity to such friends only as do not abound in the gifts of fortune, and whose situation denies them the means of indulging their tastes. By them such acts of kindness will be duly appreciated and gratefully remembered; and the article presented will have a double value if it is to them a novelty.

When a young lady of fortune is going to be married her friends are all expected to present her with bridal gifts. It is a custom that sometimes bears heavily on those whose condition allows them but little to spare. And from that little it may be very hard for them to squeeze out enough to purchase some superfluous ornament, or some article for a centre table, when it is already covered with the gifts of the wealthy—gifts lavished on one who is really in no need of such things, and whose marriage confers no benefit on any one but herself.

When the young couple have not an abundance of the "goods of this world," the case is different; and it may then be an act of real kindness for the opulent friends of the bride to present her with any handsome article of dress or of furniture that they think will be acceptable. What we contend is, that on the occasion of a marriage in a wealthy family the making of presents should be confined to the immediate relatives of the lady, and only to such of them as can well afford it.

At christenings it is, fortunately, the sponsors only that are expected to make gifts to the infant.

The presentation of Christmas and New Year's gifts is often a severe tax on persons with whom money is not plenty. It would be well if it were the universal custom to expect and receive no presents from any but the rich.

In making gifts to children choose for them only such things as will afford them somewhat of lasting amusement. For boys, kites, tops, balls, marbles, wheelbarrows, carts, gardening utensils, and carpenters' tools, &c.

Young ladies should be careful how they accept presents from gentlemen. No truly modest and dignified woman will incur such obligations. And no gentleman who really respects her will offer her anything more than a bouquet, a book, one or two autographs of distinguished persons, or a few relics or mementoes of memorable places—things that derive their chief value from associations. But to present a young lady with articles of jewelry, or of dress, or with a costly ornament, ought to be regarded as an offence rather than a compliment, excusable only in a man sadly ignorant of the refinements of society. And if he is so, she should set him right, and civilly, but firmly, refuse to be his debtor.

In presenting a dress to a friend whose circumstances are not so good as your own, and who you know will gladly receive it, select one of excellent quality, and of a color that you think she will like. She will feel mortified if you give her one that is low-priced, flimsy, and of an unbecoming tint.

3

When you give a dress to a poor woman it is far better to buy for her a substantial new one than to bestow on her an old thin dress of your own. The poor have little time to sew for themselves, and second-hand fine clothes last them but a very short time before they are fit only for the rag-bag.

Dressing for Hotel Dinners.—In dressing for a hotel dinner it is not in good taste to adopt a full evening costume, and to appear as if attired for a ball; for instance, with a colored velvet robe, or one of a splendid brocade, or a transparent gauze material over a satin, or with short sleeves and bare neck in cold weather, or with flowers or jewels in the hair. Such costumes should be reserved for evening parties. If worn at the *table d'hote*, it may be suspected that you have no other place in which to display them. Your dress need not be more showy than you would wear when dining at a private house. There is no place where dress escapes with less scrutiny than at a hotel. Still it is in bad taste to go to the dinner table in ungenteel and unbecoming habiliments, such as a figured or party-colored *mousseline-de-laine*, a thing which has always the effect of calico, and like calico gives an unladylike look even to the most decided lady.

A profusion of jewelry at a public table is in very bad taste, particularly if the jewelry is palpably false; for instance, a brooch with mock diamonds, or a string of wax beads, meant for pearls, or glass things imitating topazes or garnets. A large imitation gem always betrays its real quality by its size.

Endeavor to make your arrangements so as to be dressed for dinner, and seated in the ladies' drawing-room about ten or fifteen minutes before the dining hour, that you may be ready to go in with the rest of the company.

In seating yourself, look down for a moment to see if you have placed the foot of your chair on the dress of the lady sitting next to you; and, if you have done so, remove it instantly, that her dress may not be torn when she attempts to rise.

Sit close to the table, but never lean your elbows upon it. To sit far from it and reach forward is very awkward. Having unfolded your napkin, secure it to your waist by a pin to pre-

vent its slipping down and falling under the table. This may
be done so that the pinning will not be perceptible.

Refrain from loud talking or loud laughing. Young ladies
are never conspicuously noisy at a dinner table or anywhere
else. Still more carefully refrain from whispering or ex-
changing significant glances. Whispers are always overheard,
and glances are always observed.

In the best society, fish is now usually eaten with a silver
fish knife and fork. The method of eating it by the aid of a
piece of bread held in the left hand, while the fork is kept in
the right, is now fast becoming obsolete. Servants and all
other persons should be taught that butter-sauce should not
be poured over the fish, but put on one side of the plate, that
the eater may use it profusely or sparingly, according to taste,
and be enabled to mix it conveniently with the sauce from the
fish-castors.

Do not attempt removing a cover from the dish that you
may help yourself before the rest of the company. Leave all
that to the waiters; tell them what you want in a distinct but
not in a loud, conspicuous voice. Where servants are numerous, they should always go by their surnames, which will prevent the confusion arising from half a dozen Johns or as many
Williams.

If the waiters are attentive, and in sufficient number, you
will have, at a good hotel, little or no occasion to help yourself to anything. Do not under any circumstances reach across
the table, or rise on your feet to get at any particular dish you
may want. Trouble no one of the company; but wait till you
see a servant at hand. If in turning to speak to a waiter you
find him in the act of serving some one else, say, "When you
are at leisure I will thank you for some ——." It is selfish to
be continually sending out of the room the man who waits near
you for the purpose of bringing extra things for yourself; try
to be satisfied with what you find on the table, and recollect
that you are depriving others of his services while you are sending him back and forward on errands to the kitchen.

Many persons hold silver forks awkardly as if not accustomed to them. It is fashionable to use your knife only while
cutting up the food small enough to be eaten with the fork

alóne. While cutting keep your fork in your left hand, the hollow or concáve side downward, the fork in a very slanting pósitión, and your forefinger far down upon its handle. When you have done cutting up what you are going to eat, lay aside your knife, transfer the fork to your right hand, and take a small piece of bread in your left. If eating anything soft, use your silver fork somewhat as a spoon, turning up the hollow side that the cavity may hold the food. If engaged in talking, do not meanwhile hold your fork bold upright, but incline it downward, so as to be nearly on a level with your plate. Remember always to keep your own knife, fork, and spoon out of the dishes. It is an insult to the company, and a disgrace to yourself to dip into a dish anything that has been, even for a moment, in your mouth. To take butter and salt with your own knife is an abomination.

Sometimes these errors are committed out of pure abstraction, and by people who have been accustomed all their lives to good society. We once dined with a professor who actually ate a delicious-looking beef steak pie out of the very dish in which it was brought to table, and was so engaged in giving utterance to his profound learning that he never noticed that he had been guilty of the least impropriety. Fortunately for the company, we remember, there was a fine shoulder of mutton at the other end of the table; so the professor had the pie all to himself. But fits of abstraction are no excuse. Good habits should be so formed, and should so become part of our nature, that we follow them even when the mind is engrossed with other, and it may be more important, affairs.

In eating bread at dinner break off little bits, instead of putting the whole piece in your mouth and biting at it.

No lady looks worse than when gnawing a bone, even of game or poultry. Few ladies do it. In fact, nothing should be sucked or gnawed in public. Always pare apples and peaches, and crack no nuts with the teeth. In eating cherries, put your half-closed hand before your mouth to receive the stones; then lay them on one side of your plate.

Do not eat incongruous and unsuitable things from the same plate, telling the waiter that "he need not change it, as it will do very well."

If a lady wish to eat lobster, let her request the waiter that attends her, to extract a portion of it from the shell, and bring it to her on a clean plate, also to place a castor near her. Novices in lobster sometimes eat it simply with salt, or with vinegar only, or with black pepper. To prepare it according to the the usual custom—cut up, very small, the pieces of lobster, and on another plate make the dressing. First, mash together some hard-boiled yoke of egg, and some of the red coral of the lobster, with a little salt and cayenne. Mix in, with a fork, mustard to your taste, and then a liberal allowance of salad oil, finishing with vinegar. Transfer the bits of lobster to the plate that has the dressing, and combine the whole with a fork. Lettuce salad is dressed in the same manner.

At a public table a lady should never volunteer to dress salad for others of the company. Neither should she cut up a pie and help it round. These things ought only to be done by a gentleman, or a servant.

If a gentleman with whom you are acquainted has dressed a salad, and offers the plate to you, take what you want, and immediately return to him the remainder, and do not pass it on to persons in your vicinity. It is his privilege and not yours to offer it to others, as he has had the trouble of dressing it. And it is just that he should have a portion of it for himself, which will not be the case if you officiously hand it about to people around you.

It was formerly considered ill-bred to refuse to take wine with a gentleman. Now it is no longer an offence to decline these invitations. If you have no conscientious scruples, and if you are acquainted with the gentleman, or have been introduced to him, you may comply with his civility; and when both glasses are filled, look at him, bow your head, and taste the wine.

If a stranger, whom you do not know, and to whom you have had no introduction, takes the liberty of asking you to drink wine with him, refuse at once, positively and coldly, to prove that you consider it an unwarrantable freedom. And so it is.

If you are helped to anything whose appearance you do not like, or in which you are disappointed, when you taste it, you, of course, at a hotel table, are not obliged to eat it. **Merely** leave it on your plate, without audibly giving the reason, and then, in a low voice, desire the waiter to bring you something else. It is well, while at table, to avoid any discussion of the demerits of the dishes. On the other hand, you may praise them as much as you please.

In refusing to be helped to any particular thing, never give as a reason that, "You are afraid of it," or "that it will disagree with you." It is sufficient simply to refuse, and then no one has a right to ask why. While at table all allusions to dyspepsia, indigestion, or any other disorders of the stomach, are vulgar and disgusting. The word stomach should never be uttered at any table, or, indeed, anywhere else, except to your physician, or in a private conversation with a female friend interested in your health. It is a disagreeable word (and so are all its associations) and should never be mentioned in public to "ears polite." Also make no remark on what is eaten by persons near you (except they are children and under your care), such as its being unwholesome, indigestible, feverish, or in any way improper. It is no business of yours, and, besides, you are not to judge of others by yourself. When the finger-glasses are sent round, dip a clean corner of the napkin into the water, and wet round your lips with it, but omit the singular foreign fashion of taking water into your mouth, rinsing and gurgling it round and then spitting it back into the glass. Wait till you can give your mouth a regular and efficient washing up-stairs. Dip your fingers into the glass, rub them with the slice of lemon that may be floating on the surface, and then wipe them on the napkin.

At hotels the interval between dinner and tea is usually short; the tea hour being early that the guests may have ample time to prepare for going to places of amusement. Yet there are ladies who, though spending all the evening at home, will remain sitting idly in the parlor till eight o'clock, keeping the table standing and servants waiting in attendance. This is very inconsiderate. The servants certainly require rest, and should be exempt from all unnecessary attendance.

On the subject of rest for hotel servants good feeling suggests that we should say a few words. No one who has had much experience of hotel life can have failed to notice the wearied look which the domestics in these large establishments too often wear. To the visitor fresh from seeing every day the blythe faces of country folk, their jaded look invariably suggests that they would be all the better for going off to bed and sleeping for a week. We should do everything in our power to lessen their labors by refraining from making unreasonable demands on their time. Consideration for others is the first mark of the lady, and the fact that a woman observes all the mere forms of etiquette will never convince us that she is one of the true nobility so long as we can see that she has no consideration for the rest of those to whom fortune has granted but little repose.

In making acquaintance with a stranger at a hotel, there is no impropriety (but quite the contrary) in inquiring of her from what place she comes. In introducing yourself give your name audibly, or, what is better, if you have a card with you, present that, and she should do the same in return. Before you enter into conversation on any subject connected with religion it will be well to ask her to what church she belongs. This knowledge will guard you from indulging inadvertently in sectarian remarks that may be displeasing to her, besides producing a controversy which may be carried too far.

When you give a gratuity to a servant—for instance, to the man who waits on you at table, or he that attends your room, or to the chambermaid or messenger—give it at no regular time, but whenever you think proper or find it convenient. It is injudicious to allow them to suppose that they are to do you no particular service without being immediately paid for it. It is, at the same time, right and customary to pay them extra for carrying your baggage up and down stairs when you are departing from the house or returning to it. If you are a permanent boarder, and, from ill health, require extra attendance, it is well to give a certain sum monthly to each of the servants who wait upon you, and then they will not expect anything more except on extraordinary occasions.

All persons who go to hotels are not able to lavish large and frequent gratuities on the servants. But all, for the price they pay to the proprietor, are entitled to an ample share of attention from the domestics.

In all hotels it is against the rule to take out of the ladies' drawing-room any books that may be placed there for the general convenience of the company, such as dictionaries, guide-books, directories, magazines, &c. If you borrow a file of newspapers from the reading room, get done with it as soon as you can, lest it should be wanted by others, and as soon as you have finished ring for a servant to carry the file back.

.Correspondence.—Much time is wasted, particularly by young ladies, in writing and answering such epistles as are termed "letters of friendship"—meaning long documents filled with regrets at absence, asseverations of affection, modest de-precations of self, and flattering references to the correspon-dent, or else anticipations of what may be coming and lamen-tations of what may be past, which are of no manner of use but to foster a sickly, morbid feeling, to encourage nonsense, and destroy a relish for such true friendship as is good and whole-some.

A still worse species of voluminous female correspondence is that which turns entirely on love, or rather on what are called "beaux," or entirely on hate—for instance, hatred of stepmothers. This topic is considered the more piquant from its impropriety, and from its being carried on in secret.

Then there are young ladies born with the organ of letter-writing amazingly developed and increased by habitual prac-tice, who can scarcely become acquainted with a gentleman possessing brains, without volunteering a correspondence with him. And then ensues a long epistolary dialogue about nothing, or, at least, nothing worth reading or remembering; trenching closely on gallantry, but still not quite that; affected simplicity on the part of the lady, and an unaffected imperti-nence on that of the gentleman, alternating with pretended poutings on her side and half or whole laughing apologies on his. Sometimes there are attempts at moralizing or criticizing, or sentimentalizing—but nothing is ever elicited that, to a third person, can afford the least amusement or improvement, or ex-cite the least interest.

No young lady ever engages in a correspondence with a gentleman who is neither her relative nor her betrothed without eventually lessening herself in his eyes. Of this she may rest assured. With some men it is even dangerous for a lady to write a note on the commonest subject. He may show the superscription or the signature, or both, to his idle friends, and make insinuations much to her disadvantage, which his comrades will be sure to circulate and exaggerate.

Above all, let no lady correspond with a married man, unless she is obliged to consult him on business, and from that plain, straightforward path let her not diverge. Even if the wife sees and reads every letter, she will, in all probability, feel a touch of jealousy (or more than a touch) if she finds that they excite interest in her husband or give him pleasure. This will inevitably be the case if the married lady is inferior in intellect to the single one, and has a lurking consciousness that she is so.

Having hinted what the correspondence of young ladies ought not to be, we will try to convey some idea of what it ought. Let us premise that there is no danger of any errors in grammar or spelling, and but few faults of punctuation, and that the fair writers are aware that a sentence should always conclude with a period, or full stop, to be followed by a capital letter beginning the next sentence, and that a new paragraph should be allotted to every change of subject, provided that there is room on the sheet of paper. And still it is well to have always at hand a dictionary and a grammar, in case of unaccountable lapses of memory. However, persons who have read much, and read to advantage, generally find themselves at no loss in orthography, grammar, and punctuation. To spell badly is disgraceful to a lady or gentleman, and it looks as if they had finished reading as soon as they left school.

The wording of your letter should be as much like conversation as possible, containing, in a condensed form, just what you would be most likely to talk about if you saw your friend. A letter is of no use unless it conveys some information, excites some interest, or affords some improvement. It may be handsomely written, correct in spelling, punctuation, and grammar, and yet stiff and formal in style—affectedly didactic, and, therefore tiresome, or mawkishly sentimental, and, therefore, foolish. It may be refined and high-flown in words, but flat and barren

in ideas, containing nothing that a correspondent cares to
know.

Inexperienced letter writers often feel provoked with themselves when they have filled a sheet without touching upon
some topics that they fully intended to introduce, and perceive
they have spread out one of inferior importance over half their
paper. This may be avoided by considering before you begin
all that you wish to write about, and allowing to each topic its
proper space.

If your correspondent requires that her letters be kept
private from all friends, make it a point of honor to comply
with her wishes, only make an exception in favor of your
mother, in case she should desire to see the correspondence,
for young ladies shold gracefully acknowledge their parents'
right of inspection; though, where there is a proper confidence
on both sides, it will rarely be enforced.

The more rational and elevating the topics are on which
you write, the less will you care for your letters being seen, or
for paragraphs being read out of them, and where there is no
need of any secrecy it is best not to bind your friend by
promises, but to leave it to her discretion.

Do not feel bound to write to every one who begs you to do
so, but choose carefully whom you will have in that relation,
and when you have a few choice correspondents do not neglect them, and begin every letter with an apology, but write in
due season, and waste no paper on commonplace excuses.

Madame de Sevigne praises her daughter for her attention
to dates, which, she says, shows an interest in the correspondence; a dateless letter certainly loses much of its value, and
they are but too common.

Remember the liability of a letter to miscarry, to be opened
by the wrong person, to be seen by other eyes than those for
whom it is meant, and be very careful what you write to the
disadvantage of any one. Praise and admire, but beware of
blame. Your judgment may be wrong, and you know not
when or where it may come up against you and make you
sorry you ever penned it.

As you finish each page of your letter read it over to see
that there are no errors. If you find any, correct them care-

fully. In writing a familiar letter, a very common fault is tautology, or a too frequent repetition of the same word—for instance, "Yesterday I received a letter from my sister Mary, which was the first letter I have received from my sister since she left." The sentence should be, "Yesterday I received a letter from my sister Mary, the first since she left us."

Unless you are writing to one of your own family, put always the pronoun "my" before the words "sister," "father," "mother," and not without it, as if they were also the relatives of your correspondent.

To end a sentence with the word "left" (for departed) is awkward and unsatisfactory—for instance, "It is two days since he left." Left what? It is one of the absurd innovations that have crept in among us of late years, and are supposed to be fashionable.

Avoid in writing, as in talking, all words that do not express the true meaning. Unless you know that your correspondent is well versed in French, refrain from interlarding your letters with Gallic words or phrases.

Do not introduce long quotations from poetry. Three or four lines of verse are sufficient; one line or two are better still. Write them rather smaller than your usual hand, and leave a space at the beginning and end, marking their commencement and termination with inverted commas, thus " ".

Unless to persons living in the same house, do not enclose one letter to another. And even then it is not always safe to do so. Let each letter be transmitted on its own account by mail, with its own full direction and its own postage stamp. Confide to no one the delivery of an important letter intended for another person.

To break the seal of a letter directed to another person is punishable by law. To read secretly the letter of another is morally as felonious. A woman who would act thus meanly is worse than those who apply their eyes or ears to key-holes or door cracks, or who listen under windows, or who, in a dusky parlor, before the lamps are lighted, ensconce themselves in a corner, and give no note of their presence while listening to a conversation not intended for them to hear.

We do not conceive that, unless he authorizes her to do so

(which he had best not), a wife has a right to open her husband's letters, or he to read hers. Neither wife nor husband has any right to entrust to the other the secrets of their friends; and letters may contain such secrets. Unless under extraordinary circumstances, parents should not consider themselves privileged to inspect the correspondence of grown-up children. Brothers and sisters always take care that their epistles shall not be unceremoniously opened by each other. In short, a letter is the property of the person to whom it is addressed, and nobody has a right to read it without permission. If you are shown an autograph signature at the bottom of a letter, be satisfied to look at that only, and do not open out and read the whole, unless desired.

The letters of a regular correspondent should be endorsed and filed as regularly by young ladies as by merchants; this facilitates your reference to any one of them, prevents their being lost or mislaid, or exposed to curious eyes, saves your table from being strewn, and your letter-case from being crowded with them.

The letters of past years should either be destroyed or carefully locked up, with directions on the box that in case of your death they are to be returned unread to the writers, or if that cannot be done, that they should be burnt unread. This disposal of letters after death is often the only important part of a young girl's last wishes, and yet it is rarely provided for. It is best to be always so prepared by making the necessary arrangements whilst in health.

The letters of very young persons rarely have any interest beyond the period in which they are written; they are very seldom read after they are a year old; and the idea of keeping them for future perusal is altogether chimerical. Life is too much crowded with novel interests to allow time for reading over quires of paper filled with the chat of young girls, however good it may have been in its day; and, therefore, the wisest plan is to agree with your correspondent to make each a bonfire of the other's letters when they shall be more than a year old. A year's letters are enough for a memorial of your friend, if she be taken from you; and by keeping the latest you will have her most mature compositions.

Notes of invitation should always designate both the day of the week and that of the month. If that of the month only is specified, one figure may, perhaps, be mistaken for another; for instance, the 13th may look like the 18th, or the 25th like the 26th. We know instances where, from this cause, some of the guests did not come till the day after the party.

There are some very sensible people who, in their invitations, tell frankly what is to be expected, and if they really ask but a few friends, they at once give the names of those friends, so that you may know who you are to see. If you are to meet no more than can sit around the tea table, they signify the same. If they expect twenty, thirty, or forty persons they say so, and do not leave you in doubt whether to dress for something very like a party, or for a mere family tea-drinking.

If it is a decided music party, by all means specify the same, that those who have no enjoyment of what is considered fashionable music, may stay away.

Always reply to a note of invitation the day after you have received it. To a note on business send an answer the same day. After accepting an invitation, should any thing occur to prevent your going, send a second note in due time.

Do not take offence at a friend because she does not invite you every time she has company. Her regard for you may be as warm as ever, but it is probably inconvenient for her to have more than a certain number at a time. Believe that the omission is no evidence of neglect, or of a desire to offend you; but rest assured that you are to be invited on other occasions. If you are not, then indeed you may take it as a hint that she is no longer desirous of continuing the acquaintance. Be dignified enough not to call her to account; but cease visiting her without taking her to task and bringing on a quarrel. But if you must quarrel let it not be in writing. A paper war is always carried too far, and produces bitterness of feeling, which is seldom, if ever, entirely eradicated, even after apologies have been made and accepted. Still, when an offence has been given in writing, the atonement should be made in writing also.

Avoid giving letters of introduction to people whose acquaintance cannot possibly afford any pleasure or advantage to those whose civilities are desired for them, or who have not leisure to attend to strangers. Professional people, to whom "time is money," and whose income stops whenever their hands and eyes are unemployed, are peculiarly annoyed by the frequency of introductory letters brought by people with whom they can feel no congeniality, and whom they never would have sought. Many men of worth are not in a situation to entertain strangers handsomely, which means expensively. They may be in straightened circumstances through a thousand causes, and, therefore, unable to bear incessant demands on their time, attention, and purse. And in numerous instances letters are asked and given with no better motive than the gratification of idle curiosity.

Bores are particularly addicted to asking letters of introduction in accordance with their system of bestowing their tediousness upon as many people as possible. The kind friends from whom these missives are required are to be pitied, as they appear to have not the courage to refuse, or address enough to excuse themselves plausibly from complying.

In obtaining an introductory letter to a public favorite, say to a painter, for instance, ascertain before presenting it what branch of the art he professes. Also, no one should presume to request an introduction to an authoress if they are ignorant whether she writes prose or verse. Not that they are expected to talk to her immediately on literary subjects. Far from it. But if they know nothing of her works they deserve no letter. Letters of introduction should not be sealed. To do so is rude and mean. If you wish to write on the same day to the same person, take another sheet, write as long an epistle as you please, seal it, and send it by mail.

It is best to deliver an introductory letter in person, as the lady or gentleman whose civilities have been requested in your behalf may thus be spared the trouble of calling at your lodgings, with the risk of not finding you at home. This is very likely to happen if you send instead of taking the letter yourself. If you do send it, enclose a card with your address upon it.

On farewell cards it is usual to write with a pencil the letters "T. T. L.," "to take leave;" or P. P. C.," "*pour prendre congé;*" or "P. D. A.," *pour dire adieu*," "to bid adieu." In writing upon business exclusively your own, for instance, to make a request, to ask for information, to petition for a favor, or to solicit an autograph, it it but right not only to pay the postage on your own letter, but to enclose a stamp for the answer. This is always done by really polite and considerate people. You have no right, when the benefit is entirely your own, to cause any extra expense to the receiver of the letter not even the cost of the postage back again.

Courtship.—By the custom of society, man has been awarded the privilege of making the first advance towards matrimony, it is the safest and happiest way for woman to leave the matter entirely in his hands. She should be so educated as to consider that the great end of existence may be equally attained in married or single life; and that no union but the most perfect one is at all desirable. Matrimony should be considered as an incident in life, which, if it comes at all, must come without any contrivance of yours; and, therefore, you may safely put aside all thoughts of it till some one forces the subject upon your notice by professions of a particular interest in you.

Lively, ingenious, conversable, charming girls often spoil into dull, bashful, silent young ladies, and all because their heads are full of nonsense about beaux and lovers. They have a thousand thoughts and feelings which they would be ashamed to confess, though not ashamed to entertain; and their preoccupation with a subject which they had better let entirely alone prevents their being the agreeable and rational companions of the gentlemen of their acquaintance, which they were designed to be.

Women are happily endowed with a sense of propriety and a natural modesty which will generally guide them aright in their intercourse with the other sex, and the more perfectly well-bred and discreet you are in your intercourse with female friends, the easier it will be for you to acquit yourself well with your male ones.

As soon as young ladies go into general society, they are liable to receive attentions that indicate a particular regard, and long before they are really old enough to form any such ties, often receive matrimonial overtures; it is, therefore, highly necessary to know how to treat them,

The offer of a man's heart and hand is the greatest compli-ment he can pay you, and, however undesirable to you those gifts may be, they should be courteously and kindly declined; and since a refusal is, to most men, not only a disappointment, but a mortification, it should always he prevented, if possible. Men have various ways of cherishing and declaring their at-tachment; those who indicate the basis of their feelings in many intelligible ways can generally be spared the pain of a refusal. If you do not mean to accept a gentleman who is paying you very marked attentions you should avoid receiving him whenever you can. You should not allow him to escort you; you should show your displeasure when joked about him; and, if sounded by a mutual friend, let your want of reciprocal feelings be very apparent.

You may, however, be taken entirely by surprise, because there are men who are so secret in these matters that they do not even let the object of their affections suspect their prefer-ence until they suddenly declare themselves lovers and suitors. In such a case you will need all your presence of mind, or the hesitation produced by surprise may give rise to false hopes. If you have any doubt upon the matter, you may fairly ask time to consider of it, on the grounds of your never having thought of the gentleman in the light of a lover; but if you are resolved against the suit, endeavor to make your answer so decided as to finish the affair at once. Inexperienced girls sometimes feel so much the pain they are inflicting that they use phrases which feed a lover's hopes; but this is mistaken tenderness; your answer should be as decided as it is court-eous.

Whenever an offer is made in writing, you should reply to it as soon as possible; and, having in this case none of the embarrassment of a personal interview, you can make such a careful selection of words as will best convey your meaning. If the person is estimable you should express your sense of his merit and your gratitude for his preference in strong terms; and put your refusal of his hand on the score of your not feel-ing for him that peculiar preference necessary to the union he seeks. This makes a refusal as little painful as possible, and soothes the feelings you are obliged to wound. The gentleman's letter should be returned in your reply, and your lips should be closed upon the subject for ever afterwards. It is his secret, and you have no right to tell it to any one; but if your parents are your confidential friends, on all other occasions, he will not blame you for telling them.

Your young female friends should never be allowed to tease or banter you into the betrayal of this secret. You cannot turn your ingenuity to better account than by using it to baffle their curiosity. Some girls are tempted to tell of an offer and refusal in order to account for a cessation of those attentions on the part of the gentleman which have before been so constant and marked as to be observed by their friends. But this is not a sufficient reason for telling another person's secret. You cannot always prevent a suspicion of the truth, but you should never confirm it by any disclosure of yours.

If you are so situated as to meet the gentleman whose hand you have refused, you should do so with frank cordiality, and put him at ease by behaving as if nothing particular had passed between you. If this manner of yours is so far mistaken as to lead to a renewal of the offer, let him see as soon as possible that he has nothing to hope from importunity, and that if he would preserve your friendship he must seek for nothing more. Always endeavor to make true friends of your rejected lovers by the delicacy and honor with which you treat them. If, when your own conduct has been unexceptionable, your refusal to marry a man produces resentment, it argues some fault of character in him, and can only be lamented in silence.

Never think the less of a man because he has been refused, even if it be by a lady whom you do not value highly. It is nothing to his disadvantage. In exercising their privilege of making the first advances, the wisest will occasionally make great mistakes, and the best will often be drawn into an affair of this sort against their better judgment, and both are but too happy, if they escape with only the pain of being refused. So far from its being any reason for not accepting a good and wise man when he offers himself to you, it should only increase your thankfulness to the Power which reserved him for you, and to the lady through whose instrumentality he is still free to choose.

4

Bridal Etiquette.—Assuming that the important day is fixed, and that the bidden guests have accepted the invitation, the grand preoccupation of the female part of the lady's family is to prepare the bridal outfit or trousseau, which must be in accordance with the circumstances of the bride's family. Nevertheless, as it is an expense that few mothers grudge, they generally take an affectionate pride in rendering the outfit as complete as possible. We have heard of outfits in the class of wealthy merchants comprising twelve dozen chemises, trimmed with lace, a large assortment of slips, trimmed with embroidered bands, others plainer for morning use, an endless abundance of elegant night-caps, and countless pairs of stockings, from the silk hose and the gossamer-like open-work stockings, down to the solid stocking for a country ramble. Dressing-gowns, muslin and silk dresses, and mantillas, should also be comprised in the outfit, as well as several bonnets, or hats, and suitable wrappings for winter. Those who cannot afford such luxuries must substitute fewer articles of a more modest and durable kind. Such a stock is an invaluable groundwork to start with, and, by supplying gradually each article as it wears out, the lady's wardrobe can be renewed without great expense.

BRIDAL GIFTS.—Jewels are not comprised in an outfit. These should be presented by the bridegroom. Still, in families where there are family jewels, the daughter may have a portion set for her, according to the fashion of the day, over and above what her future husband may offer. Such, however, are exceptional cases. In less wealthy classes the husband would offer trinkets according to his means. Besides the latter, a watch, fan, a smelling bottle, or any elegant article for the toilet or boudoir table, such as an ornamental candlestick, a desk of inlaid wood, or a fanciful standish, would be appropriate gifts. Any good old lace which the elders among the bride's female relations may happen to have amongst their stores is a most welcome present on such an occasion; but, if no aunts or other relations volunteer anything of the kind, the bride's mother should then supply the want, if she can afford it, or, in default of real lace, that pretty substitute, Irish point. A dress of black lace, and another of white lace, whether real or imitation, would likewise be a most useful addition to a trousseau, as well as feathers, ribbons, and any of those articles that can scarcely go out of fashion, and form an excellent *fonds-de-toilette.* But if the donors of bridal gifts really wish to benefit a bride, not in affluent circumstances, we would suggest that they hold council together, so as not to double any superfluous article.

BRIDESMAIDS.—A bride may have one or six bridesmaids at her choice. No particular number being fixed, it is often determined by the number of sisters, or of intimate friends, she may have. The bridesmaids should be dressed in white, and all alike, and may wear orange flower bouquets; they should avoid dressing like brides, which is out of place.

THE CEREMONY.—The bride uniformly goes to church in the same carriage with her parents, or with those who stand in their place; as, for instance, if the father is deceased, an elder brother or uncle, or even guardian, accompanies her mother and herself. If unhappily she is an orphan, and has no relations, a middle-aged lady and gentleman, friends of her parents, should be requested to take their place. A bridesmaid will also occupy a seat in the same carriage.

The bridegroom finds his way to church in a separate carriage, with his friends, or on foot, as the case may be; and he will show his gallantry by handing the bride from her carriage, and paying every attention to those who accompany her. Any omission in this respect cannot be too carefully avoided.

When before the altar, the father of the bride, or, in default of such relation, the nearest connection or some old friend, gives away the bride. The bridesmaids stand near the bride; and either her sister or some favorite friend will hold the gloves or handkerchief, as may be required, when she ungloves her hand for the wedding ring. When the ceremony is completed, and the names of the bride and bridegroom are signed in the vestry, they first leave the church together, occupying, by themselves, the carriage that waits to convey them to the house of the bride's father, or that of the guardian or friend by whom the bridal breakfast is given.

BRIDAL BREAKFAST.—The wedding cake uniformly occupies the centre of the table. It is often tastefully surrounded with flowers, among which those of the orange are conspicuous. After being cut according to the usages observed on such occasions, the oldest friend of the family proposes the lady's health; that of the bridegroom is generally proposed by some friend of his own, if present, but, if not so, by his father-in-law, or any of his new relatives, who will deem it incumbent upon them to say something gratifying to him while proposing his health, which courtesy he must acknowledge as best he can. The bride will retain her bridal costume during the breakfast. She occupies, with her husband, the centre of the table, and sits by his side—her father and mother taking the top and bottom, and showing all honor to the guests. When every compliment and kind wish has been proffered and acknowledged, the bride, attended by her friends, withdraws and exchanges her bridal costume for a walking dress, before she starts for her wedding tour. Good taste points out that all bridal attributes should now be entirely discarded. Peculiarities that pertain to past days should be guarded against; mysteries concerning knives, forks, and plates, or throwing "an old shoe" after the bride, have long been exploded.

Bridal Dress.—This, like all the rest of the outfit, must depend on her fortune and position in life; still, whatever be the material, it should be white. If a widow likes to wear a colored silk, let her do so by all means, there is almost a modest propriety on her part in declining to play the bride a second time in her life; and, if those of limited means prefer to choose their dress for its solidity rather than its beauty, we can but respect their economical motives, but where no such reasons exist, we cannot fancy any young maiden dressed otherwise than in white.

A Brussels lace dress over white satin, or a rich *moire-antique* with point lace flounces, would each form a beautiful costume for a bride. As to the head-dress, a veil is usually preferred, as being elegant and forming a decided costume peculiar to brides. There is something charmingly poetical in a veil and orange flower wreath, rendered doubly attractive by its being only on one occasion through life that such a *coiffure* can be worn. The veil may be of Brussels or of point lace, or of simple *tulle* with a plain hem, each pretty in their way. The bride, with a veil, should wear an orange flower wreath upon her head. This flower, we may observe, which France first taught us to dedicate entirely to the service of brides, no longer holds its undivided privilege there. Jasmine, white roses, and other white flowers, are now mixed up with the orthodox orange flower wreath by some of the most eminent artificial florists of Paris.

ETIQUETTE AND DRESS AFTER MARRIAGE.—No particular dress is required on the days the newly-married pair receive their friends. If it be winter, a rich silk or velvet dress, made high like a morning one, would be an appropriate attire for the lady. If it be summer, a light silk or barege would be suitable, but no flowers should be worn in the hair, though lace lappets and velvet bows are admissible. Wedding cake and wine should be handed to all comers. This is generally the only form in which wedding cake is distributed to one's friends in London. Persons in the country, not being able to assemble their friends so easily, still maintain the old custom of sending parcels of wedding cake to all the near connections of the family; or, if they receive, pieces of cake are, nevertheless, despatched to distant friends and relatives. Some Londoners send cake to their country connections, but far the larger portion neglect this friendly old custom. Formerly, the cake was passed through the wedding ring, or the charm was not complete; but this antiquated piece of superstition is now discarded, or, at most, would only be found in existence in some old farm house remote from town.

The visits may be returned at the end of above a week or ten days.

At the parties the young couple may attend during the first month, there is nothing inappropriate in the bride's wearing some little badge of her new state, such as a dress looped up with orange flowers or a few orange blossoms in her hair.

A new-married couple are not expected to give parties at their house for the first year; but after that time they must no longer play the part of exceptional beings, but give and take, as others.

As to the dress of a young matron, we expect it to be somewhat richer than that of an unmarried girl. The Parisians show admirable tact in the shades that distinguish the toilette of mademoiselle and madame. The girlish simplicity that adds a grace to the youthful attractions of the former would be out of place on the part of the latter, who, being possessed of jewels (which the French deem a superfluous ornament to the unmarried young lady), must dress in a corresponding style of luxury. Besides, she now assumes a position in society as the mistress of a house; her fate is fixed; she knows she can spend, and acts accordingly. But, if the young lady, having rich parents, launches at once into the full blaze of jewels and expensive dresses, and then marries some poor captain on half-pay, she will feel humiliated at having to modify her toilette to suit her altered circumstances. This change would be less perceptible were our young ladies equally as judicious with the Parisian ones, in adopting a simple style of adornment.

Should there be no settlement, and the couple be in easy circumstances, we would advise the fixing a sum for pin money, which would avoid a number of disputes, particularly among touchy people. We would avise the wife never to exceed the sum agreed upon, as some men would make that a fertile theme for expiating on the extravagance of ladies. Many ladies prefer that their dressmaker, silk mercer, shoemaker, and others, should send in their bills to their husband, calculating that the brunt of his ill temper, if such is called forth, will fall on the tradespeople for allowing the running up of such accounts; but this is a habit that only encourages profuse expenditure where, perhaps, there is not adequate fortune to meet it.

A cheerful home is the best security for happiness. There is not only a moral, but a physical cheerfulness that should be attended to. A well-lighted room, a neatly-served dinner, everything clean and tidy and bright, predispose the mind to pleasant impressions. Let the prudent wife strive to attain this state of things, if she values her domestic happiness.

Always receive your husband with smiles, leaving nothing undone to render home agreeable, and gratefully reciprocate his kindness and attention. Study to gratify his inclinations in regard to food and cookery, in the management of the household, in your dress, manners, and deportment. Never attempt to rule, or appear to rule, your husband. Such conduct degrades husbands, and wives always partake largely in the degradation of their husbands. In everything reasonable comply with his wishes with cheerfulness, and even, as far as possible, anticipate them. Avoid all altercations or arguments leading to ill-humor, and more especially before company. Few things are more disgusting than the altercations of the married when in the company of friends or strangers. If a lady understands that her duties are obedience, complaisance, an entire surrender of her will to that of her husband, and attention to his happiness as the first consideration, she has the spirit of the religious and civil idea of marriage.

Evening Parties.—A list of the persons you intend to invite having been made out, proceed to write the notes, or have them written, in a neat, handsome hand by an experienced caligrapher. Fashion, in its various changes, sometimes decrees that these notes and their envelopes should be perfectly plain (though always of the finest paper), and that the wax seals shall, of course, be very small. At other times the mode is to write on embossed note paper, with bordered envelopes secured by fancy wafers, transparant, medallion, gold or silver. If the seals are gold or silver, the edges or borders of the paper should be also gilt or silvered. Sometimes, for a very large or splendid party, the notes are engraved and printed on cards.

The notes are usually sent either eight, seven, or six days before the party; if it is to be very large, ten days or two weeks. In the notes always specify not only the day of the week, but also the day of the month, when the party is to take place. It is very customary now to designate the hour of assembling, and then the company are expected to be punctual to that time. People really genteel do not go ridiculously late. When a ball is intended, let the words "Dancing" be introduced, in small letters, at the lower left-hand corner of the note.

In preparing for a party, it is well (especially if you have had but little experience yourself) to send for one of the public waiters and consult with him on the newest style of "doing these things." He can also give you an idea of the probable expense. We do not, of course, allude to magnificent entertainments such as are celebrated in the newspapers and become a nine days' wonder.

In engaging your presiding genius it is well to desire him to come on the morning of the party; he will be found of great advantage in assisting with the final preparations. He will attend to the silver, and china and glass; and see that the lamps are all in order, and that the fires are in proper trim for evening. He will bring with him (at whatever hour you indicate) his young men, as he calls them, and these are his apprentices that he has in training for the profession.

One of these men should be stationed in the vestibule, or just within the front door. On that evening (if not at other times) let this door be furnished with a lamp, placed on a shelf or bracket in the fanlight, to illumine the steps and shine down upon the pavement where the ladies cross it on alighting from their carriages. If the evening prove rainy, let another man attend, with an umbrella, to assist in sheltering them on their way into the house. The ladies should all wear overshoes, to guard their thin slippers from the damp, in their transit from the coach to the vestibule.

At the top, or on the landing-place of the first staircase, let another man be posted to show the female guests to their dressing room, while still another waiter stays near the gentleman's room till the company have arrived.

In the apartment prepared as a dressing room for the ladies, two or more women should be all the evening in attendance; the room being well warmed, well lighted, and furnished with all that may be requisite for giving the last touches to head, feet, and figure, previous to entering the drawing room. When ready to go down, the ladies meet their gentlemen in the passage between the respective dressing rooms.

If any lady is without an escort, and has no friends at hand, she should send for the master of the house to meet her near the door and give her his arm into the drawing room. He will then lead her to the hostess and to a seat. Let her then bow, as a sign that she releases him from further attendance, and leaves him at liberty to divide his civilities among his other guests.

In the ladies' room, beside two toilette glasses with their

branches lighted, let a Psyche or cheval glass be also there; likewise a hand-mirror on each toilette, to enable the ladies to see the back of their heads; with an ample suppy of pins, combs, brushes, hair-pins, &c., and a workbox containing needles, thread, &c. Let there be bottles of fine *eau-de Cologne*, and camphor, and hartshorn, in case of faintings. Among the furniture have a sofa and several footstools for the ladies to sit on if they wish to change their shoes.

The women attending must take charge of the cloaks, shawls, overshoes, &c., rolling up together the things that belong to each lady, and putting each bundle in some place they can easily remember when wanted at the breaking-up of the assembly.

It is now the custom for the lady of the house (and those of her own family) to be dressed rather plainly, showing no desire to eclipse any of her guests on this her own night. But her attire, though simple, should be handsome, becoming, and in good taste. Her business is, without any bustle or apparent officiousness, quietly and almost imperceptibly to try and render the evening as pleasant as possible to all her guests, introducing those who, though not yet acquainted, ought to be, and finding seats for ladies who are not young enough to continue standing.

The custom that formerly prevailed, in the absurd days of crowds and jams, when dense masses were squeezed into small apartments, of removing every seat and every piece of furniture from the room, is now obsolete. A hard squeeze is no longer a high boast. Genteel people no longer go to parties on the staircase or in the passages.

In houses where space is not abundant, it is now customary to have several moderate parties in the course of the season, instead of inviting everybody you know on the same night.

When the hour of assembling is stated in the notes of invitation (as it always should be) the guests, of course, will take care to arrive as nearly as possible about that hour. At large parties tea is usually omitted, it being supposed that every one has already taken that beverage at home previous to commencing the business of the toilette. Many truly hospitable ladies still continue the custom, thinking that it makes a pleasant beginning to the evening and exhilarates the ladies after the fatigue of dressing and arriving. So it does. For a large company, a table with tea, coffee, and cakes may be set in the ladies' room, attendants being there to supply the guests with refreshments before they go down. If there is no tea, refreshments are sent round soon after the majority of the company has come.

After a little time allotted to conversation, music is generally introduced by one of the ladies of the family, if she plays well; otherwise, she invites a competent friend to commence. A lady who can do nothing "without her notes," or who cannot read music and play at sight, is scarcely enough of a musician to perform in a large company, for this incapacity is an evidence that she has not a good ear, or rather a good memory, for melody, or that her musical talent wants more cultivation. A large party is no time or place for practising or for risking attempts at new things, or for vainly trying to remember old ones.

Some young ladies rarely sit down to a piano in any house but their home without complaining that the instrument is out of tune. We have known a fair amateur, to whom this complaint was habitual and never omitted, even when we know that, to provide against it, the piano had really been tuned that very day. The tuning of a harp immediately before playing is sometimes a very tedious business. Would it not be well for the harpist to come a little earlier than the rest and tune the instrument previous to their arrival? And let the tuning be deemed sufficient for a while, and not repeated more than once again in the course of the evening, especially in the midst of the first piece.

Unless a gentleman is himself familiar with the air, let him not volunteer to turn over the leaves for a lady who is playing. He will certainly turn them over too soon or too late, and therefore annoy and confuse her. Still worse, let him not attempt to accompany her with his voice unless he is an excellent musician or accustomed to singing with her.

For the hearers to crowd closely round the instrument is smothering to the vocalist. Let them keep at a proper distance, and she will sing the better and they will hear the bet-

ter. It is so rude to talk during a song that it is never done in
company; but a little low conversation is sometimes tolerated
in the adjoining room during the performance of one of those
interminable pieces of instrumental· music whose chief merit
lies in its difficulty, and which (at least to the ears of the un-
initiated) is rather a bore than a pleasure.

It is very old-fashioned to return thanks to a lady for her
singing or to tell her she is very kind to oblige the company
so often. If she is conscious of really singing well, and sees
that she delights her hearers, she will not feel sensible of
fatigue, at least till the agreeable excitement of conscious success is over.

At a dancing party the ladies of the house decline joining
in it, out of politeness to their guests, till towards the latter
part of the evening, when the company begin to thin off and
the dancers are fatigued. Ladies who are strangers in the
place are, by courtesy, entitled to particular attention from
those who know them. A deformed woman dancing is a
"sorry sight." She should never consent to any such exhibition of her figure. She will only be asked out of mere
compassion, or from interested and unworthy motives.

When a lady has the misfortune to have a crooked or
misshapen person, it is well for her to conceal it as much as
possible by wearing a shawl, a large cape, a mantilla, and on
no account a tight bodied dress.

A distinguished lady appeared at an evening assemblage so
judiciously attired that her personal defects did not prevent
her from looking really well. Over a rich black satin
dress she wore a long, loose sacque of black lace, lined with
grey silk. From beneath the short sleeves of her sacque
came down long, wide sleeves of white lace, confined with
bracelets round her fair and delicate little hands. Her throat
was covered closely with a handsome collar of French embroidered muslin, and her beautiful and becoming cap was of
white lace, white flowers, and white satin ribbon; her light
hair being simply parted on her broad and intellectual forehead. With her lively blue eyes and the bright and pleasant
expression of her countenance, no one seemed to notice the
faults of her nose, mouth, and complexion, and those of her

figure were so well concealed as to be scarcely apparent; and then her lady-like ease and the total absence of all affectation rendered her graceful and prepossessing. True it is that, with a good heart and a good mind, no woman can be ugly; at least they soon cease to be so considered, even if nature has been unkind to them in feature, figure, and complexion. An intelligent eye and a good-humored mouth are excellent substitutes for the want of regular beauty.

Now, as a deformed lady may render herself very agreeable as a conversationist, she has no occasion to exhibit the defects of her person in a dance, more especially going down in a country dance.

At a large party, or at a wedding, there is generally a supper table, lemonade and cake having been sent round during the evening. The host and hostess should see that all the ladies are conducted thither, and that none are neglected, particularly those that are timid and stand back. It is the business of the host to attend to those himself, or to send the waiters to them.

If the party is so large that all the ladies cannot go to the table at once, let the matrons be conducted thither first, and the young ladies afterwards. If there is a crowd, it is not unusual to have a cord (a handsome one, of course) stretched across the door of the supper room and guarded by a servant, who explains that no more are allowed to pass till after that cord is taken down. Meanwhile the younger part of the company amuse themselves in the adjacent rooms. No lady should take the liberty of meddling with the flowers that ornament the table.

At a summer evening party the refreshments are of a much lighter description than at a winter entertainment, consisting chiefly of ice-creams, water-ices, fresh fruits, and cake.

At a fashionable dinner party the following were the arrangements: The guests were twenty-four in number, and they began to assemble at half-past seven punctually. They were received in the library, where the host and hostess were standing ready to receive them, introducing those who were strangers to each other. When all had arrived the butler entered, and, going up to the lady of the house, told her, in a

low voice, that dinner was served. The hostess then arranged
those that were not previously acquainted, and the gentlemen
conducted the ladies to the dining room, the principal
stranger taking the mistress of the house, and the master giving
his arm to the chief of the female guests. Going into the
dining room, the company passed by the butler and eight foot-
men, all of whom were stationed in two rows.

The table was set for twenty-six, and standing on it were
elegant gilt candelabra. All the lights were wax candles.
Chandeliers were suspended from the ceiling. In the middle
of the table was a magnificent plateau or centre ornament of
gold, flowers surmounted the summit, and the circular stages
below were covered with confectionery, elegantly arranged.
On each side of the plateau, and above and below, were tall
china fruit baskets. In the centre of each basket were im-
mense pine-apples of hot-house growth, with their fresh green
leaves. Below the pine-apples were large bunches of purple
and white hot-house grapes, beautifully disposed with leaves
and tendrils hanging over the sides of the baskets. Down
each side of the whole long table were placed large, round,
saucer-shaped fruit dishes, heaped up with peaches, nectarines,
pears, plums, ripe gooseberries, cherries, currants, and strawberries. All the fruits not in season were supplied from hot
houses. And, alternating with the fruit, were all the *entremets*
in covered dishes, placed on long slips of damask the whole
length of the table. All the plate was superb. The dinner
set was of French china, gilt and painted with roses. At
every plate was a carafe of water, with a tumbler turned down
over it, and several wine glasses. The napkins were large.
The sideboard held only the show silver and the wine. The
side-tables were covered with elegant damask cloths. On
these were ranged, laid along in numerous rows, the knives
forks, and spoons to be used at dinner. The dessert spoons
were in the form of hollow leaves, the stems being the
handles. The fruit knives had silver blades and pearl
handles. There were two soups (white and brown) standing
on a side table. Each servant handed the dishes in his white
kid gloves, and with a damask napkin under his thumb. They
offered (mentioning its name in a low voice) a plate of each

soup to each guest. After the soup, Hock and Moselle were offered to each guest, that they might choose either. A dish of fish was then placed at each end of the table—one was salmon, the other turbot. These dishes were immediately taken off to be helped by the servants, both sorts of fish being offered to each person; then the appropriate sauce for the fish, also cucumbers to eat with the salmon. No castors were on the large table, but they were handed round by the servants. Directly after the fish came the *entremets*, or French dishes. The wine following the fish was Madeira and sherry.

Afterwards a saddle or haunch of Welsh mutton was placed at the master's end of the table, and at the lady's end a boiled turkey. These dishes being removed to the side tables, very thin slices of each were handed round. The poultry was not dissected—nothing being helped but the breast. Ham and tongue was then supplied to those who took poultry; and currant jelly to the eaters of mutton. Next came the vegetables, handed round on dishes divided into four compartments, each division containing a different sort of vegetable.

Next, two dishes of game were put on—one before the master of the house, and the other before the mistress. The game (which was perfectly well done) was helped by them and sent round with appropriate sauce. Then placed along the table were the sweet things—Charlottes, jellies, frozen fruit, &c. A lobster salad, dressed and cut up large, was put on with sweets. On a side table were Stilton and cream cheese, to be eaten with the salad. After this, port wine—the Champagne being early in the dinner. Next, the sweets were handed round. With the sweets were frozen fruits—fruits cut up and frozen with isinglass jelly (red, in molds). Next, a dessert plate was given to each guest, and on it a ground glass plate, about the size of a saucer. Between these plates was a crochet-worked white doyly, of the size of the under plate, the crochet-work done with thread, so as to resemble lace. These doylies were laid under the ground glass plate to deaden the noise of their collision. Then was brought from the side table a ground glass plate of ice cream or water ice, which you took in exchange for that before you. The water ice was frozen in molds in the form of fruit, and suitably colored. The baskets containing the fruit were then removed to the side tables.

After sitting awhile over the fruit, the lady of the house gives the signal by looking and bowing to the ladies on each side, and the ladies, at this signal, prepare to retire. The gentlemen all rise and remain standing while the ladies depart —the master of the house holding the door open. The servants then all retire, except the butler, who remains to wait on the gentlemen while they linger awhile (not more than a quarter of an hour) over the fruit and wine.

The Toilette.—A great object of importance to every lady is the care of her complexion. There is nothing more pleasing to the eye than a delicate, smooth skin, and besides being pleasing to the eye is an evidence of health, and gives additional grace to the most regular features. The choice of soaps has considerable influence in promoting and maintaining this desideratum. These should invariably be selected of the finest kinds and used sparingly, and never with cold water, for the alkali which, more or less, mingles in the composition of all soaps, has an undoubted tendency to irritate a delicate skin; warm water excites a gentle perspiration, thereby assisting the skin to throw off those natural secretions which, if allowed to remain, are likely to accumulate below the skin and produce roughness, pimples, and even eruptions of an obstinate and unpleasant character. Those soaps which ensure a moderate fairness and flexibility of the skin are the most desirable for regular use.

Pomades, when properly prepared, contribute, in an especial manner, to preserve the softness and elasticity of the skin, their effect being of an emollient and congenial nature; and, moreover, they can be applied on retiring to rest, when their effects are not liable to be disturbed by the action of the atmosphere, muscular exertion, or nervous influences.

The use of paints has been very correctly characterized as "a species of corporeal hypocrisy as subversive of delicacy of mind as it is of the natural complexion," and has been, of late years, discarded at the toilette of every lady.

THE HANDS.—A fine hand contributes greatly to the elegance of the personal appearance. Its shape depends, of course, in a great measure, upon physical conformation, though, doubt-lessly, exertion early in life, such as continual musical practice, may disturb its symmetry. We refer more especially to the harp, which makes the fingers crooked and render their tips hard and thick. This may also apply to many kinds of me-chanical employment and manual labor. A white, soft hand, small in proportion to the height of the person, moderately muscular, with slender, straight fingers, and well-formed, trans-parent nails, is, perhaps, as near the standard of beauty as any given outline can be.

The texture and color of the skin, and the appearance of the nails, show how much care and culture the possessor has bestowed upon them, and, consequently, may be regarded as evidence of his or her taste. To preserve the hands soft and white, they should be washed with fine soap in warm water, and carefully dried with a moderately coarse towel. The rub-bing should excite a brisk circulation, which alone will pro-mote a soft and transparent surface. The palm of the hand and the tips of the fingers should be of the color of the inner leaves of a moss rose, with the blue veins distinctly visible. The transparency of the nails may be preserved by the use of a firm brush, and the skin which encroaches upon the fine circle forming their base may be pushed back by a firm towel while the hand is wet. The nails worn moderately long form not only a protection to the fingers, as intended by nature, but look graceful and finished. Exposed, as the hands often are in accidental pursuits, to discoloration, their whiteness may, for the time, be restored by a little lemon juice, and, when washing, by the use of lemon soap. In preserving the delicacy of the hands almond paste will be found serviceable and agree-able. Gloves should always be worn on exposure to the at-mosphere, and are graceful at all times for a lady in the house, except at meals.

THE FEET.—If simply considered as the organ of locomo-tion, the foot is one of the most important members of the human frame. When suffered to exhibit the untrammeled for-mation and proportion of nature it is, indeed, beautiful, but as it is, is an appropriate and elegant finish to the figure. The usages of society in modern Europe, at once judiciously com-

bining health, comfort, and elegance, forbid the exhibition of
the unclothed foot; but the exquisite sculptures of Greece and
Rome sufficiently attest the accuracy of our assertion. We see
there the finely-proportioned feet only protected by the simple
sandal; the arched and muscular instep; the dimpled joints,
and stright, slender toes falling equally to the ground. As we
look upon them we feel at once their perfect adaption to the
purpose of graceful exercise, their peculiar beauty of formation and finish in themselves, and their capability of supporting the superstruction of which they form so elegant a part.
Yet a small foot, meaning a narrow, shapeless one, is now so
generally admired—and such excessive pains are taken to obtain it by restricting the growth of the foot in early life by the
use of small and unyielding shoes—that in the upper and middle classes of society a really handsome foot is rarely found to
accompany figures of even faultless proportions otherwise.
This absurd prejudice exists chiefly among ladies, who, heed-
less of medical advice to the contrary, continue to wear shoes
smaller in size than the dimensions of their feet actually require, and do, in many instances, cheerfully submit to the most
cruel self-imposed restraint rather than the world should say
that nature had given them feet properly proportioned to the
development of their persons. Now, the truth is, that feet
larger than they really require to be for the size and weight of
the rest of the body very rarely occur, and, when they do, are
by no means more inelegant in appearance than such as are
disproportionately small; and were these self-doomed sufferers
to reflect that a foot can only be handsome so long as it is
suitable for the performance of its natural functions, and that
such as approach to the Chinese idea of beauty must ensure a
most ungraceful carriage, they would certainly cease their endeavors to attain an end so closely approaching to deformity.
Besides, in attempting to reduce the feet to an unnatural narrow compass, the confinement to which they are subjected
necessarily leads to their ultimate distortion; crooked and un-
even toes, projecting joints, irritable corns and bunions, and
crippled motions, are the results of the endeavors to cramp the
feet into fashionable neatness ! And yet all the squeezing and
compressing which can be brought to bear upon a foot by

5

shoes of ordinary materials will tend but little to lessen it in size, one quarter of an inch being, we may safely state, the utmost extent of the diminution that can for any time be borne. Reflection, too, will show how slight the change can be which if effected in this way upon the appearance of an ordinary sole, and, also, how little the advantages keep pace with the annoyances undergone.

A foot which is flatly formed appears much larger to the eye than one which is finely arched, although, in reality, its surface may not be greater, and a judicious method of reducing its bulk in appearance, and perhaps improving its shape, is to adopt those coverings which, by form and color, are calculated to produce that effect by optical delusion. White and fancy stockings should be avoided by those whose feet possess this peculiar development, as white and other light colors, from their well-known power of reflecting light, give the form of the object to which they are applied a peculiar distinctness. Black, on the other hand, sends back few, if any, rays of light to meet the eye, and, consequently, the feet, if clothed in this color, will appear themselves sensibly diminished. Black stockings and dark-colored boots and shoes, invariably black, whatever their material may be, should, therefore, be worn by those who have large and flat feet, and, by skillful management, will not appear out of keeping with the rest of the dress. The shoe, moreover, should be made to come high upon the instep, for nothing tends so much to give a degree of awkwardness to the feet as their being allowed to overflow, as it were, the leather, since they are certain to look large if anything in the vicinity should happen to be disproportionately small. The heel should, in addition, be considerably elevated, with a view to increase the height of the arch, by which, in turn, the general flatness is diminished, and the appearance of breadth consequently lessened. Such, we doubt not, our fair readers will find on trial to be a better way of remedying apparent and even real defects in size than the ordinary method by compression; let greater attention be paid to the color of the stocking and the form of the shoe, and less to the thinness of the former and smallness and lightness of the latter, and benefits greater than may appear at first sight will, we firmly believe, result to those who alter their line of procedure. A walking shoe should be particularly easy and of firm materials, with a thick sole; boots are not well adapted for this purpose, as they are usually tight and do not admit of the free play of the muscles of the foot and ankle so necessary to walk with either grace or comfort; a slight shoe with a slight sole induces fatigue, from its inability of yielding a firm support to the foot. Ladies are too much in the habit of neglecting the practice of walking as a means of healthful exercise, although part of the blame attaches to their natural protectors, who have absurd ideas of the impropriety of women being frequently seen out doors. Those, indeed, who possess carriages do not confine themselves so rigorously, but walking is by far the most preferable mode of taking the air. Our continental neighbors differ from us in no respect more than in their fondness for exercise in the open air, and to the opportunities of thus fulfilling the dictates of nature we may ascribe the elegance which marks the movements of their wives and daughters. The women of Paris and Madrid are celebrated for the elegance of their feet, but then they cultivate them properly by constant walking, which they look upon as a graceful accomplishment. In both capitals the utmost care is bestowed upon the decoration of the feet; and from this results that symmetrical form which fixes the attention of the English stranger.

THE TEETH.—Many reasons combine to render early and persevering attention to the cleanliness and care of the teeth an imperative duty; a white, regular dental arch is, besides being beautiful in itself, a most advantageous accompaniment to the finest features and renders even homely ones agreeable, and is necessary in order to preserve the contour of the face. The teeth are usually thirty-two in number, sixteen in each jaw; they are divided into three classes: 1st. The incisors, which are the four cutting teeth in front of each jaw. 2nd. The canine, or cuspidati, the longest of all the teeth, derive their name from their resemblance to the tusks of a dog, and are four in number, one appearing on each side of the upper and lower row of incisors. 3rd. The molars, or grinders, of which there are ten in each side, five above and the same number below, so called from being, as to size, figure, and situa-

tion, best calculated for the mastication of our food. The
teeth of the first and second classes have only one fang each;
the three last molars two fangs, and the same teeth in the
upper, three. Each tooth is divided into two parts—its body,
or that part which is above the gum, covered with the hard,
white, peculiar substance called enamel, and its fangs, or root,
which is fixed in the socket; the boundary between these two,
called the neck of the tooth, is formed by a small, circular depression immediately above the edge of the gum. The teeth
should be washed with a moderately soft brush and tepid water
every morning, taking care that the brush operates also on the
gum, for the purpose of keeping up a brisk circulation and at
the same time rendering its surface firm and healthy. The
mouth should also be carefully rinsed with tepid water after
meals, as the small particles of food which may remain in the
interstices of the teeth are liable, by their decomposition, to
impart an unpleasant odor to the breath, and this precaution
should be particularly attended to after supper, with a few
strokes of the brush, as a very slight roughness of the surface
materially assists the accumulation of tartar. Tartar appears
to be a residuum of the saliva, as it is found to invade those
teeth more particularly which are in the immediate vicinity of
the openings of the salivary ducts; these are the inner sides of
the front teeth in the lower jaw and the outer surfaces of the
molars in the upper jaw; it is, therefore, a natural source of
annoyance peculiar to every human being; in some constitutions it is more largely deposited than in others; but never so
obstinately as to resist the brush, if constantly used; we do not
mean to say that a brush can remove tartar when once suffered
to effect a lodgment and acquire consistence, but we are certain
that the daily use of the brush will, in most individuals, prevent its being deposited altogether. The operation for removing the tartar is called scaling, and in the hands of an experienced dentist, is both a simple and a safe one. In some
instances, however, the teeth will be so loaded with tartar that
it is unsafe to remove it at one time. Where this is the case,
that part which is next the gums should be first removed, that
they may be thoroughly relieved. This being accomplished,
the patient should be directed to use some proper application

to the gums for a week, which will tend to their eventual restoration. When the gums are relieved and the teeth show signs
of fastening, the remaining tartar should be removed, either at
one or more sittings, until the teeth are perfectly freed from it
and no roughness is felt to the patient's tongue. After the
tartar is removed the teeth assume a dark lead color, which
only disappears after the use of tooth powder for some time
once or twice a day. "The best tooth powders," says an eminent dentist (Mr. Snell), "are, in my opinion, composed of such
ingredients as the following: Prepared chalk, finely levigated,
three drachms; Spanish soap, one drachm; Florentine iris-root,
one drachm; carbonate of soda, one drachm. I have often
found, after the teeth have been perfectly cleaned with instruments, that if constantly brushed once or twice a day with
this powder they are kept free from tartar. Tinctures and
other fluid applications to the gums are often extremely useful
when they are in an unhealthy state. As a simple application
to the mouth I know of no better thing than soap liniment.
Where the teeth are not much disposed to collect tartar or become discolored they may be kept in good order by this alone,
without the aid of any powder."

"The various opinions which are held relative to the shape
and texture of tooth-brushes would lead us to suppose that
the matter was a much more important one that it really is.
There are even patent tooth brushes. A brush too hard is as
useless, from having no elasticity, as one too soft is from its
having no firmness; a medium between the two should be
chosen. The brush should be used as much as possible in a
perpendicular direction, not as regards the brush, but the
teeth."

Metal tooth picks have a pernicious effect on the teeth, and
those made from quills irritate the gum; indeed, the only
safe article to use is a piece of cane or slip of light wood cut
to a nice point.

To the toilette a dental mirror will be found a useful appendage. It is usually of an oval shape, formed of either glass or
steel, cased in silver, and so small as to admit of being placed
in the mouth without the slightest inconvenience. Those con-
cave mirrors made expressly for the use of dentists are the best,

and are easily obtained. By shifting the mirror as occasion requires a complete view is obtained of those parts of the teeth which, even in the most regular and well-proportioned mouth, cannot be seen, either by the individual herself on examination in the dressing glass or by another person on looking into the mouth itself. For the individual, the dressing glass must, of course, be combined with the use of the dental mirror. Thus the complete cleanliness and general condition of every part of the teeth is ascertained, and the first indication of disease is instantly discoverable; consequently, the means of remedy will have all the advantage of early application.

THE MOUTH.—The mouth requires to be rinsed and the throat well gargled with tepid water, to which a few drops of Eau-de-Cologne may be added with advantage, every morning, for a kind of mucus gathers upon the surface of the mouth, and particularly on the tongue, during the hours of sleep, which, if not removed, obscures the nice perception of the palate and impairs the appetite. Sometimes this unpleasant matter is more thickly deposited than at others, owing, perhaps, to changes of food, of temperature, or any other cause upon the stomach. When it requires the aid of a scraper to remove it, one made of thin cane, or nicely-prepared whalebone, is infinitely preferable to those ivory or even silver articles with which dressing boxes are usually supplied. If the mouth feels clammy during the day, after walking or other exercise, one part of port wine mingled with three parts of water forms a refreshing lotion to rinse it with. A comfortable sensation is produced by drinking a wineglassful of spring water after the usual routine of the toilette is completed, and to take a seidlitz powder occasionally is an excellent preventive if subject to headache.

THE BREATH.—Purity of breath is an unspeakable personal comfort, and its value in social intercourse is literally beyond that of rubies. Yet, although it may be said to be peculiar to almost every healthy person, it is a precarious possession, easily forfeited at any time, and many causes more particulary tend to affect it as years advance. The natives of eastern countries seem to be particularly sensible to this; and, considering the sweetness of the breath to depend chiefly upon the condition of the mouth, are in the habit of chewing mastic and other odoriferous substances with a view to its preservation. This is at best a troublesome practice, and, while subject to immediate detection, has not always the effect hoped for. The breath is, however, dependent upon other organs and causes, as well as the mouth and teeth, for its odor; and almost every incident which can affect the general health extends its influence to the breath. Thus fatigue, induced either by immoderate exercise or repeated and protracted vigils, will render it impure. Deep study, combined with anxiety and restless nights, will have an equal effect. Sometimes disease of the lungs affects the breath; the impurity of the latter is then only a symptom and will meet due attention in the medical treatment of the disease. Habitual sacrifices to the "jolly god" may almost invariably be detected by the fetid odor of the breath; the derangement of the digestive organs being the inevitable result of the abuse of fermented liquors, the cause must be removed ere the effect can cease. When the breath is affected by the teeth an opiate has been recommended, which may be prepared by immersing eight ounces of the best honey with two ounces of rose water over a gentle fire for a few minutes, and then adding as much powdered myrrh and Armenian bole as will form a soft paste; it is applied to the teeth on a brush, and is generally successful in removing any unpleasant odor from them at the time. Tincture of myrrh, combined with tepid water, forms an effectual gargle when the affection does not proceed from the stomach. A gargle is also made for this purpose by pouring boiling water upon bruised charcoal and filtering it when cold; but it is most unpleasant to use and can only confer a temporary benefit. Vitiated breath may be a source of annoyance when its cause cannot be ascertained; but the measures so often insisted upon by physicians in order to promote health on other accounts will always exercise a beneficial influence upon it. We may mention, among others, early rising, exercise in the open air especially, equestrian exercise, strict temperance, and constant attention to the economy of the stomach and bowels; perseverance in these will, if not remove it altogether, at least ameliorate the evil.

THE LIPS.—The thinness of the skin which forms the out-

ward covering of the lips, although contributing in itself to
their peculiar beauty, renders them particularly susceptible of
injury from cold; and chaps and excoriation from this cause
are to many ladies a constant source of annoyance during
winter. Otherwise the lips are almost independent of assistance from the toilette. When tenderness of the face and lips
occurs from taking exercise in cold weather, and the skin is
rendered rough, though not actually broken, a little cold cream
is a most soothing application on returning to the house, as it
immediately allays the smarting and restores the natural
smoothness to the surface. Cold cream, for this particular
purpose, should be prepared thus:

Melt two ounces of the finest white wax with eight ounces
of oil of almonds over a very slow fire, and add gradually half
a pint of distilled rose water, stirring it until cold. By gentlemen who are habitually exposed to the action of the atmosphere the following lip salve will be found most useful as a
prophylactic against the effects of frost: Take four ounces of
the oil of almonds, one ounce of spermaceti, and one drachm
of prepared suet, with any simple vegetable coloring according
to fancy; simmer these until thoroughly mingled; as soon as
taken off the fire stir into the mixture fifteen drops of tincture
of capsicum, and, when nearly cold, twenty drops of oil of
rhodium.

A pleasing and efficacious lip salve is made thus: Put four
ounces of the best olive oil into a wide-mouthed bottle, with
one ounce of alkanet root well bruised, stop the bottle carefully, and place it in the heat of the sun until the color becomes a rich crimson; then strain the oil into a pipkin, with
two ounces each of fine white wax and new lamb suet; melt
the whole slowly, and, when almost cold, add six drops of otto
of roses, carefully stirred in, and put the salve up in small
ivory pots. The use of cayenne losenges deepens the natural
crimson of the lips; the effect of this carminative preparation
upon the stomach and the breath are at the same time correc-
tive and grateful, and it should be had immediate recourse to
upon the slightest symptom of sore throat. The habit of
smoking, now so generally adopted by gentlemen, is a decided
enemy both to the color and the contour of the lips. Nor are

these its only evils. In the first place, the stem of the pipe is very liable to excoriate the lips by its unyielding harshness, when, if not laid aside for the time, a painful and obstinate sore may be the result; as, among other causes of irritation, lead enters largely into the glazing portion of the stem, and its deleterious qualities are now too well known to require to be particularized here. Besides the disfiguring effects of a recent sore upon the lip, permanent disease may be reasonably dreaded, since a reference to any medical gentleman will confirm the startling truth that in a large proportion of cases of cancer occurring in the face and throat among the poorer classes, the first indication of the disease may be clearly traced to the obstinate excoriation caused by the use of a tobacco pipe.

THE HAIR.—The culture and decoration of the hair, as it is one of the first objects of personal adornment, naturally forms a very important branch of the toilette. In youth the hair is generally abundant and glossy, requiring little assistance from art to improve its appearance. Perfect cleanliness is indispensable for the preservation of its beauty and color, as well as its duration; this is attained by frequently washing it in tepid water, using those soaps which have the smallest portion of alkali in their composition, as this article renders the hair too dry, and by depriving it of its moist coloring matter impairs at once its strength and beauty. After washing, the hair should be immediately and thoroughly dried, and, when the towel has ceased to imbibe moisture, brushed constantly in the sun or before the fire until its lightness and elasticity are fully restored; and in dressing it a little marrow, pomatum, bears' grease, or fragrant oil should be used, yet as sparingly as possible.

The belief entertained by many persons that washing the hair induces catarrh, or headache, or injures the hair, is erroneous, as the application of water to the skin is the most natural and effectual method of cleansing it, and of keeping open the pores through which the perspiration must pass in order to ensure its healthy condition; besides, scabs naturally come around the roots of the hair of the most cleanly person, and these can only be completely detached by the use of soap. Wearing an oiled silk cap to prevent the hair and head from being wetted in sea bathing is an injurious custom, and usually causes headache at least, and often more serious though unsuspected evil. Thus, for the sake of avoiding a little trouble or saving a little time, that member of the frame, that truly requires it, is deprived of the invigorating influence of the sea water—denied an application more truly repellant of catarrh and rheumatic and neuralgic affections than all the coverings and artificial means of warmth and cure in use in the fashionable world. The constant and persevering use of the brush is a great means of beautifying the hair, rendering it glossy and elastic, and encouraging a disposition to curl. The brush produces further advantages in propelling and calling into action the contents of the numerous vessels and pores which are interspersed over the whole surface of the head, and furnish vigor and nourishment to the hair; five minutes, at least, every morning and evening should be devoted to its use. Two brushes are necessary for the toilette of the hair—a penetrating and a polishing brush; the penetrating brush, especially for a lady's use, should be composed of strong elastic hairs cut into irregular lengths, but not so hard or coarse as to be in any danger of irritating the skin; after being passed once or twice through the hair, to ensure its smoothness and regularity, the brush should be slightly dipped in Eau-de-Cologne, or sprinkled with a little perfumed hartshorn, as either of these preparations are beneficial in strengtheing the hair. The polishing brush should be made of firm, soft hairs, thickly studded. Combs should only be resorted to for the purpose of giving a form to the hair or assisting in its decoration, as their use is more or less prejudicial to the surface of the skin and the roots of the hair. The small toothed ivory comb is particularly injurious, as, besides its irritating effect on the skin, it has a tendency to split and crush the hair as it passes through it; surely this comb is not necessary at the toilette of a lady?

The growth of the hair is best promoted by keeping it scrupulously clean, and by cutting it frequently.

A moderate profusion of hair, gracefully arranged, is a characteristic adornment of women, and its appearance and condition will be found to convey conclusive evidence of the habits and taste of the wearer. In the disposition of the hair attention should always be paid to the style of the features and the formation of the face; yet it would be scarcely possible to imagine a countenance whose symmetry would not be injured by adopting any *outre* method. Braiding the hair, though a simple and unpretending method of dressing it, yet requires extremely regular features to relieve its formality, and is becoming perhaps only to those ladies whose style of face resembles the Grecian. Braids are, however, indispensable in deep mourning, when decoration is least in the thoughts of the wearer. Curls and ringlets generally harmonize with the female face, and seem really to be the most tasteful method of dressing the hair. Papillotes, the usual and best way of curling, should be put up gently and secured from coming out by a small pin run through the paper, because if they are too tightly twisted they not only occasion headache and uneasy sleep, but actually injure the hair by drawing it out by the roots; and in plaiting or tying the hair with a ribbon care should be taken not to draw it so tightly as to render the head uncomfortable, for anything that prevents the natural, easy flow of the hair tends to deprive it of its moisture, and thus, by checking its growth, renders it weak and thin. If the hair be very soft and fine, pomatum or oil is not required to dress it, but a fluid composition, such as either of the following, will be serviceable, both in giving it a fine gloss and imparting strength to it: Grate carefully down a pound and a half of good white soap, and put it with six ounces of potash and three pints of alcohol into a jar, which place in a hot water bath, stirring the mixture until it is thoroughly melted, then leave it to settle; pour off the clear liquor; perfume it with essence of violets, and put it up in well-corked bottles for use. The other excellent curling fluid is made by dissolving in the same manner, two pounds of soap, eight ounces of potash in a pint and a half each of water, adding to the liquor, when cold and clear, twenty drops of essence of amber.

The hair is subject to changes peculiar to its nature and structure as disease or the approach of age alter the constitution. Loss of color is perhaps the earliest source of annoyance, and many recipes have been set forth as a means of its restoration. These consist chiefly of hair dyes; preparations which at best are of doubtful service, and, in some instances, positively dangerous from the metallic agents employed in their composition; at the same time, they are extremely troublesome to use.

The remote causes of premature grey hair are anxiety, disappointment, protracted grief, great mental exertion, fear, fright, headache, and some others. Great care should be taken after sea bathing to wash the hair in soft water, to free it from the saline particles which form so large a constituent of the sea water, as these are very active in producing grey hair by extraction of the natural color. Among the best applications to the hair, with a view to prevent its becoming grey, are prepared marrow, bear's grease and honey water; the latter should be made thus: Take two quarts of the best French brandy; one pound of virgin honey; half a pound of coriander seeds; one ounce of cloves; half an ounce each of nutmeg, benzoin, and storax; the rind of two lemons, and two vanilloes; digest forty-eight hours, and distil with a gentle heat; add a pint each of rose water and orange-flower water; with three grains of ambergris; digest again forty-eight hours, and then filter and keep the water in closely stopped bottles.

There may possibly be a few instances where the adoption of false hair is excusable if not justifiable, but the matron whose tresses have become sprinkled with silver, commits an offence against beauty of the most interesting order in 'removing or concealing them, and assuming in their place substitues prepared by the artist, since the latter, however elegant and even natural in their appearance, are ever too youthful to harmonize with the faded complexion and altered features of advancing years.

The hair exercises considerable influence upon the health; and the consequence of cutting it depends upon the state of the circulation in the head at the time, and the quantity removed; to a person in health cold in the head, ear ache, head ache, and sometimes sore throat is the result when much is taken off suddenly, unless a covering is substituted, and worn for some time afterwards. Those who are strongly constituted, and who take regular exercise in the open air, may not perhaps experience inconvenience by the neglect of this precaution, but to the weak, or with convalescents, it will be otherwise. "Cutting off the hair," says Dr. Copland, "in cases of inflammatory excitement of the brain, or under any circumstances calling for cold applications, can seldom be productive of injury, though it seems doubtful if it be so beneficial as is generally supposed." On the other hand, keeping the hair closely cut is often productive of good effects; it is serviceable in head aches; frequent cutting promotes the growth of the hair, and admits of the usual operations of combing and brushing acting more efficiently on the scalp. In cases where cold sponging or the shower bath is necessary short hair is a decided advantage.

Depilatories are preparations for removing superfluous hair; but to have the desired effect they require to be compounded of such powerful ingredients that their use is attended with extreme danger to the skin. They are chiefly in the form of powders, of which a small quantity is made into a paste with rose water, Eau-de-Cologne, or even simple water, and applied on a piece of cambric.

Bad Practices.—It may be well to caution our young friends against certain bad practices, easily contracted, but sometimes difficult to relinquish. The following are things not to be done: Biting your nails. Slipping a ring up and down the finger. Sitting cross-kneed and jogging your feet. Drumming on the table with your knuckles; or, still worse, tinkling on a piano with your forefinger only. Humming a tune before strangers. Singing as you go up and down stairs. Putting your arm round the neck of another young girl, or promenading the room with arms encircling waists. Holding the arm of a friend all the time she sits beside you; or kissing or fondling her before company. Sitting too closely.

Slapping a gentleman with your handkerchief or tapping him with your fan. Allowing him to take a ring off your finger, to look at it. Permitting him to unclasp your bracelet or, still worse, to inspect your brooch. When these ornaments are to be shown to another person, always take them off for the purpose.

To listen at door cracks and peep through key holes is

vulgar and contemptible. So it is to ask children questions concerning their parents, though such things are still done.

However smart and witty you may be considered, do not exercise your wit in rallying and bantering your friends. If you do so, their friendship will soon be worn out, or converted into positive enmity. A jest that carries a sting with it can never give a pleasant sensation to the object. The bite of a mosquito is a very little thing, but it leaves pain and inflammation behind it, and the more it is rubbed the longer it rankles in the blood. No one likes to have their foibles or mishaps turned into ridicule, before other persons especially. And few can cordially join in a laugh that is raised against themselves.

The slightest jest on the personal defects of those you are conversing with is an enormity of rudeness and vulgarity. It is, in fact, a sneer at the Creator that made them so. No human creature is accountable for being too small or too large; for an ill-formed figure, or for ill-shaped limbs; for irregular features or a bad complexion.

Still worse to rally any person (especially a woman) on her age, or to ask indirect questions with a view of discovering what her age really is. If we continue to live, we must continue to grow old. We must either advance in age, or we must die. Where, then, is the shame of surviving our youth? And when youth departs, beauty goes along with it. At least as much beauty as depends on complexion, hair, and teeth. In arriving at middle age (or a little beyond it) a lady must compound for the loss of either face or figure. About that period she generally becomes thinner or fatter. If thin, her features shrink and her skin shrivels and fades, even though she retains a slender and perhaps girlish form. If she grows fat, her skin may continue smooth and her complexion fine, and her neck and arms may be rounder and handsomer than in girlhood; but then symmetry of shape will cease, and she must reconcile herself to the change as best she can. But a woman with a good mind, a good heart, and a good temper, can never, at any age, grow ugly—for an intelligent and pleasant expression is in itself beauty, and the best kind of beauty.

Sad, indeed, is the condition of women in the decline of life when "no lights of age adorn them;" when, having neglected in the spring and summer to lay up any stores for the winter that is sure to come, they find themselves left in the season of desolation with nothing to fall back upon but the idle gossip of the day—striving painfully to look younger than they really are; still haunting balls and parties, and enduring all the discomforts of crowded watering-places, long after all pleasure in such scenes must have passed away. But then they must linger in public because they are miserable at home, having no resources within themselves, and few enduring friends to enliven them with their society.

The woman who knows how to grow old gracefully will adapt her dress to her figure and her age, and wear colors that suit her complexion.

HOUSEHOLD.

The Kitchen.—One of the finest house-keepers in the United States says: "If scrimping must be done, scrimp parlor and sitting-room, but have the kitchen and bedrooms as comfortable as possible." Another writer observes: "The kitchen is to the house what the stomach is to the body, and should be the most spacious, best lighted, and best ventilated apartment in the house." This remark, however, is aimed mainly at city homes, where the kitchen is too often a mere little basement cellar, badly lighted and illy supplied with pure air, from which it is no wonder that the servants are continually rising to the upper regions to "give warning." In the country the average kitchen is far more decent, but still the erring house-keeper, anxious to "have things like other people," is prone to pinch the poor kitchen in order to furnish the parlor in gim-cracks.

This is all wrong. If one's house were intended for entertainment and continual festivity, then it would be well to place its parlor and dining-room first and foremost; but in a farm house, where the house-mother's work lies mainly in the kitchen and dairy, and where are needed all the aids and conveniences for making this work pleasant as well as profitable, it is simply silly to deny one's self valuable and useful every-day things for the sake of what-nots, upholstered chairs and Nottingham-lace curtains, that must necessarily be shut up, and of no benefit to anybody nine-tenths of the year.

The room should be of good size, with windows on opposite sides, as they thus give a peculiarly cheerful light. The ceiling and walls should be whitened or calcimined in some cheerful tint, and the woodwork oiled and varnished. For the floor—if it is even and of decent quality of lumber—nothing is better than two or three coats of oil, put on one after the other as fast as absorbed. Such a floor needs no scrubbing, a weekly mopping with plenty of warmish water, being sufficient to keep it clean. Comfortable little rugs should be placed before the sink and the ironing table, and, if this room must do duty as a dining-room, there should be, in winter, a large square of carpeting under the dining-table. A neat screen, made by tacking chintz or furniture calico upon a light wooden frame, about five feet high and six feet wide, might be placed between the table and the cook-stove, not only to temper the heat, but to shut off the not always attractive view of saucepans, spiders, and kettles used in the dinner-getting.

The sink should be capacious, lined with zinc. provided with drain-pipes, and flanked by pumps connected with cistern and well. Underneath may be a cupboard for pots and kettles, and above it a row of pegs on which to hang a dishcloth holder, a stiff brush for cleaning vegetables, a little mop for washing bottles and narrow-necked pitchers and jars, the lamp scissors, and such small articles as are in daily use in this department of the kitchen. Two small shelves should be placed at either end for soap dishes. A large, conveniently arranged sink goes a great way in making kitchen work easy.

A good-sized, substantial table of white-wood or pine is needed for ironing and baking days. It should have three drawers—a large one for ironing sheets, shirt-board and holders, and two smaller ones for baking-tins, spoons and knives used in cooking, and boxes of spices, salt, etc. Having once used such a table, no housekeeper will like to be without it. Above this table can be fastened a hanging rack for ironed clothes. These are much more convenient than the sort which stand on the floor, and when not in use can be folded back against the wall, entirely out of the way.

For washing days are needed a long bench two and a half feet wide, and of the right height, two or three tubs, a wringer, and, for heavy clothes, a washer. The latter, which costs $5 or $6, can be fitted to any tub, and ought to be an indispensable article. It is to washing-day what a reaping-machine is to an eighty-acre wheat field; and no farmer should neglect to provide one for his kitchen, unless he is willing to settle down to his harvesting with merely the sickle and the "cradle" of his forefathers! These items come under the head of kitchen furniture, but are, of course, kept in the cellar, or in a closet opening from the kitchen.

Along with a first-class cooking-stove, for it is not economy to have a poor one, should be selected the following quite necessary articles: Wash-boiler, tea-kettle, soup-pot, frying-kettle, spider, two or three granitized saucepans of different sizes, four bread-tins, two gem irons, coffee and tea-pots, large and small iron spoons, wire steak-broiler, wire toaster, steamer, pudding mold, patty pans, potato masher, skimmer, cream whipper, gravy strainer, egg-beater, half a dozen cake and pie tins, large and small graters, a dozen muffin rings, or a muffin pan, which is more convenient than the rings, a colander, a quart measure, and a griddle. No doubt other items will readily suggest themselves, but these, at any rate, are essential, if good housekeeping is the object. A proper and convenient place to keep them is a large, deep-shelved cupboard, with close doors, in which the common crockery and glass can also be kept.

The best arrangement is to have cupboard room for all table and cooking ware, and keep food and provision stores in a cool, well ventilated closet, that can be effectually closed to dust and flies.

Let the farmer provide a large, pleasant kitchen and interest himself in its conveniences for work—being as enthusiastic in furnishing labor-saving machines for this department of farming as for his outside fields—and he will find that he makes an investment that pays an hundred fold. Let the farmer's wife make the kitchen a bright and sweet-aired realm, and be proud to be its intelligent and efficient queen. Let her beautify her work as much as possible, and lift it above the dull, discouraging slough of drudgery. With conveniences for work, and a cheerful, comfortable place to work in, the women are few who will not make their homes "the dearest spot on earth" to all who dwell within them.

The Dining-room.—Although there are many country kitchens so shining and orderly and clean aired that it is a pleasure to break bread in them, there are many others which, owing to a large family and a pressure of work, cannot always be nice and orderly at meal times; so it is well, if it can be afforded, to have a small cheerful room opening from the kitchen, easily warmed in winter, and from which heat and flies can be excluded in summer, where meals can be eaten in the healthful serenity and comfort which is almost as essential as the food itself. What can be more refreshing to the laborer than to enter from the blistering glare of a harvest day into a cool, softly lighted room, in which the fragrance of freshly gathered flowers, or the aroma of leafy boughs, mingles its poetry with the cheerful prose of the beef and vegetables? And how pleasant and restful it is for his helpmate to lay aside her kitchen cares and kitchen apron together, and come smiling and tidy to her little throne behind the tea-service.

Such a room requires very little furniture. The walls should be of neat and quiet tint, with two or three pleasing pictures and some brackets for pots of ferns, or such vines as will grow prettily in the shade during the hot summer weather. In winter a few petunias and two or three foliage plants will fill the sunny windows with brightness and bloom. There should be a long, substantial table, with plenty of elbow room for all, and a side-board or cupboard for table-crockery. A small table will be found a convenience—if there is no side-board—for holding such dishes as are used toward the end of a meal at dinner time, when the varieties of food have a tendency to crowd each other. The window curtains may be plain shades of color suited to the walls of the room. Nothing can be better for the floor in summer time than an oiled surface, like that of the kitchen, which can be made comfortable to the feet in winter by a large " crumb-cloth " of drugget or home-made carpeting.

In more opulent farm homes, where the wife has liberty to devote more time and means to house decoration and furnishing, very handsome dining-rooms can be achieved with a moderate outlay. There should be high walls, a fire place, and a fine large window looking to the south or east. All the rest is in the hands of the mistress. If the floor has been laid in light and dark woods, well and good. It will be a thing of beauty through more than one life time, and always look genuine and substantial, as everything about a dining-room should. If, however, the floor is of pine, it may be stained in blocks or stripes, in a bordering two feet in width, covered with two coats of the best varnish, and the centre adorned with three or more breadths of pretty carpeting.

Have a carpenter construct a side-board of simple but substantial form, faced with oak or maple, or else made of the best pine. Glue artificial wood carvings of fruits in the centre of the top, and upon each door and drawer, and finish the whole with oil and varnish.

The table may also be home-made, and large and solid, with rounded corners, and substantial turned legs with casters. If not of real oak, the legs should be nicely stained to imitate it. If colored table-linen is used, it should be buff and white, with green borders, or buff and green in any neat, small patterns. These cloths, however, are generally covered with plain white ones at meal time.

Above this table there should be a handsome hanging lamp or small chandelier, with perhaps a little basket of Kennelworth ivy, or other gracefully growing vine, suspended from it. Such a light glorifes the plainest tea table.

As for chairs, there are a great many ways for achieving handsome ones without paying five dollars apiece for them at furniture shops. If a dozen oak chairs without seats can be obtained "in the rough" at the factory, they can be transformed into something pretty and substantial at small cost. They should first be oiled and varnished. Then with some stout sacking or canvas, some rich, dark cretonne, some gimp and furniture tacks, and either hair or wool for stuffing the seats— being careful to fasten the canvas securely in place and to cut the cretonne to fit neatly—even the cheap "splint-bottoms" which cost much less than oak, can be made into handsome chairs by painting the wood-work black, ornamenting it with gilt and scarlet lines, and varnishing—the seats to be upholstered in cretonne, striped linen, or common chintz.

The Parlor.—If means are small, and best room furniture seems to be among the things never to be obtained, let not the whole house be made dismal because of it; but rejoice that there is a kitchen, that there are comfortable bedrooms, and that there is a bit of Heaven in the form of a flower garden under the windows !

Even if one have but a small room to devote to this purpose, it can be made very pleasing, and has the advantage of requiring less furniture. A fire-place, with a mirror above it and a large wide-ledged window opposite, make the room already half-fitted up. The ceiling calcimined with the palest blue, and the walls with a tint two shades deeper, will have the effect to make the room appear more spacious. A border of dark and light blue, or of bluish-green and gold, should be used on such walls. The wood-work should be stained walnut color and varnished. The most suitable carpet would be an ingrain in small figures of blue and gray, with perhaps a bit of yellow or a bit of rose-colored scattered through it. Plain blue or gray lambrequins should be used for the windows, trimmed with fringe of the same color. For the curtains beneath them, sheer Swiss muslin is always pretty and graceful. Sometimes they are made with a knife plaiting or a fluted ruffle down the inner edges and across the bottom; but they look well when finished with simple hems, and are much easier laundried.

The fire place should be treated after the manner described in a previous chapter, and will be found the most effective feature in the room, especially if furnished with a good sized mirror, which will reflect back all the light and beauty of the apartment, and, like the cool color on the walls and ceiling, enhance its size. All those tasteful but restricted house-keepers who are anxious to have really attractive parlors, should aim for simply these three things—a large, wide-silled window, a fire-place, and a generous-sized mirror to place above it—letting curtains and carpet and chairs come about as they can; or using for a while plain shades for the windows, and a neat matting for the floor. Adding two or three pictures, a few books, some growing vines, and an easy chair to such a room, it is already cosy and hospitable in its aspect. In this room, as in all others, one should avoid a cluttered, crowded appearance. Do not afflict the wall with a general outbreak of small pictures, brackets, and fancy articles, as if a notion store were being fitted up. It is better to distribute such things throughout the house, that each room may have its two or three touches of graceful fancy.

For a table obtain something in a round or oval shape. It may be of pine or whitewood, but must be strong and substantial. Paint the legs black and varnish them. The top can be covered with a blue or gray cloth, embroidered about the edges, if one has time, with silk or white zephyr wool. Above the table suspend a pretty hanging lamp with shade.

Sometimes old chairs can be purchased at an auction, or dragged out of a garret, and transformed into beautiful things, with paint and varnish, decalcomania-gildings, and stuffed seats of rep or cretonne. These, with a light willow rocker, or a camp-chair and a handsome foot-stool or two, will comfortably complete the furnishing.

Remarks.—The dining or breakfast-room should be cool, light, and airy, with not much more than the indispensable furniture.

In summer, the floor covered with a staw-matting or an oil-cloth; in winter, with a dark, warm-looking carpet.

A sideboard, or narrow tables, at the side or end of the room, for the convenience of dessert and changes of dishes; or else have dumb waiters (which are stands supporting large trays).

Most modern houses are built with sliding closets; when the dining room is above the kitchen, this is almost indispensable; or the waiters' pantry—between the dining room and kitchen—has an open communication with it, that the dishes may be passed to and fro from the cook, without the delay and awkwardness of opening and shutting the doors; or, when there are no servants in attendance, it is convenient to have the dessert arranged on a tray, covered with a white napkin, and placed on a stand or small table at the left hand of the mistress or head of the table, and one on the other hand for receiving empty plates, etc.

For Breakfast.—Have a white cloth, with the folds regular and perceptible; let each dish be polished with a soft napkin, as it is placed upon the table, otherwise there is apt to be a dimness from having been put together before they were perfectly dried; and, further, to remove the traces of the necessary handling, in putting them to their places and returning them to the table.

The plates may be put in a pile at the left hand of the carver or at regular intervals around the table. A vast differ-ance may be made in the appearance and neatness of the table, by the manner in which the knives and forks, and spoons, and other paraphernalia, are placed.

The coffee-urn or pot should have on its brightest face, and all the recommendative warmth of its nature—ready for a free outpouring; the cream or boiled milk should not lack heat, and, not to "waste its sweetness" on the unappreciating air, should be contained in a covered pitcher of tin or other metal; the sugar-basin, whether the same as the other dishes, or of metal, should be bright and covered, with a large-sized tea or sugar-spoon beside it; the cups and saucers may be placed in heaps of three, within the circle of the sugar, slop, and cream vessels. Let the urn or coffee-pot be set at the right hand side of the person who serves it; and, if tea is used, let it be placed on the same side in a line with it; the one to be least called for, to stand at the outer corner of the tray—which may be placed at the middle of the broadside of the table, or at one end.

Before putting the dishes on it, the tray should be covered with a white napkin, fringed at the ends. Small napkins or doyles, folded in four and ironed very smoothly, may be laid at each plate; which should be reversed, or turned the bottom side up, and the knife and fork at the right side, or the knife at the side and a silver fork in front of the plate. Since so it is, that many Americans dislike the use of a silver fork—find-ing it exceedingly clumsy and awkward—it is best to place the one belonging to the knife with it, at the side of the plate, leaving it optional which to make use of.

Let the cruet-stand or castor occupy the centre of the table. If there are more than five or six persons, have two small plates of butter, one at either end of the table, and opposite each other. Let there be two plates of bread or rolls, or one of either of these, and the other place for hot griddle-cakes, or corn-bread, or toast.

Opposite the tray or head of the table, let the steak, or fry, (or whatever principal dish,) be placed, with the carving-knife and fork before it, and dishes of hominy, or boiled rice, or mashed potatoes, and boiled eggs, or hash, opposite each other, and the plates of bread between the steak dish and tray, having one of the plates of butter between each two, and the castor in the centre; also one or two salt stands filled with fine salt, and neatly marked with a teaspoon or otherwise, and a salt-spoon across each, and may be placed diagonally opposite each other. These, with a pitcher of ice-water and several tumblers, occupying the corners of the table on either side of the carver, complete the breakfast-table.

If there is a servant or waiter in attendance, let such stand at the left hand of the mistress, or head of the table, with a small tray, and pass the cups to and from her, presenting it at the left hand.

The Dinner Table.—Without a perfect knowledge of the art of carving, it is impossible to perform the honors of the table with propriety; and nothing can be more disagreeable to one of a sensitive disposition, than to behold a person, at the head of a well-furnished board, hacking the finest joints, and giving them the appearance of having been gnawed by dogs.

It also merits attention in an economical point of view; a bad carver will mangle joints so as not to be able to fill half a dozen plates from a sirloin of beef, or a large tongue; which, besides creating a great difference in the daily consumption of families, often occasions disgust in delicate persons, causing them to loathe the provisions, however good, which are set before them. One cannot, therefore, too strongly urge the study of this useful branch of domestic economy.

Carving.—An ox is divided by the butcher into the following joints, London style:

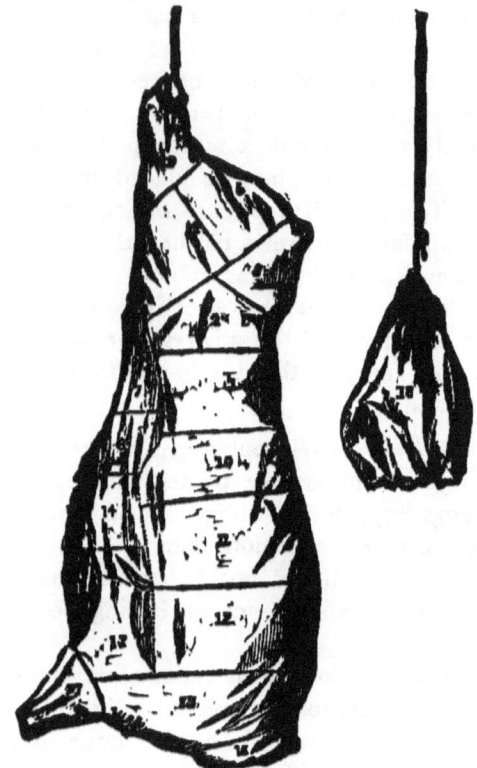

1. Sirloin.	7. Thick flank.	13. Shoulder, or leg-of-mutton piece.
2. Top, or aitch-bone.	8. Thin flank.	
3. Rump.	9. Leg.	14. Brisket. 15. Clod.
4. Buttock, or round.	10. Fore-rib (5 ribs).	16. Sticking.
5. Mouse buttock.	11. Middle rib (4 ribs).	17. Shin.
6. Veiny piece.	12. Chuck rib (3 ribs).	18. Cheeks, or Head.

Fish is cut with a silver fish-slice, or the more modern large

TURBOT.

MIDDLE-CUT OF SALMON.

silver-fish knife and fork. Large flat fish, as turbot, brill, John Dorey, etc., must first be cut from head to tail down the middle, and then in portions across to the fin, which, being considered a delicacy, is helped with the rest. (See cut.)

Salmon is cut in slices down the middle of the upper side, as from A to B, and then in slices across D to C, and a little of the "thick," or upper side, and "thin," or under side, are put on each plate.

A mackerel divides between four people; the fish-knife is passed between the upper and under side from head to tail, and each side is halved to help. A cod is cut cross-ways, like

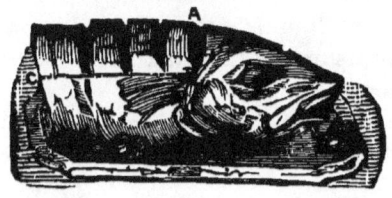

COD FISH.

salmon, from C to B, and in down slices as from A to B, and a small piece of the sound is sent with each helping. Small fish, as smelts, are sent whole, one on each plate, as are whiting.

Fried soles are cut across right through the bone. The "shoulder" or head end, should be first helped.

A sirloin of beef is cut across for the under-cut, and lengthways for the upper. You should ask your guest if he or

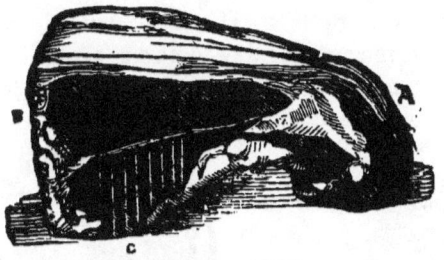

SIRLOIN OF BEEF.

she prefers the under-cut, which is by some considered the most delicate part of the beef, and is disliked by others. Slices from the under cut should be thick.

Rolled ribs and a round of beef are easily carved in hori-

zontal slices over the whole surface. The slices should be
very thin.

Boiled beef should also be cut in thin horizontal slices the

AITCH-BONE.

size of the joint itself in length and breadth. (See cut.)

Mutton appears on the table in four forms—the saddle, the
leg, the shoulder, the loin.

The saddle is the joint ordered for a large dinner party. It
is cut in very thin slices close to the backbone; B to A and

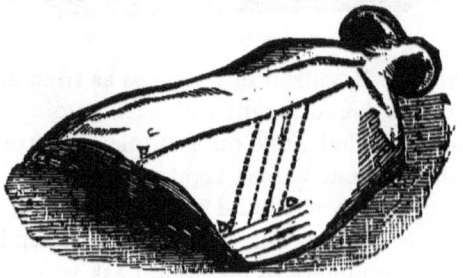

SADDLE OF MUTTON.

then downwards from A to D and C; but a lady is scarcely
ever required in the present day to carve a saddle of mutton.

A shoulder must lie with the knuckle towards your right,
and the blade-bone towards your left hand.

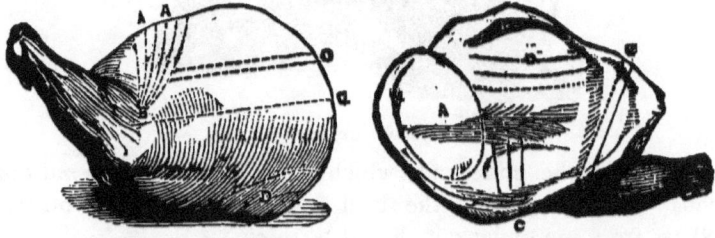

SHOULDER OF MUTTON.   SHOULDER OF MUTTON.

In the middle of the edge of the part farthest from you

place the fork, and then give one sharp cut from the edge to the bone. The meat flies apart, and you cut rather thick slices on each side of the opening A to B till you can cut no more.

You will then find two or three slices from the centre bone to the end B to C. Afterwards the joint must be turned over, and slices cut from the under side.

Some people, instead of cutting the joint in this manner, begin with slices cut lengthways near the middle of the joint from the end to the knuckle, and it is the better way.

A leg of mutton must be placed with the knuckle towards your left hand; you then cut into the side farthest from you

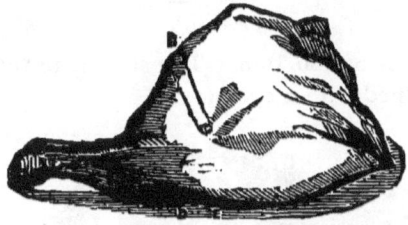

LEG OF MUTTON.

towards the bone B to C, helping thin slices from the right and thick slices towards the knuckle. The little tuft of fat near the thick is a delicacy, and must be divided among your guests.

A loin of mutton is carved either through the joints, which brings it into the form of "chops," or it is cut lengthways, in a parallel line with the joints. The latter is the best mode for a lady, but a loin is rather for family consumption than for guests.

A fore-quarter of lamb consists of a shoulder, the breast, and the ribs, and, alas! when the carver has to dissect it! If a lady is obliged to carve this joint, she must first place her knife upon the shoulder, draw it through horizontally, and then

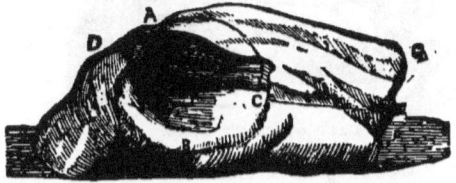

FORE-QUARTER OF LAMB.

remove the joint whole, placing it on a separate dish, which is held for its reception. She must then cut off the breast and separate the ribs (see cut); but the cook should always cut off the shoulder, and leave it on the joint.

The hind-quarter consists of a leg and loin.

A fillet of veal is cut in horizontal slices like a **round of**

FILLET OF VEAL.

beef; they must not be too thin. The stuffing in the centre is taken out and helped with a spoon.

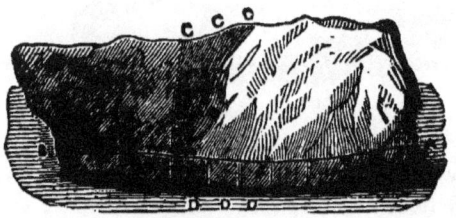

BREAST OF VEAL.

In a breast of veal the ribs should be first separated from the brisket, after which either or both may be sent round.

A calf's head must be cut down the centre in rather thin slices on each side. The meat round the eye is scooped out;

HALF OF CALF'S HEAD.

it is considered a delicacy. A small piece of the palate and accompanying sweetbread must be sent on each plate.

Roast pork is never seen at dinner parties, but is occasionally served at a family dinner.

The leg is carved like a leg of mutton, but the slices should be thicker and not so large.

A ham may be cut in three ways—1st. By beginning at the knuckle, which must be turned towards your left hand and cut

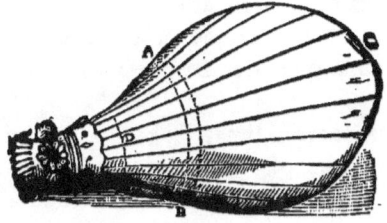

HAM.

in a slanting direction; or at the thick end, which is then turned towards your left; or in the ordinary manner, like a leg of mutton, beginning in the centre.

The slices must be as thin and delicate as you can possibly cut them. One slice is given as accompaniment to fowl or veal.

A rabbit has the legs and shoulders removed with a sharp-

BOILED RABBIT.

pointed knife, then the back is broken into three or four pieces at the joints.

Hare is thus carved: First, take off the legs. Cut two long thin slices off each side of the back B to A; then take off the shoulders, and break the back into four pieces with the fork. Cut off the ears, insert the point of the knife exactly in the

HARE.

centre of the palate, and drawing it to the nose, split the head

in two. But when only a small portion of the hare is eaten, and it is only served at second course, it is more elegant for a lady to help a portion of the side with a spoon, as we have often seen done.

The best parts of a hare are the slices from the back, the head, and ears. But ladies never eat the two latter. They should be sent to any gentleman guest who is known to be an epicure.

A chicken is carved thus: Take off the wings, cut slices from the breast, take off the merrythought and side !bones. The liver wing is the best part of the chicken after the breast;

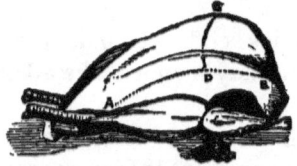

ROAST FOWL.

BOILED TURKEY.

but you should help the breast first, then both wings. If you have many to help, manage to reserve a slice of white meat to send with the legs and sides.

A partridge is carved like a fowl; so is a pheasant.

A pigeon is cut in halves right down the middle, and half is sent at once to the guest.

A snipe is treated in the same way.

Very small birds are sent whole.

A turkey and goose are helped by cutting slices off the breast, and then the wings and legs are taken off. Wild duck is helped in the same manner.

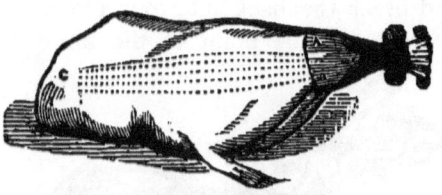

HAUNCH OF VENISON.

A haunch of venison should be cut from A to B close to the knuckle. (See cut first.) Then from C to A.

Coffee is sent to the gentlemen in the dining-room. Tea

only is handed after dinner, when the gentlemen have left the dinner-table.

A few hints are prefixed on the etiquette of the dinner-table, which will be found useful. In that, however, much must be left to a quick and observant eye, and a determination to render yourself as agreeable as possible.

As Host.—The important day on which you feast your friends being arrived, you will be duly prepared to receive the first detachment. It were almost needless to observe that the brief interval before dinner is announced may be easily filled up by the common-place inquiries after health, and observations on the weather; as the company increases, provided they were previously acquainted, you will find your labors in keeping up the conversation very agreeably diminished.

While your guests are awaiting the announcement of dinner, it will be expedient that you should intimate to the gentlemen of the party, as unobtrusively as possible, which lady you wish each to take in charge, that, when the moment arrives for your adjournment to the dining-room, there may not be half a dozen claimants for the honor of escorting *la plus belle* of the party, while some plain *demoiselle* is under the painful necessity of escorting herself. Such a scene as this should be carefully provided against by the mode above suggested.

When dinner is announced, you will rise and request your friends to proceed to the dining-room, yourself leading the way, in company with your most distinguished female visitor, followed immediately by the hostess, accompanied by the gentleman who has the best claim to such an honor. The remainder of the guests then follow, each gentleman accompanied by the lady previously pointed out to him.

Arrived at the dining-room, you will request the lady whom you conducted, to take her seat on your right hand; then, standing behind your chair, you will direct your visitors to their respective seats.

Having taken your seat, you will now dispatch soup to each of your guests, from the pile of plates placed on your right hand, without questioning any whether you shall help them or not; but, dealing it out silently, you will first help the person

7

at your right hand, then at your left, and so throughout the table. You will not ask to be allowed to help your guests, but supply a plate in silence, and hand it to your servants, who will offer it to such of the company as are unprovided. Never offer soup or fish a second time.

If a dish be on the table, some parts of which are preferred to others, according to the taste of the individuals, all should have the opportunity of choice. You will simply ask each one if he has any preference for a particular part; if he replies in the negative, you are not to repeat the question, nor insist that he must have a preference. Do not attempt to eulogize your dishes, or apologize that you cannot recommend them,— this is extremely bad taste; as is also the vaunting of the excellence of your wines, etc., etc. Do not insist upon your guests partaking of particular dishes. Do not ask persons more than once, and never force a supply upon their plates. It is ill-bred, though common, to press any one to eat; and, moreover, it is a great annoyance to be crammed like turkeys. Neither send away your plate, nor relin uish your knife and fork, till your guests have finished.

Soup being removed, the gentleman who supports the lady of the house on the right, should request the honor of taking wine with her. This movement will be the signal for the rest. Should he neglect to do this, you must challenge some lady. Until the cloth be removed, you must not drink wine except with another. If you are asked to take wine, it is a breach of etiquette to refuse. In performing this ceremony, (which is very agreeable if the wine be good,) you catch the person's eye and bow politely. It is not necessary to say any· thing.

If you have children, never introduce them after dinner, unless particularly asked for, and then avoid it if possible.

Never make any observations to your servants at dinner, other than to request them to provide you with what you require, or take away that which may be removed.

With the dessert, you will have a small plate, two wine-glasses, and *doyles*, placed before each guest. If fresh fruit be on the table, as pears, apples, nectarines, etc., a knife with a silver or silver-plated blade should be placed by the side or each plate; a steel blade, in addition to being discolored by the juice, imparts an unpleasant flavor to the fruit.

As Guest.—To dine out, it is usually understood that you must be invited. There are, however, some gentlemen who have attained to that high degree of refinement which enables them to dispense with such a stupid ceremony. They drop in as dinner is being served up, when it is impossible that the party on whom they intrude can do other than to request them to stay and dine, though we suspect he has a much stronger inclination to kick the unwelcome guest into the street. We would recommend you to eschew such practices; but when invited, return an answer in plain terms, accepting or declining. If you accept, be there at the appointed time. It is inconvenient, on many accounts, to yourself and your friends, to be either too late or too early. You will probably have to wait a little time before dinner is announced. During this short period, render yourself as agreeable as possible to the assembled company.

Your host will doubtless point out to you the lady he wishes you to escort to the dining room. You will be in readiness to attend upon her the moment you are summoned to adjourn. Offer her your right arm, and follow in order. Should you have to pass down stairs, you will give the lady the wall. You will take your seat at the table on the right hand of the lady you conducted. Being seated, soup will be handed round. When offered, take it; but if you prefer fish, pass it on to your neighbor. You must not ask for soup or fish a second time; it will not be offered—you would not be so rude or selfish as to keep the company waiting for the second course, that you may have the pleasure of demolishing a double portion of fish.

Fish must be eaten with a silver fork, as the acid in the sauce, acting on the steel of an ordinary fork, gives an unpleasant flavor to the dish. For this reason, also, a knife should not be used in eating fish.

If asked whether you have a preference for any dish, or any particular part of a dish, answer plainly and distinctly as you wish.

Pay as much attention to your companion on your left, as politeness requires, but do not be unnecessarily officious.

People do not like to be stared at when eating. When you are helped to anything, do not wait until the rest of the company are provided. This is very common in the country but shows a want of good breeding.

Do not allow your plate to be overloaded with a multifarious assortment of vegetables, but rather confine yourself to one kind. When you take another sort of meat, or a dish not properly a vegetable, you must change your plate.

If you have the honor of sitting on the right hand of the hostess, you will, immediately on the removal of soup, request the honor of taking wine with her.

Finally, to do all these things well, and to be au fait at a dinner party, be perfectly at your ease. To be at ease is a great step towards enjoying your own dinner, and making yourself agreeable to the company. Fancy yourself at home; performing all the ceremonies without any apparent effort. For the rest, observation and your own judgment will be the best guide, and render you perfect in the etiquette of the dinner table.

Condiments and Beverages.—Condiments are simply seasoning or flavoring agents, and, though hardly coming under the head of food, yet have an important part to play. As food by their use is rendered more tempting, a larger amount is consumed, and thus a delicate or uncertain appetite is often aided. In some cases they have the power of correcting the injurious character of some foods.

Salt stands foremost. Vinegar, lemon juice, and pickles owe their value to acidity; while mustard, pepper, black and red, ginger, curry-powder, and horseradish, all depend chiefly upon pungency. Under the head of aromatic condiments are ranged cinnamon, nutmegs, cloves, allspice, mint, thyme, fennel, sage, parsley, vanilla, leeks, onions, shallots, garlic, and others, all of them entering into the composition of various sauces in general use.

Salt is the one thing indispensable. The old Dutch law condemned criminals to a diet of unsalted food, the effects being said to be those of the severest physical torture. Years ago an experiment tried near Paris demonstrated the necessity of its use. A number of cattle were fed without the ration of salt; an equal number received it regularly. At the end of a specified time, the unsalted animals were found rough of coat, the hair falling off in spots, the eyes wild, and the flesh hardly half the amount of those naturally fed.

A class of extreme Grahamities in this country decry the use of salt, as well as any form of animal food; and I may add that the expression of their thought, in both written and spoken speech, is as savorless as their diet.

Salt exists, as we have already found, in the blood; the craving for it is a universal instinct, even buffaloes making long journeys across the plains to the salt-licks, and its use not only gives character to insipid food, but increases the flow of the gastric juice.

Black pepper, if used profusely, as is often done in American cooking, becomes an irritant, and produces indigestion. Red pepper, or cayenne, on the contrary, is a useful stimulant at times; but, as with mustard, any overuse irritates the lining of the stomach.

So with spices and sweet herbs. There should be only such use of them as will flavor well, delicately, and almost imperceptibly. No one flavor should predominate, and only a sense of general savoriness rule. Extracts, as of vanilla, lemon, bitter almond, etc., should be used with the greatest care, and if possible always be added to an article after it cools, as the heat wastes the strength. Tea is valuable chiefly for its warming and comforting qualities. Taken in moderation, it acts partly as a sedative, partly as a stimulant, arresting the destruction of tissue, and seeming to invigorate the whole nervous system. The water in it, even if impure, is made wholesome by boiling, and the milk and sugar give a certain amount of real nourishment. Nervous headaches are often cured by it, and it has, like coffee, been used as an antidote in opium-poisoning

Pass beyond the point of moderation, and it becomes an irritant, precisely in the same way that an overdose of morphine will, instead of putting to sleep, for just so much longer time prevent any sleep at all. The woman who cannot eat, and who braces her nerves with a cup of green-tea,—the most powerful form of the herb,—is doing a deeper wrong than she may be able to believe. The immediate effect is delightful. Lightness, exhilaration, and sense of energy are all there; but the reaction comes surely, and only a stronger dose next time accomplishes the end desired. Nervous headaches, hysteria in its thousand forms, palpitations, and the long train of nervous symptoms, own inordinate tea and coffee drinking as their parent. Taken in reasonable amounts, tea can not be said to be hurtful; and the medium qualities, carefully prepared, often make a more wholesome tea than that of the highest price, the harmful properties being strongest in the best. If the water is soft, it should be used as soon as boiled, boiling causing all the gases which give flavor to water to escape. In hard water, boiling softens it. In all cases the water must be fresh, and poured boiling upon the proper portion of tea, the teapot having first been well scalded with boiling water. Never boil any tea but English breakfast tea; for all others, simple steeping gives the drink in perfection.

The most valuable property of coffee is its power of relieving the sensation of hunger and fatigue. To the soldier on active service, nothing can take its place; and in our own army it became the custom often, not only to drink the infusion, but, if on a hard march, to eat the grounds also. In all cases it diminishes the waste of tissue. In hot weather it is too heating and stimulating, acting powerfully upon the liver, and, by producing over-activity of that organ, bringing about a general disturbance.

So many adulterations are found in ground coffee that it is safest for the real coffee-lover to buy the bean whole. Roasting is usually more perfectly done at the grocers', in their rotary roasters, which give every grain its turn; but, by care and constant stirring, it can be accomplished at home. Too much boiling dissipates the delicious aroma we all know; and the best methods are considered to be those which allow no boiling, after boiling water has been poured upon it, but merely a standing to infuse and settle. The old fashion, however, of mixing with an egg, and boiling a few minutes, makes a coffee hardly inferior in flavor. In fact, the methods are many, but results, under given conditions, much the same; and we may choose urn or old-fashioned tin pot, or a French biggin, with the certainty that good coffee, well roasted, boiling water, and good judgement as to time, will give always a delicious drink. Make a note of the fact that long boiling sets free tannic acid, powerful enough to literally tan the coats of the stomach, and bring on incurable dyspepsia. Often coffee without milk can be taken, where, with milk, it proves harmful; but, in all cases, moderation must rule. Taken too strong, palpitation of the heart, vertigo, and fainting are the usual consequences.

In chocolate—a preparation of cocoa—the cocoa is carefully dried and roasted, and then ground to a smooth paste, the nuts being placed on a hot iron plate, and so keeping the oily matter to aid in forming a paste. Sugar and flavorings, as vanilla, are often added, and the whole pressed into cakes. The whole substance of the nut being used, it is exceedingly nutritious, and made more so by the milk and sugar added. Eaten with bread, it forms not only a nourishing but a hearty meal; and so condensed is its form, that a small cake carried in traveling, and eaten with a cracker or two, will give temporarily the effect of a full meal.

Alcohol is last upon our list, and scientific men are still uncertain whether or not it can in any degree be considered as a food; but we have not room for the various arguments for and against. You all know, in part, at least, the effects of intemperance; and even the moderate daily drinker suffers from clouded mind, irritable nerves, and ruined digestion.

This is not meant as an argument for total abstinence; but there are cases where such abstinence is the only rule. In an inherited tendency to drink, there is no other safe road; but to the man or woman who lives by law, and whose body is in the best condition, wine in its many forms is a permissible occasional luxury, and so with beer and cider and the wider range of domestic drinks. In old age its use is almost essential, but always in moderation, individual temperament modifying every rule, and making the best knowledge an imperative need. A little alcoholic drink increases a delicate appetite; a great deal diminishes or takes it away entirely, and also hinders, and, in many cases, stops, digestion altogether. In its constant over-use the membranes of the stomach are gradually destroyed, and every organ in the body suffers. In ales and beers there is not only alcohol, but much nitrogeneous and sugary matter, very fattening in its nature. A light beer, well flavored with hops, is an aid to digestion, but taken in excess produces biliousness. The long list of alcoholic products it is not necessary to give, nor is it possible to enter into much detail regarding alcohol itself.

Soyer's Cafe au Lait.—One cup of best coffee, freshly roasted, but unground, two cups of boiling water, one quart of boiling milk. Put the coffee in a clean, dry kettle, or tin pail; it on a close top, and set in a sauce-pan of boiling water. Shake it every few minutes, without opening it, until you judge that the coffee grains must be heated through. If, on lifting the cover, you find that the contents of the inner vessel are very hot and smoking, pour over them the boiling water directly from the tea-kettle. Cover the inner vessel closely, and set on the side of the range, where it will keep very hot, without boiling, for twenty minutes. Then add the boiling milk; let all stand together for five minutes more, and strain through thin muslin into the coffee urn. Use loaf sugars for sweetening.

Vienna Coffee.—With very little extra trouble morning coffee can be greatly improved. Beat the white of an egg to a stiff froth, mix with an equal quantity of whipped cream, and use in coffee instead of cream· put in cream first, then coffee, and lastly this mixture.

Good New England Coffee.—For a family of six, take six large tablespoonfuls of best Java coffee, well browned and ground (not too fine), beat into it half an egg and one cup of cold water. After it is thoroughly beaten, let it stand half an hour well covered. Then put into coffee-pot, pour on two and a half quarts of boiling water and put on the stove; stir once or twice at first, to prevent burning. Let it scald fifteen or twenty minutes. If desired to be very nice, beat up eight instead of six tablespoonfuls of coffee; put six in the pot to boil for twenty minutes, and about five minutes before it is done, throw in the rest and cover quickly.

Cream and Milk for Coffee.—Sweet, rich cream, well beaten to free from lumps, is best for coffee, but boiling fresh milk is a good **substitute.** The white of an egg, thoroughly beaten and added (California coffee) to thin cream or rich milk, is also very fine.

Tea.—Tea is made variously as the taste of people require. Black, green, Japan, and English breakfast, all require different methods. For green or Japan tea, scald the tea-pot and allow from one-half to one teaspoonful for each person, as the strength of the herb may indicate. Pour over this one-half a cup of boiling water, steep in a hot place (but do not let it boil) ten minutes, then turn in water at a keen boil, in proportion one quart to every three persons.

English Breakfast, or Oolong.—Take two teaspoonfuls for three persons, and proceed as above, only letting the tea boil for ten minutes.

An English gentleman, whose tea was quite famous, put it to steep in cold water, as soon as the one o'clock dinner was over, and left it steeping until supper time, when it was brought to a boil. Others put it on to steep when the fire is made for supper, and let it stand until the meal is announced; served boiling hot.

Iced Tea.—To each glass of tea add the juice of half a lemon; fill up the glass with pounded ice, and sweeten.

Chocolate.—Four heaping tablespoonfuls grated chocolate, one of sugar, and wet with one of boiling water; rub this smooth. Then stir into one pint of boiling water; then add one pint of boiling milk. Let this boil three minutes. It is greatly improved by milling, while boiling, with a Dover egg-beater. If desired sweet, add to the boiling milk one heaping teaspoonful of sugar.

A dainty addition is two tablespoonfuls of whipped cream, that has been sweetened and flavored with vanilla, laid on the top of each cup.

Stock and Seasoning.—The preparation called stock is, for some inscrutable reason, a stumbling-block to average cooks, and even by experienced housekeepers is often looked upon as troublesome and expensive. Where large amounts of fresh meat are used in its preparation, the latter adjective might be appropriate; but stock in reality is the only mode by which

5

every scrap of bone or meal, whether cooked or uncooked, can be made to yield the last particle of nourishment contained in it. Properly .prepared and strained into a stone jar, it will keep a week, and is useful in the making of hashes and gravies as in soup itself.

The first essential is a tightly-covered kettle, either tinned iron or porcelain lined, holding not less than two gallons, three being a preferable size. Whether cooked or uncooked meat is used, it should be cut into small bits, and all bones broken or sawn into short pieces. that the marrow may be easily extracted.

To every pound of meat and bone allow one quart of cold water, one even teaspoonful of salt, and half a saltspoonful of pepper. Let the meat stand till the water is slightly colored with its juice; then put upon the fire, and let it come slowly to a boil, skimming off every particle of scum as it rises. The least neglect of this point will give a broth in which bits of dark slime float about, unpleasant to sight and taste. A cup of cold water, thrown in as the kettle boils, will make the scum rise more freely. Let it boil steadily, but very slowly. allowing an hour to each pound of meat. The water will boil away leaving, at the end of the time specified, not more than half or one-third the original amount. In winter this will become a firm jelly, which can be used by simply melting it, thus obtaining a strong, clear broth; or can be diluted with an equal quantity of water, and vegetables added for a vegetable soup.

The meat used in stock, if boiled the full length of time given, has parted with all its juices, and is therefore useless as food. If wanted for hashes or croquettes, the portion needed should be taken out as soon as tender, and a pint of the stock with it, to use as gravy. Strain, when done, into a stone pot or crock kept for that purpose, and, when cold, remove the cake of fat which will rise to the top. This fat, melted and strained, serves for many purposes better than lard. If the stock is to be kept for several days, leave the fat on till ready to use it.

Fresh and cooked meat may be used together, and all remains of poultry or game, and trimmings of chops and steaks, mav be added. mutton being the only meat which can not as well be used in combination; though even this, by trimming off all the fat, may also be added. If it is intended to keep the stock for some days, no vegetables should be added, as vegetable juices ferment very easily. For clear soups they must be cooked with the meat; and directions will be given under that head for amounts and seasonings.

The secret of a savory soup lies in many flavors, none of which are allowed to predominate; and, minutely as rules for such flavoring may be given, only careful and frequent tasting will insure success. Every vegetable, spice, and sweet herb, curry-powders, catchups, sauces, dried or fresh lemon peel, can be used; and the simple stock, by the addition of these various ingredients, becomes the myriad number of soups to be found in the pages of great cooking manuals like Gouffee's or Francatelli's.

BROWN SOUPS are made by frying the meat or game used in them till thoroughly brown on all sides, and using dark spices or sauces in their seasoning.

WHITE SOUPS are made with light meats, and often with the addition of milk or cream.

PUREES are merely thick soups strained carefully before serving, and made usually of some vegetable which thickens in boiling, as beans, peas, &c., though there are several forms of fish purees in which the foundation is thickened milk, to which the fish is added, and the whole then rubbed through a common sieve, if a regular puree sieve is not to be had.

Browned flour is often used for coloring, but does not thicken a soup, as, in browning a, the starchy portion has been destroyed; and it will not therefore mix, but settles at the bottom. Burned sugar or caramel makes a better coloring, and also adds flavor. With clear soups grated cheese is often served, either Parmesan or any rich cheese being used. Onions give a better flavor if they are fried in a little butter or dripping before using, and many professional cooks fry all soup vegetables lightly. Cabbage and potatoes should be parboiled in a separate water before adding to a soup. In using wine or catchup, add only at the last moment, as boiling dissipates the flavor. Unless a thick vegetable soup is desired, always strain into the tureen. Rice, sago, macaroni, or any cereal may be used as

thickening; the amounts required being found under the different headings. Careful skimming, long boiling, and as careful removing of fat, will secure a broth especially desirable as
a food for children and the old, but almost equally so for any
age; while many fragments, otherwise entirely useless, discover
themselves as savory and nutritious parts of the day's supply
of food.

RECIPES.

Soups.—Beef Soup with Vegetables.—For this very excellent soup take two quarts of stock prepared before hand, as
already directed. If the stock is a jelly, as will usually be the
case in winter, an amount sufficient to fill a quart measure can
be diluted with a pint of water, and will then be rich enough.
Add to this one small carrot, a turnip, a small parsnip, and two
onions; all chopped fine; a cupful of chopped cabbage; two
tablespoonfuls of barley or rice; and either six fresh tomatoes
sliced, or a small can of sealed ones. Boil gently at least one
hour: then add one saltspoonful each of pepper, curry powder
and clove. If the stock has been salted properly, no more will
be needed; but tasting is essential to secure just the right flavors. Boil a few minutes longer, and serve without straining.

This is an especially savory and hearty soup, and the combinations of vegetables may be varied indefinitely. A cup of
chopped celery is an exceedingly nice addition, or, if this is not
to be had, a teaspoonful of celery salt, or a saltspoonful of celery seed. A lemon may also be sliced thin, and added at the
last. When tomatoes are used, a little sugar is always an improvement; in this case an even tablespoonful being sufficient.
If a thicker broth is desired, one heaped tablespoonful of corn-
starch or flour may be first dissolved in a little cold water; then
a cup of the hot broth gradually mixed with it, and the whole
added to the soup and boiled for five minutes.

Perfect Mock Turtle Soup.—Endeavor to have the
head and the broth ready for the soup, the day before it is to
be eaten. It will take eight hours to prepare it properly.

Hours.

	Hours.
Cleaning and soaking the head	1
To parboil it to cut up	1
Cooling, nearly	1
Making the broth and finishing the soup	5
	8

Get a calf's head with the skin on (the fresher the better); take out the brains, wash the head several times in cold water, let it soak for about an hour in spring water, then lay it in a stewpan, and cover it with cold water, and half a gallon over; as it becomes warm, a great deal of scum will rise, which must be immediately removed; let it boil gently for one hour, take it up, and, when almost cold, cut the head into pieces about an inch and a half by an inch and a quarter, and the tongue into mouthfuls; or rather make a side dish of the tongue and brains.

When the head is taken out, put in the stock meat (about five pounds of knuckle of veal), and as much beef; add to the stock all the trimmings and bones of the head; skim it well, and then cover it close and let it boil five hours (reserve a couple of quarts of this to make gravy sauces); then strain it off and let it stand till the next morning; then take off the fat, set a large stewpan on the fire with half a pound of good fresh butter, twelve ounces of onions sliced, and four ounces of green sage; chop it a little; let these fry an hour; then rub in half a pound of flour, and by degrees add your broth till it is the thickness of cream; season it with a quarter of an ounce of ground allspice, and half an ounce of black pepper ground very fine, salt to your taste, and the rind of one lemon peeled very thin; let it simmer very gently for an hour and a half, then strain it through a hair sieve; do not rub your soup to get it through the sieve, or it will make it grouty; if it does not run through easily, knock your wooden spoon against the side of your sieve; put it in a clean stewpan with the head, and season it by adding to each gallon of soup two tablespoonfuls of Tarragon vinegar, and two tablespoonfuls of lemon juice; let it simmer gently till the meat is tender; this may take from half an hour to an hour; take care it is not overdone; stir it frequently to prevent the meat sticking to the bottom of the stewpan, and when the meat is quite tender the soup is ready.

A head weighing twenty pounds, and ten pounds of stock meat, will make ten quarts of excellent soup, besides the two quarts of stock you have put by for made dishes.

OBSERVATIONS.—If there is more meat on the head than you wish to put in the soup, prepare it for a pie, with the addition of a calf's foot boiled tender; it will make an excellent ragout pie; season it with zest and a little minced onion, put in half a teacupful of stock, cover it with puff paste, and bake it one hour; when the soup comes from table, if there is a deal of meat and no soup, put it into a pie dish, season it a little, and add some little stock to it; then cover it with paste, bake it one hour, and you have a good mock-turtle pie.

To Season the Soup.—To each gallon put four table-spoonfuls of lemon juice, two of mushroom catsup, and one teaspoonful of mace, a teaspoonful of curry powder, or a quarter of a drachm of cayenne, and the peel of a lemon pared as thin as possible; let it simmer for five minutes more, take out the lemon peel, add the yolks of four hard boiled eggs, and the soup is ready for the tureen.

While the soup is doing, prepare for each tureen a dozen and a half of mock-turtle forcemeat balls, and put them into the tureen. Brain balls, or cakes, are a very elegant addition, and are made by boiling the brains for ten minutes, then putting them in cold water and cutting them into pieces about as big as a large nutmeg; take savory or lemon thyme dried and finely powdered nutmeg grated, and pepper and salt, and pound them all together; beat up an egg, dip the brains in it, and then roll them in this mixture, and make as much of it as possible stick to them; dip them in the egg again, and then in finely grated and sifted bread crumbs; fry them in hot fat, and send them up as a side-dish.

A veal sweet-bread, not too much done or it will break, cut into pieces the same size as you cut the calf's head, and put in the soup just to get warm before it goes to the table, is a superb "*bonne bouche;*" and pickled tongue, stewed till very tender, and cut into mouthfuls, is a favorite addition. We order the meat to be cut into mouthfuls that it may be eaten with a spoon; the knife and fork have no business in a soup plate.

N. B.—In helping this soup, the distributer of it should serve out the meat, forcemeat and gravy in equal parts; however trifling and needless this remark may appear, the writer has often suffered from the want of such a hint being given to the soup-server, who has sometimes sent a plate of more gravy without meat, at others, of meat without gravy, and sometimes scarcely anything but forcemeat balls.

OBSERVATIONS.—This is a delicious soup within the reach of those who "eat to live;" but if it had been composed expressly for those who only "live to eat," I do not know how it could have been more agreeable; as it is, the lover of good eating will "wish his throat a mile long, and every inch of it a palate."

SUMMER OR WINTER CORN SOUP.—Boil a leg of mutton or shank of beef in six quarts of water for four hours. After the meat and fat have been removed (it is better to stand over one day to cool, so that the grease may all be taken off), add a quart or more of sweet corn nicely cut from the cob, and boil twenty or thirty minutes. In cutting the corn (with a sharp knife) take off only the point of the kernels, and scrape the milk or pulp, thus avoiding the hull or skin, which is indigestible and unpalatable. Just before serving, add to the soup a coffee-cup of cream, with two tablespoonfuls of flour stirred smoothly in and boil for a minute. This can be made in winter by using the Yarmouth canned corn or the dried corn soaked over night, and boiled till tender.

CORN SOUP.—Cut the grains from twelve ears of sweet corn and scrape the milk; add one pint of water. Let it boil until quite done—thirty to forty minutes—then add two quarts of new milk, and when it boils stir in one-quarter pound of butter rubbed into two tablespoonfuls of flour, pepper and salt. Beat the yolks of two eggs in the tureen and pour the soup in boiling, stirring all the time.

TURKEY SOUP.—Place the rack of a cold turkey and what remains of dressing or gravy in a pot, and cover with cold water. Simmer gently three or four hours, and let it stand until the next day. Take off what fat may have risen, and take out with a skimmer all the bits of bones. Put the soup on to heat till boiling, then thicken slightly with flour wet up in water, and season to the taste. Pick off all the turkey from the bones, put them in the soup, boil up and serve.

CALF'S HEAD SOUP.—Take the head, pluck and feet. Put them into a pot with cold water. Be careful to skim well when it boils. Chop a dozen small onions and let them all boil together until the meat cleaves from the bones. Then strain it. After putting the liquor into the pot again, add thyme, cloves, salt, pepper and cayenne to your taste. But all the meat from the head and feet, half the liver and lights, the whole of the heart and tongue; put all into the pot and boil about three-quarters of an hour. Before it is done take half a pound of butter with as much flour as will make into balls; stir until dissolved. Then add two tablespoonfuls of tarragon vinegar, four hard boiled eggs cut in slices, and a lemon to improve the flavor. This will make two gallons, and may be kept several weeks, to be used as occasion requires.

TOMATO SOUP.—One quart of water, eight good-sized ripe tomatoes cut up; boil twenty minutes and add one half teaspoonful of soda; then boil and add one pint or more of milk, and season as you do oysters.

BLACK BEAN SOUP.—One quart of black beans, soaked over night in four quarts of water, one pound of beef, half pound of salt pork. Grate one large or two small carrots, and slice one large onion, and add to the beans and the water in which they were soaked. Boil all together for three or four hours, then strain through a colander. When in the tureen add one tablespoonful of mushroom sauce, one sliced lemon and one sliced or chopped boiled egg.

PEA SOUP.—Soak one quart of peas (split, if you can get them) over night; next morning early put them over the fire with one pound of corned beef or pork (beef is the best to my taste, however), and let them boil hard for three hours. Then add a chopped carrot and turnip, and an onion, if liked, a teaspoonful of celery seed or a handful of celery tops, and boil another hour or more; then strain through a sieve, season with pepper, and cut up two thin slices of toasted bread in the shape of small dice; put in the tureen, turn on your soup and serve. A cup of milk boiled in it for twenty minutes is an improvement. Small, white beans can be substituted for peas and made in the same manner.

OYSTER SOUP.—For four cans of oysters, have twelve crackers rolled fine, two quarts of boiling water, one pint of good rich milk. Let the milk and water come to a boil, add the crackers, salt and pepper, boil one minute briskly; pour in the oysters and let all come to a scald; add about a quarter of a pound of butter as they are poured into a tureen.

OYSTER SOUP, No. 2.—To one quart of oysters add one quart of water; pour the water on the oysters and stir them; take them out one at a time, so that no small particle of shell may adhere to them; strain the liquor through a sieve and put it in a stew-pan over the fire, with two or three blades of mace, and season with red pepper and salt to taste; when this boils put in your oysters, add a teaspoonful of flour rubbed to a paste with one ounce of butter; let them scald again, then add one half pint of cream and serve hot.

Fish.—The most essential point in choosing fish is their freshness, and this is determined as follows: If the gills are red, the eyes prominent and full, and the whole fish stiff, they are good; but if the eyes are sunken, the gills pale and the flesh flabby, they are stale and unwholesome, and, though often eaten in this condition, lack all the fine flavor of a freshly-caught fish.

The fish being chosen, the greatest care is necessary in cleaning. If this is properly done, one washing will be sufficient; the custom of allowing fresh fish to lie in water after cleaning destroys much of their flavor.

Fresh-water fish, especially the cat-fish, have often a muddy taste and smell. To get rid of this, soak in water strongly salted; say a cupful of salt to a gallon of water, letting it heat gradually in this, and boiling it for one minute; then drying it thoroughly before cooking.

All fish for boiling should be put into cold water, with the exception of salmon, which loses its color unless put into boiling water. A tablespoonful each of salt and vinegar to every two quarts of water improves the flavor of all boiled fish, and also makes the flesh firmer. Allow ten minutes to the pound after the fish begins to boil, and test with a knitting needle or sharp skewer. If it runs in easily, the flesh can be taken off. If a fish-kettle with strainer is used, the fish can be lifted out without danger of breaking. If not, it should be thoroughly dredged with flour, and served in a cloth kept for the purpose. In all cases drain it perfectly, and send to table on a folded napkin laid upon the platter

In frying, fish should, like all fried articles, be immersed in the hot lard or drippings. Small fish can be fried whole; larger ones boned, and cut in small pieces. If they are egged and crumbed, the egg will form a covering, hardening at once, and absolutely impervious to fat.

Pan-fish, as they are called—flounders and small fish generally—can also be fried by rolling in Indian meal or flour, and browning in the fat of salt pork.

Baking and broiling preserve the flavor most thoroughly.

Cold boiled fish can always be used, either by spicing as in the rule to be given, or by warming again in a little butter and water. Cold fried or boiled fish can be put in a pan, and set in the oven till hot; this requiring not over ten minutes; a longer time giving a strong oily taste, which spoils it. Plain boiled or mashed potatoes are always served with fish where used as a dinner course. If fish is boiled whole, do not cut off either tail or head. The tail can be skewered in the mouth if liked; or a large fish may be boiled in the shape of a letter S by threading a trussing-needle, fastening a string around the head, then passing the needle through the middle of the body, drawing the string tight, and fastening it around the tail.

To Fry or Broil Fish Properly.—After the fish is well cleansed, lay it on a folded towel and dry out all the water. When well wiped and dry, roll it in wheat flour, rolled crackers, grated stale bread, or Indian meal, whichever may be preferred; wheat flour will generally be liked.

Have a thick-bottomed frying-pan or spider with plenty of sweet lard salted (a tablespoonful of salt to each pound of lard), for fresh fish which have not been previously salted; let it become boiling hot, then lay the fish in and let it fry gently, until one side is a delicate brown, then turn the other; when both are done take it up carefully and serve quickly, and keep it covered with a tin cover, and set the dish where it will keep hot.

To Broil.—Have a clean gridiron, and a clear but not fierce fire of coals; rub the bars with a bit of beef suet, that the fish may not stick; fish must be broiled gently and thoroughly. There are few things more offensive than undone

For the broil, have ready a dish with a good bit of butter in which is worked a little salt and pepper, enough for the fish. Lay the fish upon it, when both sides are nicely done, and with a knife-blade put the butter over every part; fish should be turned with a broad-bladed knife or a pancake turner.

All salt fish require to be soaked in cold water before cooking, according to the time it has been in salt. When it is hard and dry it will require thirty-six hours soaking before dressing; the water must be changed three or four times. When fish is not very salt or hard, twenty-four hours will be sufficient.

For frying fish, beef suet or dripping or sweet oil may be used in place of lard. Butter is not good; it spoils the color and tastes strong.

Fish have a fine appearance prepared in the following manner: Clean and wash them, and wipe them dry with a nice soft towel; then wet them over with beaten egg, and dip them in bread crumbs or rolled crackers. If done twice over with egg and cracker or crumbs, it will have a finer appearance.

The largest sized pan fish, weighing nearly or quite a pound each, should be scored or cut across each side from the head to the tail, nearly to the bone, and about an inch apart, that it may be well done. Garnish with sprigs of parsley. Have ready a thick-bottomed frying pan, with plenty of lard salted; let it become boiling hot; lay the fish carefully in and let them fry gently, until one side is a rich yellow brown, then turn the other and do likewise; when both are done, take them carefully up on a hot dish and serve. Garnish with fried parsley.

DRIED CODFISH.—This should always be laid in soak, at least one night before it is wanted; then take off the skin and put it in plenty of cold water; boil it gently (skimming it meanwhile) for one hour, or tie it in a cloth and boil it. Serve it with egg sauce; garnish with hard boiled eggs cut in slices, and sprigs of parsley. Serve plain boiled or mashed potatoes with it.

STEWED SALT COD.—Scald some soaked cod by putting it over the fire in boiling water for ten minutes; then scrape it white, pick it in flakes, and put it in a stewpan, with a tablespoonful of butter worked into the same of flour, and as

much milk as will moisten it; let it stew gently for ten minutes;
add pepper to taste, and serve hot; put it in a deep dish, slice
hard boiled eggs over it, and sprigs of parsley around the edge.

This is a nice relish for breakfast, with coffee and tea, and
rolls or toast.

CODFISH CAKES.—First boil soaked cod, then chop it fine,
put to it an equal quantity of potatoes boiled and mashed;
moisten it with beaten eggs or milk, and a bit of butter and a
little pepper; form it in round small cakes, rather more than
half an inch thick, flour the outside, and fry in hot butter or
beef drippings until a delicate brown. Like fish, these must be
fried gently, the lard being boiling hot when they are put in;
when one side is done turn the other. Serve for breakfast.

TO BAKE A DISH OF COLD BOILED COD.—Chop fine some
cold boiled cod, put to it an equal quantity or more of boiled
potatoes chopped and mashed; add a good bit of butter and
milk to make it moist, and put it in a stewpan over a gentle
fire; cover it, and stir it frequently until it is thoroughly
heated, taking care that it does not burn; then take it up,
make it in a roll or any other form, mark the surface, take a
pinch of ground pepper between your finger and thumb, and
put spots at equal distances over it; or wet it over with melted
butter, and brown it in an oven before the fire.

FRESH COD.—Fresh cod, when good, are firm, and the
gills red, and the eyes are full; if at all soft and flabby it is
not good. A fine fish is thick at the back; the shoulder or
piece near the head of a large cod is better for boiling than
a small fish.

TO BOIL FRESH COD.—If you. have not a fish kettle,
after cleaning the fish properly, lay it on a plate in a circle,
and tie a clean towel about it; to a gallon of hot water put
a tablespoonful of salt and a gill of vinegar; put in the fish
and boil according to its weight. Serve with plain boiled
potatoes and drawn butter, parsley, or egg sauce. Garnish
with sprigs of parsley. Lay a folded napkin on the dish under
the fish.

FRIED CODFISH STEAKS.—Cut the fish in steaks of about

one inch thickness; or it may be split as for broiling; dip each piece in wheat flour or rolled cracker, or Indian meal; have some lard, (which is salted in proportion, a tablespoonful of salt to a pound,) let it become boiling hot in a frying pan; lay in the steaks; let them fry gently, without stirring them, until one side is a fine brown, then turn each steak carefully with a broad knife; when both sides are done, serve hot, with sprigs of parsley over it.

BAKED COD.—Clean a good sized fish, weighing four or five pounds; wash it and dry it well in a cloth; rub it inside and out with a mixture of pepper and salt; cut a slice from a loaf of bread, spread it thickly with butter; moisten it with hot water, and fill the body of the fish; tie a thread around it to keep the dressing in, then put bits of butter, the size of a hickory nut, all over the surface; dredge flour over it until it looks white; then lay a trivet on some muffin rings in a dripping-pan, and lay the fish on; put in a pint of water to baste with, then put it in a hot oven, and baste frequently; in one hour it will be done. Take it up on a hot dish, add a gill of vinegar to the gravy, or a lemon cut in very thin slices; dredge in a little flour; let it boil up once; stir it well; add a very little hot water if necessary, then strain into a gravy-boat, lay the slice over the fish, and serve.

HADDOCK.—These are chosen and dressed the same as cod.

SHAD.—These are in season from the last of March until May; they are chosen by the same rules as other fish.

These fish may be fried, baked, boiled or salted.

FRIED SHAD.—Scale the fish, and cut off the head, then split it open down the back, at the side of the backbone; take out the entrails; keep the roe or eggs to be fried with the fish; then cut it in two from head to tail, and cut each side in pieces two or three inches wide; rinse them in cold water, wipe them dry, and dip each in wheat flour, and fry in salted lard; when the inside, which must always be cooked first (of any fish), is done a fine brown, turn the other; the fat must be boiling hot when the fish is put in, and then fried gently, that it may not be too dark colored.

BROILED SHAD.—Cut the fish the same as for frying, or

merely split it in two; lay it on a gridiron over a bright steady fire of coals; let it broil gently; put the inside to the fire first that it may be done through; have ready a steak dish with nearly a quarter of a pound of sweet butter, and a teaspoonful of salt and pepper each, worked into it; when both sides of the fish are done, lay it on the dish, turn it several times in the butter, cover it with a tin cover, and set the dish where it will keep hot, until ready to serve.

BAKED SHAD.—Scale the shad clean, cut off the head, and split the fish half way down the back; scrape the inside perfectly clean; make a stuffing thus: Cut two slices of a baker's loaf of wheat bread, spread each thickly with butter; sprinkle with pepper and salt, and a little pounded sage if liked; moisten it with hot water; fill the belly with this; wind a cord around it to keep in the stuffing, dredge the outside well with flour; stick bits of butter, the size of a hickory nut, all over outside; mix a teaspoonful each of salt and pepper together, and sprinkle it all over the whole surface; then lay the fish on a trivet or muffin rings in a dripping pan; put in a pint of water to baste with, and keep the gravy from burning; if this all wastes before the fish is done, add more hot water; bake for one hour in a quick oven; baste frequently. When done, take the fish on a steak dish; if there is not enough gravy in the pan (there should be at least half a pint), add more hot water; dredge in a heaping teaspoonful of flour, then put to it a bit of butter, and, if liked, a lemon sliced thin, and the seeds taken out. Stir it smooth with a spoon, and pour it through a gravy-strainer into a gravy-boat; lay the slices of lemon over the fish, and serve with mashed potatoes.

TO FRY BLACK FISH.—Scale the fish, and scrape the inside clean to the backbone; wash in water, with a little vinegar; wipe it dry with a clean towel; then dip it in wheat flour, or rolled crackers. Have in a thick-bottomed frying pan plenty of lard salted (a large tablespoonful of salt to a pound of lard), let it become boiling hot; then lay in the fish and fry it gently, until one side is a fine brown; then turn it carefully. When both sides are done, take it up and serve.

Fried fish may be garnished or ornamented with sprigs of green or fried parsley, or thin slices of lemon, sliced.

STEWED BLACK FISH.—Put a fish weighing abou five pounds on a fish-drainer; after having properly cleansed it, put it into the fish-kettle with hot water to cover it; add to it a few blades of mace, a large teaspoonful of salt, and a wineglass of port wine; let it simmer or boil gently for half an hour; then skim it clear; work into a smooth mass a quarter of a pound of sweet butter, and a heaping tablespoonful of wheat flour; take from the fish part of the water in which it was boiled, leaving it scarcely covered; then add the flour and butter, with a teaspoonful of pepper; dip a bunch of parsley into boiling water, cut it small and add it to the stew; cover it close for twenty minutes, and let it simmer gently; then take the fish up on a dish, and serve with the gravy or sauce over. A sliced lemon without the pits may be added with the parsley by those who like it. Served with plain boiled or mashed potatoes. Black fish dressed in this manner is very delicious.

PERCH.—Clean these fish well, wash and wipe them dry, then fry them as directed

STRIPED BASS.—These fish are best fried or boiled. See directions for boiling or frying fish.

HALIBUT.—This fish is fine, whether cut in steaks and broiled or fried; or the thick part boiled. Fry or broil as directed for codfish. Steaks or fillets cut from the tail part are very fine, and may be fried or broiled more nicely than any other.

TO BOIL HALIBUT.—Take a piece weighing four or five pounds, scrape the skin clean, dredge flour over it, and boil according to its weight—ten minutes to a pound. Serve with plain boiled potatoes, and drawn butter, or egg, or parsley sauce. Cold boiled halibut may be served the same as codfish; any of the sauce which may remain may be put with the cold fish.

SALMON.—When salmon is fresh and good, the gills and flesh are of a bright red, the scales clear, and the fish stiff. When first caught, there is a whiteness between the flakes, which, by keeping, melts down, and the fish becomes richer. Salmon requires to be well broiled. When underdone it is unwholesome.

BROILED SALMON.—Cut some slices about an inch thick, and broil them over a gentle, bright fire of coals for ten or twelve minutes. When both sides are done, take them on to a hot dish; butter each slice well with sweet butter; strew over each a little salt and pepper to taste, and serve.

SPICED SALMON (PICKLED).—Boil a salmon, and, after wiping it dry, set it to cool; take of the water in which it was boiled, and good vinegar each equal parts, enough to cover it; add to it one dozen cloves, as many small blades of mace, or sliced nutmeg, one teaspoonful of whole pepper, and the same of allspice, make it boiling hot, skim it clear, add a small bit of butter (the size of a small egg), and pour it over the fish; set it in a cool place. When cold it is fit for use and will keep a long time, covered close, in a cool place. Serve instead of pickled oysters for supper. A fresh cod is very nice done in the same manner; as is also a striped sea bass.

BOILED SALMON.—Run a long needle with a packthread through the tail, centre and head of a fish, to bring it in the form of a letter S. Put it in a fish-kettle, with hot water to cover it, and a teaspoonful of salt (cut three or four slanting gashes in each side of the fish before making it into the form, otherwise the skin will break and disfigure it); allow ten minutes gentle boiling for each pound of fish. Or a piece of a large fish may be boiled. Serve with lobster, or anchovey, or draw butter sauce, and plain boiled or mashed potatoes.

A DISH OF SALT SALMON.—Salmon is often put down in brine. It is to be soaked and boiled, as directed for salt codfish, or it may be boiled for breakfast. Or pull off the skin, and pick in flakes the thickest side of a salmon; pour scalding hot water over it, let it stand for a few minutes; then pour it off; add to it enough milk or hot water to moisten it; put it over the fire and let it simmer for five minutes; then add a tablespoonful of butter, shake over it a little wheat flour and pepper to taste, stir it for a few minutes, and it is done. A fine relish for breakfast or supper.

EELS.—Eels, to be good, must be as fresh caught as possible; skin them, cut off the heads, cut them open and scrape them clean to the back bone.

For frying or boiling, the middle-sized fat ones are best·

those caught in fresh water have a muddy taste, and should be put in salted water a short time before cooking. Eels may be boiled and served with drawn butter or parsley sauce, and boiled potatoes.

FRIED EELS.—After cleaning the eels well, cut them in pieces two inches long; wash them and wipe them dry; roll them in wheat flour or rolled cracker, and fry as directed for other fish, in hot lard or beef dripping, salted. They should be browned all over and thoroughly done.

FRESH MACKEREL.—These fish to be good must be cooked as soon as possible after they are caught. They may be broiled, fried, or baked, the same as shad—also salted.

DRIED MACKEREL.— Take fresh caught mackerel, scale them and cut them down the back to the tail; leave the heads on; then hang them by the tail in a cool place to drain; strew some salt on the bottom of the pan; sprinkle the fish plentifully with it, and lay them two by two, the insides together, in a pan; let them lie twelve hours, then rinse off the salt and hang them to drain for half an hour, after which pepper the insides a little and lay them on stones, aslant towards the sun, to dry; take care never to put them out when the sun is not hot on them, nor until the stones are heated and dry; lay the insides to the sun—they will be perfectly cured in one week; stretch them open with two sticks. Or, instead of drying, after having prepared them in this manner, smoke them.

SALT MACKEREL.—Split fresh caught mackerel down the back, scrape the inside clean, spread them open on a board, and strew them plentifully with salt; then strew salt over the bottom of a tub; lay the fish two by two, the insides together, and lay them in the tub; strew salt between each layer; half coarse and half fine salt; then cover them close—put plenty of salt above the last layer of fish.

TO DRESS SALT MACKEREL.—Take mackerel from the salt, and lay them inside downward in a pan of cold water for two or three days, change the water once or twice, and scrape the fish clean without breaking it. When fresh enough, wipe one dry and hang it in a cool place; then fry or broil, or lay one in a shallow pan, the inside of the fish down; cover it with hot water, and set it over a gentle fire or in an oven for twelve or fifteen minutes; then pour off the water, turn the fish, put bits of butter in the pan, and over the fish, sprinkle with pepper, and let it fry for five minutes, then dish it.

TROUT.—These may be stewed, fried, boiled, or baked.

PIKE OR PICKEREL.—These may be stewed, fried or broiled.

There are many more fine fish not mentioned herein, but as the process of stewing, boiling, broiling, and frying is very nearly the same for all sorts of fish, it does not seem necessary to mention more.

HERRINGS.—These are eaten in three varieties—fresh, salted, smoked, or red herrings. Salted herrings are to be soaked in clean water before boiling, the same as mackerel. Red herrings are to be skinned, split in two, and the insides and the backbone to be taken out; or they may first be broiled, then skinned. To cook fresh herrings, scale and prepare them the same as any other fish.

CHOWDER.—Slice some salt pork very thin, strew it over with onions chopped small, and some fine pepper; then cut a haddock, fresh cod, or any other firm fish, in thin steaks; take out the bones; lay some of the sliced pork at the bottom of the kettle with some of the seasoning; then put a layer of fish, then put over some soaked crackers or biscuit, then another layer of the seasoned pork, after which fish and crackers and a few bits of butter, and so on alternately, pork, fish and crackers, until the kettle is two-thirds full; then put in about a pint of water, and cover the pot with a thick iron cover with a rim; set it over a gentle fire, put coals and ashes on the cover, and bake two or three hours, or more, if the pot is large. When done, turn it out on a dish and serve with pickles. It may be baked in an oven.

Shell Fish.—TO CHOOSE LOBSTERS.—These are chosen more by weight than size; the heaviest are best. A good small sized one will not unfrequently be found to weigh as heavily as one much larger. If fresh, a lobster will be found lively, and the claws have a strong motion when the eyes are pressed with the finger. Hen lobsters are preferred for sauce or salad, on account of their coral. The head and small claws are never used.

To Boil Lobsters.—Put in a large kettle water enough to cover the lobster, and salt—a dessertspoonful to a quart of water; when it boils fast put in the lobster, head first, which kills it instantly; keep boiling briskly for half an hour, then take it from the water with the tongs and lay it to drain; wipe off the scum from it and rub it over with a bit of butter tied in a cloth, or some sweet oil; break off the large claws, and crack each shell without shattering, but so that they may come easily to pieces; lay a napkin on a large steak dish; with a sharp knife split the body from head to tail, and lay it open on the napkin; put a large claw at either end, and serve with melted butter sauce. Or else take out all the meat from the shells, and lay it neatly on a dish, and serve with melted butter.

Lobster Salad.—Break apart one or two heads of white heart lettuce, lay the leaves in cold water, rinse them well, then shake the water from each leaf, and lay them, the largest first, in a salad bowl, the stalk inwards. Lay the delicate small leaves around the edge; or cut it all small before putting it in the bowl.

Having boiled a hen lobster, take the meat from the shell and cut it small; rub the coral to a smooth paste, with the green inside if liked, and a tablespoonful of oil or melted butter; add to it a teaspoonful of made mustard, and a saltspoonful of black pepper; add a gill of sharp vinegar; stir it smooth, then mix it with the minced lobster and salad, and serve with cold butter and crackers or rolls. The lobster and dressing must not be put with the lettuce until ready to serve.

To Choose Crabs.—If fresh, the joints of the claws will be stiff, and the inside have an agreeable smell; the heaviest for their size are best; the light ones are watery. Crabs are stale when the eyes look dull.

To Boil Crabs.—Have a pot of boiling water in which is salt (a tablespoonful to the quart), throw the crabs in and keep them boiling briskly for twelve minutes, if large; then take them out, wipe the shells clean, and rub them over with a bit of butter; break off the small claws, spread a napkin on a large dish, and lay the crabs on it in regular rows, beginning at the outside. Serve with cold butter and rolls.

To Boil Soft Shell Clams.—Wash the shells clean, and put the clams, edges downwards, in a kettle; then pour about a quart of boiling water over them; cover the pot and set it over a brisk fire for three quarters of an hour. Pouring boiling water over them causes the shells to open quickly and let out the sand which may be in them. Take them up when done; take off the black skin which covers the hard part, trim them clean, and put them in a stewpan; put to them some of the liquor in which they were boiled; put to it a good bit of butter, and pepper and salt to taste; make them hot; serve with cold butter and rolls

To Fry Soft Shell Clams.—Get them from the shell, as they are very troublesome to clean; wash them in plenty of water, and lay them on a thickly folded napkin to dry out the water; then roll a few at a time in wheat flour, until they will take up no more; have a thick bottomed frying pan one-third full of boiling hot lard, and salted (in proportion, a tablespoonful of salt to a pound of lard); lay the clams in with a fork, one at a time; lay them close together and fry gently, until one side is a delicate brown; then turn carefully and brown the other; then take them off on a hot dish. When fried properly, these clams are very excellent.

Hard Shell Clams.—Hard shell clams may be prepared for table in a variety of ways. The sand clams, either large or small, are preferable to any other, being whiter and more tender. Those called Quahogs are least delicate eating of all.

To Boil Hard Shell Clams.—Wash the shells until they are perfectly clean, then put them into a kettle, with the edges downwards; add a pint of water, cover the pot and set it over a brisk fire; when the shells open wide they are done. Half an hour is generally enough for them; if a strong taste to the juice is not liked, put more than a pint of water to them. When done, take the clams from the shells into a deep dish; put to them some of the juice, a good bit of butter, and some pepper, or toast some thin slices of bread, butter them and cut them small, and put them in the dish before putting in the clams and juice.

Stewed Clams.—Take fifty large sand clams from their

shells, and put to them their own liquor and water in equal parts, nearly to cover them; put them in a stewpan over a gentle fire for half an hour; take off any scum as it rises, then add to them a teacup of butter in which is worked a table-spoonful of wheat flour, and pepper to taste; cover the stew-pan, and let them simmer for fifteen minutes longer, then serve. Pour it over toast if preferred. Substituting milk for water makes them more delicate and white. Any other than sand clams, require one hour to stew; that is, three-quarters of an hour before putting in the seasoning.

FRIED HARD SHELL CLAMS.—Get the large sand clams; wash them in their own liquor; dip them in wheat flour or rolled crackers, as may be preferred, and fry in hot lard or beef dripping, without salt; or dip each one in batter made as for clam fritters.

CLAM CHOWDER.—Butter a deep tin basin, strew it thickly with grated bread crumbs or soaked crackers; sprinkle some pepper over, and bits of butter the size of a hickory nut, and, if liked, some finely chopped parsley; then put a double layer of clams, season with pepper, put bits of butter over, then another layer of soaked cracker; after that clams and bits of butter; sprinkle pepper over, add a cup of milk or water, and lastly a layer of soaked crackers. Turn a plate over the basin, and bake in a hot oven for three-quarters of an hour; use half a pound of soda biscuit, and a quarter of a pound of butter with fifty clams.

OYSTERS.—Oysters must be fresh and fat to be good. They are in season from September to May.

The small ones, such as are sold by the quart, are good for pies, fritters, or stews; the largest of this sort are nice for fry-ing or pickling for family use.

OYSTER FRITTERS.—Take a quart of oysters from their own liquor, strain it and add to it half a pint of milk and two well beaten eggs, stir in it by degrees flour enough to make a smooth but rather thin batter; when perfectly free from lumps put the oysters to it, have some lard or beef dripping made hot in a frying pan, salt it a little, and when it is boiling hot put in the butter with a large spoon, having one or more oysters in each;

hold it over a gentle fire until one side is a delicate brown—turn each fritter separately. When both sides are done, take them on a hot dish and serve for breakfast or supper.

FRIED OYSTERS.—Take large oysters from their own liquor into a thickly folded napkin to dry them off; then make a tablespoonful of lard or beef fat hot, in a thick-bottomed frying pan, add to it a half saltspoonful of salt; dip each oyster in wheat flour, or cracker rolled fine, until it will take up no more, then lay them in the pan, hold it over a gentle fire until one side is a delicate brown; turn the other by sliding a fork under it; five minutes will fry them after they are in the pan. Oysters may be fried in butter, but it is not so good; lard and butter half and half is very nice for frying. Some persons like a very little of the oyster liquor poured in the pan after the oysters are done; let it boil up, then put it in the dish with the oysters; when wanted for breakfast this should be done.

BROILED OYSTERS.—Take the large oysters from their own liquor, lay them on a folded napkin to dry off the moisture, then dip each one in wheat flour or rolled cracker, or first into beaten egg and then into rolled cracker; have a gridiron made of coarse wire, put it over a bright but not fierce fire of coals, lay the oysters carefully on; when one side is done turn the other, put some sweet butter on a hot plate, sprinkle a little pepper over, lay the oysters on and serve with crackers.

TO STEW OYSTERS.—Put the oysters with the broth to boil, and when they begin to curl, skim them out of the kettle into a pan of cold water; let them lie in the water until the broth has been skimmed and seasoned with butter, salt and pepper, add mace if you like; then drain off the water and return the oysters to the broth. When they begin to boil up again they are ready to serve, and will be found to be more plump and hard by the process.

GRIDDLED OYSTERS.—Heat a griddle very hot, butter it and lay oysters all over it; when brown on one side, turn as you do griddle cakes. They should be washed first from the liquor, and this must be boiled and skimmed, and turned over the oysters when served, first seasoning it with butter, salt and pepper; serve on bread or cracker toast.

PANNED OYSTERS.—Take the oysters from their liquor, and

put them in a saucepan or spider that is hot. Let them cook quickly, season with salt and pepper, and a little butter, and lay upon toast. A little juice will exude from the oysters while cooking, which will keep them from getting too dry, and they will prove very palatable to all who will try it.

To FRY OYSTERS WITH BATTER.—Take fine large oysters, beat as many eggs with cream (say two eggs to a cup of cream) as will moisten all the oysters required; dip the oyster thoroughly into this r 'xture and then cover well with cracker crumbs which have been seasoned with salt, pepper and a little mace, if desired. Put into your frying pan or spider equal quantities of butter and lard, and when hot fry the prepared oysters to a delicate brown tint and serve hot. If preferred, add three tablespoonfuls of flour to the eggs and cream, and omit the cracker crumbs.

OYSTERS BROILED ON THE SHELL.—The oysters should be of the largest size. Clean the shells with a stiff brush, then open and save the juice; turn boiling water over the oysters for only a minute or two; drain it off, and lay the oysters on one-half of the shell, putting it on a well-heated gridiron over a very hot fire. Boil the liquor that came from the oysters when opened, add it to the shell with a sprinkle of salt, pepper, and a bit of butter, serve hot on the shells, laid on large platters.

UNSURPASSED FRICASSEED OYSTERS.—For one can of oysters use one pint of thin cream; clean all the liquor from the oysters and put them over steam until hot; at the same time thicken the cream with flour and season with salt, pepper and a small pinch of mace, and the same of cinnamon and a very little butter; cook this well, and when done thoroughly, add to it the liquor of the oysters which has been scalded and well skimmed until clear; then add the oysters, letting them remain just long enough to get plump (if left too long they grow tough). Have ready some toast on a platter and pour the whole over it, or have leaves and triangles of rich paste around the dish and partially moistened by the fricassee. Your platter must be very hot, as fricasseed oysters chill like a new-born baby.

OYSTER PIE.—Two cans of oysters, or three pints of solid

oysters, one quart of cream, one dozen rolled crackers, pepper, salt, etc. Stir all together and pour into a dish lined with thick puff paste, cover with another paste and bake three-quarters of an hour. This is a delicious mode of cooking oysters.

OYSTER PATTIES.—Put the oysters in a saucepan with enough of the liquor to cover them; let them come to a boil, skim well, add two teaspoonfuls of butter for one quart of oysters, season with pepper and a little salt. Two or three spoonfuls of cream will add to the richness. Have ready small tins lined with puff-paste; put three or four oysters in each, according to the size of the patty; cover with paste and bake in a quick oven twenty minutes; when done wash over the top with beaten egg and set in the oven for two minutes to glaze.

SCALLOPED OYSTERS.—Have plenty of fine crushed cracker crumbs—either soda or butter crackers; put a layer in the bottom of a buttered pudding dish; wet slightly with oyster liquor and milk, mixed; next a layer of oysters; season with salt and pepper and small bits of butter; then more crumbs and oysters, alternately, until the dish is full. Let the top layer be of crumbs. Beat an egg and mix it with a little milk to pour over the top; place little lumps of flour all over the top, cover the dish and bake half an hour; remove the cover a few minutes before taking from the oven to let it brown.

CHICKEN AND OYSTER CROQUETTES.—Take equal quantities of chicken and oysters, chopped fine, with a cup of sifted bread crumbs and a piece of butter; season with salt and pepper, and, if liked, a little mace. Moisten with one or two well beaten eggs. Form into long, slender rolls, and fry in lard to a light brown; serve on a napkin, and garnish with celery tops or parsley, and slices of lemon.

PICKLED OYSTERS.—Strain the liquor from the oysters; boil and skim until clear; drop in the oysters and let them come to a boil; skim them out and put them in a jar. Take about half the liquor remaining, add vinegar until it tastes sharp, a few whole cloves and allspice; boil and pour over the oysters hot; cover them and let them stand two or three days before using. If you wish to use them any sooner take a little more vinegar.

Sauces and Salads.—The foundation for a large proportion of sauces is in what the French cook knows as a *roux*, and we as "drawn butter." As our drawn butter is often lumpy, or with the taste of the raw flour, we give the French method as a security against such disaster.

To MAKE A ROUX.—Melt in a saucepan a piece of butter the size of an egg, and add two even tablespoonfuls of sifted flour; one ounce of butter to two of flour being a safe rule. Stir till smooth, and pour in slowly one pint of milk, or milk and water, or water alone. With milk it is called *cream roux*, and is used for boiled fish and poultry. Where the butter and flour are allowed to brown, it is called a *brown roux*, and is thinned with the soup or stew which it is designed to thicken. Capers added to a *white roux*—which is the butter and flour, with water added—give *caper sauce* for use with boiled mutton. Pickled nasturtiums are a good substitute for capers. Two hard-boiled eggs, cut fine, give egg sauce. Chopped parsley or pickle, and the variety of catsups and sauces, make an endless variety; the *white roux* being the basis for all of them.

BREAD SAUCE.—For this sauce boil one pint of milk, with one onion cut in pieces. When it has boiled five minutes, take out the onion, and thicken the milk with half a pint of sifted bread-crumbs. Melt a teaspoonful of butter in a frying-pan; put in half a pint of coarser crumbs, stirring them till a light brown. Flavor the sauce with half a teaspoonful of salt, a saltspoonful of pepper, and a grate of nutmeg; and serve with game, helping a spoonful of the sauce and one of the browned crumbs. The boiled onion may be minced fine and added, and the browned crumbs omitted.

CELERY SAUCE.—Wash and boil a small head of celery, which has been cut up fine, in one pint of water, with half a teaspoonful of salt. Boil till tender, which will require about half an hour. Make a *cream roux*, using half a pint of milk, and adding a quarter of a saltspoonful of white pepper. Stir into the celery; boil a moment, and serve. A teaspoonful of celery salt can be used, if celery is out of season, adding to it the full rule for *cream roux*. Cauliflower may be used in the same way as celery, cutting it very fine, and adding a large cupful to the sauce. Use either with boiled meats.

MINT SAUCE.—Look over and strip off the leaves, and cut them as fine as possible with a sharp knife. Use none of the stalk but the tender tips. To a cupful of chopped mint allow an equal quantity of sugar, and half a cup of good vinegar. It should stand an hour before using.

CRANBERRY SAUCE.—Wash one quart of cranberries in warm water, and pick them over carefully. Put them in a porcelain-lined kettle, with one pint of cold water and one pint of sugar, and cook without stirring for half an hour, turning then into molds. This is the simplest method. They can be strained through a sieve, and put in bowls, forming a marmalade, which can be cut in slices when cold; or the berries can be crushed with a spoon while boiling, but left unstrained.

EGG SAUCE.—Cut up three hard boiled eggs in small dice, salt, pepper, minced onions (one teaspoonful), parsley and thyme; add all these to the drawn butter recipe. It is very nice for boiled chickens, fish or leg of mutton.

OYSTER SAUCE.—Scald one pint of large fresh oysters just enough to plump them, adding a tablespoonful of pepper, vinegar, a little black pepper and salt; pour this into a recipe of well made drawn butter (as above) at boiling point; stir thoroughly, and serve.

TOMATO SAUCE.—Scald and peel six large, ripe tomatoes; cut them up and stew slowly; cream together one tablespoonful of butter, one tablespoonful of sugar, one tablespoonful of flour; when the tomatoes are thoroughly done and reduced to a fine pulp, add pepper and salt; stir the butter, sugar and flour in; let boil up, and serve. In winter this sauce may be made from nice canned tomatoes.

PEPPER VINEGAR.—Fill a quart bottle or jar with small peppers, either green or ripe; put in two tablespoonfuls of sugar and fill with good cider vinegar. Invaluable in seasoning sauces, and good to eat with fish or meat.

CHILI SAUCE.—Twelve ripe tomatoes, four ripe peppers, two onions, two tablespoonfuls of salt, two of sugar, three teacups of vinegar, a little cinnamon, chopped tomatoes, peppers and onions, very fine; boil one hour.

WHITE SAUCE FOR FOWLS.—Take tne neck, gizzard and liver of fowls, with a piece of veal or calf's foot; boil in one quart of water with a few whole peppers, and salt, till reduced to one pint; then thicken with two tablespoonfuls of flour mixed with two tablespoonfuls of butter; boil five or six minutes; have ready the yolks of two eggs beaten with one teacup of cream from the morning's milk; pour into the saucepan and shake a moment until done.

MUSHROOM SAUCE.—Wash and pick one pint of fresh mushrooms (or one can of French mushrooms), put in a saucepan with a little salt, nutmeg (three grates), one blade of mace, one pint of very sweet cream, a lump of butter (size of a pullet's egg) rubbed in one teaspoonful of flour; boil up, stir until cooked, and serve with chickens.

HORSE-RADISH SAUCE.—One teacupful of grated norseradish, one tablespoonful of ground mustard, one tablespoonful of sugar, four tablespoonfuls of vinegar and one of olive oil, pepper and salt.

MINT VINEGAR.—Take a glass can and put loosely into it enough nice, clean mint leaves to fill it; then pour over enough good vinegar to fill the bottle full. Cork tight and let stand for three weeks; then pour off into another bottle and keep to flavor mint sauce, etc.

DUTCH SAUCE.—FOR FISH.—One-half teaspoonful of flour, two ounces of butter, four tablespoonfuls of vinegar—tarragon vinegar is best—yolks of two eggs, juice of half a lemon, salt to the taste. Put all the ingredients except the lemon juice into a stewpan. Set it over the fire and stir constantly until it heats (but not boils). Scald the lemon.

Meats.—BEEF.—The best beef is of a clear red color, slightly marbled with fat, and the fat itself of a clear white. Where the beef is dark red or bluish, and the fat yellow, it is too old, or too poorly fed, to be good. The sirloin and ribs, especially the sixth, seventh and eighth, make the best roasting pieces. The ribs can be removed and used for stock, and the beef rolled or skewered firmly, making a piece very easily carved, and almost as presentable the second day as the first. For steaks sirloin is nearly as good, and much more economi-

cal, than porter-house, which gives only a small eatable portion, the remainder being only fit for the stock-pot. If the
beef be very young and tender, steaks from the round may be
used; but these are usually best stewed. Other pieces and
modes of cooking are given under their respective heads.

MUTTON.—Mutton should be a light, clear red, and the fat
very white and firm. It is always improved by keeping, and
in cold weather can be hung for a month, if carefully watched
to see that it has not become tainted. Treated in this way,
well-fed mutton is equal to venison. If the fat is deep yellow,
and the lean dark red, the animal is too old; and no keeping
will make it really good eating. Four years is considered the
best age for prime mutton.

PORK.—Pork should have fine, white fat, and the meat
should be white and smooth. Only country-fed pork should
ever be eaten, the pig even then being liable to diseases
unknown to other animals, and the meat, even when carefully
fed, being at all times less digestible than any sort. Bacon,
carefully cured and smoked, is considered its most wholesome
form.

Poultry.—Poultry come last. The best turkeys have black
legs; and, if young, the toes and bills are soft and pliable.
The combs of fowls should be bright colored, and the legs
smooth.

Geese, if young and fine, are plump in the breast, have
white, soft fat, and yellow feet.

Ducks are chosen by the same rule as geese, and are firm
and thick on the breast.

Pigeons should be fresh, the breast plump, and the feet
elastic. Only experience can make one familiar with other
signs; and a good butcher can usually be trusted to tide one
over the season of experience, though the sooner it ends the
better for all parties concerned.

Boiled Meats and Stews.—All meats intended to be boiled
and served whole at table must be put into boiling water, thus
following an entirely opposite rule from those intended for
soups. In the latter, the object being to extract all the juice,

cold water must be used first, and then heated with the meat in it, and half an hour to the pound allowed. In the former, all the juice is to be kept in; and by putting into boiling water, the albumen of the meat hardens on the surface and makes a case or coating for the meat, which accomplishes this end. Where something between a soup and a plain boiled meat is desired, as in *beef bouilli*, the meat is put on in cold water, which is brought to a boil very quickly, thus securing good gravy, yet not robbing the meat of all its juices. With corned or salted meats, tongue, etc., cold water must be used. If to be eaten cold, such meats should always be allowed to cool in the water in which they were boiled; and this water, if not too salt, can be used for dried bean or pea soup.

BOILED MEATS.—In boiling meat, simply for the meat's sake, or the use of it, you follow an opposite rule, in the beginning, from that in regard to boiling meat for soup. You put it into boiling, instead of cold, water.

Cold water draws the juice of meat, which is precisely what you want in broth and soup. Boiling water contracts and coagulates the surface, and keeps in the juice; which again is precisely what you want.

Certain preparations of meats, however, which are, in character, between a soup and a boiled dish, as will appear in detail, are covered at first with cold water, and then brought to a quick boil. This method steers between the two results, and secures at once a good gravy and an eatable, nourishing piece of meat. Corn and salted meats are put on to boil in cold water.

BEEF BOUILLI.—This is one of the dishes, just now referred to, which comes between a soup and a simple boiled meat. It is, in fact, merely a whole stew.

Take a nice round of fresh meat. Trim off almost all the fat—all the gristle and hard, outside, scrappy bits—and take out the bone. Wash it, and lay it in a deep stew-pan, or soup-pot; cover it once and a half with cold water, and set it on the fire where it will come quickly to a boil. Take off the scum carefully, as it rises. Cut up in small bits and slices two carrots, two small turnips, or one large one, two onions, and a large head, or two small ones, of celery. If you have no celery, you can do without it by adding celery seed or celery salt to the spicing. When the scum is well removed, put in some vegetables and set the pot where it will only boil, or simmer, very gently, yet steadily, like soup. Scatter in a dozen whole cloves. Keep closely covered. Allow four hours; cook it till quite tender. One hour before it is done, put in a teaspoonful of made mustard, a large spoonful of any fine catsup or sauce, and a gill or more of wine if you choose. Still keep closely covered. When the beef is done, take it carefully on a deep dish, hot, and set it near the fire until you finish your gravy. Do this by stirring in a little smooth flour thickening. `Prepare two teaspoonfuls of flour to a quart, mixed with a little cold water, and added gradually, till you are sure you want it all. The vegetables will already have partly thickened the soup. Boil up and turn over the meat.

Scatter some bits of nice mixed pickles—cauliflower, sliced gherkin, with bits of some red pickle for the color—over the meat, before it goes to table.

CORNED BEEF.—Salted and corned meats are put to boil in cold water.

Buy corned beef from the round of a large, well-fed creature. Put to soak over night in cold water. Early in the morning wash and wipe, and put into the pot to boil. Cover twice deep with cold water, and set where it will heat up gradually and come to a very gentle boil. Take the scum off as it comes up. Boil four hours—a large solid piece may take from four to five—and be sure that it is tender when you take it off. If it is to be served hot for dinner, cook it in time to allow of removing it from the flour and letting it stand in the liquor it was boiled in until cooled down from the boil as far as will still be palatable. This makes it richer and more tender. Make a smooth drawn butter sauce to eat with it.

If it is to be eaten cold, take it from the fire and from the pot as soon as done. With a knife and fork, chiefly with the fork, divide and shred it into small pieces; mix these, fat and lean —disregarding all undesirable bits—equally together; pack all down into a pan; set a pan, just a little smaller, inside, upon the meat, so as to press it down, and put a heavy weight

—flatirons answer the purpose very well—into the upper pan, and set all away for some hours, or over night. It will cut in delicious, tender, marbled slices, and is excellent for a Sunday lunch with hot vegetables.

BOILED TONGUE.—Smoked tongue is best.

Wash, and lay in cold water over night. Put on to boil in cold water, and boil, not furiously, but steadily, for four hours. Take out, peel off the skin, and put back into the hot liquor, and set away to grow cold. It may remain in the water through the rest of the day and over night, if not wanted sooner. Cut tongue in lengthwise slices, beginning at the outside of the bend. This makes a wonderful difference in tenderness and flavor.

BOILED VEAL.—Take out the bone from a fillet of veal. Make a stuffing, as for roast meat. Fill the place of the bone with the stuffing, and draw the ends of the meat as tight as possible with a needle and a coarse, strong thread. Scald and flour a cloth, as for boiled mutton, and sew or tie the meat in it tightly. Boil three hours, or until tender, trying with a knitting-needle. Make an oyster' sauce, by soup recipe, to serve with it. Well cooked, it is much like boiled turkey similarly served.

BOILED MUTTON.—A shoulder of mutton will boil in an hour, or a little more. A leg will take from an hour and a half to two hours, according to size. Try with a knitting-needle, to ascertain when it is tender. Have a cloth to boil it in. Wring this out of scalding water, dredge it thickly with flour, and tie up the meat tightly in it. Put it into a large kettle of boiling water, and throw in two heaping tablespoonfuls of salt. When done, put it, rag and all, into a pan, and turn cold water over it enough to cover. Let it stand a few minutes, but not long enough to cool too much. Then take off the cloth, and send at once to table. Serve with it a smooth butter sauce, with capers separately.

BOILED LAMB.—Same way, allowing about a fourth less time. It must depend upon the size, however. Eight minutes to the pound, then try it.

To CHOOSE BEEF.—When beef is good it may be known by

its texture and color; the lean will have a fine, open grain of a deep coral or bright carnation red; the fat rather inclining to white than yellow; and the suet firm and white. Very yellow fat is generally sufficient proof of inferior beef.

The better roasting pieces of beef are the prime ribs, sirloin, and what is known as the porter-house piece; it may be recognized by the bone.

The best steaks are cut from the sirloin and porter-house. The last mentioned cut probably took its name from having been the most highly esteemed steak, and so dished for the palate of the epicure at porter-houses, which were formerly the only eating-houses. Fine steaks may be cut from between the ribs

The round of tender, fat beef, cuts very good steaks, as does also the cross-ribs, but they are juiceless compared with the other pieces. The lean of fat beef is the most juicy and tender.

The neck, shin, or marrow bone, leg or head make good soups.

Beef skirts are good for sausage meat, stewing, hashes, or for mince-pie meat; or they may be broiled or fried.

To Fry Tripe.—Take prepared tripe, lay it in a little water over night; in the morning scrape the rough side clean, then wipe it dry; then dip in wheat flour or rolled crackers. Have a thick-bottomed frying pan, put into it a cup of lard or beef dripping; let it become boiling hot; then lay the tripe in, the rough side down first, let it fry gently; when this side is a delicate brown turn the other and do likewise; then take it from the pan, add to it the fat in which it was fried a wineglass of vinegar, let it boil up once, then pour it in the dish with the tripe; or you may use water instead of vinegar.

Beef Liver.—Cut the liver in thin slices; dip each slice in wheat flour or rolled crackers, and fry in hot lard or beef dripping; season with pepper and salt. It must be thoroughly cooked and a fine brown.

To Stew a Round of Beef.—Boil the beef till it is rather more than half done; gash it with a sharp knife, then rub it over with salt and pepper and sweet herbs chopped small; one sliced carrot, also a leek or onion sliced small; dredge it white with flour; strew bits of butter over it, and put it into a dinner pot with a pint or more of the water in which it was boiled; cover it close, and let it bake or stew slowly for two hours; add a little hot water when it may be necessary to keep it from burning; turn it once; when it is nicely browned take it up, add a little boiling water to the gravy, stir it well together, let it boil up once, then pour it over the meat.

BEEF HEART BAKED OR ROASTED.—Cut a beef heart in two; take out the strings from the inside; wash it with warm water; rub the inside with pepper and salt, and fill it with a stuffing of bread and butter moistened with water, and seasoned with pepper and salt, and, if liked, a sprig of thyme made fine; put it together and tie a string round it; rub the outside with pepper and salt; stick bits of butter on, then dredge flour over and set it on a trivet or muffin rings, in a dripping pan; put a pint of water in to baste with, then roast it before a hot fire or in a hot oven; turn it round and baste frequently. One hour will roast or bake it; when done take it up, cut a lemon in thin slices, and put it in a pan with a bit of butter; dredge in a teaspoonful of flour; let it brown, add a small teacupful of boiling water; stir it smooth, and serve in a gravy tureen.

BEEF KIDNEYS.—These may be split and fried, or broiled, or they may be chopped small and made a hash or stew. Cut them in half, or mince them, and put them in a stewpan with enough hot water to moisten them; then cover them close and let them simmer gently until tender; add a good bit of butter, pepper and salt to taste, and some browned flour; a wineglass of wine or catsup may be added, if liked. Toast some thin slices of bread delicately brown, take off the crust and lay them in a dish, and put the stew or hash over. A finely chopped onion or leek may be added to it, if liked.

HASHED BEEF.—Take some very rare done or uncooked beef, chop it fine, one-fourth as much fat as lean, and moisten it with water or gravy; if with water, add a bit of butter rolled in flour; put it in a closely covered stewpan over a gentle fire for half an hour; then dredge in a little browned flour, add salt and pepper to taste, and cover it for fifteen minutes, and

serve. Or, cut some thin slices of toast in neat squares, put
them in the dish and put the hash on it; or serve it on boiled
rice. Some persons like a teaspoonful of made mustard or
catsup put to it before dishing it.

BEEF STEAKS.—Sirloin, and what is known in New York
markets as porter-house steaks, are the choicest cuts. If the
beef is not very tender and young, it may be improved by beating gently with a rolling-pin or potato-beetle before cooking;
the steaks should be nearly the thickness of an inch; beef
steaks must on no account be washed. By keeping beef as
long as possible without tainting, it may be improved in flavor,
and will become more tender; broiling is by far the best manner of cooking beef steaks.

FRIED BEEF STEAKS.—Cut some of the fat from the steak
and put it into a frying-pan and set it over the fire; if the
steaks are not very tender, beat them with a rolling-pin, and
when the fat is boiling hot, put the steak evenly in, cover the
pan and let it fry briskly until one side is done; sprinkle a little
pepper and salt over, and turn the other; let it be rare or well-
done, as may be liked; take the steak on a hot dish, add a wineglass or less of boiling water or catsup to the gravy; let it boil
up once and pour it in the dish with the steak.

BEEF AND ONION STEW.—Cut two pounds of meat in pieces
the size of an egg, and put it into a stewpan with enough warm
water nearly to cover it; cover the stewpan and let it simmer
slowly for half an hour; then skim it clear, peel five or six small
onions and cut them in thick slices; pare half a dozen large
potatoes and cut them in half, or quarters; add a tablespoonful of salt, and a small teaspoonful of pepper to the stewed
meat; then put in the potatoes and onions. If the meat is
lean, (it is best to have a small portion of fat,) add a bit of
butter the size of a large egg; shake over it a tablespoonful of
wheat flour, or work it into the butter; cover the stewpan close,
and let it stew gently that it may brown without burning; one
hour is required for making this stew. If the potatoes are cut
smaller than halves, they should be put in twenty minutes
before it is done; half an hour will be required to cook them
if cut in two.

To Roast Beef.—Have a bright, clear fire before putting down the roast; if it is large, have a fire according; let it be a clear, steady fire, with a bed of coals at the bottom—this is for a wood fire; for a coal fire, make one large enough to last the length of time required for the roast (fifteen minutes for each pound of meat); make the front of the fire clear from ashes, and brush up the hearth; rinse the meat in cold water, wipe it dry; mix salt and pepper, a teaspoonful of salt, and a saltspoonful of pepper for each pound of meat; rub it over every part, then put it evenly on the spit, taking care not to run it through the best parts; or if it is done in a reflector, set it on a trivet or muffin rings, and turn the pan about as occasion may require; then put it down at a little distance from the fire, that the outside may not be too much done before the inside is cooked; put at least a pint of water into the dripping-pan, with which to baste; replenish with boiling water, so that there shall not be less than a pint of gravy when the meat is done, for a piece weighing five or six pounds; when about half done, clear the front of the fire and set it a little nearer; turn the meat so that all sides may be done evenly; fifteen minutes before it is done, if you please, dredge with the fat of the meat wheat flour until it looks white; baste it freely and set it to finish; when done, take it on to a large dish and cover with a tin cover; set the dripping over the fire, dredge in a small tablespoonful of flour, stir it smooth; when it is a fine brown, add a teacupful of boiling water, let it boil up, stirring it meanwhile; then pour it through a gravy strainer into a tureen; if there is much fat skim nearly all of it off; or, instead of dredging in flour, make a thin, smooth batter of a tablespoonful of flour, and a small cup of cold water; let the gravy in the pan become boiling hot before stirring it in; then stir it smooth, and when it is a fine rich brown, strain it into the tureen and serve with the meat.

The vegetables most proper with roast beef are plain boiled or mashed potatoes, with boiled spinach, beets or dressed celery, and turnips mashed, or squash. If you please, pickles, or grated horseradish, may also be served with roast beef instead of spinach or celery, with made mustard and catsup in the castor. In roasting meat it should be so placed as to bring the largest or thickest part nearest the fire. In roasting meat its juiciness depends on the frequency of basting it, after it has fairly begun to roast.

VEAL.—Veal should not be kept long before dressing, as it by no means improves by keeping. The loin is apt to taint under the kidney. When soft and slimy it is stale; it will be cool and firm and have an agreeable smell when fresh.

In the shoulder, if the vein is a clear red, it is good. When there are any yellow or dark spots it is stale. The breast and neck, when good, look white and clear. Veal must always be well cooked. The leg of veal is generally boiled or made soup of. The loin also may be boiled, but it is best roasted, and cut into chops and broiled and fried. The shoulder may be roasted; it may be boned and stuffed and then roasted, or it may be split, after having been boned, and fried or broiled. The breast may be roasted, stewed, or broiled, or made a pie. Steaks are cut from leg or shoulder. The neck, or scrag, may be cut in chops and fried, broiled, or stewed; or a dish of soup may be made of it.

Calf's liver is cut in steaks, and fried like beef liver, or it may be broiled and buttered.

Veal sweet-breads are roasted with the breast, or they may be fried or stewed.

Calf's head may be boiled and served with a sauce, and a soup made of the liquor in which it is boiled.

The head and feet are used for making jellies.

To BROIL VEAL.—Put in hot water (not boiling) to cover it, put to it a teaspoonful of salt, cover the pot, and let it boil very gently, taking off the scum as it rises; allow fifteen minutes for each pound of meat; four pounds of meat will require one hour gentle boiling. Serve boiled veal with drawn butter, or oysters, or lemon, or parsley sauce, and plain boiled potatoes with pickles, or lettuce, or celery. Boil the loin and serve with egg sauce.

CALF'S HEAD.—Clean it very nicely and soak it in salt and water, that it may look white (clean as directed for beef tripe), take out the eyes, take out the tongue to salt, and the brains to make a little dish; boil the head very tender, and serve with a sauce, or take it up, put bits of butter all over it, dredge with flour, **and season** with pepper and finely **sifted sweet herbs,** if liked, set it in a hot oven or before the fire; baste **with some** of the water in which it was boiled, or squeeze the juice of a lemon over; roast it a fine brown; then take it on a hot dish and put on a tin cover; add a piece of butter, the size of an egg, to the gravy; cut a small lemon in thin slices, and make the gravy boiling hot; add them to it; let them fry brown, then put a teaspoonful of browned flour, and a teacup of boiling water to the gravy, and serve with the meat. The lemon may be dispensed with if preferred—it will generally be liked.

To Make a Dish of Calf's Brains.—Wash them in salt and water, then boil them tender, and take them in a dish; put butter and pepper over, and serve. Or, after washing the brains in salt and water, wipe them dry, and dip them in wheat flour, or in beaten egg, and then into bread crumbs, and fry in hot lard or beef dripping; season with pepper and salt, and slices of lemon fried, if liked.

Calf's Head Cheese.—Boil a calf's head in water enough to cover it, until the meat leaves the bones, then take it with a skimmer into a wooden bowl or tray; take from it every particle of bone; chop it small; season with pepper and salt, a heaping teaspoonful of salt, and a teaspoonful of pepper will be sufficient; if liked, add a teaspoonful of finely chopped sweet herbs; lay a cloth in a cullender, put the minced meat in it, then fold the cloth closely over it, lay a plate over, and on it a gentle weight. When cold it may be sliced for supper or sandwiches. Spread each slice with made mustard.

Calf's Head (a fine dish).—Boil a calf's head (after having cleaned it), until tender, then split it in two, and keep the best half (bone in it if you like); cut the meat from the other in uniform pieces, the size of an oyster; put bits of butter the size of a nutmeg all over the best half of the head; sprinkle pepper over, and dredge on flour until it looks white, then set it on a trivet or muffin rings in a dripping pan; put a cup of water into the pan and set it in a hot oven or before a hot fire; turn it that it may brown evenly; baste once or twice, whilst this is doing, dip the prepared pieces of the head in wheat flour or batter, and fry in hot lard or beef dripping, a delicate brown; season with pepper and salt, and slices of lemon, if liked. When the roast is done put it in a hot dish, lay the fried pieces around it and cover with a tin cover; put the gravy from the dripping pan into the pan in which the pieces were fried, with the slices of lemon, and a teaspoonful of browned flour, and, if necessary, a little hot water. Let it boil up once, and strain it into a gravy boat and serve with the meat.

VEAL CHOPS.—Cut your chops about an inch thick; beat them flat with a rolling pin, put them in a pan, pour boiling water over them, and set them over the fire for five minutes; then take them up and wipe them dry; mix a tablespoonful of salt and a teaspoonful of pepper for each pound of meat; rub each chop over with this, then dip them, first into beaten egg, then into rolled crackers as much as they will take up; then finish by frying in hot lard or beef dripping; or broil them. For the broil have some sweet butter on a steak dish; broil the chops until well done, over a bright, clear fire of coals (let them do gently that they may be well done) then take them on to the butter, turn them carefully over once or twice in it, and serve. Or, dip the chops into a batter, made of one egg beaten with half a teacup of milk, and as much wheat flour as may be necessary. Or, simply dip the chops without parboiling into wheat flour; make some lard or beef fat hot in a frying pan; lay the chops in, and when one side is a fine, delicate brown, turn the other. When all are done, take them up, put a very little hot water into the pan, then put it into the dish with the chops.

Or, make a flour gravy thus: After frying them as last directed, add a tablespoonful more of fat to that in the pan, let it become boiling hot; make a thin batter, of a small tablespoonful of wheat flour and cold water; add a little more salt and pepper to the gravy, then gradually stir in the batter; stir it until it is cooked and a nice brown; then put it over the meat, or in a dish with it; if it is thicker than is liked, add a little boiling water.

VEAL STEWED WITH VEGETABLES (*Ragout*).—Wash three pounds of veal in cold water, then cut it small and put it in a stewpan with water nearly to cover it; add a tablespoonful of salt and a teaspoonful of pepper; cover the stewpan, and let it simmer for twenty minutes, then skim it clear. Whilst the meat is stewing, scrape one large or two small carrots and cut them in thin slices, a quarter of an inch thick, notch the edges, and put them in a stewpan, with boiling water to cover them, and set it over the fire until they are tender; dip a bunch of parsley into boiling water and mince it fine; cut a leek into thin slices; pare and cut six small potatoes in halves or quarters, then take the carrot from the water with a skimmer; put quarter of a pound of sweet butter to the meat; dredge over it a tablespoonful of browned flour, and add the vegetables; cover the stewpan and let it stew gently for an hour; then take the meat on a dish, put the vegetables around it, pour the gravy over, and serve.

To Roast Veal.—Rinse the meat in cold water; if any part is bloody, wash it off; make a mixture of pepper and salt, allowing a large teaspoonful of salt and saltspoonful of pepper for each pound of meat; wipe the meat dry; then rub the seasoning into every part, shape it neatly and fasten it with skewers, and put it on a spit, or set it on a trivet or muffin rings, in a pan; stick bits of butter over the whole upper surface; dredge a little flour over, put a pint of water into the pan to baste with, and roast it before the fire in a Dutch oven or reflector, or put it into a hot oven; baste it occasionally, turn it if necessary that every part may be done; if the water wastes, add more, that the gravy may not burn; allow fifteen minutes for each pound of meat; a piece weighing four or five pounds will then require one hour or an hour and a quarter. When it is nicely browned and done, take it up; add a bit of butter the size of a large egg to the gravy, dredge in a tablespoonful of flour, stir it smooth, let it brown, add a cup of boiling water to it; then strain it into a gravy-boat, and serve with the meat; serve plain boiled or mashed potatoes with the meat, with such green vegetables as may be liked.

Plain boiled or mashed potatoes, with any other vegetable which may be liked may be served with roast veal; also pickles of any kind.

Veal Hashed.—Cut a pound of cold veal small, season it to taste with pepper and salt, dredge a small teaspoonful of wheat flour over it, add a bit of butter the size of an egg, put it in a stewpan, put water enough to make it moist; then cover it close and set it over a gentle fire for half an hour; stir it occasionally; if liked, a bunch of parsley may be cut small and added to it; when half done, toast some thin slices of bread delicately brown, cut it in small squares or diamonds, and serve the hash on it, for breakfast.　A glass of wine may be added.

VEAL PIE.—Cut a breast of veal small and put it in a stew-pan, with hot water to cover it; add to it a tablespoonful of salt and set it over the fire; take off the scum as it rises; when the meat is tender, turn it into a dish to cool; take out all the small bones, butter a tin or earthen basin or pudding-pan, line it with a pie paste (see clam pie), lay some of the parboiled meat in to half fill it, put bits of butter the size of a hickory nut all over the meat, shake pepper over, dredge wheat flour over until it looks white; then fill it nearly to the top with some of the water in which the meat was boiled, roll a cover for the top of the crust, puff paste it, giving it two or three turns, and roll it to nearly half an inch thickness; cut a slit in the centre and make several small incisions on either side of it; lay some skewers across the pie, put the crust on, trim the edges neatly with a knife, bake one hour in a quick oven.　A breast of veal will make two quart basin pies; half a pound of nice corned pork, cut in thin slices and parboiled with the meat, will make it very nice, and little, if any, butter will be required for the pie; when pork is used no other salt will be necessary.

POTATO AND VEAL PIE.—Peel and cut small some cold boiled potatoes; cut some cold veal small; put some of the meat in the bottom of a baking dish, or tin basin, put on a layer of potatoes, sprinkle pepper and salt over and bits of butter; then another layer of meat and potatoes and seasoning, and so con-tinue until the pan is nearly full, then add to it water or gravy to moisten it; cover it with a pie crust, and bake in a quick oven for three-quarters of an hour.

TO BOIL PICKLED BEEF.—Put on the fire in cold water; let it simmer slowly, allowing fifteen minutes to every pound; do not let it boil; keep skimming or it will look dirty; if it is left in the pot until the water is cold it will be much more tender.

SPICED BEEF.—Take a piece of beef from the fore-quarter,

weighing ten pounds. Those who like fat should select a fatty piece; those who prefer lean may take the shoulder clod, or upper part of the fore-leg. Take one pint of salt, one teacup of molasses or brown sugar, one tablespoonful of ground cloves, allspice and pepper, and two tablespoonfuls of pulverized salt-petre. Place the beef in a deep pan; rub with this mixture; turn and rub each side twice a day for a week; then wash off the spices; put in a pot of boiling water, and, as often as it boils hard, turn in a teacupful of cold water. It must simmer for five hours, on the back part of the stove. Press under a heavy weight until it is cold, and you will never desire to try corned-beef of the butcher again. Your pickle will do for another ten pounds of beef, first rubbing into it a handful of salt. It can be renewed and a piece kept in preparation every day. This is good to pickle tongues also.

BEEF.—To pickle for drying or boiling, thoroughly rub salt into it, and let it remain twenty-four hours to draw off the blood; after which drain and pack as desired; have ready a pickle prepared as follows: For every one hundred pounds of beef, seven pounds of salt, one ounce of saltpetre, one quart of molasses, eight gallons of soft water; boil and skim well; when cold pour it over the beef. Pieces designed for drying should be taken out in two weeks, and soaked over night, to take the salt from the outside.

REMAINS OF ROAST BEEF.—Take off with a sharp knife all the meat from the bones, chop it fine, take cold gravy without the fat, put it in the spider to heat; if you have not this, some of the water in which the bones were boiled; when it boils up, sprinkle in salt and put in the minced meat; cover it and let it stand upon the fire long enough to heat it thoroughly, then stir in a small piece of butter, toast bread, and lay in a dish; put the meat over it; serve hot.

BOILING MEAT.—There is all the difference in the world between boiling meat which is to be eaten, and meat whose juices are to be extracted in the form of soup. If the meat is required as nourishment, of course you want the juices kept in. To do this, it is necessary to plunge it into boiling water, which will cause the albumen in the meat to coagulate suddenly,

10

and act as a plug or stopper to all the tubes of the meat, so that the nourishment will be tightly kept in. The temperature of the water should be kept at boiling point for five minutes, and then as much cold water must be added as will reduce the temperature to one hundred and sixty-five degrees. Now if the hot water, in which the meat is being cooked, is kept at this temperature for some hours, we have all the conditions united, which give to the flesh the quality best adapted for its use as food. The juices are kept in the meat, and, instead of being called upon to consume an insipid mass of indigestible fibres, we have a tender piece of meat, from which, when cut, the imprisoned juice runs freely. If the meat be allowed to remain in the boiling water, without the addition of any cold water to it, it becomes in a short time altogether cooked, but it will also be almost indigestible, and therefore unpalatable.

To Bake a Ham.—Most persons boil a ham, but a first-rate Virginia housewife tells us it is much better if baked properly. Soak it for an hour or more and wipe dry. Next spread it all over with a batter made of flour and water; put it into a deep pan with muffin rings or bits of oak wood under it to keep it out of the gravy. When fully done—it will take from five to seven hours—take off the skin and batter crusted upon the flesh side and set it away to cool, or glaze it by the following recipe:

Glazed Ham.—Beat the yolks of two eggs very light. Spread them all over your ham; then sift over fine cracker crumbs, and set in the oven to brown. Currant jelly may be used instead of yolks of eggs, and is very nice.

Poultry and Game.—To Clean Poultry.—First be very careful to singe off all down by holding over a blazing paper, or a little alcohol burning in a saucer. Cut off the feet and the ends of the wings, and the neck as far as it is dark. If the fowl is killed at home, be sure that the head is chopped off, and never allow the neck to be wrung, as is often done. It is not only an unmerciful way of killing, but the blood has thus no escape, and settles about all the vital organs. The head should be cut off, and the body hang and bleed thoroughly before using.

Pick out all the pin-feathers with the blade of a small knife.

Turn back the skin of the neck, loosening it with the finger and thumb, and draw out the windpipe and crop, which can be done without making any cut. Now cut a slit in the lower part of the fowl, the best place being close to the thigh. By working the fingers in slowly, keeping them close to the body, the whole intestines can be removed in a mass. Be especially careful not to break the gall-bag, which is near the upper part of the breastbone, and attached to the liver. If this operation is carefully performed, it will be by no means so disagreeable as it seems. A French cook simply wipes out the inside, considering that much flavor is lost by washing. We prefer to wash in one water, and dry quickly, though in the case of an old fowl, which often has a strong smell, it is better to dissolve a teaspoonful of soda in the first water, which should be warm, and wash again in cold, then wiping dry as possible. Slit and wash the gizzard, reserving it for gravy.

Dressing for Poultry.—One pint of bread or cracker crumbs, into which mix dry one teaspoonful of pepper, one of thyme or summer savory, one even tablespoonful of salt, and, if in season, a little chopped parsley. Melt a piece of butter the size of an egg in one cup of boiling water, and mix with the crumbs, adding one or two well-beaten eggs. A slice of salt pork chopped fine is often substituted for the butter.

For ducks two onions are chopped fine, and added to the above; or a potato dressing is made, as for geese, using six large boiled potatoes, mashed hot, and seasoned with an even tablespoonful of salt, a teaspoonful each of sage and pepper, and two chopped onions.

Game is usually roasted unstuffed, but grouse and prairie-chickens may have the same dressing as chickens and turkeys, this being used also for boiled fowls.

Roast Turkey.—Prepare by cleaning, as in general directions above, and, when dry, rub the inside with a teaspoonful of salt. Put the gizzard, heart, and liver on the fire in a small saucepan, with one quart of boiling water and one teaspoonful of salt, and boil two hours. Put a little stuffing in the breast, and fold back the skin of the neck, holding it with a stitch or with a small skewer. Put the remainder in the body, and sew it up with darning cotton. Cross and tie the legs down tight, and run a skewer through the wings to fasten them to the body. Lay it in the roasting-pan, and for an eight-pound turkey allow not less than three hours' time, a ten or twelve pound one needing four. Put a pint of boiling water with one teaspoonful of salt in the pan, and add to it as it dries away. Melt a heaping tablespoonful of butter in the water and baste very often. The secret of a handsomely-browned turkey lies in this frequent basting. Dredge over the flour two or three times, as in general roasting directions, and turn the turkey so that all sides will be reached. When done, take up on a hot platter. Put the baking-pan on the stove, having before this chopped the gizzard and heart fine, and mashed the liver, and put them in the gravy-tureen. Stir a tablespoonful of brown flour into the gravy in the pan, scraping up all the brown, and add slowly the water in which the giblets were boiled, which should be about a pint. Strain on to the chopped giblets, and taste to see if salt enough. The gravy for all roast poultry is made in this way. Serve with cranberry sauce or jelly.

ROAST OR BOILED CHICKENS.—Stuff and truss as with turkeys, and to a pair of chickens weighing two and a half pounds each, allow one hour to roast, basting often, and making a gravy as in precedent recipe. Boil as in rule for turkeys.

ROAST DUCK.—After cleaning, stuff as in rule given for poultry dressing, and roast—if game, half an hour; if tame, one hour, making gravy as in directions given, and serving with currant jelly.

BIRDS.—Small birds may simply be washed and wiped dry, tied firmly, and roasted twenty minutes, dredging with flour, basting with butter and water, and adding a little currant jelly or wine to the gravy. They may be served on toast.

BOILED TURKEY.—Clean, stuff, and truss the fowl selected, as for a roasted turkey. The body is sometimes filled with oysters. To truss in the tightest and most compact way, run a skewer under the leg-joint, between the leg and the thigh, then run through the body and under the opposite leg-joint in the same way; push the thighs up firmly close to the sides; wind a string about the ends of the skewer, and tie it tight. Treat the wings in the same way, though in boiled fowls the points are sometimes drawn under the back, and tied there. The turkey may be boiled with or without cloth around it. In either case use boiling water, salted as for stock, and allow twenty minutes to the pound. It is usually served with oyster sauce, but parsley or capers may be used instead.

BONED TURKEY.—This is a delicate dish, and is usually regarded as an impossibility for any ordinary house-keeper; and, unless one is getting up a supper or other entertainment, it is hardly worth while to undertake it. If the legs and wings are left on, the boning becomes more difficult. The best plan is to cut off both them and the neck, boiling all with the turkey, and using the meat for croquettes or hash.

Draw only the crop and windpipe, as the turkey is more easily handled before dressing. Choose a fat hen turkey of some six or seven pounds weight, and cut off legs up to second joint, with half the wings and the neck. Now, with a very sharp knife, make a clean cut down the entire back, and, holding the knife close to the body, cut away the flesh, first on one side, and then another, making a clean cut around the pope's nose. Be careful, in cutting down the breastbone, not to break through the skin. The entire meat will now be free from the bones, save the pieces remaining in legs and wings. Cut out these, and remove all sinews. Spread the turkey skin-side down on the board. Cut out the breasts, and cut them up in long, narrow pieces, or as you like. Chop fine a pound and a half of veal or fresh pork, and a slice of ham also. Season with one teaspoonful of salt; a saltspoonful each of mace and pepper; half a saltspoonful of cayenne and the juice of a lemon. Cut half a pound of cold boiled smoked tongue into dice. Make layers of this force-meat, putting half of it on the turkey and then the dice of tongue, with strips of the breast between, using force-meat for the last layer. Roll up the turkey in a tight roll, and sew the skin together. Now roll it firmly in a napkin, tying at the ends and across in two places to preserve the shape. Cover it with boiling water, salted as for stock, putting in all the bones and giblets, and two onions stuck with two cloves each. Boil four hours. Let it cool in the liquor. Take up in a pan, lay a tin sheet on it, and press with a heavy weight. Strain the water in which it was boiled, and put in a cold place. Next day take off the napkin and set the turkey in the oven a moment to melt off any fat. It can be sliced and eaten in this way, but makes a handsomer dish served as follows:

Remove the fat from the stock, and heat three pints of it to boiling-point, adding two-thirds of a package of gelatine which has been soaked in a little cold water. Strain a cupful of this into some pretty mold—an ear of corn is a good shape —and the remainder in two pans or deep plates, coloring each with caramel—a teaspoonful in one, and two in the other. Lay the turkey on a small platter turned face down in a larger one, and, when the jelly is cold and firm, put the molded form on top of it. Now cut part of the jelly into rounds with a pepper-box top, or a small star-cutter, and arrange around the mold, chopping the rest and piling about the edge, so that the inner platter or stand is completely concealed. The outer row of jelly can have been colored red by cutting up, and boiling in the stock for it, half of a red beet. Sprigs of parsley or delicate celery-tops may be used as garnish, and it is a very elegant-looking as well as savory dish. The legs and wings can be left on and trussed outside, if liked, making it as much as possible in the original shape; but it is no better, and much more trouble.

JELLIED CHICKEN.—Tenderness is no object here, the most ancient dweller in the barnyard answering equally well, and even better than " broilers."

Draw carefully, and, if the fowl is old, wash it in water in which a spoonful of soda has been dissolved, rinsing in cold. Put on in cold water, and season with a tablespoonful of salt and a half teaspoonful of pepper. Boil till the meat slips easily from the bones, reducing the broth to about a quart. Strain, and, when cold, take off the fat. Where any floating particles remain, they can always be removed by laying a piece of soft paper on the broth for a moment. Cut the breast in long strips, and the rest of the meat in small pieces. Boil two or three eggs hard, and, when cold, cut in thin slices. Slice a lemon very thin. Dissolve half a package of gelatine in a little cold water; heat the broth to boiling-point, and add a saltspoonful of mace, and, if liked, a glass of sherry, though it is not necessary, pouring it on the gelatine. Choose a pretty mold, and lay in strips of the breast; then a layer of egg slices, putting them close against the mold. Nearly fill with chicken, laid in lightly; then strain on the broth till it is nearly full, and set in a cold place. Dip for an instant in hot water before turning out. It is nice as a supper or lunch dish, and very pretty in effect.

TURKEY AND CHICKEN STUFFING.—Three teacups of grated bread crumbs (no crust and not a drop of water), one cup finely chopped suet, two-thirds of a cup of chopped parsley, a tablespoonful of sweet marjoram and summer savory, one-half teaspoonful of pepper, one teaspoonful of salt, one or two eggs, beaten.

TO BOIL A CHICKEN OR TURKEY.—It is not every housewife who knows how best to boil a chicken. Plain, artless boiling is apt to produce a yellowish, slimy looking fowl. Before cooking, the bird should always be well washed in tepid water and lemon juice, and to insure whiteness, delicacy and succulence, should be boiled in a soup of flour and water; after being put in the boiling water should be allowed to simmer slowly. This method is very effectual in preserving all the juices of the fowl, and the result is a more toothsome and nourishing morsel than the luckless bird which has been " galloped to death" in plain boiling.

ESCALLOPED TURKEY.—Take the remains of cold turkey, from which remove all the bones and gristle; chop the meat in small pieces. Place in an earthen dish a layer of powdered cracker, moistened with milk; then add a layer of turkey seasoned with pepper and salt, then another layer of powdered cracker, and then 'one of turkey, and so on until the dish is filled; over that pour the gravy you may have left, or a little hot water and butter. Finish the top with the powdered cracker, moisten with a beaten egg and sweet milk, bake one hour. Cover the dish for the first half hour, that the top may not become too brown.

PRAIRIE CHICKENS, PARTRIDGES AND QUAIL.—Clean nicely, using a little soda in the water in which they are washed; rinse them and drain, and fill with dressing, sewing them up nicely, and binding down the legs and wings with cord. Put them in a steamer and let them cook ten minutes. Then put them in a pan with a little butter, set them in the oven and baste frequently until of a nice brown. They ought to brown in about thirty-five minutes. Serve them in a ᵖlatter with sprigs of parsley alternated with currant jelly.

A NICE WAY TO COOK PIGEONS.—Stuff the birds with a rich bread dressing; place compactly in an iron or earthen dish; season with salt, pepper, and butter (or, if you like best, thin slices of salt pork over the top), dredge thickly with flour and nearly cover them with water. Then put over a closely fitting plate or cover, and place the dish in a moderate oven, from two to four, or even five, hours, according to the age of the birds. If the birds are old and tough, this is the best way they can be cooked, and they may be made perfectly tender and much sweeter than by any other process. If the gravy is insufficient, add a little water before dishing.

TO POT BIRDS.- -Prepare them as for roasting. Fill each with a dressing made as follows: Allow for each bird of the size of a pigeon one-half of a hard boiled egg, chopped fine, a tablespoonful of bread crumbs, a teaspoonful of chopped pork; season the bird with pepper and salt; stuff them, lay them in a kettle that has a tight cover. Place over the birds a few slices of pork, add a pint of water, dredge over them a little flour, cover and put them in a hot oven. Let them cook until tender, then add a little cream and butter. If the sauce is too thin, thicken with flour. **One pint of water is sufficient for twelve birds.**

QUAIL ON TOAST.—After the birds are well cleaned, cut them open on the back, salt and pepper them, and dredge them very lightly with flour. Break them down so they will lie flat, and broil them on a gridiron, or place them in a pan with a little butter and a little water in a hot oven, covering them closely for awhile, until about done. Then take them up and place in a spider on top of the stove, and let them fry a nice brown. Have ready slices of baker's bread well toasted and slightly buttered. The toast should be broken down with a carving knife to make the crust tender; on this place your **quails. Make a gravy of the drippings in the pan, thickened** very lightly with browned flour, and pour over each quail. The quails should only be allowed to fry just long enough to brown nicely, and not long enough to dry out; five minutes ought to be sufficient.

FRICASSEE CHICKEN.—Cut up, wash and dry a pair of chickens, put into a stewpan a tablespoonful of butter; let it boil; lay the chickens into this and shake them about, turning them and giving each piece a little glazed look; then add water enough to cover the fowls, and let stew slowly from forty minutes to an hour. Just before serving let it come to a keen boil, and stir in a teacupful of milk or sweet cream, in which a heaping tablespoonful of flour has been stirred. Let it cook five minutes and pour into a dish over which some freshly baked powder biscuits have been opened and spread. Season with salt and pepper.

ESCALLOPED CHICKEN.—Cold chicken, chiefly the white meat, one cup of gravy, one tablespoonful of butter, and one egg, well beaten, one cup of fine bread crumbs, pepper and salt· Take from the chicken all gristle and skin, and cut, not chop, into pieces not less than half an inch long. Have ready the gravy, or some rich drawn butter in a saucepan on the fire. Thicken it well, and stir into it the chicken; boil up once, take it off and add the beaten egg; cover the bottom of a buttered dish with bread crumbs, pour in the mixture, and put in another thick layer of crumbs on top, sticking butter all over it. Bake to a delicate brown in a quick oven. Turkey may be used instead of chicken; also veal.

CHICKEN PIE.—Stew until tender two chickens in just enough water to stew them. Make a nice crust, line a deep dish with it; when the chickens are done remove all the bones; put the chickens into the dish in which they are to be baked; thicken the gravy with a little flour and cream; add a can of oysters; season with salt, pepper and butter; cover the pie with a crust, and bake quickly. This is very nice.

RICE AND CHICKEN PIE.—Boil a pint or more of rice; stir in a teaspoonful of butter, a little milk, two eggs and a little salt. Fricassee two chickens; cover the bottom of a long dish with rice, then a layer of chicken, and so on, until it ʍ full; save out some of the gravy of the fricassee to eat on the rice; cover the whole with the yolk of an egg and brown it. Curry may be put into the chicken if liked. One chicken makes a good sized dish.

CHICKEN JELLY.—Boil the chicken until tender; cut with a knife fine, put it in a dish or mold; season with salt, pepper, a little summer savory and a teaspoonful of vinegar; boil the bones in the broth awhile and pour over. When cold it will turn out.

TO CHOOSE A GOOSE.—Be careful in choosing a goose that it is young; an old goose is very poor fare. If the skin and joints are tender and easily broken with the finger, it is young; a fat goose is best. The feet and bill of a young goose are yellow; in an old one they are red. When fresh killed, the feet are pliable; if stale, they will be dry and stiff. The loose fat from the inside of a goose should be taken out, and the fat from the lower part of the back. Goose grease may be used medically, but not for eating. Some persons use it for making pie crust and for common molasses cake instead of other shortening.

TO ROAST A GOOSE.—Pick it perfectly clean, cut off the legs at the joints, and singe it nicely; cut off the vent, cut a slit from the breast bone to it, or across, below the breast bone; draw out the entrails, take off that leading to the vent; take out all the loose fat; save the heart and liver; cut a slit at the back of the neck, and draw out the crop; cut off a part of the neck, leave enough of the skin to fasten over against the back; wash the inside of the body with cold water, wipe it dry, and rub it well with a mixture of salt and pepper; prepare the stuffing.

Cut a sixpenny loaf of wheat bread in slices; pour hot water over to wet them; then add a teaspoonful of salt and the same of ground pepper, and quarter of a pound of sweet butter, with a tablespoonful of finely powdered sage or thyme, if liked. Fill the body, then sew up the slit, tie the ends of the legs together, or cut a place and put them in the body; pass a skewer through the hips; put the heart and liver between the wings and the body, and fasten close to it with a skewer; spit it; put a pint of water in the pan to baste with; have a bright, steady and clear fire, with a bed of coals at the bottom, and set the goose at a little distance at first, until it is heated through; put a teaspoonful of salt to the water in the pan, and baste freely with it after it has begun to roast; put one side to the fire first, then the other; after that the back, and lastly the breast, that it may be evenly done; gradually draw it nearer the fire; when nearly done, stir up the fire, put quarter of a pound of butter in the pan and baste with it; dredge a little flour over it; turn it that every part may be browned; allow fifteen minutes for each pound of meat. It must be well done, which will depend on the state and management of the fire.

If the gravy is very fat, take some of it off; put the pan over the fire, let it become hot, then stir into it a thin batter made of a tablespoonful of wheat flour and cold water; stir it until it is brown and smooth; if it is thicker than is liked, add a little boiling water; stir it in and pour it through a gravy-strainer into a tureen.

A goose may be equally well dressed in a hot oven or stove. Prepare it as directed for roasting; set a trivet or muffin rings in a dripping-pan, and place the goose with its back upon the trivet or rings; put a pint of hot water in the pan; put bits of butter the size of a large hickory nut over the body; dredge wheat flour over, and set in a thoroughly heated brick or stove oven; baste it freely and often; when done, take it from the pan; cover it, and set it before the fire to keep hot; put the pan over the fire; take out the rings or trivet; add a bit of butter the size of an egg, and when it is hot stir it into a thin batter made of a tablespoonful of wheat flour and cold water; if too thick, add hot water to thin it; stir it smooth, and pour through a gravy-strainer into a tureen. A lemon sliced thin and fried in the gravy before putting in the batter and served over the goose, or put in the tureen with the gravy, is liked by some persons.

The stuffing may be made of boiled potatoes, chopped or mashed, instead of bread, and moistened with milk. An onion or leek, finely minced, may be added to the gravy, if liked. Half a pound of fat corned pork chopped small may be put with the stuffing instead of butter for ordinary occasions, if preferred.

A young goose may be cut up and made in a pie or potpie.

An old goose may be rendered eatable thus: Empty it and

put it in hot water to cover it, and let it boil until tender, then roast it or make a fricassee.

The vegetables to be served with roast goose are as follows: Plain boiled or mashed potatoes, mashed yellow turnips or winter squash, apples stewed with sugar, or cranberry jam, boiled onions, pickles and dressed celery.

Dessert—Apple, pumpkin, custard or mince pies.

To Choose Ducks.—Ducks must be fat and plump and thick on the breast. If a duck is young, the skin can be easily broken with the finger, and the feet are pliable. Tame ducks are prepared for the table the same as young geese. For roasting, have a hot fire, and baste freely and often; half an hour will be sufficient for the smallest, the larger in proportion. Wild ducks should be fat, the claws small, reddish and supple; if they are not fresh, on opening the beak there will be a disagreeable smell. The flesh of the hen is the most delicate. Pick them clean without scalding; cut the wings close to the body and empty it; cut off a part of the neck, and singe them nicely.

Having drawn wild ducks, wipe them well inside with a cloth, rub each outside and in with a mixture of pepper and salt, cut a slice of white bread, dip it in hot water, spread it thick with butter, sprinkle pepper over and put it in the body, sew it up, truss the legs close to the body and fasten them with skewers; then split them or lay them on a trivet in a dripping-pan; have a bright, clear fire that they may roast quickly; put half a pint of water in the pan, put to it a teaspoonful of salt and an onion sliced thin, baste with this ten or twelve minutes (to take off the fishy taste peculiar to wild ducks) throw it away, put half a pint of hot water in its place, put in a little pepper, baste the ducks with butter, dredge a little flour over and baste with the water in the pan; turn them that every part may be done. Half an hour, with a hot fire and frequent basting, will roast them nicely. Serve the ducks as hot as possible.

Whilst the ducks are roasting, boil the giblets tender in a little water, chop or mince them fine, add to the mince pepper and salt, a small bit of butter and a tablespoonful of browned flour, when the ducks are done put it in the pan with the gravy, set it over the fire, stir it for a few minutes, then serve in a tureen. Make a glass of wine hot, put to it a tablespoonful of currant jelly and white sugar each, and serve with ducks, or put a wineglass of port in the pan; a few minutes before taking them up baste the ducks once or twice with it; add a table-spoonful of jelly and the gravy.

Or half roast wild ducks without seasoning. When they are brought to the table slice the breast, strew over pepper and salt, pour a little port wine over, or squeeze the juice of an orange or lemon over; add a bit of butter the size of an egg, sprinkle over a teaspoonful of fine white sugar, cut up the bird and set it over a chafing dish, turn it that it may be nicely done; or prepare it in this manner and set it on coals before a hot fire.

CANVAS BACK DUCKS.—Canvas back ducks are served in the same manner as wild ducks, without the onion in the basting; as there is no disagreeable taste to destroy, that is not necessary. Canvas back ducks may be served the same as goose or tame duck. Roast them according to their size.

Venison.—The choice of venison is regulated by the fat, which when young is thick, clear and close. As it always begins to taint first towards the haunches, run a knife into that part; if it is tainted you will perceive a rank smell, and it will have a greenish appearance.

VENISON STEAK FRIED.—Cut venison steaks from the leg or loin, half an inch thick, dip them in rolled crackers or wheat flour; make of lard and sweet butter equal parts, or beef drippings, half the size of an egg, hot in a frying pan, rub the steaks over with a mixture of pepper and salt, cover the pan and let them fry quickly, until one side is a fine brown, then turn the other, and finish frying without the cover; take care that they are not over done, then add to the gravy a glass of red wine, or a wineglass of hot water, with a tablespoonful of currant jelly, stir it over the fire for a few minutes, then put it in the dish with the meat, and serve as hot as possible. Steak dishes of block tin, with heaters, are used for beef or venison. Lean steaks of fat beef cooked in this way are equal to venison, for which the beef should be kept till ready to taint, then rinse them in cold water, wipe them dry, and finish as directed; the steaks should be cut small like venison.

Pork.—SPARE-RIB. — Broil the blade-bone and spare-rib nicely over a bright clear fire of coals; let it be well done. It is best to cover it whilst on the gridiron, as by so doing it is sooner done and the sweetness is kept in. Put the inside to the fire first, and let it be done nearly through before turning it; when done, take it on a hot dish, butter it well, season with pepper and salt, and serve hot.

SAUSAGE MEAT.—Take of pork three-quarters, and one of beef, chop it fine, put four ounces of fine salt, and one of pepper to every ten pounds of meat; mix the seasoning well into the meat; then put it in small muslin bags, tie them close, and hang them in a dry, cool cellar. When wanted for use, cut it in slices, or form it in small cakes, flour the outside of each, and fry in hot lard. Let them be nicely browned. Serve with boiled vegetables. Fine hominy may be boiled and served with them for breakfast.

PORK SAUSAGES.—Take such a proportion of fat and lean pork as you like, chop it quite fine, and for every ten pounds of meat take four ounces of fine salt, and one of fine pepper; dried sage or lemon thyme, finely powdered, may be added, if liked; a teaspoonful of sage, and the same of ground allspice and cloves, to each ten pounds of meat. Mix the seasoning through the meat, pack it down in stone pots, or put it in muslin bags. Or fill the hog's or ox's guts, having first made them perfectly clean, thus: empty them, cut them in lengths, and lay them three or four days in salt and water, or weak lime water; turn them inside out once or twice; scrape them; then rinse them and fill with the meat.

TO ROAST A PIG.—Thoroughly clean the pig; then rinse it in cold water, wipe it dry; then rub the inside with a mixture of salt and pepper, and, if liked, a little pounded and sifted sage; make a stuffing thus: cut some wheat bread in slices half an inch thick, spread butter on to half its thickness, sprinkled with pepper and salt, and, if liked, a little pounded sage and minced onion; pour enough hot water over the bread to make it moist or soft, then fill the body with it and sew it together, or tie a cord around it to keep the dressing in, then spit; put a pint of water in the dripping-pan, put into it a tablespoonful of salt, and a teaspoonful of pepper, let the fire be hotter at

each end than in the middle, put the pig down at a little distance from the fire, baste it as it begins to roast, and gradually
draw it nearer; continue to baste occasionally, turn it that it may
be evenly cooked; when the eyes drop out it is done; or a better rule is to judge by the weight, fifteen minutes for each
pound of meat, if the fire is right.

Have a bright, clear fire with a bed of coals at the bottom;
first put the roast at a little distance, and gradually draw it
nearer; when the pig is done stir up the fire, take a coarse cloth
with a good bit of butter in it, and wet the pig all over with it,
and when the cracking is crisp take it up; dredge a little flour
into the gravy, let it boil up once, and having boiled the heart,
liver, etc., tender, and chopped it fine, add to it the gravy,
give it one boil, then serve.

To BAKE A PIG.—Prepare a pig as for roasting, and lay it
on a trivet or on muffin rings in a dripping-pan, stick bits of
butter all over it, sprinkle pepper and salt over, and dredge
some flour over; put in a pint or more of water in the pan, then
set it in a quick or hot oven, baste frequently, when nearly
done, baste with a spoonful of butter, and close the oven to
finish; then take it up, dredge a tablespoonful of flour to the
gravy, set it over the fire to brown, stir it smooth, and if necessary add a little hot water, let it boil up once, then strain it
and serve with the pig. Pig to roast or bake may be stuffed
with boiled potatoes, seasoned with butter, pepper and salt,
and made soft with a cup of milk.

SAUCES TO SERVE WITH ROAST PIG OR PORK.—Mashed
potatoes, boiled onions, turnips mashed, pickled beets, man-
goes of cucumbers, or dressed celery and cranberry sauce,
stewed apples or currant jelly.

To ROAST A LOIN.—Take a sharp penknife and cut the
skin across, then cut over it in the opposite direction so as to
form small squares or diamonds; rub every part of it with a
mixture of salt and pepper, put bits of butter the size of a
hickory nut over the skin side, and roast or bake it; serve with
the gravy, boiled potatoes mashed, turnips mashed, and dressed
celery or pickles, and tart apples stewed without sugar.

PORK TENDER LOIN.—This part of pork is the most delicate; it may oe got where pork is cut up for packing or salting. It may be fried or broiled; if it is too thick, split it in two. Steaks cut from the tender-loin are nice, but not equal to the tender-loin which is cut with the grain; steaks are cut across it. The chine of pork may be roasted.

PIG'S FEET SOUSED.—Scald and scrape clean the feet; if the covering of the toes will not come off without, singe them in hot embers until they are loose, then take them off. Many persons lay them in a weak lime-water to whiten them. Having scraped them clean and white, wash them and put them in a pot of hot (not boiling) water, with a little salt, and let them boil gently, until, by turning a fork in the flesh, it will easily break, and the bones are loosened. Take off the scum as it rises. When done, take them from the hot water into cold vinegar, enough to cover them; add to it one-third as much of the water in which they were boiled; add whole pepper and allspice, with cloves and mace, if liked; put a cloth and tight-fitting cover over the pot or jar. Boil until the bones are loose. Soused feet may be eaten cold from the vinegar, split in two from top to toe; or, having split them, dip them in wheat flour and fry in hot lard, or broil and butter them. In either case, let them be nicely browned.

To BOIL HAM.—Wash the ham in cold water two or three times, and put it into a kettle of hot (not boiling) water to cover it; let it boil gently according to its weight (fifteen minutes to each pound); it must be kept slowly boiling all the time; keep the pot covered, except to take off the scum as it rises; if it is likely to boil over, take the lid partly off.

Putting meat down to boil in cold water draws out its juices. Hard or fast boiling makes it tough and hard. Ham which has been smoked a long time, should be soaked over night. When it is done, take off the skin, trim off the under side neatly, and put spots of pepper, and stick cloves at regular intervals, over the whole upper surface; or dredge it well with wheat flour or rolled crackers, and brown it in a hot oven, or before a hot fire. Serve hot with the gravy from it and boiled vegetables; or it may be served cold. Trim the bone with parsley, or the delicate leaves of celery, and put sprigs of the same around it on the dish; lemon sliced and dipped in flour or batter and fried, may be laid over the ham and on the dish. Mashed potatoes, stewed apple, or cranberry, celery, or boiled spinach, or cauliflower and mashed turnips are served with hot ham.

With cold ham serve pickles or dressed celery, or both, and bread and butter sandwich.

To Boil a Leg of Pork.—Take a leg of pork which has been in pickle for three or four days, soak it for half an hour in cold water to make it look white; then tie it in a nicely floured cloth, and put it in hot water to cover it. Boil the same as ham. When done, take a small sharp knife, and cut through the skin in a straight line about a quarter of an inch apart; put spots of pepper over and serve with the same vegetables as for ham; or with mashed potatoes, turnips mashed, and pickles or tart apples stewed without sugar. Currant jelly or cranberries may be served with ham or leg of pork.

Pig's Cheek—Is smoked and boiled like ham with vegetables; boiled cabbage or fried parsnips may be served with it.

Pork Chops, Steaks and Cutlets.—Fry or stew pork chops, after taking off the rind or skin, the same as for veal. Cutlets and steaks are also fried, broiled, or stewed, the same as veal.

To Fry or Broil Salt Pork and Bacon.—Cut some slices from corned pork, or streaked bacon (fat and lean), put them in a pan, pour boiling water over, set it over the fire, and let it boil up once; then pour the water off, and fry them in their own fat, sprinkle with pepper, and, if liked, a little dried sage, or thyme, pounded fine; when both sides are nicely browned, take them up, put a little hot water or some vinegar in the pan, let it boil up once, and put it in the dish with the meat. Or, having fried the meat, dredge a teaspoonful of flour into the gravy; while it is hot, stir it about; then add a little hot water, stir it smooth, and pour into the dish with the meat.

To Broil.—After having parboiled the slices with plenty of water in the pan, lay them on a gridiron, over a bright fire of coals; sprinkle a little pepper over; when both sides are done, put them on a hot dish, put a little butter over and serve. Or, whilst broiling, dip the slices several times into a dish of hot water.

Salt pork is very nice fried thus: Cut it in thin slices, put them in the frying-pan with hot water to cover them; set it over the fire, let it boil up once, then pour off the water, shake a little pepper over the meat, and fry it nicely in its own fat, both sides; then take it up, add to the gravy a large teaspoonful of flour, stir it smooth; then put to it a cup of milk, stir over the fire for a few minutes, shake pepper over, and put it in the dish with the meat.

Cold boiled potatoes, sliced thin, may be fried in the pan, after pork or bacon, and served with it; parsnips boiled, cut in thin slices and fried, may also be served with fried salt meat. Or, having boiled some cabbage or spinach, and pressed all the water from it, cut it small, put it on a steak dish, lay the fried meat on it, and pour the gravy over. Vinegar is generally eaten with the vegetables.

To Fry Ham.—Cut some large slices from the large end of the ham, take off the skin, put them in a frying-pan, and pour hot water over; set if over the fire and let it boil up once, then pour the water off, take the slices up, put a spoonful of lard in the frying-pan and let it become hot; dip the slices in rolled cracker or wheat flour, and fry them a nice brown; when one side is done, turn the other; then take them on a dish, put a very little water in the pan, let it boil up once, put it over the meat. Or, if a flour gravy is wanted, make a thin batter with a teaspoonful of flour and cold water, and stir it into the gravy in the pan, let it brown, and, if too thick, put a little hot water to it, stir it smooth, and serve with the meat.

To Broil Ham.—Cut some slices of ham, quarter of an inch thick, lay them in hot water for half an hour, or give them a scalding in a pan over the fire, then take them up and lay them on a gridiron over bright coals; then take the slices on a hot dish, butter them freely, sprinkle pepper over and serve. Or, after scalding them, wipe them dry, dip each slice in beaten egg, and then into rolled crackers and fry or broil.

Ham Gravy.—When a ham is almost done with, cut off what meat remains on the bone, break or saw the bones small, and put it into a saucepan with hot water to cover it;

set the stewpan over the fire and let it simmer gently; then strain it, add a little pepper and fine sage, if liked, dredge in a tablespoonful of browned flour, and add a bit of butter; stir it over the fire for a few minutes; then, having toasted some slices of bread a nice brown, lay them in a dish and serve the gravy over. Or, serve ham gravy with boiled vegetables.

HAM AND EGGS FRIED.—Cut some nice slices of ham, put them in a frying-pan, cover them with hot water, and set the pan over the fire, let it boil up once or twice, then take out the slices and throw out the water; put a bit of lard in the pan, dip the slices in wheat flour or rolled crackers, and, when the fat is hot, put them in the pan, sprinkle a little pepper over; when both sides are a fine brown, take them on a steak dish, put a little boiling water into the pan, and put it in the dish with the meat.

Now put a bit of lard the size of a large egg into the pan, add a saltspoonful to it, let it become hot; break six or eight eggs carefully into a bowl, then slip them into the hot lard, set the pan ever a gentle fire; when the white begins to set, pass a knife blade so as to divide an equal quantity of white to each yolk, cut it entirely through to the pan that they may cook the more quickly; when done, take each one up with a skimmer spoon, and lay them in a chain around the meat on the dish. Fried eggs should not be turned in the pan.

POACHED EGGS WITH FRIED HAM.—Fry the ham as above directed, take a clean frying or omelet pan, nearly fill it with boiling water, set it over a gentle fire, break the eggs singly into a cup and slip each one into the boiling water, cover the pan for four or five minutes; when done, take them up with a skimmer on to a dish, sprinkle a little pepper and salt over, add a small bit of butter, and serve in a dish or over the ham.

PORK AND BEANS.—Take two quarts of dried white beans (the small ones are best), pick out any imperfections, and put them to soak in hot water, more than to cover them, let them remain one night; the next day, about two hours before dinner time, throw off the water, have a pound of nicely corned pork; a rib piece is best; put the beans in an iron dinner-pot, score the rind or skin of the pork in squares or diamonds, and lay it on the beans, put in hot (not boiling) water to cover them, add a small dried red-pepper, or a saltspoonful of cayenne, cover the pot close, and set it over a gentle fire for one hour; then take a tin basin or earthen pudding-pan, rub the inside over with a bit of butter, and nearly fill it with the boiled beans, lay the pork in the centre, pressing it down a little, put small bits of butter over the beans, dredge a little flour over them and the pork, and set it in a moderately hot oven for nearly one hour.

Serve in the dish in which it was baked, thus: Lay a nicely fringed small napkin on a dinner plate, set the basin or pan on that, turn the corners of the napkin up against it, and keep it in place by sprigs of green parsley or celery leaves on the plate under it, and so continue a wreath around the dish, concealing the pan entirely. Serve pickles and mashed potatoes with it.

SUCCOTASH.—Take of dried sweet corn and white beans, one quart of dried sweet corn to one or two of beans. Put the beans to soak in a basin with water to cover them; rinse the corn in cold water, and put them in a basin with water to cover it, let them remain until the next day; within two hours of dinner time, pour the water from the beans, pick out any imperfections, and put them with the corn, with the water in which it is soaked, into a dinner-pot; cut a pound of nicely corned pork in thin slices, put it to the corn and beans, and put over them hot water, rather more than to cover them, add a very small red pepper, or a saltspoonful or cayenne, and cover the pot close; set it where it will boil very gently, for an hour and a half, then put it in a deep dish, add a bit of butter to it and serve. The pork may be scored, and not cut up, if preferred, and served in a separate dish.

TO BOIL SALTED OR CORNED BEEF.—Wash the brine from a piece of corned beef and put it in a pot of hot (not boiling) water, take off the scum as it rises, then try if it is tender; let it boil gently. When it is done, take it up and press it between two plates.

Cabbage, or spinach, or some other greens, are generally boiled with salt beef; put down the beef in time that it may be done before it is time to boil the vegetables, and set it to press while the vegetables are boiling.

To Prepare the Cabbage.—Take off the discolored out-side leaves, and cut each head in four; look well between the leaves to see that no insects are secreted; wash the quarters, and put them in the water in which the meat was boiled; set it over the fire and let it boil fast for three quarters of an hour; if you wish the potatoes boiled with it, choose large, equal sized ones, and put them in with the cabbage; when they are done take the potatoes into a covered dish, put the cabbage into a cullender, press out all the water. If you wish to have the meat hot, after pressing it, put it into the pot ten minutes before taking up the vegetables. Serve the cabbage and pota-toes in covered dishes, and the meat on an oval dish.

Parsnip Stew.—Cut half a pound of fat salt pork or bacon in slices, and a pound of beef or veal in bits, put them in a dinner-pot with very little water. Scrape some parsnips, and cut them in slices an inch thick, wash and put them to the meat; pare and cut six small sized potatoes in halves. Cover the pot close and set it over a bright fire for half an hour; then dredge in a tablespoonful of wheat flour, add a small bit of butter, and a small teaspoonful of pepper, stir it in, and set it over the fire to brown for fifteen minutes. Take the stew into a dish and serve.

Lamb.—To Choose Lamb.—The vein in the neck of a fore-quarter of a lamb will be a fine blue, if it is fresh; if it is of a green or yellowish color it is stale.

The hind-quarter first becomes tainted under the kidney.

A fore-quarter includes the shoulder, neck and breast.

The pluck is sold with the head, liver, heart and lights. The melt is not used with us.

The fry contains the sweet-breads, skirts, and some of the liver.

Lamb may be hashed, stewed, roasted, fried, broiled, or made in a pie, the same as veal.

To Broil a Breast of Lamb.—Have a clear, bright fire of coals; when the gridiron is hot rub it over with a bit of suet, then lay on the meat, the inside to the fire first, let it broil gently; when it is nearly cooked through turn the other side, let it brown nicely, put a good bit of butter on a steak dish, work a large teaspoonful of salt and a small one of pepper into it, lay the meat upon it, turn it once or twice, and serve hot. The shoulder may be broiled in the same manner.

LAMB STEWED WITH PEAS.—Cut the scrag or breast of lamb in pieces, and put it in a stewpan with water enough to cover it. Cover the stewpan close, and let it simmer or stew for fifteen to twenty minutes; take off the scum, then add a tablespoonful of salt and a quart of shelled peas; cover the stewpan and let them stew for half an hour; work a small tablespoonful of wheat flour with a quarter of a pound of butter, and stir it into the stew; add a small teaspoonful of pepper; let it simmer together for ten minutes. Serve with new potatoes, boiled. A blade of mace may be added if liked.

QUARTER OF LAMB ROASTED.—Wash a quarter of lamb with cold water, mix a large tablespoonful of salt, and a heaping teaspoonful of pepper, and rub it well over every part of the meat; then split it, or lay it on muffin rings or a trivet in a dripping-pan; put a pint of water in the pan to baste with, set it before the fire in a Dutch oven or reflector, or in a hot stove oven, baste very often after it begins to roast; lay it so that the thickest part may be nearest the fire; allow fifteen minutes for each pound of meat; baste with the water in the pan until nearly done; add more to it as it wastes, then put to it a quarter of a pound of butter, baste the meat with it, dredge it white with flour, stir up the fire to brown it.

TO PREPARE A QUARTER OF LAMB FOR BROILING.—Wash a quarter of lamb in cold water, then rub it all over with a mixture of salt and pepper, dredge well with wheat flour, and put in a pot of hot (not boiling) water; cover the pot and let it boil gently, allowing fifteen minutes for each pound of meat; take off the scum as it rises. Served with boiled potatoes and parsley, or drawn butter sauce, and mint sauce, and lettuce dressed. Break the leaves from some white heart lettuce and rinse each one in cold water, then cut them small, put a teaspoonful of made mustard with a teaspoonfnl of sugar, and the same of oil, beat them together in a cup; then add enough vinegar to fill a cup, and pour it over the lettuce.

Mutton.—OBSERVATIONS ON MUTTON.—The pipe which runs along the bone inside of a chine or saddle of mutton, must be taken out. If it is to be kept any length of time, wipe the meat perfectly dry, and rub pepper over it in every part. Whenever you find any moisture, wipe it dry, rub it with pepper, and dredge flour over. The kernels should be taken out by the butcher.

Mutton for roasting or steaks should hang as long as it will keep without tainting. Let it hang in the air in a cool, dry place. Pepper will keep flies from it. The chine or rib bones should be wiped every day. The bloody part of the neck should be cut off. In the breast the brisket changes first. In the hind quarter, the part under and about the kidneys is first to taint. Mutton for stewing or broiling should not be so long kept. It will not be so fine a color if it is. The lean of mutton should be a clear red, fine, close grain, and tender to the touch. The fat should be firm and white. Skewer a piece of letter paper over the fat of mutton whilst roasting. When nearly done, take it off.

HAUNCH OF MUTTON.—Keep the haunch as long as you can, and have it sweet, wash it in vinegar and water before dressing it. Before putting the meat to the fire, rub it all over with a mixture of pepper and salt; make a stiff paste of wheat flour and water, roll it thin, and put it over the meat; have a large, bright fire, and set the meat at a little distance from it (allow fifteen minutes to each pound of meat); when half done, take off the paste, draw it nearer the fire, and baste freely with water from the pan; turn it so that every part may be done; half an hour before taking it up, stir up the fire, put quarter of a pound of butter in the pan, baste with it, dredge the meat white with flour, baste again, turn the meat over, baste freely, and dredge more flour over, and baste again; the fire must be bright for finishing. When done, take it up, put the dripping-pan over the fire, cut a lemon in thin slices into it, dredge in a large tablespoonful of browned flour, stir it smooth for ten minutes, then strain into a gravy tureen, and serve with the slices of lemon. Or, instead of a lemon, put a wineglass of port wine to the gravy.

Boiled potatoes, asparagus; or spinach, dressed celery, and currant jelly, is served with roast mutton.

Putting the paste over the meat keeps in its juices, and therefore makes it sweeter. A gravy may be made of a pound of loin of mutton, cut small and simmered in a pint of water till reduced to half; salt it a little, stir in a teaspoonful of browned flour and a little pepper; let it boil up once, then strain it, and serve with the meat and currant jelly.

A SHOULDER OF MUTTON.—Broil a shoulder of mutton over a clear, bright fire of coals, let it broil gently, putting the inside to the fire first, cover it with a tin; when nearly done through, turn it; let it brown nicely; when it is done, take it on to a hot steak dish, sprinkle a small tablespoonful of salt and a teaspoonful of pepper over; butter it freely, turn it once or twice in the seasoning, turn the inside down, cover it with a tin cover, and serve hot, with boiled hominy, or potatoes, for breakfast. The shoulder may be boned, before broiling.

TO BROIL A BREAST OF MUTTON.—Parboil a breast of mutton, then wipe it dry, and broil it as directed for shoulder.

MUTTON CHOP FRIED.—Cut some fine mutton chops without much fat; rub over both sides with a mixture of salt and pepper, dip them in wheat flour or rolled crackers, and fry in hot lard or beef drippings; when both sides are a fine brown, take them on a hot dish, put a wineglass of hot water in the pan, let it become hot, stir in a teaspoonful of browned flour, let it boil up once, and serve in the pan with the meat. A tablespoonful of currant jelly may be stirred into the gravy, or a wineglass of port wine instead of water. Or, cut a lemon in thin slices, take out the pits, and fry them brown with a bit of butter in the pan, dredge in a teaspoonful of browned flour, add a wineglass of hot water, stir it for a few minutes over the fire, then serve in the dish with the meat.

LEG OF MUTTON BOILED.—Wash a leg of mutton, dredge it well with flour, and wrap it in a cloth, then put it in a pot of hot water, and boil according to its weight. Serve with drawn butter or parsley sauce, with boiled vegetables and pickles.

Eggs.—TO CHOOSE EGGS.—Fresh eggs, when held to the light, the white will look clear, and the yellow distinct; if not good, they will have a clouded appearance.

When eggs are stale, the white will be thin and watery, and

the yolk will not be a uniform color, when broken; if there is no mustiness, or disagreeable smell, eggs in this state are not unfit for making cakes, puddings, etc.

Eggs for boiling should be as fresh as possible; a new laid egg will generally recommend itself, by the delicate transparency of its shell.

To Boil Eggs.—Wash the shells clean in cold water before boiling; have a stewpan of boiling water, into which put the eggs; keep it boiling—four minutes for very soft—five, that the yolk only may be soft—six minutes will boil the yolk hard, for eating. Eight minutes are required to boil eggs for salad or garnish. When done, take them from the boiling water, into a basin of cold water, which will prevent the yolk turning dark or black.

Egg Omelet.—Five well-beaten eggs, one and a half cups of milk, three tablespoonfuls of flour; mix the flour in a little milk, and rub smooth, then add milk and flour to eggs, and beat well together; grease well with lard a frying-pan; put in when not very hot, a large teaspoonful, it will cover about half; turn with knife when light brown, and roll up as it browns.

Ham Omelet.—One-half pint of milk, two teaspoonfuls of flour, three teaspoonfuls of cracker crumbs, six eggs. Put thinly and evenly over the griddle; then immediately scatter over it finely minced ham. Double it, then fold again in a quarter circle.

Omelet.—Set a smooth frying-pan on the fire to heat; break five eggs into a bowl; put butter the size of an egg into a heated pan, give twelve strong beats to your eggs, and, when the butter begins to boil, pour in the eggs. Draw up the eggs from the bottom of the pan, but do not stir, simply shake the pan. When the bottom is well done, and the top a little soft, fold over and put on a platter. Serve immediately. This may be varied by the addition of three tablespoonfuls of milk.

Baked Eggs.—Six eggs, four tablespoonfuls of good gravy, veal, beef or poultry; the latter is particularly nice; one handful of bread crumbs, six rounds of buttered toast or fried bread. Put the gravy into a shallow baking dish, break the eggs into this, pepper and salt them, and strew the bread crumbs over them. Bake for five minutes in a quick oven. Take up the eggs carefully, one by one, and lay upon the toast, which must be arranged on a hot, flat dish. Add a little cream, and, if you like, some very finely chopped parsley and onion to the gravy left in the baking dish, and turn it into a saucepan. Boil up once quickly, aud pour over the eggs.

EGGS SUR LE PRAT.—Six eggs, one tablespoonful of butter, or nice dripping, pepper and salt to taste. Melt the butter on a stone china or tin plate, or shallow baking dish. Break the eggs carefully into this, dust lightly with pepper and salt, and put into a moderate oven until the whites are well set. Serve in the dish in which they were baked.

EGGS POACHED IN BALLS.—Put three pints of boiling water into a stewpan; set it on a hot stove or coals; stir the water with a stick until it runs rapidly around, then having broken an egg into a cup—taking care not to break the yolk— drop it into the whirling water, continue to stir it until the egg is cooked; then take into a dish with a skimmer and set it over a pot of boiling water; boil one at a time, until you have enough. These will remain soft for a long time. Or, put some hot water in a frying pan; break in the eggs; let it set over the fire, without boiling, until they are done; then serve on toast

Sweet-Breads.—VEAL SWEET-BREADS—Spoil very soon; the moment they come from the butcher's they should be put in cold water to soak for about an hour; lard them or draw a lardoon of pork through the centre of each one; put into salt boiling water or stock and let boil for fifteen or twenty minutes; throw them into cold water for only a few moments, they will now be firm and white; remove carefully the skinny portion and pipes.

SWEET-BREADS STEWED.—Wash carefully, remove all bits of skin and fatty matter, cover with cold water and heat to a boil; pour off the hot water and cover with cold until the sweet-breads are firm. If liked, add butter as for frying before you put in the second water; stir in a very little water the second time. When they are tender, add for each sweet-bread a heaping teaspoonful of butter, a little chopped parsley, pepper, salt, and a little cream. Let them simmer in this gravy for five minutes. Send to table in a covered dish with the gravy poured over them.

SWEET-BREADS ROASTED. — Parboil and put into cold water for fifteen minutes; change to more cold water for five minutes longer; wipe perfectly dry, lay them in a dripping-pan and roast, basting with butter and water until they begin to brown; then withdraw them for an instant, roll in beaten egg, then in cracker crumbs, and return to the fire for ten minutes longer, basting meanwhile twice with melted butter. Keep hot in a dish while you add to the dripping half a cup of hot water, some chopped parsley, a teaspoonful of browned flour and the juice of half a lemon. Pour over the sweet-breads and serve at once.

BROILED SWEET-BREADS. — Parboil and blanch by putting them first in hot water and keeping it at a fast boil for five minutes. Then plunging it into ice cold water, a little salted. When the sweet-breads have lain in this ten minutes, wipe them very dry, and with a sharp knife split them each in half lengthwise. Broil on a clear, hot fire, turning every minute as they begin to drip. Have ready on a deep plate some melted butter, well salted and peppered, mixed with catsup or pungent sauce. When the sweet-breads are done to a fine brown, lay them in this, turning them over several times, and set covered in a warm oven. Lay toast upon a plate or chafing-dish and a sweet-bread on each, and pour the hot butter, in which they have been lying, over them, and send to the table.

Vegetables. — POTATOES. — To be able to boil a potato perfectly is one of the tests of a good cook, there being nothing in the whole range of vegetables which is apparently so difficult to accomplish. Like the making of good bread, nothing is simpler when once learned. A good, boiled potato should be white, mealy, and served very hot. If the potatoes are old, peel thinly with a sharp knife; cut out all spots, and let them lie in cold water some hours before using. It is more economical to boil before peeling, as the best part of the potato lies next the skin; but most prefer them peeled. Put on in boiling water, allowing a teaspoonful of salt to every quart of water.

Medium sized potatoes will boil in half an hour. Let them be as nearly of a size as possible, and, if small and large are cooked at the same time, put on the large ones ten or fifteen minutes before the small. When done, pour off every drop of water; cover with a clean towel, and set on the back of the range to dry for a few minutes before serving. The poorest potato can be made tolerable by this treatment. Never let them wait for other things, but time the preparation of dinner so that they will be ready at the moment needed. New potatoes require no peeling, but should merely be well washed and rubbed.

POTATO SNOW.— Mash fine, and rub through a colander into a very hot dish, being careful not to press it down in· any way, and serve hot as possible.

BROWNED POTATO.—Mash well boiled potatoes finely; mix with them, as you do so, a palatable allowance of butter and salt; nice beef dripping will do instead of butter; put into tin baking plates, and set in a hot oven till well browned. Give them twenty minutes' time.

CREAM POTATO.—Mash finely; salt well; stir in a cupful of scalded cream to a dishful made with ten large sized potatoes; add a little butter, by taste. Do all this in the hot pan they were steamed off in. Keep hot over the fire, where it cannot burn. Serve as soon as possible.

RICE.—Wash and rinse repeatedly in cold water, till very white. Pick out all discolored grains, and other refuse articles. The best rice ought not to need much picking over. Let it soak in the last water an hour or more. Drain off all the water, and dry the rice on a large towel. Prepare it long enough beforehand to allow of its remaining awhile spread out on the cloth to dry more perfectly. It must not dry hard; simply let all the actual water be absorbed from it, leaving the kernels separate, and with a beginning of swelling and softning from the moisture. Have a kettle with a good deal of boiling water in it. The rice must have room to scatter in it as it boils. See that it does scatter, by frequently stirring it up from the bottom with a fork. Never stir rice with a spoon. Let it boil fifteen minutes; then try a grain or two by tasting;

the moment you find it tender enough to bite through without any feeling of hardness or rawness, take the kettle off, and pour the water away through a fine colander or vegetable strainer. Set the strainer, with the rice in it, on the back of the stove for about ten minutes, to let the grains dry perfectly.

All depends upon the plenty of water, and the instant watching of the rice to detect the exact point of its sufficient softening. It must not boil a minute after you can bite it as before said.

MACARONI.—Wash and soak like rice, having broken it up into lengths of six or eight inches. Wipe dry and put into a plenty of boiling water. Boil half an hour, in salted water. Meanwhile, for an average dishful, cream two tablespoonfuls of butter, scald a teacupful of cream, or rich milk, stir the hot cream gradually to the butter, adding a heaping saltspoonful of salt. Do not mix these till the macaroni is ready to be taken up. Turn off all the water carefully from the macaroni, pour the butter and cream upon it in the kettle, and set it back on the fire to turn it over in the dressing. Then dish for the table.

TOMATOES.—Stewed: Pour boiling water over them, to take the skins off. Peel them nicely and cut them up. Put them into a saucepan with a little butter, allow a round table-spoonful to half a dozen tomatoes; salt, half a teaspoonful to as many; and a sprinkle of pepper. Stew three quarters of an hour. As they boil, after cooking about half an hour, dredge over, and stir in, two or three sprinkles of flour. Or, if you prefer, scatter and stir in fine cracker crumbs, until thickened a little.

Fried: Mix together in a dish a little flour, pepper, and salt. A pinch of pepper and a large saltspoonful of salt to three tablespoonfuls of flour. Slice the tomatoes without skinning; lay each slice in the flour, turning it over to flour it well; or put your flour, pepper, and salt into a little sifter or sprinkler, and dredge each tomato slice on both sides.

Put enough butter into a frying-pan to cover the bottom when melted, let it heat till it sizzles, and then lay in the slices of tomato. Fry brown.

Broiled: **Slice** the tomatoes without peeling. See that your fire is clear and hot. Put the slices in a wire toaster, and toast, carefully, like bread, or like broiling steak; turning often, to keep the juice in. Bring them to a nice, decided brown on both sides. Lay the slices in a dish, dropping on the middle of each one a bit of butter, and giving it a dust of salt and pepper. Send to the table as hot as possible.

Baked: Scald, peel, and slice. Butter a baking dish. Have ready a cupful of fine cracker crumbs. Put a layer of tomatoes in the dish, sprinkle them with pepper and salt, the former cautiously; drop a bit of butter on each slice, and strew cracker crumbs over the whole. Proceed in this way until you have used all your tomatoes, or filled the dish. Finish with a good sprinkle of crumbs, and drop bits of butter over the top. Bake an hour.

Canned tomatoes: May be stewed or baked in the same way as fresh ones.

CAULIFLOWER.—Pick off the leaves; trim down the stalk; put the cauliflower in cold water. An hour before dinner, put it into a large porcelain kettle, or nice tin boiler, with a great deal of boiling water, salted. Let it boil steadily, but not in a furious manner, to toss and bruise it, for one hour. Prepare for it a cream butter sauce, without the spicing of mace. Take up the cauliflower carefully, with a large vegetable skimmer or wire ladle. Put it in the dish for table, and pour over it the cream sauce.

CABBAGE.—Wash it, examining it carefully, and stripping off the old outside leaves. Let it lie for an hour or two, as convenient, in cold water. Put it into a large potful of boiling water. Have a plenty more of boiling water, to renew with, as below. When it has boiled half long enough—see "Time-Table," for old and young cabbages—turn away all the water, and fill the pot with more; throwing in two or three spoonfuls of salt. Let it boil the remainder of the time, then take it out carefully upon a drainer, let the water run from it, and serve. A drawn butter sauce is nice, poured over it. Or, when well boiled, chop it fine, put it in a saucepan, stir butter with it, and sprinkle in a little pepper, put it on the fire, and stir it till boiling hot again. Or, chop and dress like cauliflower.

FRIED POTATOES.—Pare and slice the potatoes thin—if sliced in small flakes they look more inviting than when cut in larger pieces—keep in ice water two or three hours; then drain them dry, or dry them on a crash towel, and drop them into boiling lard; when nearly done take them out with a skimmer and drain them. Let them get cold, and then drop them again into boiling lard, and fry until well done. This last operation causes them to swell up and puff out; sprinkle with salt, and serve hot—our recipe says; but many like them cold as a relish for tea or with cold meats.

SARATOGA POTATOES.—Peel good sized potatoes and cut as thin as your cabbage cutter will slice them, and throw into cold water. After soaking an hour wipe them dry, and drop into boiling lard until a light brown. Skim them out into a colander and sprinkle with salt while hot. A wire basket is better to boil in, if you have it.

POTATO PUFF.—Stir two cupfuls of mashed potatoes, two tablespoonfuls of melted butter and some salt to a light, fine and creamy condition; then add two eggs, well beaten (separately) and six tablespoonfuls of cream; beat it all well and lightly together; pile it in a rocky form on a dish; bake it in a quick oven until nicely colored; it will puff up quite light

CREAMING POTATOES.—Slice cold boiled potatoes very thin, have ready a saucepan of boiling milk, in which place the potatoes, with salt, a good sized piece of butter, and while boiling, thicken with flour, mixed with water, stirring until delicate and creamy; when ready dish for the table. The goodness of this dish depends much upon catering, just when ready; ten minutes being sufficient to prepare it.

OYSTER PLANT.—Scrape the root, dropping each into cold water as soon as cleaned. Exposure to the air blackens them. Cut in pieces an inch long, put into a saucepan with hot water to cover them, and stew until tender. Turn off the water and add soup stock enough to cover them. Stew ten minutes after this begins to boil; put in a great lump of butter cut into bits and rolled in flour. Boil up once, and serve.

FRIED SALSIFY OR MOCK OYSTERS. — Scrape the roots thoroughly and lay in cold water ten or fifteen minutes. Boil whole until tender, and, when cold, mash with a wooden spoon to a smooth paste, picking out all the fibers. Moisten with a little milk, add a tablespoonful of butter, and an egg and a half for every cupful of salsify. Beat the egg light. Make into round cakes, dredge with flour and fry brown.

COOKING CARROTS.—Cut the carrots in small pieces and stew in a little water until tender; pour off what water is left; put in milk enough to make a sauce, and a good lump of butter rolled in flour; boil up again altogether, having added salt and pepper to taste. Celery is excellent prepared in the same way.

POTATO FRITTERS.—Mash and rub through a colander six good boiled potatoes; add a little salt, two tablespoonfuls of flour, one egg and the yolks of two others; beat the reserved whites to a stiff froth and stir it into the other ingredients, after they are well mixed; have ready a spider of hot lard, and drop by the spoonful, and boil as other fritters. This is a delicious breakfast dish.

MASHED POTATOES.—Potatoes are not good for mashing until they are full grown; peel them and lay them in water for an hour or more before boiling, for mashing.

Old potatoes, when unfit for plain boiling, may be served mashed; cut out all imperfections, take off all the skin and lay them in cold water for one hour or more; then put them into a dinner pot or stewpan, with a teaspoonful of salt, cover the stewpan and let them boil for half an hour unless they are large, when three-quarters of an hour will be required; when they are done, take them up with a skimmer into a wooden bowl or tray, and mash them fine with a potato-beetle; melt a piece of butter the size of a large egg into half a pint of hot milk, mix it with the mashed potatoes until it is thoroughly incorporated, and a smooth mass; then put it in a deep dish, smooth the top over, and mark it neatly with a knife; put pepper over and serve. The quantity of milk used must be in proportion to the quantity of potatoes.

Mashed potatoes may be heaped on a flat dish; make it in a crown or pineapple; stick a sprig of green celery or parsley in the top; or, first brown it before the fire or in an oven. Mashed potatoes may be made a highly ornamental dish; after shaping it as taste may direct, trim the edge of the plate with a wreath of green celery leaves or parsley; or first brown the outside before the fire or in an oven.

HASHED POTATOES.—Peel and chop some cold boiled potatoes, put them into a stewpan with a very little milk or water to moisten them, put to them a small bit of butter and pepper and salt to taste, cover the stewpan close, and set it over a gentle fire for ten or fifteen minutes; stir them once or twice whilst cooking. Serve hot for breakfast.

SWEET, OR CAROLINA POTATOES.—The best sweet potatoes are from the Southern States; those raised in New Jersey are not nearly as sweet as those from the South.

The best manner of serving sweet potatoes is roasted or baked.

TO BAKE SWEET POTATOES.—Wash them perfectly clean, wipe them dry, and bake in a quick oven, according to their size—half an hour for quite small-sized, three-quarters for larger, and a full hour for the largest. Let the oven have a good heat, and do not open it unless it is necessary to turn them, until they are done.

ROASTED SWEET POTATOES.—Having washed them clean and wiped them dry, roast them on a hot hearth as directed for common potatoes, or put them in a Dutch oven, or tin reflector. Roasted or baked potatoes should not be cut, but broken open and eaten from the skin, as from a shell.

TO BOIL SWEET POTATOES.—Wash them perfectly clean, put them into a pot or stewpan, and pour boiling water over to cover them; cover the pot close, and boil for half an hour, or more if the potatoes are large; try them with a fork; when done, strain off the water, take off the skins, and serve.

Cold sweet potatoes may be cut in slices across or lengthwise, and fried or broiled as common potatoes; or they may be cut in half and served cold. Sweet potatoes are made pie of, the same as pumpkin pie.

YOUNG TURNIPS.—Cut off the green leaves of new turnips, leaving an inch or more of the stalk; pare them, and trim them neatly, put them into a pot of boiling water, with a teaspoonful of salt; cover the pot, and let them boil fast for half an hour

or until perfectly tender; put butter and pepper over, and serve **hot.** Or serve with drawn butter over.

RUTA BAGA—Or large winter turnip, may be cut in quarters **or** slices, and boiled with meat, and served with a little butter and pepper over; or boil in water with a little salt; take off the thick outside rind, and cut them in quarters and slices, and boil them for half an hour or more, until they are soft; then drain off the water and mash them fine, add a bit of butter and pepper to taste, work them smooth, then put them into a covered dish, smooth the upper surface over, and mark it with a knife-blade in flutes, meeting in the centre, or make it in a pyramid or pineapple, and serve.

SUMMER SQUASH.—Young green squashes must be fresh to be fit for eating; if they are so, the outside will be crisp when cut with the nail. Cut them in quarters, and if not very tender, pare off the outside skin; take the seed and strings from the inside, and cut the squashes small; then put them into a stewpan, with a teaspoonful of salt to a common-sized squash; pour boiling water on nearly to cover them, cover the stewpan, and let them boil fast, until they are tender; half an hour is generally enough; take them from the water into a colander with a skimmer, press the water from them, then take them on to a dish, mash them smooth, add a bit of butter and pepper to taste, put them into a dish and serve.

WINTER SQUASH.—Cut the large yellow or winter squash small, take off the outside skin and the inside strings and seeds; then put it into a stewpan, with hot water to cover it; cover the stewpan for half an hour or longer until they are tender; take them into a colander with a skimmer, press out the water; then take them into a dish and mash them perfectly smooth; add a good bit of butter, and pepper and salt to taste; make it in a neat form, the same as mashed turnips or potatoes, but do not brown it; put pepper over in spots, and garnish with sprigs of parsley, or celery leaves, if you wish it ornamental.

SPROUTS AND GREENS.—Cabbage sprouts, young beet tops, and the green leaves of young turnips, or boiled with salt meats, or in clear water, with a little salt.

BEETS.—Winter beets should be put in cold water over

night to take off the earthy taste which they are apt to have; before boiling wash them clean, put them into a pot of boiling water, and boil fast; if not very large, one hour will be sufficient for them; should they be very large, one hour and a half or two hours will be required; when done, take them into a pan of cold water, rub the skins off with the hands, and cut them in thin slices; put them into a deep dish, strew a little salt and pepper over, and pour on cold vinegar nearly to cover them; prepare them an hour before serving, with roasted or fried meat; if to be served with cold or boiled meat, make a cup of vinegar hot, put a large tablespoonful of butter to it; add pepper and salt to taste, and serve hot. Winter beets may be cut in halves or quarters, and pickled by covering them with cold vinegar.

Beets must be washed, but never cut before boiling, else they will lose their fine color.

SPINACH.—Take off every discolored leaf from the bunches; put them into a large pan or pail of water, and wash each cluster of leaves separately, shaking it well in the water, otherwise it will be gritty and sandy; washing it in this way through two waters, will generally be enough; have a large kettle of water boiling fast, put in the spinach; cover the pot and let it boil fast for fifteen minutes, it will sink when done; then take it into a colander with a skimmer, press the water from it, cut it small with a knife, press it again, put a good bit of butter and a little pepper to suit; put it into a deep dish, smooth the surface over, let it rise high in the center, cut a cold boiled egg in slices and lay them over, serve hot with a cover; or it may be served on a flat dish; put it neatly on, lay hard boiled and sliced egg over. Spinach is boiled with salt beef, pork or ham. After the meat is done, take it up and press it between two plates that it may be cut nicely; meanwhile put the spinach into the pot, let it boil fast for fifteen minutes, then take it into a colander, press all the water from it, cut it small and serve with the meat. To be served with fried meat and gravy; boil it in water with a teaspoonful of salt, press the water from it and serve.

GREEN PEAS.—Shell green peas until you have a quart; half a peck in the shells will generally produce a quart of shelled peas. Put boiling water to cover them, add a teaspoonful of salt, cover the stewpan, and boil fast for half an hour; then take one between your fingers, if it will mash easily they are done; drain off the water, take them into a deep dish, put to them a teacupful or less of sweet butter, and a little pepper; a small teaspoonful of white sugar is a great improvement; serve hot. Small young potatoes, nicely scraped, may be boiled and served with them, or in a separate dish with a little butter over.

Lamb and peas are a favorite dish in the spring of the year; they are nice with poultry, veal and mutton. A bit of saleratus or carbonate of soda, the size of a pea, put with green vegetables, improves the color and renders them more healthful: fast boiling keeps the color good.

ASPARAGUS.—Choose green stalks of asparagus, the largest are best; cut off the white, tough part, wash the green in cold water, and tie it in small bundles that they may be taken up without danger of breaking, put them in hot water with a tea·spoonful of salt, and let them boil for half an hour; toast some thin slices of bread a delicate brown, cut off the extreme outside crust, butter each slice frequently; and then lay them on small oval dishes; untie the asparagus and lay it on the toast, butter it a little, sprinkle pepper over and serve. Or it may be served without the toast; the toast may be moistened by puting a little of the water in which the asparagus, was boiled, over it.

Vinegar is eaten with asparagus; it is generally added at table by such as like it. Asparagus may be laid on plain toast, and a little drawn butter poured over both.

GREEN BEANS.—Cut the bud and stem end off, and take the strings from the sides of stringed beans, cut them in inch lengths, wash them in cold water, then put them into a stewpan of hot water, add a teaspoonful of salt, cover the stewpan and let them boil fast for half or three-quarters of an hour; take one up, if it will mash easily when pressed between the thumb and finger, they are done. Drain off the water, add sweet butter and pepper to taste, cut some nicely toasted bread in squares or diamonds, lay them on a dish, and serve the beans over. Green beans, when good, will be a bright color, and crisp, when broken. They should be fresh picked.

BEANS AND CORN, CALLED SUCCOTASH.—Take the husks

and silk from a dozen ears of sweet corn, and with a sharp knife cut the kernels from the cob, scrape gently what remains on the cob with the knife blade, string a quart or more of green beans and cut them in inch lengths or shorter; wash them and put them to the corn; put them with the corn into a stewpan, add half a pint of boiling milk or water, cover it close and let them boil rather gently for three-quarters of an hour, then add a tea-cupful of butter, a teaspoonful of salt, and a saltspoonful of pepper; stir them well together, cover it for ten minutes, take the beans and corn into a dish, with more or less of the liquids as may be liked.

This may be made without butter by substituting half a pound of nicely corned fat pork, washed in cold water, and cut in slices as thin as a knife blade. No other salt is required. Lima beans and sweet corn make the finest succotash.

LIMA BEANS.—Lay a quart of shelled Lima beans in cold water for one hour, then put them into a stewpan and pour water over to cover them, cover the stewpan and let it boil fast for half an hour; then take one between your finger and thumb; if it will mash easily, it is done; drain off nearly all the water, add a small teacupful of butter, a teaspoonful of salt, and a little pepper; cover them for a few minutes over the fire, then serve hot.

OLD OR WINTER CARROTS—Must be scraped and washed clean, then boil them tender, slice them, and serve with butter, pepper and salt over. Carrots may be sliced before boiling, and served in the same manner. Carrots are mostly used for soups.

GREEN CORN.—Cut the center of kernels through length-wise with a sharp knife; scrape the inside out with the back of the knife; put over and boil with a very little water. After cooking ten minutes, add milk, salt, a very little sugar, and plenty of butter, and let boil gently for five or ten minutes more.

CORN OYSTERS.—One dozen grated ears of sweet corn, three tablespoonfuls of cream, two do. of flour, one do. of melted butter, one egg well beaten; mix and bake in small cakes on a griddle. These are very nice for tea when made from cold boiled ears of corn left over from dinner.

EGG PLANT.—Slice the egg plant about half an inch thick, parboil in salt and water for about a quarter of an hour; then take out and fry in part butter and part lard. These are nice also when each plant is dipped in beaten egg and bread crumbs, and then fried.

BOILED CAULIFLOWER.—To each half a gallon of water allow one heaped teaspoonful of salt. Choose cauliflowers that are close and white. Trim off the decayed outside leaves, cut the stalks off flat at the bottom. Open the flowers a little to remove the insects, and let lie in salt and water, with the head down, for an hour before cooking; then put them into fast boiling water, with the addition of salt as above. Skim well and boil till tender. Serve with melted butter or delicate drawn butter poured over.

CABBAGE JELLY.—Boil a cabbage in the usual way, and squeeze in a colander till perfectly dry, then chop fine; add a little butter, pepper and salt; press the whole very closely into an earthenware mold, and bake one hour, either in an oven or in front of the fire.

COLD SLAW.—Sprinkle a quart of finely chopped cabbage with salt, and let it stand an hour; drain off the brine into a saucepan; pour half a pint of strong vinegar, a piece of butter (size of a hickory nut), a teaspoonful of strong mustard (after it has been stirred with water), and half the same of pepper; when it boils stir in two well-beaten eggs, and three table-spoonfuls of sweet cream; pour hot on the cabbage, and have it cold when it is to be served. A very delicious relish with meats.

ONIONS.—If milk is plenty, use equal quantities of skim-milk and water, allowing a quart of each for a dozen or so large onions. If water alone is used, change it after the first half-hour, as this prevents their turning dark; salting as for all vegetables, and boiling young onions one hour; old ones, two. Either chop fine, and add a spoonful of butter, half a teaspoonful of salt, and a little pepper, or serve them whole in a dressing made by heating one cupful of milk with the same butter and other seasoning as when chopped. Put the onions in a hot dish, pour this over them, and serve. They may also be half-boiled; then put in a buttered dish, covered with this sauce and a layer or bread crumbs, and baked for an hour.

STRING BEANS.—String, cut in bits, and boil an hour if very young. If old, an hour and a half, or even two, may be needed. Drain off the water, and season like green peas.

SHELLED BEANS.—Any green bean may be used in this way, Lima and butter 'beans being the nicest. Put on in boiling, salted water, and boil not less than one hour. Season like string beans.

GREEN CORN.—Husk, and pick off the silk. Boil in well-salted water, and serve on the cob, wrapped in a napkin, or cut off and seasoned like beans. Cutting down through each row gives, when scraped off, the kernel without the hull.

GREEN CORN FRITTERS.—One pint of green corn grated. This will require about six ears. Mix with this half a cupful of milk, two well-beaten eggs, half a cupful of flour, one tea-spoonful of salt, half a teaspoonful of pepper, and a table-spoonful of melted butter. Fry in very small cakes in a little hot butter, browning well on both sides. Serve very hot.

CORN PUDDING.—One pint of cut or grated corn, one pint of milk, two well-beaten eggs, one teaspoonful of salt and a saltspoonful of pepper. Butter a pudding dish, and bake the mixture half an hour. Canned corn can be used in the same way.

SPINACH.—Not less than a peck is needed for a dinner for three or four. Pick over carefully, wash, and let it lie in cold water an hour or two. Put on in boiling, salted water, and boil an hour, until tender. Take up in a colander, that it may drain perfectly. Have in a hot dish a piece of butter the size of an egg, half a teaspoonful of vinegar. Chop the spinach fine, and put in the dish, stirring in this dressing thoroughly. A teacupful of cream is often added. Any tender greens, beet or turnip tops, kale, etc., are treated in this way; kale, however, requiring two hours boiling.

ARTICHOKES.—Cut off the outside leaves; trim the bottom; throw into boiling, salted water, with a teaspoonful of vinegar in it, and boil an hour. Season, and serve like turnips, or wit drawn butter poured over them.

TOMATOES STEWED.—Pour on boiling water, to take off the skins; cut in pieces, and stew slowly for half and hour; adding for a dozen tomatoes a tablespoonful of butter, a teaspoonful of salt, a saltspoonful of pepper, and a teaspoonful of sugar. Where they are preferred sweet, two tablespoonfuls of sugar will be necessary. They may be thickened with a tablespoon-ful of flour or corn-starch dissolved in a little cold water, or with half a cupful of rolled cracker or bread crumbs. Canned tomatoes are stewed in the same way.

Bread-Making and Flour.—Much of the health, and conse-quently much of the happiness, of the family depends upon good bread; therefore, no pains should be spared in learn-ing the best method of making, which will prove easiest in the end.

Yeast, flour, kneading, and baking must each be perfect, and nothing in the whole range of cooking is of such prime importance.

Once master the problem of yeast, and the first form of wheat bread, and endless varieties of both bread and breakfast cakes can be made.

The old and the new process flour—the former being known as the St. Louis, and the latter as Haxall flour—are now to be had at all good grocers; and from either good bread may be made, though that from the latter keeps moist longer. Potapsco flour is of the same quality as the St. Louis. It con-tains more starch than the St. Louis, and for this reason requires, even more than that, the use in the family of coarser, or graham flour, at the same time; white bread alone not being as nutritious or strengthening.

Flour made by the new process swells more than that by the old, and a little less quantity—about an eighth less—is therefore required in mixing and kneading. As definite rules as possible are given for the whole operation; but experience alone can insure perfect bread, changes of temperature affect-ing it once, and baking being also a critical point.

Pans made of thick tin, or, better still, of Russia iron, ten inches long, four or five wide, and four deep, make the best shaped loaf, and one requiring a reasonably short time to bake.

YEAST.—Ingredients: One teacupful of lightly broken

hops; one pint of sifted flour; one cupful of sugar; one table-spoonful of salt; four large or medium-sized potatoes; and two quarts of boiling water.

Boil the potatoes and mash them fine. At the same time, having tied the hops in a little bag, boil them for half an hour in two quarts of water, but in another saucepan. Mix the flour, sugar, and salt well together in a large mixing-bowl, and pour on the boiling hop-water, stirring constantly. Now add enough of this to the mashed potato to thin it till it can be poured, and mix all together, straining it through a sieve to avoid any possible lumps. Add to this, when cool, either a cupful of yeast left from the last, or of baker's yeast, or a Twin Brothers' yeast cake, dissolved in a little warm water. Let it stand till partly light, and then stir down two or three times in the course of five or six hours, as this makes it stronger. At the end of that time it will be light. Keep in a covered stone jar, or in glass cans. By stirring in corn meal till a dough is made, and then forming it in small cakes and drying in the sun, dry yeast is made, which keeps better than the liquid in hot weather. Crumb, and soak in warm water half an hour before using.

Potato yeast is made by omitting hops and flour, but mashing the potatoes fine with the same proportion of other ingredients, and adding the old yeast, when cool, as before. It is very nice, but must be made fresh every week; while the other, kept in a cool place, will be good a month.

BREAD.—For four loaves of bread of the pan-size given above, allow as follows: Four quarts of flour; one large cupful of yeast; one tablespoonful of salt, one of sugar, and one of butter or lard; one pint of milk mixed with one of warm water, or one quart of water alone for the "wetting."

Sift the flour into a large pan or bowl. Put the sugar, salt, and butter in the bottom of the bread pan or bowl, and pour on a spoonful or two of boiling water, enough to dissolve all. Add the quart of wetting and the yeast. Now stir in slowly two quarts of the flour; cover with a cloth, and set in a tempera-ture of about 75 degrees to rise until morning. Bread mixed at nine in the evening will be ready to mold into loaves or rolls by six the next morning. In summer it would be necessary to find a cool place; in winter a warm one—the chief point being to keep the temperature even. If mixed early in the morning, it is ready to mold and bake in the afternoon, from seven to eight hours being all that it should stand.

The first mixture is called a sponge; and, if only a loaf of graham or rye bread is wanted, one quart of it can be measured and thickened with other flour, as in the rules given hereafter.

To finish as wheat bread, stir in enough flour from the two quarts remaining to make a dough. Flour the moulding-board very thickly, and turn out. Now begin kneading, flouring the hands, but after the dough is gathered into a smooth lump, using as little flour as may be. Knead with the palm of the hand as much as possible. The dough quickly becomes a flat cake. Fold it over, and keep on kneading not less than twenty minutes; half an hour being better.

Make into loaves; put into the pans; set them in a warm place, and let them rise from thirty to forty-five minutes, or till they have become nearly double in size. Bake in an oven hot enough to brown a teaspoonful of flour in one minute; spreading the flour on a bit of broken plate, that it may have an even heat. Loaves of this size will bake in from forty-five to sixty minutes. Then take them from the pans; wrap in thick cloths kept for the purpose, and stand them tilted up against the pans till cold. Never lay hot bread on a pine table, as it will sweat, and absorb the pitchy odor and taste; but tilt so that air may pass around it freely. Keep well covered in a tin box, or large stone pot, which should be wiped out every day or two, and scalded and dried thoroughly now and then. Pans for wheat bread should be greased very lightly; for graham or rye, much more, as the dough sticks and clings.

Instead of mixing a sponge, all the flour may be molded in and kneaded at once, and the dough set to rise in the same way. When light, turn out. Use as little flour as possible, and knead for fifteen minutes; less time being required, as part of the kneading has already been done.

Graham Bread.—One quart of wheat sponge; one even quart of graham flour; half a teacupful of brown sugar or molases; half a teaspoonful of soda dissolved in a little hot water; and half a teaspoonful of salt.

Pour the sponge in a deep bowl; stir in the molasses, etc.; and lastly the flour, which must never be sifted. The mixture should be so stiff that the spoon moves with difficulty. Bake in two loaves for an hour or an hour and a quarter, graham requiring longer baking than wheat.

If no sponge can be spared, make as follows: One pint of milk or water; half a cupful of sugar or molasses; half a cupful of yeast; one teaspoonful of salt; one cupful of wheat flour; two cupfuls of graham. Warm the milk or water; add the yeast and other ingredients, and then the flour; and set in a cool place—about 60 degrees Fahrenheit—over night, graham bread souring more easily than wheat. Early in the morning stir well; put into two deep, well-greased pans; let it rise an hour in a warm place and bake one hour.

OLD SCHOOL PRESBYTERIAN YEAST.—Boil two good handfuls ot good hops in three quarts of water. Strain. When cool stir in one quart of flour, one cupful of sugar, and a handful of salt. Cover this in a stone jar, and let it stand three days in a warm place, stirring it occasionally. On the fourth day add one quart of nicely mashed potatoes. Let it stand until the day following, when it will be ready for use. A small teacupful is sufficient for five loaves of bread.

This yeast, which has proved most reliable, needs nothing to start it, as it is self-raising, and, if kept in a cool place, will keep six weeks in the summer, and three months in cold weather.

It does not foam as do other kinds of yeast, so that one who had not used it would think it worthless, but if once used its excellency will not be doubted.

In making bread, a tablespoonful of white sugar to a quart of flour is a great improvement to all kinds of bread.

HOP YEAST.—Of pressed hops, break up fine about enough to make a teacupful; boil them in one quart of water for half an hour. At the same time boil in another kettle ten or twelve potatoes (peeled) in a quart of water; when thoroughly done mash the potatoes and pour the water back over them. If the water is boiled away, restore the quantity. Have ready two quart of sifted flour; strain the hop water on to it, and add the potato gruel; when lukewarm put in a teacupful of good yeast, or a yeast cake, and a little salt. After it is thoroughly light it should be kept in a stone jug or jar in a cool place.

BROWN BREAD.—One quart of corn meal, one pint of rye or graham flour, one quart of sour milk, one teacupful of molasses, and one teaspoonful of soda. Steam four hours, or bake one hour. This quantity will make two loaves.

CORN BREAD.—One quart of Indian meal, two ounces of butter, as much warm milk as will make a stiff batter, four eggs, a little salt. Beat the whole well together, and bake in shallow tins in a moderate oven.

TO MAKE TWIST BREAD.—Let the bread be made as directed for baker's or for wheat bread, then take three pieces as large as a pint bowl each; strew a little flour over the pasteboard or table, roll each piece under your hands, to twelve inches length, making it smaller in circumference at the ends than in the middle; having rolled the three in this way, take a baking tin, lay one part on it, join one end of each of the other two to it, and braid them together the length of the rolls, and join the ends by pressing them together; dip a brush in milk, and pass over the top of loaf; after ten minutes or so, set it in a quick oven, and bake for nearly an hour.

WHEAT AND INDIAN BREAD.—Put three pints of water over the fire; when it is boiling hot, add a large tablespoonful of salt, stir into it sweet white corn meal, until it is a thick batter; continue to stir it for ten minutes, that it may not burn, then turn it into a dish, stir into it a quart of cold water; when it is cool enough to bear your hand in it, pour it into a bowl, in which is seven pounds of wheat flour, heaped around the sides so as to leave a hollow in the centre; add to it a gill of baker's yeast, and half a teaspoonful of saleratus, dissolved in a little hot water, then work the whole into a smooth dough, work it, or knead, for nearly an hour, then strew a little flour over it, lay a thickly folded cloth over, and set it in a warm place for five or six hours in summer, or mix at night in winter; when light, work it down, set it to rise again for one hour, then heat the oven, work the bread down, and divide it in loaves, and bake, according to their size, in a quick oven; when taken from the oven, turn them over in the pans, and set them to become cold;

if the crust is hard, wrap them in a towel as soon as taken from the oven.

RYE BREAD.—Make the same as wheat and Indian bread, substituting rye flour for wheat. Or,'thus: To a quart of warm water stir as much wheat flour as will make a smooth batter, stir into it half a gill of baker's yeast, and set it in a warm place to rise; this is called setting a sponge; let it be mixed in some vessel which will contain twice the quantity; in the morning put three pounds and a half of rye flour into a bowl or tray; make a hollow in the centre, pour in the sponge, add a dessert spoonful of salt, and half a small teaspoonful of saleratus, dissolved in a little water; make the whole into a smooth dough with as much warm water as may be necessary; knead it well, cover it, and let it set in a warm place for three hours, then knead it again, and make it in two or three loaves; bake in a quick oven one hour, if made in two loaves, and less if the loaves are smaller.

BREAD-CAKE OR BISCUIT.—Take from risen bread dough, the size of a small loaf, work into it one egg and a large table-spoonful of lard when it is thoroughly amalgamated, flour the hands and make it in balls the size and shape of a hen's egg; rub a tin pan over with a bit of sponge dipped in butter, lay them in so as to touch each other until the pan is full, wet the tops over with milk, then set them into a quick oven for twenty minutes; serve hot for breakfast or tea. When eaten, break them open—to cut them would make them heavy.

These cakes are very nice, when cold, for breakfast or tea.

INDIAN GRIDDLE CAKES.—Beat two eggs light, stir them into a quart of sweet milk with a teaspoonful of salt and enough corn meal to make a good batter; bake as soon as mixed, on a hot griddle rubbed over with a bit of suet or fat pork; a tablespoonful of butter for each cake.

JOHNNY CAKE.—Put a quart of fresh corn meal into a basin, add a heaping teaspoonful of salt, stir into it boiling water until it is all moistened, then with your hands make it in cakes half an inch thick, and bake them on a hot griddle rubbed over with a bit of pork fat or beef suet; let them do slowly; when one side is done turn the other; they may be baked in an oven for twenty minutes; or, put the cake on a flat board or iron plate, and slant it in front of the fire; when one side is done, turn the other; serve hot, split them open and butter freely; they are eaten with fried pork.

INDIAN MEAL MUFFINS.—Pour boiling water into a quart of yellow corn meal, stirring it all the time until it is a thick batter; let it cool; when only warm, add a small teacupful of butter, a teaspoonful of salt, and a tablespoonful of yeast, with two well-beaten eggs; set it in a warm place for two hours, then stir it smooth, and bake in small cakes on a hot griddle; when one side is a rich brown, turn the other, lay them singly on a hot dish, and serve. These may be made without the yeast, and baked as soon as mixed.

BUCKWHEAT GRIDDLE CAKES.—Put three pints of warm water into a stone pot or jar, add a gill of baker's yeast, or an inch square of turnpike cake dissolved in a little warm water; add a heaping teaspoonful of salt, and half a small teaspoonful of saleratus, have a pudding stick, or spatula, and gradually stir in enough buckwheat flour to make a nice batter, beat it perfectly smooth, then cover it and set it in a moderately warm place until morning; a large handful of corn meal may be put with the flour, and it is by many persons considered an improvement.

TO BAKE BUCKWHEAT CAKES.—Set a griddle over a gentle, steady fire; when it is hot, rub it over with a bit of suet or fat fresh pork on a fork; the griddle must be hot but not scorching; put the batter on in small cakes; when one side is nicely browned and about half cooked through, turn them.

These cakes, to be in perfection, must be not much thicker than a dollar piece, and both sides a delicate brown. Should the batter prove too thick, it may be made thinner with sweet milk; this will also make them bake a finer color. The best of sweet butter and syrup to be served with buckwheat cakes hot from the griddle. Should the cakes be preferred thicker than mentioned in this recipe, it is an easy matter to make them so; take care that they are baked through.

Buckwheat may be mixed the same as wheat muffins, and baked on a griddle.

MUFFINS.—Mix with a pint of warm milk two well beaten eggs, half a teaspoonful of melted butter, and half a gill of baker's yeast, with a teaspoonful of salt and a bit of saleratus the size of a large pea (dissolved in hot water); stir in enough sifted wheat flour to make a thick batter, set it in a warm place to rise, for three hours in warm weather, or longer in winter; it may be mixed at night for breakfast next morning; put a griddle over the fire; when it is hot, rub it over with some fat, grease the inside of the rings, set them on and half fill them with the batter, or they may be done without rings; when one side is done, turn the other; bake a light color; as they are done break each one open, put a bit of butter in each, and set them in front of the fire until served; muffins should never be cut open. Cold muffins may be toasted and served hot.

TEA RUSK.—To a pint of warm milk put half a gill of baker's yeast, a teaspoonful of salt, and half a small teaspoonful of saleratus, dissolved in a little hot water; put to it enough wheat flour to make a soft dough; mix well and smooth; cover it, and set it in a warm place for two hours, to rise; when light, add half a teacupful of sugar, and a cupful of melted butter; work them well into the dough, flour your hands well, and make it in small cakes (the size of a large egg, or a trifle larger), lay them close together in a buttered pan; dip your hand in a little sweetened milk, and pass it lightly over the tops of the rusks, set them in a quick oven for half an hour; serve hot.

COMMON BUNS.—Rub four ounces of butter into two pounds of flour, with four ounces of fine sugar and a teaspoonful of carraway seeds, and the same of salt; add half a gill of yeast, and as much warm milk as will make a soft dough; set it in a warm place to rise (it will be light after about three hours); strew a paste-slab and rolling pin with flour, and roll out the dough to half an inch thickness, and cut them in large, round cakes; lay them on baking tins, wet the tops over with milk, strew sugar over each, and put them on tins in a quick oven for fifteen minutes.

MILK BISCUITS.—Warm two ounces of sweet butter in a gill of sweet milk, and with it wet a pound of flour into a very stiff paste; beat it with a rolling-pin, and work it very smooth; roll it a quarter of an inch thick; cut it in small, round cakes; stick each with a fork, and bake ten minutes in a quick oven.

To Fry Doughnuts and Crullers.—Have a small iron or porcelain kettle; put into it a pound of lard, set it over a gentle fire; when it is boiling hot, drop a bit of dough in to try it; if the fat is not hot enough, the cakes will absorb it, and thereby be rendered unfit for eating; if too hot, it will make them a dark brown outside before the inside is cooked; boiling hot is about the heat the fat should be; if it is at a right heat, the doughnuts will in about ten minutes be of a delicate brown outside, and nicely cooked inside; five or six minutes will cook a cruller; try the fat, by dropping a bit of the dough in; if it is right, the fat will boil up when it is put in; keep the kettle in motion all the time the cakes are in, that they may boil evenly; when the cakes are a fine color take them out with a skimmer on to an inverted sieve.

Doughnuts.—Take a pound of flour, a quarter of a pound of butter, three-quarters of a pound of clean brown sugar rolled fine, one nutmeg, grated, and a tablespoonful of ground cinnamon; mix these well together; then add a tablespoonful of baker's yeast, with as much warm milk, with saleratus the size of a pea dissolved in it, as will make a smooth dough; knead it for a few minutes, cover it, and set it in a warm place to rise for three hours or more, until it is light; then roll it out to a quarter of an inch in thickness; cut it in small squares or diamonds, and fry as directed.

Indian Muffins.—One quart of milk, eight eggs, one and a half cupfuls of butter, one cupful of flour, two cupfuls of Indian meal, one teaspoonful of soda, two teaspoonfuls of cream of tartar, and a little salt; two teaspoonfuls of sugar. Beat well together and bake in muffin rings.

(This recipe is from a reliable source, but we can only recommend it to those who have eggs and butter in abundance.)

Rice Muffins.—Two cups of milk, four tablespoonfuls of yeast, one tablespoonful of white sugar, two tablespoonfuls of melted butter, nearly a cupful of well boiled rice, four cupfuls of flour, or enough to make a good batter; salt to the taste; one-quarter teaspoonful of soda, dissolved in hot water, added just before baking. Beat the ingredients well together, set to rise for six hours, or until very light; put into muffin rings, let it stand fifteen minutes, and bake quickly; eat hot.

FLANNEL CAKES.—One cupful of sweet milk, one-half cupful of yeast, whites of two eggs, two-thirds of a cupful of butter, flour, enough to make a thick batter; set to rise over night and in the morning add whites and butter. Bake in cups.

PANCAKES.—Add enough flour to one quart of sour milk to make a rather thick batter. Let it stand over night and in the morning add two well beaten eggs, salt, and half a teaspoonful of soda dissolved in one tablespoonful of warm water. Bake immediately.

RICE PANCAKES.—One and a half pints of boiled rice, the same of flour, one-half teacupful of sour milk, one teacupful of sweet milk, one teaspoonful of soda, salt, three eggs, and butter the size of a walnut.

Salads.—CHICKEN SALAD.—Mix the celery and chicken together, and then stir well into them a mixture in the proportion of three tablespoonfuls of vinegar to one of oil and one (level) of salt, a pinch—the smallest pinch—of cayenne, about what would lie on the point of a penknife, and a teaspoonful of mustard. Let the chicken stand in this mixture an hour or two; drain off what may be in the bottom of the bowl; ten or twenty minutes before serving pour over a mild mayonnaise. Little strips of anchovy rolled up are used with pickles, hard boiled eggs, and lettuce heads, or tender yellow celery tops to garnish.

As minute directions as possible are given for the various methods and tastes in mixing the·dressing.

An eight-pound turkey, rubbed with a fresh lemon, and boiled in well salted water (having two tablespoonfuls of raw rice in it), is used and preferred by many to a pair of chickens. The flavor is radically different, but quite delightful. Every one of the recipes given will make a nice salad, unless our scholars fall into the error of a well-meaning lady, who set her dish of salad into the hot oven for half an hour. The colder your salad is the crisper and fresher it will taste, and the thicker and better will be your dressing.

CHICKEN SALAD.—One chicken, three bunches of celery, four eggs (whites and yolks beaten seperately), one or two tablespoonfuls of mixed mustard, two teaspoonfuls of salt, one level teaspoonful of pepper, one tablespoonful of butter (hard), six or eight tablespoonfuls of vinegar. Set the dish with these ingredients into a pan of boiling water on the stove, and stir until it thickens like custard; then set off to cool. Cut the chicken that has been carefully boiled into little pieces, and the celery also, and pour over them the dressing, adding, if you please, a little olive oil and sweet cream.

DRESSING FOR SALAD.—Four eggs beat ʌight, yolks and whites together; two tablespoonfuls of mixed mustard, one teaspoonful of salt, one teaspoonful of black pepper, or one-third of a teaspoonful of red pepper, one tablespoonful of butter, and nearly one teacupful of sharp vinegar. Float the pan containing the ingredients in a pan of boiling water on the stove and stir until thick like custard. When cold pour over the salad, adding cold vinegar if needed.

Pies.—PASTRY.—One pound and a quarter of flour, one pound of shortening and a little salt, all put together, sufficient cold water to mix with; no more flour. Put upon the molding-board, roll out and cut in strips, put one upon another, then cut off in squares, roll out, and put upon plates.

PLAIN PIE-CRUST.—One pound of flour, half a pound of butter; mix thoroughly with a knife or a spoon. Pour in very cold water, just enough to form a dough for rolling out; flour the board and rolling-pin, using a knife to handle the dough (the warmth of the hand makes it heavy); roll out the size of one plate at a time, so as to work it as little as possible. Bake in a quick oven.

TART CRUST.—The white ot one egg beaten to a stiff froth, one tablespoonful of white sugar, one cupful of lard, a little salt, five tablespoonfuls of water, three cupfuls of sifted flour; roll quite thin for tarts; cut out with a cooky cutter—a scalloped one will look best; take an open-top thimble, make five holes in one, lay on a whole one, which makes one tart; proceed with all the dough in the same way; bake lightly; when done split open the tart and lay a slice of nice jelly between the layers; squeeze up the jelly through the holes; place them on the table on a plate, and you have a splendid looking dish for the tea table, and something that will keep two months. Do not put your jelly in till you wish them for the table.

RICH MINCE PIE.—Three pounds of beef, one beef's tongue, four (or six) pounds of suet, three and a half pounds of raisins three pounds of currants, three-quarters of a pound of citron, ei, it pounds of chopped apples, four and a half pounds of sugar. three pints of molasses, three ounces of cinnamon, two ounces of cloves, a nutmeg, one teacupful of the Mace Compound, one and a fourth ounces of salt, half an ounce of pepper, one gallon and a half of sweet cider. When mixed, put into a kettle and scald, stirring it all the time. Put it hot into Hero or Mason jars—and the longer you keep it the nicer it will be.

GRANDMOTHER'S APPLE PIE.—Line a deep pie-plate with plain paste. Pare sour apples—greenings are best; quarter, and cut in thin slices. Allow one cup of sugar, and quarter of a grated nutmeg mixed with it; fill the pie-plate heaping full of the sliced apple, sprinkling the sugar between the layers. It will require not less than six good sized apples. Wet the edges of the pie with cold water; lay on the cover, and press down securely, that no juice may escape. Bake three-quarters of an hour, or a little less, if the apples are very tender. No pie in which the apples are stewed beforehand can compare with this in flavor. If they are used, stew till tender, and strain; sweeten and flavor to taste; fill the pies, and bake half an hour.

DRIED-APPLE PIES.—Wash one pint of dried apples, and put in a porcelain kettle with two quarts of warm water; let them stand all night. In the morning put on the fire, and stew slowly for an hour; then add one pint of sugar, a teaspoonful of dried lemon or orange rind, or half a fresh lemon sliced, and half a teaspoonful of cinnamon. Stew half an hour longer, and then use for filling the pies. The apple can be strained if preferred, and a teaspoonful of butter added. This quantity will make two pies. Dried peaches are treated in the same way.

LEMON PIES.—Three lemons, juice of all and the grated rind of two; two cupfuls of sugar, three cupfuls of boiling water, three tablespoonfuls of corn starch dissolved in a little cold water, three eggs, a piece of butter the size of an egg.

Pour the boiling water on the dissolved corn starch, and boil for five minutes. Add the sugar and butter. the yolks of the eggs beaten to a froth, and last the lemon juice and rind. Line the plates with crust, putting a narrow rim of it around each one; pour in the filling, and bake half an hour. Beat the whites to a stiff broth; add half a teacupful of powdered sugar and ten drops of lemon extract, and, when the pie is baked, spread this on. The heat will cook it sufficiently, but it can be browned a moment in the oven. If to be kept a day. do not make the frosting till just before using. The whites will keep in a cold place. Orange pie can be made in the same way.

SWEET-POTATO PIE OR PUDDING.—One pound of hot, boiled sweet pototo rubbed through a sieve; one cupful of but-ter, one heaping cupful of sugar, half a grated nutmeg, one glass of brandy, a pinch of salt, and six eggs.

Add the sugar, spice, and butter to the hot potato. Beat whites and yolks seperately, and add, and last the brandy. Line deep plates with nice paste, making a rim of puff paste. Fill with the mixture, and bake till the crust is done, about half an hour. .Wickedly rich, but very delicious Irish pota-toes can be treated in the same way, and are more delicate.

SQUASH OR PUMPKIN PIE.—Prepare and steam. Strain through a sieve. To a quart of the strained squash add one quart of new milk, with a spoonful or two of cream, if possible; one heaping cupful of sugar, into which has been stirred a teaspoonful of salt, a heaping one of ginger, and half a one of cinnamon. Mix this with the squash, and add from two to four well beaten eggs. Bake in deep plates lined with plain pie-crust. They are done when a knife-blade, on being run into the middle, comes out clean. About forty minutes will be enough. For pumpkin pie half a cupful of molasses may be added, and the eggs can be omitted, substituting half a cupful of flour mixed with the sugar and spice before stirring in. A teaspoonful of butter can always be added.

CHERRY AND BERRY PIES.—Have a very deep plate, and either no crust under, save a rim, or a very thin one. Allow a cupful of sugar to a quart of fruit, but no spices. Stone cherries. Prick the upper crust half a dozen times with a fork, to let out the steam.

For rhubarb or pie-plant pies, peel the stalks; cut them in little bits, and fill the pie. Bake with an upper crust.

CUSTARD PIE.—Line and rim deep plates with pastry, a thin custard pie being very poor. Beat together a teacupful of sugar, four eggs, and a pinch of salt, and mix slowly with one quart of milk. Fill the plate up to the pastry rim after it is in the oven, and bake till the custard is firm, trying, as for squash pies, with a knife blade.

COCOANUT PIE.—One teacupful of sugar, one-half cupful of butter, three eggs, one grated cocoanut, one pint of scalded milk poured on the cocoanut, underlined with pastry.

ORANGE PIE.—Rub the yellow of two oranges with lumps of sugar, add juice of three, and one cupful of white sugar, one finely rolled cracker, a small piece of butter, four eggs, one cupful of sweet milk. Line pudding dish with paste, and bake until firm; nice either hot or cold. With or without a meringue.

PIE-PLANT PIE.—Peel a bunch of pie-plant, put it into your chopping-bowl and chop into pieces the size of your little finger nail; grate the rind, and squeeze the juice of a lemon over this; add sugar.

STRAWBERRY PIE.—Make a nice puff paste, with which line a baking plate; half bake in a quick oven. Have ready sugared strawberries to fill the plate, and the white of an egg beaten and sweetened as a meringue with which to cover the berries. Return to the oven long enough to brown slightly.

PUMPKIN PIE.—One pint of well stewed and strained pumpkin, one good quart of scalding hot, rich milk, and one and one-half cupfuls of sugar, four eggs, one-half teaspoonful of salt,

one tablespoonful of ginger, and one of ground cinnamon.
Bake in pie-plates lined with good paste; do not let the mixture stand after it is put together, but bake at once.

Puddings.—For boiled puddings a regular pudding-boiler,
holding from three pints to two quarts, is best, a tin pail with a
very tight-fitting cover answering instead, though not as good.
For large dumplings a thick pudding-cloth—the best being of
Canton flannel, used with the nap-side out—should be dipped
in hot water, and wrung out, dredged evenly and thickly with
flour, and laid over a large bowl. From half to three-quarters
of a yard square is a good size. In filling this, pile the fruit
or berries on the rolled-out crust which has been laid in the
middle of the cloth, and gather the edges of the paste evenly
over it. Then gather the cloth up, leaving room for the dump-
ling to swell, and tying very tightly. In turning out, lift to a
dish; press all the water from the ends of the cloth: untie and
turn away from the pudding, and lay a hot dish upon it, turning over the pudding into it, and serving at once, as it darkens
or falls by standing.

In using a boiler, butter well, and fill only two-thirds full
that the mixture may have room to swell. Set it in boiling
water, and see that it is kept at the same height, about an inch
from the top. Cover the outer kettle, that the steam may be
kept in. Small dumplings, with a single apple or peach in
each, can be cooked in a steamer. Puddings are not only
much more wholesome, but less expensive than pies.

Apple Dumplings.—Make a crust, as for biscuit, or a po-
tato-crust, as follows: Three large potatoes, boiled and
mashed while hot. Add to them two cupfuls of sifted flour and
one teaspoonful of salt, and mix thoroughly. Now chop or cut
into it one small cupful of butter, and mix into a paste with about
a teacupful of cold water. Dredge the board thick with flour,
and roll out, thick in the middle, and thin at the edges. Fill,
as directed, with apples pared and quartered, eight or ten good-
sized ones being enough for this amount of crust. Boil for
three hours. Turn out as directed, and eat with butter and
syrup or with made sauce. Peaches pared and halved, or
canned ones drained from the syrup, can be used. In this

case, prepare the syrup for sauce. Blueberries are excellent in the same way.

ENGLISH PLUM PUDDING.—One pound of raisins stoned and cut in two; one pound of currants washed and dried; one pound of beef-suet chopped very fine; one pound of bread-crumbs; one pound of flour; half a pound of brown sugar; eight eggs; one pint of sweet milk; one teaspoonful of salt; a tablespoonful of cinnamon; two grated nutmegs; a glass each of wine and brandy.

Prepare the fruit and dredge thickly with flour. Soak the bread in the milk; beat the eggs and add. Stir in the rest of the flour, the suet, and last the fruit. Boil six hours either in cloth or large mold. Half the amounts given make a good-sized pudding; but, as it will keep three months, it might be boiled in two molds. Serve with a rich sauce.

ANY-DAY PLUM PUDDING.—One cup of sweet milk; one cup of molasses; one cup each of raisins and currants; one teaspoonful of salt, and one of soda, sifted with three cups of flour; one teaspoonful each of cinnamon and allspice.

Mix milk, molasses, suet, and spice; add flour and then the fruit. Put in a buttered mold and boil three hours. Eat with hard or liquid sauce. A cupful each of prunes and dates or figs can be substituted for the fruit, and is very nice; and the same amount of dried apples, measured after soaking and chopping, is also good. Or the fruit can be omitted altogether, in which case it becomes "Troy Pudding."

BATTER PUDDING, BOILED OR BAKED.—Two cups of flour in which is sifted a heaping teaspoonful of baking powder, two cups of sweet milk, four eggs, one teaspoonful of salt. Stir the flour gradually into the milk, and beat hard for five min-utes. Beat yolks and whites separately, and add to batter. Have the pudding-boiler buttered. Pour in the batter, and boil steadily for two hours. It may also be baked an hour in a buttered pudding-dish. Serve at once, when done, with a liquid sauce.

TAPIOCA PUDDING.—Put into one quart of milk two-thirds of a cupful of tapioca that has soaked over night, one saltspoon-ful of salt; set it on the back part of the stove and heat gently until the tapioca becomes clear; then beat the yolks of four eggs with one cupful of sugar and the rind and juice of one lemon; stir this into the boiling milk and tapioca; of the whites of the eggs make a frosting with one cupful of pulverized sugar. Add the juice of a lemon, or other flavoring, spread over the top of the pudding in a baking dish, and let it just brown to a cream tint in the oven. It is best eaten cold.

CHEAP APPLE PUDDING.—In the first place select two deep earthen dishes, of the same size and shape, that will hold two or three quarts, according to the family. Then fill one with nice apples, peeled and sliced thin. Add a teacupful of cold water. Cover the apples with a tender crust, then turn the empty dish, after it has been well buttered, over the one in which you have the pudding, and place them both in a hot oven. It will require about half an hour to bake. Let the pudding be just ready for the dessert, and do not remove the upper dish until the minute the pudding is to be eaten.

It is nice with sugar and butter, but with rich cream, sweetened, it is a very delicious dessert.

RICE PUDDING.—Half a teacupful of rice in three pints of milk; set it in a tin pail in a kettle of boiling water; let it simmer till the rice is cooked soft; while hot, stir in two tablespoonfuls of butter; set it by to cool; beat five eggs, leaving out two whites, and a teacupful of sugar; stir into the rice and milk when cold, and set in the oven to bake; take out as soon as it forms a custard; do not wait for the custard to set or it will whey; one-quarter of a pound of stoned raisins added to this is very nice. Make a meringue of the two whites of eggs and six tablespoonfuls of pulverized sugar beaten to a stiff froth; pile up on the top and set in the oven just two minutes.

GINGER PUDDING.—Five eggs, two teacupfuls sugar, one and one-half teacupfuls butter, four teacupfuls of flour, after being sifted, one of molasses, one of sour milk, with a teaspoonful of soda dissolved in it, two teaspoonfuls ground ginger, a little cinnamon, a pinch of salt, unless the butter is salt enough; beat the eggs and sugar together, set the molasses and butter over the fire to melt the latter; mix alternately the eggs, and flour; lastly, milk, soda and spice; bake slowly. Eat with the following sauce: One-half pint of molasses, one pint of sugar, lump of butter, size of an egg, a teaspoonful of ginger, a little water. Let all boil and serve hot.

COTTAGE PUDDING.—One egg, one pint of flour, one cupful of milk, one cupful of sugar, three tablespoonfuls of melted butter, one teaspoonful of soda, two teaspoonfuls of cream of tartar. Mix the cream of tartar in the flour, and the soda in the milk. Can be made in twenty minutes. Bake quickly, and eat with sauce. Square, shallow pans are better to bake in. Two teaspoonfuls of baking powder can be used.

MARROW PUDDING.—Grate a large loaf of baker's bread and pour on the crumbs a pint of rich milk boiling hot; when cold, add four eggs and three-quarters of a pound of beef's marrow sliced thin, four tablespoonfuls of lemon juice, in which one teaspoonful (level) of mace has been soaked and stirred, one teaspoonful of extract of nectarine, and one tablespoonful of rose water. Add two cups of raisins and one of blanched almonds, if you wish; boil three hours; or omit the fruit and use a pound of marrow instead of three-quarters, and bake it.

STEAMED GRAHAM BREAD.—One cupful of milk, three-quarters of a cupful of molasses, one cupful of water, two cupfuls of graham flour, three teaspoonfuls of baking powder, one half teaspoonful of soda dissolved in a little hot water, a little salt; steam three hours. Nice hot for a dessert with Virginia molasses sauce.

CARROT PUDDING.—One pound of grated carrots, three-quarters of a pound of chopped suet; one-half pound of raisins and currants, four tablespoonfuls of sugar, eight tablespoonfuls of flour, spices to suit the taste; boil four hours and bake twenty minutes. This is the recipe, but we question whether we would bake it the twenty minutes if it were nice without.

WHORTLEBERRY PUDDING.—One quart of flour, one heaping tablespoonful of baking powder, a little salt, and mix with cold water, having the dough softer than for soda biscuit; roll out the paste and pour upon it one quart of whortleberries, then cover the berries by securely lapping the paste as for dumplings. The water must be boiling, the pot ample and well filled with the boiling water. Dip the pudding cloth in hot water, then flour it well; tie the pudding very closely in the cloth and let it boil steadily one hour.

Cakes.—SPICE CAKES.—Two pounds of sifted flour, three-quarters of a pound of sugar, three-quarters of a pound of butter, one tablespoonful of ground spices, one teaspoonful of salt, and two tablespoonfuls of yeast; mix it to a nice dough with warm milk, cover it, and set in a warm place for three hours; then roll it thin; cut it in small cakes, and bake ten or twelve minutes in a quick oven. These may be fried as doughnuts.

WINE CAKES.—Mix eight ounces of flour with half a pound of finely powdered sugar, beat four ounces of butter with two tablespoonfuls of wine; then make the flour and sugar into a paste with it, and four eggs, beaten light; add caraway seeds, and roll the paste as thin as paper; cut the cakes with the top of a tumbler, brush the tops over with the beaten white of an egg, grate sugar over, and bake ten or twelve minutes in a quick oven; take them from the tins when cold.

SOFT GINGERBREAD (*Molasses*).—Take half a pint of sour milk, half a pint of molasses, one teacupful of butter, or salted lard, or beef fat, one large teaspoonful of saleratus, dissolved in a little hot water, two well beaten eggs, half a nutmeg, grated, a teaspoonful of ground cinnamon, and a large spoonful of ground ginger; mix in sifted wheat flour until it is a thick batter which you can stir easily with a spoon; beat it well together for some time, then pour it in an inch deep in square tin pans, buttered; bake half an hour in a quick oven; to ascertain whether it is done, try as directed in introductory remarks.

SOFT GINGERBREAD (*without eggs*).—Make as directed for soft gingerbread, omitting the eggs, and using two teaspoonfuls of saleratus instead of one; dissolve it in a teacupful of warm water.

MOLASSES CUP CAKES.—Two cups of molasses, one cupful butter, one cupful of milk, one teaspoonful of powdered saleratus dissolved in a little hot water, one teaspoonful of lemon extract, half a nutmeg, grated, and two well beaten eggs; stir in, by degrees, enough flour to make it as stiff as you can stir easily with a spoon, beat it well until it is very light, rub a two-quart tin basin over with a bit of butter, line it with white paper, and put the cake in it; bake forty minutes in a quick oven; try if it is done, by running a broom splint in it at the thickest part; if it comes out clean it is done. This is a delicious cake.

COMMON CUP CAKE.—One teacupful of butter, two of sugar, four of flour, four well beaten eggs, one cupful of sour milk, one teaspoonful of saleratus, dissolved in a little water, one teaspoonful of lemon extract, or a wineglass of brandy, and half a nutmeg, grated; beat up the mixture well, butter two two-quart basins, line them with white paper, and divide the mixture between them; bake in a quick oven three-quarters of an hour.

POUND CAKES.—One pound and a half of flour, one pound of butter, one pound of fine white sugar, ten eggs, one gill of brandy, half a nutmeg grated, and a teaspoonful of vanilla or lemon extract, or orange flour water.

Beat the butter and sugar to a cream, beat the eggs to a high froth, then put all together, beat it until it is light and creamy, put it in basins lined with buttered paper, let the mixture be an inch and a half deep, and bake in a moderate oven for one hour, then try it; when done, turn it gently out, reverse the pan, and set the cake on the bottom until cold; let the paper remain until the cake is to be cut.

SPONGE CAKE.—One pound of sugar finely ground, half a pound of sifted flour, eight eggs, one teaspoonful of salt, one tablespoonful of rose brandy, or a teaspoonful of lemon extract.

Beat the yolks of the eggs, flour and sugar together, until it is smooth and light, beat the whites of the eggs to a high froth, then beat all together until well mixed; one teaspoonful of cream of tartar, and half a teaspoonful of soda sifted dry into the flour.

Butter a square tin pan, line it with paper, and put in the mixture more than an inch deep; bake in a moderate oven.

LOAF CAKE.—One pound of butter beaten to a cream, two pounds of sugar rolled fine, three pounds of sifted wheat flour, six well beaten eggs, three teaspoonfuls of powdered saleratus dissolved in a little hot water, one tablespoonful of ground cinnamon, and half a nutmeg grated; add one pound of currants, well washed and dried, one pound of raisins stoned and cut in two; work the whole together, divide it in three loaves, put them in buttered basins, and bake one hour in a moderate oven.

FRENCH TEA CAKE.—Beat ten eggs to a high froth, dissolve half a teaspoonful of volatile salts in a little hot water, let it stand to cool, then put it to the eggs and beat for ten minutes; add four ounces of powdered loaf sugar, and the same of sifted flour; beat them well together, line square tin pans with buttered paper, put in the cake mixture nearly an inch deep, and bake in a quick oven. When served, cut it in squares.

DROP CAKES.—Beat eight eggs very light with one pound of powdered sugar and twelve ounces of flour; flavor with lemon or rose, and half a nutmeg, grated; if the mixture is not beat enough the cakes will run into each other; make them in small, oblong cakes, on sheets of paper; grate sugar over each, bake in a moderate oven; when done, take them from the paper with a knife.

WEDDING CAKE.—One pound of flour, nine eggs, the whites and yolks beaten separately, one pound of butter beaten to a cream, one pound of sugar, one teacupful of molasses, nutmegs grated, or ground mace, one ounce, one teaspoonful of ground allspice, one teaspoonful of cinnamon and a gill of brandy; beat this mixture well.

Having picked, washed and dried three pounds of currants, and stoned, and cut in two, three pounds of raisins, strew half a pound of flour over them, mix it well through and stir them with a pound of citron cut in strips into the cake.

Line round tin pans with buttered paper, put the mixture in an inch and a half or two inches deep, and bake in a moderate oven an hour and a half or two hours. See directions for icing a cake.

PLUM CAKE.—Make a cake of two cupfuls of butter, two cupfuls of molasses, one cupful of sweet milk, two eggs well beaten, one teaspoonful of powdered saleratus, dissolved with a little hot water, one teaspoonful of ground mace or nutmeg, one teaspoonful of ground allspice, a tablespoonful of cinnamon and a gill of brandy; stir in flour to make a batter as stiff as may be stirred easily with a spoon, beat it well until it is light, then add two pounds of raisins stoned, and cut in two, two pounds of currants, picked, washed and dried, and half a pound of citron, cut in slips. Bake in a quick oven.

This is fine, rich cake, easily made and not expensive.

RICH BRIDE CAKE.—Take four pounds of sifted flour, four pounds of sweet fresh butter beaten to a cream, and two pounds of white powdered sugar; take six eggs for each pound of flour, an ounce of ground mace or nutmegs, and a tablespoonful of lemon extract or orange flower water.

Wash through several waters and pick clean from grit, four pounds of currants, and spread them on a folded cloth to dry; stone, and cut in two, four pounds of raisins, cut two pounds of citrons in slips, and chop or slice one pound of blanched almonds.

Beat the yolks of the eggs with the sugar to a smooth paste; beat the butter and flour together and add them to the yolks and sugar; then add the spice and half a pint of brandy, and the whites of the eggs beaten to a froth; stir all together for some time, strew half a pound of flour over the fruit; mix it through, then by degrees stir it into the cake.

Butter large tin basins, line them with white paper and put in the mixture two inches deep, and bake in a moderate oven two hours. The fruit should be prepared the day before making the cake.

TO MAKE ICING FOR CAKES.—Beat the white of two small eggs to a high froth; then add to them quarter of a pound of white sugar ground fine like flour; flavor with lemon extract or vanilla; beat it until it is light and very white, but not quite so stiff as kiss mixture; the longer it is beaten the more firm it will become. No more sugar must be added to make it so. Beat the frosting until it may be spread smoothly on the cake.

This quantity will ice quite a large cake over the top and sides.

TO ICE OR FROST CAKE.—Make an icing as above directed, more or less, as may be required.

Turn over the basin in which the cake was baked, and set the cake on the bottom, then spread the icing on the sides with a piece of card paper or Bristol board, about four inches long and two and a half wide, then heap what you suppose to be sufficient for the top in the centre of the cake, and with the card paper spread it evenly over, set it in a warm place to dry and harden, after which ornament it as you may fancy.

If sugar ornaments are put on, it should be done whilst it is moist or soft.

For small cakes, where a thin icing only is required, it must not be beaten as stiff. Let it be so as to flow for the last coating of a cake that it may be smooth.

ALMOND CAKE.—One-half cupful of butter, two of sugar, two and a half of flour, three-quarters of a cupful of sweet milk, one-half a teaspoonful of soda, one teaspoonful of cream of tartar, whites of eight eggs beaten to a stiff froth, one pound of soft-shelled almonds blanched by steeping in boiling water till the skins are loose enough to remove, and then sliced or rolled, adding, while crushing them, the juice of an orange; flavor with essence of bitter almond. Bake in a pan two inches deep.

COOKIES.—Two cupfuls of white sugar, one cupful of butter, three eggs, two teaspoonfuls of cream of tartar in the flour, one teaspoonful of soda, one tablespoonful of sweet milk; to the whole add flour enough to make it a soft mixture; add nutmeg.

SOFT COOKIES.—Take one cupful of butter and two of sugar; rub them to a cream; mix with them three well beaten eggs, one teacupful of milk or cream, six cupfuls of flour, one teaspoonful of saleratus, and a little nutmeg.

CURRANT SHORT CAKE.—String and sugar a quart of currants, take a quart of flour, mix well in it a large tablespoonful of butter and a tablespoonful of Snowflake baking powder, and a little salt; add milk enough to make a soft biscuit dough, roll it out three-quarters of an inch thick, and put it into dripping-pans eight by twelve inches, as this is a good size to cut. Bake, and the moment it is done turn out on to a platter, and with your carving knife open right through the center; spread well with butter the top and bottom crust, then put in your currants, strawberries or raspberries, sprinkle some more sugar over, put on the top crust, and return to the oven for ten minutes to soak.

We consider sweet cream essential for eating with these short cakes, but many people do not mind its absence.

Strawberry short cake is made as above, except that you mash one-half the strawberries and leave the other half whole.

FREEZING OF ICE CREAM AND ICES.—With a patent freezer, ice cream and ices can be prepared with less trouble than puff paste. The essential points are the use of rock-salt, and pounding the ice into small bits. Set the freezer in the centre of the tub. Put a layer of ice three inches deep, then of salt, and so on till the tub is full, ending with ice. Put in the cream, and turn for ten minutes, or till you can not turn the beater. Then take off the cover, scrape down the sides, and beat like cake for at least five minutes. Pack the tub again, having let off all water; cover with a piece of old carpet. If molds are used, fill as soon as the cream is frozen; pack them full of it, and lay in ice and salt. When ready to turn out, dip in warm water a moment. Handle gently and serve at once.

ICE CREAM OF CREAM.—To a gallon of sweet cream add two and a quarter pounds of sugar, and four tablespoonfuls of vanilla or other extract, as freezing destroys flavor. Freeze as directed.

ICE CREAM WITH EGGS.—Boil two quarts of rich milk, and add to it, when boiling, four tablespoonfuls of corn starch wet with a cup of cold milk. Boil for ten minutes, stirring often. Beat twelve eggs to a creamy froth with a heaping quart of sugar, and stir in, taking it from the fire as soon as it boils. When cold, add three tablespoonfuls of vanilla or lemon, and two quarts either of cream or very rich milk, and freeze. For strawberry or raspberry cream, allow the juice of one quart of berries to a gallon of cream. For chocolate cream, grate half a pound of chocolate; melt it with one pint of sugar and a little water, and add to above rule.

Canning and Preserving.—In canning, see first that the jars are clean, the rubbers whole and in perfect order, and the tops clean and ready to screw on. Fill the jars with hot (not boiling) water half an hour before using, and have them ready on a table sufficiently large to hold the preserving kettle, a dish-pan quarter full of hot water, and the cans. Have ready, also, a deep plate, large enough to hold two cans, a silver spoon, an earthen cup with handle, and, if possible, a can-filler—that is, a small tin in strainer shape, but without the bottom, and fitting about the top. The utmost speed is needed in filling and screwing down tops, and for this reason every thing must be ready beforehand.

In filling the can let the fruit come to the top; then run the spoon-handle down on all sides to let out the air; pour in juice till it runs over freely, and screw the top at once, using a towel to protect the hand. Set at once in a dish-pan of water, as this prevents the table being stained by juice, and also its hardening on the hot can. Proceed in this way till all are full; wipe them dry; and, when cold, give the tops an additional screw, as the glass contracts in cooling, and loosens them. Label them, and keep in a dark, cool closet. When the fruit is used, wash the jar, and dry carefully at the back of the stove. Wash the rubber also, and dry on a towel, putting it in the jar when dry, and screwing on the top. They are then ready for next year's use. Mason's cans are decidedly the best for general use.

GENERAL RULES FOR CANNING.—For all small fruits allow one-third of a pound of sugar to a pound of fruit. Make it into syrup with a teacupful of water to each pound, and skim carefully. Throw in the fruit, and boil ten minutes, canning as directed. Raspberries and blackberries are best; huckleberries are excellent for pies, and easily canned. Pie-plant can be stewed till tender. It requires half a pound of sugar to a pound of fruit.

For peaches, gages, etc., allow the same amount of sugar as for raspberries. Pare peaches, and can whole, or in halves, as preferred. Prick plums and gages with a large darning-needle to prevent their bursting. In canning pears, pare and drop at once into cold water, as this prevents their turning dark.

Always use a porcelain-lined kettle, and stir either with a silver or a wooden spoon—never an iron one. Currants are nice mixed with an equal weight of raspberries, and all fruit is more wholesome canned than in preserves.

MISCELLANEOUS RECIPES AND DIRECTIONS.

To Test the Purity of the Atmosphere.—Fill a glass tumbler with lime water, and place it in any convenient position. The rapidity with which a pellicle forms on its surface corresponds to the amount of carbonic acid, or foul air, present in the atmosphere that surrounds it.

To Clean Wall Papers.—Let the servant or man employed get on high steps, and first brush the wall all over with a perfectly clean brush. Then divide a stale loaf in large pieces and rub the paper downwards with it in firm, clear strokes; he must not go back over it with the same piece of bread, nor rub it up and down, only downwards. The bread will remove all the dirt and leave the paper like new; but it must not be used dirty, a fresh piece must be taken when the last used is soiled, otherwise dust will be carried from one breadth of the paper to the next.

To Remove Grease Spots.—If there are any grease spots on the paper, cover them with a little moist fuller's earth, and when it is dry brush it off. Repeat the application if required.

To Clean Paint.—Get some of the best whiting; powder it and then sift it, so that it may be as fine as possible. Put it in a plate for use. Get some clean, warm water in a basin, and a piece of soft flannel, and a new soft chamois leather.

Dip the flannel in the water and squeeze it nearly dry; then rub it down in the whiting, and take up as much as will adhere to it. Rub the paint gently with it and it will clean it perfectly. Next lightly wash the part done with clean water, and dry with the chamois leather. The paint will look as well as if it were just done, and the most delicate colors will be uninjured. It is a better mode than the old one of soap and water, and it is also quicker about.

Window-cleaning should be done by men, if the windows are high up. No woman should be allowed to run the risk of breaking her neck from a height, nor to stand where she is indelicately exposed to observation, but she ought to clean the inside of the windows with the footman or hired cleaner.

Plate-glass is best cleaned with wet whiting, which is afterwards washed off, and the glass is rubbed with a chamois leather.

If paint-splashes have been left on the panes of glass by the painter, it can be removed by washing the glass with soda and water, which will quite clear it from them.

14

Board Cleaning.—Boards should never be rubbed across, but up and down the boards. After being well scrubbed with soap, hot water and a brush, they should be washed over again with clean water and soft cloth, and then well dried by hard rubbing. To extract oil from boards (it is frequently upset on them by careless painters), make a lye of pearl-ashes and rain water; add to it unslacked lime as much as the water will absorb; stir well together; let it settle, and bottle for use. Dilute it with rain-water when required, and wash the greasy spots quickly with it. Do not let it remain wet, for fear of discoloring the boards. Boards may be whitened by scrubbing them with soft water, sand, and slacked lime. This will also destroy insects.

How to Clean Carpets.—Carpets should be swept the way of the pile, with wet tea-leaves, to prevent the dust from flying over the curtains and furniture. A short-handled soft brush should be used for valuable carpets, and the servant must sweep it with care once a week. Once a year carpets should be well shaken.

Bedroom carpets should be wiped over, especially under the bed, with a damp cloth every day, or at least three times a week.

The house-wife who has her carpets wiped with a damp cloth daily (if mud be on them, the spots must first be brushed off), will find that it is only necessary to sweep them once a week, and that they will last for years longer than if they were swept daily. Of course the cloth must not be wet, only damp enough to pick up flue and dust. But, however it is cleaned, be sure that it is done often and effectually, for the sake of health.

Polished floors, well varnished, with a mere strip of carpet by the side of the bed (in bedrooms), is better and healthier than our present carpeted rooms.

For Removing Grease from Carpets.—Half a wineglassful of fuller's earth, half a wineglassful of magnesia. Mix the above in a basin with boiling water; put it hot on the grease spot, or spots, and leave it on till it is dry, then brush it off, and you will find the spots are gone. Or, if the grease is recent, lay a sheet of blotting-paper over it and iron over the spot with a hot flat-iron; it will come out in the blotting-paper, but you must keep moving the paper and applying fresh parts of it till the heat has absorbed the whole of the grease.

To Remove Ink from Carpets.—If the ink is just spilled, take up as much as you can with a spoon and with blotting paper. When you have taken off all that is possible, wash well with skim milk (London milk does as it is), then wash again with hot water. As soon as the accident happens, wet the place with juice of sorrel, or lemon, or vinegar, and the best hard white soap. Old ink-stains are hard to get out; but they can be removed by first wetting the spot and then applying salts of sorrel. Wash off immediately, however.

Fuller's earth, mixed with lemon juice, will also take other stains out of carpets.

Carpets should not be swept with a whisk-brush above once a week. It wears them out if it is used oftener.

To Clean Floor Cloths.—Sweep them and wash them now and then with milk; never scour them with a brush, or use soap or hot water on them, as it would take off the paint. A soft cloth and lukewarm water are all that is required to clean them.

Oil-cloths are washed, when they require it, with a soft flannel wetted with milk; or, with a mixture of salad-oil and weak table beer. Never use soda or soap to them.

To Clean Greasy Cocoanut Matting.—Thoroughly scrub it all over with hot water and soap, then loosely fold it and put it into a large washing-tub. Pour a quantity of cold water over it, then hang it out on a line in the sun to dry.

To Clean Straw Matting.—Wash as seldom as possible; but when it becomes imperatively necessary to do so, use salt and water. Salt will prevent the matting from turning yellow. Dry as fast as you wash, and wash only a small space at a time.

Stained boards are dusted and polished as stained furniture would be.

To Clean Glass.—Tumblers and wineglasses should be washed in cold water in which a little soda is dissolved, then turned up to drain, dried with a soft, clean, and dry cloth, and finally polished with a leather or an old silk handkerchief. Chandelier or lustre glasses are washed in the same way. Decanters require careful cleaning. First have ready some strong suds of white soap and water and a little pearlash. Mash up an egg-shell well, drop it into the bottle, pour in some of the soap-suds, and shake it well about till the bottle is clean, then empty it; put in fresh suds and clean inside with a small sponge on the end of a glass-stick; rinse out twice with clean cold water. Next put them into the soap-suds, and if they are cut wash them with a regular glass-brush; next rinse the outside. Dry the inside with a clean piece of linen on the end of your glass-stick. Wipe the outside with a dry glass-cloth, and polish off with a leather or silk handerchief.

To Remove Rust.—To remove rust from steel, cover with

sweet oil, well rubbed on it; in forty-eight hours use unslacked lime, powdered very fine. Rub it till the rust disappears. To prevent the rust, mix with fat oil varnish four-fifths of well-rectified spirits of turpentine. The varnish is to be applied by means of a sponge; and articles varnished in this manner will retain their brilliancy and never contract any spots of rust. It may be applied to copper, philosophical instruments, etc.

To Distinguish Iron from Steel.—Let a drop of diluted nitric acid fall on the metal, and, after a few minutes, wash it off with water. If the metal be steel, a black spot will be left on it; if it be iron, a whitish spot will remain. The reason is that the nitric acid dissolves the iron in both cases, but the charcoal that enters into the composition of the steel remains undissolved, and constitutes the blackness.

To Clean Marble.—One ounce of potash, two ounces of whitening, and a square of yellow soap, cut into small pieces; boil altogether in a saucepan, until it begins to thicken; apply this with a large brush to the marble. If the marble is very dirty, let it remain all night; if not, one hour will be sufficient. Then wash it carefully off with plenty of cold water and a sponge. Take care the mixture is not applied too hot. Or:

Equal quantities of soft soap and pearlash.

Put the soap and pearlash on the chimney-piece with a soft flannel; let it lie on for a few minutes. Wash it off with warm water, not too hot; wash it over a second time with cold spring water. Acids act on marble. Marble is itself composed of carbonate of lime—that is, it is a compound of carbonic acid and lime. Now the carbonic acid has a comparatively weak affinity for lime, and most other acids will prevail over it and take its place when brought into contact with it; thus destroying the texture of the stone, liberating the carbonic acid, and leaving some salt of lime, in the form of a white powder, in its place.

When marble has had its polished surface eroded by acids—and even lemon juice or vinegar will do this readily—the only mode of reparation is to have the marble again polished by the use of polishing powders, such as emery.

Neither spirits nor water produce any permanent effect on marble, but fixed oils and grease soak into its substance, and it is impossible to remove them, as any agent potent enough to act on the grease will also destroy the texture of the marble. A portion of the grease may be extracted by covering with fuller's earth or pipeclay. But marble should be carefully preserved from contact with grease or oil.

To Clean Brass.—Rub it with a little sal ammoniac finely powdered and wet. Warm the brass first; polish with wash leather. Or:

Rub with a soft wash-leather dipped in sweet oil; then with finely powdered rotten-stone. Polish with wash-leather. The Americans use powdered rotten-stone, well mixed with a pint of water. Then a teaspoonful of sulphuric acid is added. This mixture is applied gently, then rubbed off, and the brass polished with powdered whiting which has been sifted through muslin. Use wash leather in all cases. Some persons wash the brass with the sulphuric acid and water, and then polish with rotten-stone, etc., etc.

To Clean Real Bronze.—Wash the ornaments gently (with a sponge) with soap and water, then rinse them in beer. Do not wipe it off or rub the ornaments at all, but place them in a spot at a little distance from the fire, until they are quite dry. Use very little soap.

Bronzed chandeliers, lamps, etc., should be only dusted with a feather brush or soft cloth. Washing takes off the bronzing.

To Clean Gilt Lamp and Chandeliers.—Wipe off the dust with a soft cloth, and wash gently with fine soap-suds and soft lukewarm water. Any wrought work may be carefully cleaned out with a very soft tooth-brush.

To Clean Steel and Iron.—One ounce of soft soap, two ounces of emery, make it into a paste; then rub the article for cleaning with wash-leather, and it will give a brilliant polish.

For Removing Paint from Wood.—Mix one pound of soda, such as is used for washing, two pounds of lime, unslacked. If the paint is very strong on the wood, add one-half pound of potash.

Mix these ingredients together, and dilute with water until the mixture becomes rather thicker than whitewash, and then rub it on the paint with a piece of wood folded up in rag. The person who uses this preparation must be careful not to touch it with his hand.

To Clean Japanned Waiters, Urns, Etc.—Rub on with a sponge a little white soap and some lukewarm water, and wash the water or urn quite clean. Never use hot water, as it will cause the japan to scale off. Having wiped it dry, sprinkle a little flour over it; let it rest awhile, and then rub it with a soft dry cloth, and finish with a silk handerchief. If there are white heat marks on the waiters, they will be difficult to remove. But you may try rubbing them with a flannel dipped in sweet oil, and afterwards in spirits of wine. Waiters and other articles of *papier mache* should be washed with a sponge and cold, water, without soap, dredged with flour while damp; and after a while wiped off, and then polished with a silk handkerchief.

Wood Furniture.—The greatest care should be taken to keep furniture fresh and clean. If the house-wife is neat and careful her property will last much longer than otherwise, and her dwelling will always possess a charm too often wanting in more pretentious dwellings.

Furniture which is French polished should be carefully dusted every day, and polished once a week, with the furniture polish to be bought at any good chemist's. Generally these polishes are better and really cheaper than any that the house-keeper can make herself. The chemical and mechanical action of different substances on articles of furniture is very little understood by persons in general, and consequently the most absurd directions are frequently issued for the preparation of cleaning materials, and also for preventing injury from certain agents. The substances from which furniture is chiefly exposed to injury are water, oils, spirits of various kinds, such as brandy, eau-de-Cologne, benzine, etc., and acids.

Varnishes, or polished surfaces of wood, are easily injured by volatile mineral spirits, such as those used for lamps, or by any alcoholic spirit, as brandy or wine. The polish is composed of gums and resins which are soluble in spirits. Many of these polishes or varnishes are made by dissolving the materials in alcohol, then when they are applied the spirit evaporates and the gum or resin is left in a thin polish or varnish on the wood. Of course, if wine, brandy, or spirits of wine fall on it, a portion of it is again dissolved, and the brilliancy of the surface is destroyed. The only remedy for these kinds of stains or marks is to have the table, or whatever it may be, re-polished.

Heat has the same effect on French polish. A hot plate, or dish, or cup, or mug, placed on it, leaves its shape as a dull mark on the table. Therefore dining tables are better not French polished, but well rubbed with oil. When furniture is not French polished, it is well to rub it with linseed oil, slightly colored with alkanet root. Every time the dinner table is rubbed all the leaves should be put in, so that the portions of the table may be of the same color, for oil darkens mahogany, and if the leaves are not rubbed every time there will soon be a great difference of shade between them and the table.

A Capital Recipe for Polishing Tables.—Cold-drawn linseed oil, one pint; spirits of wine, one ounce; white tonic vinegar, one pint; spirits of turpentine, one ounce; powdered gum arabic, one-half once; butter of antimony, one and one-half ounce; spirits of salt, one ounce.

The above ingredients to be well mixed together and shaken previous to being used.

Family Recipe for Polish for Furniture not French Pol-

ished.—Three ounces of beeswax; three ounces of hard white soap; one ounce of spermeceti, cut up small and simmered in a pint of water, keeping it stirred all the time. Pour it into a jar and keep it well covered.

French Polish.—We give the following excellent recipe, which proves experimentally to be good for those who may wish to polish a table or box for themselves, premising that the surface to which it is applied must be perfectly cleaned first:

Shellac, one ounce and a half; mastic, half an ounce; sandarac, half an ounce; rectified spirits of wine, two ounces. Pound the gums very finely in a mortar, and put them in a bottle which will rather more than hold the whole quantity; stand the bottle in a kettle of cold water, which bring slowly to a boil; let it boil for some time, until the contents of the bottle become like treacle (this requires great care), stirring the while with a wire rod. Roll several yards of flannel list into a flat coil, put a little sweet oil on it, and cover with a piece of old linen; on this apply the polish.

Furniture Polish.—Half a pint of spirits of wine; one-half ounce of gum shellac; one-half once of gum benzoin; one-half ounce of gum sandarac.

Put the whole into a bottle for a day or two, and shake it a few times. When the gums are dissolved it is fit for use. When you think the polish is laid on thick enough, take a clean wad and cloth, put a little clean spirits of wine on the wad, the same as you did the polish, and rub it up the same way, but rub very lightly, and rub until quite dry. You must put a little oil on the cloth, the same as in laying on the polish.

For Polishing Furniture.—Half a pint of vinegar; half a pint of linseed oil; two pennyworth of butter of antimony.

To Clean the Face of Soft Mahogany or other Wood.—After scraping and sand-papering in the usual manner, take a sponge and well wet the surface to raise the grain; then with a piece of fine pumice-stone, free from stony particles, rub the way of the fibres; rub the wood in the direction of the grain, keeping it moist with water; let the wood dry then; if you wet it again you will find the grain much smoother, and it will not rise so much; repeat the process, and you will find the surface perfectly smooth, and the texture of the wood much hardened. By this means common soft Honduras mahogany will have a face equal to Hispaniola. If this does not succeed to your satisfaction, you may improve the surface by using the pumice-stone with cold drawn linseed oil, in the same manner as you proceeded with water; this will be found to put a most beautiful, as well as durable, face to the wood, which must then be polished or **varnished.**

To Clean and Lay by Curtains.—In summer it is usual to lay by curtains of rep, damask, or chintz, and replace them with lace or muslin curtains, which look much cooler, and the more expensive rep and chintz are preserved by it. Rep curtains should be well brushed and shaken; wrapped in linen cloths, and put away (protected by bags of pepper, cedar shavings, or camphor, from the chance of moths) in a dry closet or a deep drawer. Chintz should be spread on a long table and rubbed all over with clean bran and flannel, which cleans the glaze nicely. Then fold and lay them by. If chintz curtains have the dust blown off them once a week by a pair of bellows, and are taken down and well shaken once a quarter, they will last seven years without requiring cleaning. The writer speaks from experience in this matter. It is wiser to have lace and muslin curtains cleaned than washed, and quite as cheap. Chintz should also be sent to be cleaned and re-glazed when dirty.

To Clean Covers which are not Silver.—Put a piece of mottled soap (about two ounces) and about the same quantity of whiting into a jug and pour boiling water on it; mix till it becomes a thick paste, quite smooth. Then rub it on the covers, let it dry, and rub off with dry whiting and a leather. This preserves the cover from being scratched. The insides and outsides of covers should be carefully wiped the moment they are brought from the table.

There are also pastes sold for cleaning covers, about the best of which is Graham's paste; but the old fashioned mode of using soap and whiting for the purpose does very well, and preserves the covers longer.

When they are plated, they are best cleaned like other plate, with gin and whiting mixed, or with rouge powder.

To Clean Tins.—Clean tins as you would clean covers, with soap and whiting mixed to a cream in boiling water. Lay it on with a piece of leather; let it dry, and then rub it off with dry whiting and a clean leather.

To Clean Copper and Brass.—Mix oil and brickdust, or oil and finely powdered rotten-stone (sifted through muslin) together; rub it on with a piece of leather; let it rest a little while on, and then rub off with a dry soft leather.

Many people use oil of turpentine and rotten-stone, but the copper very soon tarnishes after its use; others use oxalic acid, but this is so dangerous a poison, and so painful if it chance to get into the servant's eyes, that we strongly object to its use.

To Clean Lacquered Brass.—Wash with a stiff lather of soap and water; let the brass lie in it for three days, taking it out every day and brushing it with a hard brush; let it dry, and then rub it with a leather.

To Clean Stair-rods.—Mix finely powdered rotten-stone and sweet oil to a paste, then rub it on each rod with a piece of flannel or woolen. Polish with the dry powder of the rotten-stone and a nice leather.

The same mixture, carefully applied to inlaid brass or brass handles of furniture, answers very well; but care must be taken not to let it lodge in any network or hollows of the brass.

To Clean Candlesticks.—Melt all the wax or grease off with boiling water; but on no account melt it by putting the candlesticks before the fire, as it melts the solder. Tin candlesticks must be cleaned as other tins are. Plated candlesticks should be cleaned with plate-powder.

To Clean the Insides of Pots, Pans and Kettles.—Boil in the kettle or pot a little sal-ammoniac for the space of one hour, to remove the fur. Be sure to wash out a dirty saucepan with boiling water the moment you finish using it

To Clean Steel or Iron.—Make a paste of two ounces of soft soap and four of emery-powder—that is, two ounces of coarse emery-powder and two of fine. Put this paste on fire-irons, fenders, etc., and afterwards rub off with dry wash leather. Some people use crocus powder moistened with sweet oil. This is best for polished steel.

To Take Rust out of Steel.—The steel must be covered with sweet oil, and left for 48 hours, then rubbed with leather, and this must be repeated till the rust is removed. Or, you may rub it with the finest emery-paper

To Clean Cast Iron and Black Hearths.—Mix together black lead and whites of eggs to a liquid consistency; paint the stove, etc., all over with it, and rub bright with a hard brush.

To Clean Looking-Glasses.—Wash them with spirits of wine; dry them; powder slightly with whiting, and rub off with a leather. Take care that the whiting does not get into the edge of the frame.

Polish the mahogany frames with furniture paste. Beware of spilling scents on polished looking-glass frames, as it removes the polish.

To Clean Plate.—Plate should be treated with great care. Never put it into a basket or tray with knives, nor mix spoons with forks, for fear of making scratches which nothing will remove. Wash it directly it comes from table with warm water and soap, rinse it in cold water, wipe it, rub it well with a leather. Never suffer mercurial preparations to be used for silver. It is a really saving plan to boil it for half an hour in soft water, with whiting and yellow soap enough to make a lather. Rinse it with cold water, wipe with a soft towel, and rub with a leather.

Gas blackens silver sadly, and the deep stain can only be removed by a plate-powder. Rouge (which is made by the precipitation of sulphate of iron by carbonate of potash), is most generally used, and does very well. In our own household the plate is cleaned by first being nicely washed in warm water and wiped dry. Then a mixture is made of whiting and gin, or spirits of wine (which is in many respects better), and it is rubbed wet on the silver. A sponge is used to rub this mixture on, as it is soft. It is let dry very thoroughly, so that it will rub off like powder with a piece of flannel; then it is polished with a chamois leather. Be sure that the whiting is reduced to the finest possible powder. It should be ground quite fine and even, then sifted through coarse book-muslin, as any rough bits will scratch.

To Take Stains out of Silver.—Steep the plate in soap, let it lie for four hours, then cover it with whiting wet with vinegar, so that it may stick upon the silver, and dry it by the fire; after which rub off the whiting, rub it over with dry bran, and the spots will disappear, and the plate look bright.

To Remove Ink Stains from Silver.—The tops and other portions of silver ink-stands frequently become deeply discolored with ink, which is difficult to remove by ordinary means. It may, however, be completely eradicated by making a little chloride of lime into a paste with water, and rubbing it upon the stains.

An Old Family Recipe to Make Old Plate Look Like New. —Take of unslaked lime and alum a pound each; of aqua vitæ and vinegar each a pint; and of beer grounds two quarts; boil the plate in these ingredients, and it will receive a beautiful polish from them.

Plate is best polished by the naked hand, but the operation gives some pain to the rubber. Jewelers thus polish plate, but it requires the thick-skinned, yet soft palm of a practiced hand to do it.

Egg-spoons get discolored and tarnished by the sulphur in the egg uniting with the silver as soon as it is moistened by saliva. This tarnish is a sulphuret of silver, and may easily be removed by rubbing it with table salt or a little hartshorn.

Let the plate in use be counted over every night—a card

with a list being kept in the plate-basket—and the basket carried to the master's or lady's room.

To Clean Britannia Metal.—Finely powdered whiting, two tablespoonfuls of sweet oil, and a little yellow soap melted to some thickness; mix, with a little spirits of wine. Rub this cream on with a sponge or soft flannel, wipe it off with a soft cloth, and polish with a leather.

To Clean a Metal Teapot.—Pour into it a solution of common soda boiling hot; let it stand twelve hours near the fire; then pour it away, and wipe with a clean cloth.

To Clean Gilding.—Brush off dust with a feather brush. Never wipe with linen, it takes off and deadens the gilding.

To Clean Steel Knives and Forks.—The moment used knives are taken into the kitchen, they should be dipped in warm water and wiped, taking care not to wet the handles.

Knives are cleaned on a board covered with India-rubber, with brick-dust sold for the purpose. In some large families Kent's knife-cleaner is used. This machine saves labor, but requires care in putting the knives in. Printed directions and a powder for it are sold with the machine.

Knives are cleaned on the board by being rubbed smartly on it, with brick-dust spread on the surface. Steel forks are washed, dried and also rubbed on the board with brick-dust. The intervals between the prongs are cleaned with a small bit of stick wrapped in leather and rubbed in brick-dust.

Knives are often stained by fruit or vinegar. The stains can be removed by rubbing them with a piece of raw potato before they are cleaned on the board.

To make Windows like Ground Glass.—Make a hot solution of sal-ammoniac. Brush the solution over the pane or panes; the moisture will instantly evaporate and leave a beautiful radiated deposit.

Flies.—House-flies are very destructive to furniture. They may be effectually destroyed by mixing half a spoonful of ground black pepper, a teaspoonful of brown sugar, and a teaspoonful of cream. Place the mixture in a room where flies are troublesome.

Or:—Put saucers of strong green tea, sweetened, about the room. This will poison flies.

They also dislike elder leaves, and will keep away from them.

To Kill Beetles or Crickets.—Parings of cucumber strewn near their holes, or strong snuff.

To Get Rid of Ants.—A little green sage placed in their haunts will drive them away. Quick-lime scattered over their hills and watered will destroy them.

How to take Ink out of Boards.—Strong muriatic acid or spirits of salts, applied with a piece of cloth; afterwards well washed with water.

To take out Spots of Ink.—As soon as the accident happens, wet the place with juice of sorrel or lemon, or with vinegar, and then rub with best hard soap.

Cement for Glass.—Equal parts of flour, powdered chalk, and finely pulverized glass; half the quantity of brick-dust, scraped lint, and white of egg.

To Preserve Water Fresh.—Put into the barrel or cistern 3 lbs. of black oxide of maganese, powdered; stir it well, and the water will keep good an indefinite time.

To Wash Flannel Without Shrinking it.—Have plenty of hot soft water, make a suds with good soap, rub the clothes clean and rinse out all the soap. Do not let the clothes cool from the time they are wet till they are ready to put on the line. Put them into the next suds, or the rinsing water, as fast as wrung out, and let them cool in the basket before you hang them up. Wash them in the morning, on a sunshiny day, if possible, so they will have a good chance to dry.

To Wash Colored Flannels.—Make a suds of cold water and ordinary bar soup; wash the garment and rinse in cold water. Press while it is still damp. In this way children's fancy sacques and bright dresses may be kept looking like new, neither shrinking nor changing color. Don't be afraid to try it.

To Remove Grass Stains.—Pour boiling hot water on the stains before washing the garments.

Nice Glossy Starch.—To three cupfuls of water take three rounded teaspoonfuls of starch, a pinch of salt, and one teapoonful of powdered borax. Dissolve your borax in part of the water; then add starch and salt; dip your collars, cuffs and bosoms into the starch. Your irons must be good; rub them with bees-wax, and we promise you a stiff, glossy surface with never a failure.

To Remove Iron Rust Stains.—Moisten the spot with a solution of Epsom salts in a few drops of hot water, and rub in well once or twice; then fill a tin vessel with boiling water and set it on the stain; rinse in cold water.

To Remove Mildew.—Rub common brown soap on the spot, and scrape white chalk in it. Keep wet and lay in the sun.

To Remove Scorches.—Scorches made by over-heated flat irons can be removed from linen by spreading over the scorched cloth a paste made of the juice pressed from two onions, one-half ounce of white soap, two ounces of fuller's earth, and half a pint of vinegar. Mix, boil well and cool before using.

To Prevent Blue Fabrics from Fading.—Dissolve two teaspoonfuls of sugar of lead in one gallon of water, soak the stockings or cloth in this solution from half to one hour, according to material. Delicate fabrics need to soak only until saturated; rinse before washing and wash quickly.

Blueing.—One ounce of best Prussian blue, half an ounce of oxolic acid, one quart of soft water. Heat enough of the water to dissolve the acid, then stir in the blue, add cold water and bottle for use; keep in the cellar.

To Clean Silk Dresses.—Equal quantities of alcohol, molasses and soft soap; one pint of each will do two dresses; beat well together, and after spreading a breadth of silk on a clean kitchen table, scour it with an old but clean clothes brush; have three tubs or pails of water, take up the breadth of silk by the top and dip it up and down in first one pail, then the second, and then the third. When there is no color left in the water the rinsing is complete. Pin the breadths to the clothes-line without wringing. When a little damp press out with a cold iron. Before cleaning rub the grease spots with pure naptha or gasoline. We have used this horrid-looking mixture with the best success on even light silks and silk with white stripes.

Paint Spots.—When neither turpentine nor benzine will remove paint spots from garments, try chloroform. It will absorb and remove paint which has been on for six months.

A Cure for Bedbugs.—Gosoline or a strong solution of ammonia are both good remedies.

The only sure remedy that, in the course of seventeen years, we have invariably found efficacious, is a preparation of copperas, one pound to one gallon of boiling water. The most infected house we ever saw was cleared by filling a syringe with this fluid and shooting it into the cracks and crevices of the rooms and walls. Sponging or painting the bedstead with this solution will keep them away for months and forever. The only drawback to this is that it leaves a stain like iron rust.

Oil of cedar is an excellent and cleanly remedy. Salt and kerosene oil in cracks and under base boards is good.

To Drive Away Mice.—Moisten chloride of lime, and stop their holes of ingress with the paste. If the holes are inaccessible, set the chloride around on small plates. Mice do not like it.

To Get Rid of Black Ants.—Get five cents worth of tartar emetic; mix in an old saucer with sugar and water, and set in your pantry or cupboard, where the ants trouble you. In twenty-four hours every ant will have left the premises. With me the same dish of tartar emetic answered as well the second year as the first; as the water dries out add more.

Dyeing.—It may be necessary to remark, once for all, that every article to be dyed, as well as everything used about dyeing, should be perfectly clean.

In the next place, the article to be dyed should be well scoured in soap, and then the soap rinsed out. It is also an advantage to dip the article you wish to dye into warm water, just before putting it into the alum or other preparation; for the neglect of this precaution it is nothing uncommon to have the goods or yarn spotted. Soft water should always be used if possible, and sufficient to cover the goods handsomely.

As soon as an article is dyed it should be aired a little, then well rinsed, and afterwards hung up to dry.

When dyeing or scouring silk or merino dresses, care should be taken not to wring them; for this has a tendency to wrinkle and break the silk.

In putting the dresses and shawls out to dry, that have been dyed, they should be hung up by the edge so as to dry evenly.

Chrome Black.—For Woolen Goods.—For five pounds of goods, blue vitriol, six ounces; boil it a few minutes; then dip the goods three-quarters of an hour, airing often; take out the goods, and make a dye, with logwood, three pounds; boil one-half hour; dip three-quarters of an hour, and air the goods, and dip three-quarters of an hour more. Wash in strong suds. This will not impart any of its color in fulling, nor fade by exposure to the sun.

Black on Wool.—For Mixtures.—For ten pound of wool, bichromate of potash, four ounces; ground argal, three ounces; boil together, and put in wool; stir well, and let it remain in the dye four hours. Then take out the wool, rinse it slightly in clear water; then make a new dye, into which put logwood, three and one-half pounds. Boil one hour, and add chamber lye, one pint, and let the wool lie in all night. Wash in clean water.

SNUFF BROWN.—DARK, FOR CLOTH OR WOOL.—For five pounds of goods, camwood, one pound; boil it fifteen minutes, then dip the goods for three-quarters of an hour; take out the goods, and add to the dye, fustic, two and one-half pounds; boil ten minutes, and dip the goods three-quarters of an hour; then add blue vitriol, one ounce; copperas, four ounces; dip again one-half hour; if not dark enough, add more copperas. It is dark and permanent.

WINE COLOR.—For five pounds of goods, camwood, two pounds; boil fifteen minutes; then dip the goods for one-half hour; boil again, and dip one-half hour; then darken with blue vitriol, one and one-half ounce; if not dark enough, add copperas, one-half ounce.

MADDER RED.—To each pound of goods, alum, five ounces; red, or cream of tarter, one ounce; put in the goods, and bring your kettle to a boil for one-half an hour; then air them, and boil one-half hour longer; then empty your kettle, and fill with clean water; put in bran, one peck; make it milk warm, and let it stand until the bran rises; then skim off the bran, and put in madder, one half pound; put in your goods, and heat slowly until it boils and is done. Wash in strong suds.

GREEN.—ON WOOL OR SILK, WITH OAK BARK.—Make a strong yellow dye of yellow oak and hickory bark in equal quantities. Add the extract of indigo, or chemic, one tablespoonful at a time, until you get the shade or color desired.

BLUE.—QUICK PROCESS.—For two pounds of goods, alum, five ounces; cream of tartar, three ounces; boil the goods in this for one hour; then throw the goods into warm water, which has more or less of the extract of indigo in it, according to the depth desired, and boil again until it suits, adding more of the blue if needed. It is quick and permanent.

STOCKING YARN, OR WOOL, TO COLOR.—BETWEEN A BLUE AND PURPLE.—For five pounds of wool, bichromate of potash, one ounce; alum, two ounce; dissolve them, and bring the water to a boil, putting in the wool, and boiling one hour; then throw away the dye, and make another dye with logwood chips, one pound; or, extract of logwood, two and one-half ounces; and boil one hour. This also works very prettily on silk.

Whenever you make a dye with logwood chips, either boil the chips one-half hour, and pour off the dye, or tie up the chips in a bag, and boil with the wool or other goods; or, take two and one-half ounces of the extract in place of one pound of the chips is less trouble and generally the better plan. In the above recipe, the more logwood that is used, the darker will be the shade.

SCARLET, WITH COCHINEAL.— FOR YARN OR CLOTH.—
For one pound of goods, cream of tartar, one-half ounce; cochineal, well pulverized, one-quarter ounce; muriate of tin, two and one-half ounces; then boil up the dye, and enter the goods; work them briskly for ten or fifteen minutes, after which boil for one and one-half hours, stirring the goods slowly while boiling; wash in clear water and dry in the shade.

PINK.—For three pounds of goods, alum, three ounces; boil, and dip the goods one hour; then add to the dye, cream of tartar, four ounces; cochineal, well pulverized, one ounce; boil well, and dip the goods while boiling, until the color suits.

ORANGE.—For five pounds of goods, muriate of tin, six tablespoonfuls; argal, four ounces; boil, and dip one hour; then add to the dye, fustic, two and one-half pounds; boil ten minutes, and dip one-half hour; and add again to the dye, madder, one teacupful; dip again one-half hour.
Cochineal in place of madder makes a much brighter color, which should be added in small quantities until pleased. About two ounces.

PURPLE.— For five pounds goods, cream of tartar, four ounces; alum, six ounces; cochineal, well pulverized two ounces; muriate of tin, one-half teacupful. Boil the cream of tartar, alum, and tin fifteen minutes; then put in the cochineal and boil five minutes; dip the goods two hours; then make a new dye with alum, four ounces; Brazil wood, six ounces; logwood, fourteen ounces; muriate of tin, one teacupful, with a little chemic; work again until pleased.

SILVER DRAB.—LIGHT.—For five pounds of goods, alum, one small teaspoonful, and logwood about the same amount; boil well together, then dip the goods one hour; if not dark enough, add in equal quantities alum and logwood until suited.

DARK COLORS.—TO EXTRACT AND INSERT LIGHT.—This recipe is calculated for carpet-rags. In the first place let the rags be washed clean; the black or brown rags can be colored red, or purple, at the option of the dyer; to do this, take, for every five pounds of black or brown rags, muriate of tin, three-quarters of a pound, and the lac, one-half pound, mixed with the same as for the lac red; dip the goods in this dye two hours, boiling one half of the time. If not red enough add more tin and lac. The goods can then be made a purple by adding a little logwood; be careful and not get in but a small handful, as more can be added if not enough. White rags make a beautiful appearance in a carpet, by tying them in the skein, and coloring them red, green, or purple; gray rags will take a very good green; the coloring will be in proportion to the darkness of mix.

BLACK.—For five pounds of goods, sumach, wood and bark together, three pounds; boil one-half hour, and let the goods steep twelve hours; then dip in lime water one-half hour; then take out the goods, and let them drip an hour; now add to the sumach liquor, copperas, eight ounces, and dip another hour; then run them through the tub of lime-water again for fifteen minutes; now make a new dye with logwood, two and one-half pounds; by boiling one hour, and dip again three hours; now add bichromate of potash, two ounces to the logwood dye, and dip one hour. Wash in clear, cold water and dry in the shade. You may say this is doing too much. You cannot get a permanent black on cotton with less labor.

BLUE ON COTTON OR LINEN.—WITH LOGWOOD.—In all cases, if new, they should be boiled in a strong soap-suds or weak lye, and rinsed clean; then for cotton, five pounds, or linen, three pounds, take bichromate of potash, three-quarters of a pound; put in the goods and dip two hours; then take out and rinse; make a dye with logwood, four pounds; dip in this one hour, air, and let stand in the dye three or four hours, or till the dye is almost cold; wash out, and dry.

GREEN.—If the cotton is new, boil in weak lye or strong suds; then wash and dry; give the cotton a dip in the home-made dye-tub, until blue enough is obtained to make the green as dark as required; take out, dry, and rinse the goods a little; then make a dye with fustic, three-quarters pound; logwood, three ounces to each one pound of goods, by boiling the dye one hour; when cooled so as to bear the hand, put in the cotton, move briskly a few minutes, and let it lie in one hour; take out, and let it thoroughly drain; dissolve and add to the dye, for each pound of cotton, blue vitriol, one-half ounce; and dip another hour; wring out and let dry in the shade. By adding or diminishing the logwood and fustic, any shade of green may be obtained.

YELLOW.—For five pounds of goods, sugar of lead, seven ounces; dip the goods two hours; make a new dye with bichromate of potash, four ounces; dip until the color suits, wring out, and dry; if not yellow enough, repeat the operation.

RED.—Take muriate of tin, one-half of a teacupful; add sufficient water to cover the goods well, bring it to a boiling heat, putting in the goods one hour, stirring often; take out the goods and empty the kettle, and put in clean water, with nic-wood, one pound, steeping it for one-half hour, at hand heat; then put in the goods, and increase the heat for one hour, not bringing to a boil at all; stir the goods, and dip an hour as before; wash without soap.

GREEN.—VERY HANDSOME WITH OAK BARK.—For one pound of silk, yellow oak bark, eight ounces; boil it one-half hour; turn off the liquor from the bark, and add alum, six ounces; let it stand until cold; while this dye is being made, color the goods in the blue dye-tub a light blue; dry and wash; then dip in the alum and bark dye; if it does not take well, warm the dye a little.

YELLOW.—For one pound of silk, alum, three ounces; sugar of lead, three-quarter of an ounce; immerse the goods in the solution over night; take out, drain, and make a new dye with fustic, one pound; dip until the required color is obtained.

N. B.—The yellow or green for wool works equally well on silk.

CRIMSON.—For one pound of silk, alum, three ounces; dip at hand heat one hour; take out and drain, while making a new dye, by boiling ten minutes, cochineal, three ounces; bruised nut-galls, two ounces; and cream of tartar, one-quarter ounce, in one pail of water; when a little cool, begin to dip, raising the heat to a boil, continuing to dip one hour; wash and dry.

DOMESTIC PETS.

This is a very comprehensive title, and might fairly be supposed to comprise ponies, donkeys, dogs, cats, rabbits, poultry, and pigeons; but this article will be confined to animals kept in the house, and will especially relate to those which may be legitimately called pets, the care of them devolving entirely upon their owners. Out-of-door pets must necessarily be left, in a great measure, to the care of servants, and cannot be so essentially home friends. The following remarks are by a well known writer:

Squirrels, dormice, and white mice are sometimes kept in captivity by those whose lives are chiefly spent in towns, and who have no knowledge of the wild and frolicsome creatures in their native haunts; but they appear to lead very unnatural lives in confinement, and are not very desirable pets for the house. It is difficult to keep their cages quite sweet and clean. All may be domesticated, however, and are, we believe, capable of attachment to their owners. We have never kept any ourselves, but our brothers had dormice from time to time, and several small families were born and brought up under their care, but most of them came to an untimely end.

The Squirrel.—The squirrel seems so delightfully free and happy, playing about on the tops of the tallest trees in the woods, launching himself boldly into the air, and taking tremendous leaps from branch to branch, that, after seeing the pretty little creature at his ease, one does not feel inclined to deprive him of the liberty he seems so thoroughly to enjoy; but if he is captured, his life ought to be made as happy as possible, and he should be allowed as much exercise as he can have in the house. His cage should be at least three or four feet long and three or four feet high, and instead of the revolving cylinder, which is very injurious to the little prisoner, he should have a good-sized branch of a tree, to form perches for him, and be able to frisk about at pleasure in his little parlor. A little sleeping-box must be attached to this, with a door at the back, and the board forming the floor should be drawn out like that of a bird cage. Every part of the cage must be kept as clean as possible, and the moss and cotton wool, which must be put into the squirrel's bedroom, must be changed nearly every day. The active little creature does not often live long in confinement; but if taken young, and very carefully managed, it may become a very tame and a very engaging pet, and may sometimes be trusted to frolic about out of doors when tame enough to return at his owner's call. His cage should, however, be lined with tin; for he is apt to gnaw the wood with his sharp little teeth when impatient of confinement. He should be fed on nuts, almonds, filberts, beech masts, walnuts, acorns, wheat in the ear, and fir cones; and he is fond of milk, cold tea, and bread and milk. A little bit of boiled potato, and even a tiny morsel of cooked meat, may be given as a treat, and a stale crust of bread to gnaw. All creatures require variety in their food, and in his wild state the squirrel gets animal food by robbing birds' nests of their eggs occasionally. He lays up a store of food for the winter in various holes and crevices, and is much too acute ever to put by a nut in which a maggot has been, or to miss the place where his treasure is concealed, even when several inches depth of snow covers the ground. The female is a very affectionate mother, and will remain with her young in the nest even while the tree in which it is, is cut down, or will carry them, one after another, in her mouth, to a place of safety. She generally builds on the topmost branches of the fir tree, and the nest is made of dry grass and sticks, very slightly yet firmly put together, and lined with fur, which she scratches off her body before the young ones are born. This is generally in the summer, and the young squirrels remain with their parents till the following spring, when they are able to manage for themselves. They have a substantial win-

ter's nest, to which they appear to add every year fresh layers
of hay and moss, to make their habitation more and more warm
and comfortable. It is said the best time to buy a squirrel is at
the end of September, when it is fat and vigorous and its fur is
in good condition; but it is never safe to purchase those which
are sold in the street as "wonderfully tame," and which will
allow themselves to be handled by a stranger, and pulled about,
without showing any disposition to bite. The probability is
that the poor little creatures have been stupified by some drug,
and that they will either recover their natural ferocity in a few
hours, or die—poisoned by the narcotic which has been given
them.

The Dormouse.—The dormouse is very like the squirrel in
many of its habits; it lives upon much the same food, and is a
hybernating animal too, laying up a store of eatables for the
winter, and passing the greater parts of the cold months in sleep.
In a cage it is not seen to advantage; throughout the day it is
generally rolled up into a little soft ball of fur, fast asleep, and
its architectural talents are quite thrown away. It is, in its
wild state, a very clever nest-builder. A writer gives a most
fascinating description of a dormouse's nest, which he found in
a hedge four feet from the ground, in the forking of a hazel
branch, the smaller twigs of which formed a palisade round it.
The nest itself was six inches long and three wide, and constructed of grass blades and leaves of trees. The blades of the sword-
grass were chiefly used, and these were twisted round and between the twigs so as to form a hollow oval nest. Finer sorts
of grass and the slender stems (not bigger than thread) of delicate climbing weeds, interwoven with the leaves of hazel and
maple trees, were used for the bottom of the nest; the entrance
to which was most ingeniously concealed by long blades of
grass placed across it in such a manner as to spring back to
their places, after having been pushed aside to admit the dormouse into the nest. This was never used as a storehouse; the
little creature had its winter provisions carefully hidden under
a thick branch in the neighborhood of the nest. While hybernating, the dormouse does not seem to require food; but it
wakes up occasionally during the winter, perhaps when a warm
sunny day calls it into life for the time, and then it takes food

before it rolls itself up and sleeps again. It requires a good deal of warmth, and must have soft hay, moss, and wool, given it to form its bed, and it does its best with these, but cannot construct anything very beautiful out of them.

If we had a tame dormouse, we think we should try and provide it with materials which it might be induced to use for the construction of a nest like that described. The dormice we once had were kept in a cage made for dormice, wired at one end, with a little compartment at the other boarded in, the door of which was pulled up and pushed down at pleasure, so that the little creatures could be shut into their bedroom when the outer room was cleaned out. Even with this precaution they were continually getting out of the cage, they were such nimble little animals, and the whole house was often searched in vain for the truants. At last, perhaps, they would be found in the fold of a curtain or underneath the cushion of a sofa. Sometimes a worse fate befell them, and they would creep under the cushion of an arm-chair, and get crushed to death, or be trodden under foot, or be squeezed under a door in trying to escape. They sleep during the day and come out in the evening, so that they must be provided with food as soon as it grows dusk; and, if they have a large cage with sticks placed across it, they will gambol about very merrily in the open part of it as soon as night approaches. Their food should be varied as much as possible; they will eat nuts and almonds, peas and beans, canary seed, and various other grains; and they are very fond of the milky juice of a dandelion or sow-thistle. We used always to put a little tin pan of milk into the cage every night, and they would often drink it all, especi-ally when they had young ones. It is said that rabbits will be hindered from devouring their young by providing them with water, and that they would not eat them unless maddened by thirst or suffering from extreme hunger. Some dormice have the same propensity to cannibalism; and, if this theory about the rabbits be correct, it may apply also to the mother dor-mouse which devours her young. We thought she did so when alarmed for their safety, not being able to conceal them else-where; but it would be well to provide her with a constant sup-ply of water or milk when nursing. The milk is useful too in furnishing the dormouse with animal food; out of doors it eats insects. There are generally four or five young ones in a litter, born blind, but able to see in a few days, and they are soon capable of taking care of themselves. The cage must, of course, be kept perfectly clean, and the floor of the open part should be sanded like a bird cage.

Mice.—White, grey-and-white, and brown-and-white mice are sometimes kept in cages like those of the dormouse, and they must be treated in the same manner. The common brown mouse is said to be a more tractable and intelligent pet, and to be easily tamed by patient kindness. We never heard a mouse sing, but several instances are recorded of mice who have learned to imitate the chirp and even the song of a canary kept in the room in which they were; so that it might be worth while to try to give such pets the benefit of a musical education for the chance of their acquiring so curious an accomplishment. The little harvest mouse, the tiniest of British quadrpueds, has sometimes been kept in a cage, and will grow tame enough to take its favorite food, flies and other insects, from the hand. It is a most beautiful little creature, very active and agile, climbing about by means of its long tail and flexible toes, and leaping like a little Jerboa. It should have grains of wheat and maize, and canary seed, and plenty of water always. in the cage; and wool or flannel and grass for its nest, which in its wild state is the most beautiful and elaborate construction of leaves and grass woven together into a round ball and suspended from strong grass-stems, wheat-stalks, or thistle-heads. In the winter it takes refuge in corn ricks, or burrows deeply in the earth, and makes a warm bed of grass. Even in confinement the harvest mouse will show its instinctive propensity to store up food for the winter, and if a number of grains of wheat or seed are given to it, will carry them off and hide them in its nest.

Birds.—None of these little creatures, however pretty and intelligent they may be, seem to us to be such desirable pets to be kept in the house as birds, to which the remainder of this article will be devoted. We can make them so happy, and they can tell us when anything is amiss with them so plainly—so thoroughly enjoying our petting, and becoming so attached to us—that no trouble is thrown away upon our feathered pets.

On the whole, canaries flourish best in imprisonment. All the English finches do well in aviaries or cages; but one does not like to see them imprisoned while their brothers and sisters are flying about at large close by—one thinks they must envy them their liberty, and long to join them; while canaries would suffer extremly exposed to the cold of winter, if, indeed, they survived it. As regards other birds—robins, wrens, titmice, sparrows, &c.—it is much pleasanter to have them visiting us from the garden than to keep them shut up all the year round; and larks and nightingales are so completely out of their natural element in cages, that one cannot feel happy in keeping them. Any one who will take the trouble to feed the birds that congregate round the house in winter, may soon have a family of pensioners.

The robins will become our very familiar friends, hopping about at their ease on the breakfast-table, examining every article in the room with the utmost self-possession; will visit us regularly through the cold months, and, if they leave us in spring, will bring their young ones to make our acquaintance when they leave their nests. Crumbs of bread, potatoes, and scraps of fat will make a feast for the poor little hungry birds, driven by frost and snow to our doors; and the saucy tomtits and sparrows will afford us much amusement in return for our hospitality.

We may get much insight into the special characteristics of the birds by watching them when they are at their ease, and a hard winter will sometimes make them so tame, and so accustom them to our care, that they will hover about us out of doors, and peck at the windows for admittance at their usual feeding hours.

Although we do not advocate keeping English birds in confinement as a rule, it will sometimes happen that nestlings will be thrown upon our compassion, which have either fallen out of their nest, lost their parents, or have been taken captive by village boys, and are likely to come to a miserable end if not taken care of. Under these circumstances it is as well to know how to bring them up by hand. We once had several nests to

take care of, and all the young birds were reared and sent out
into the world when able to take care of themselves; all but
two bullfinches, which were given to a neighbor, who fed them
upon hemp-seed—the consequence of which was that nearly
all of their feathers fell off, and they were the most miserable
little objects that can be conceived, and their little red-hot
bodies were quite uncomfortable to touch. A course of warm
baths and plenty of cooling green food, however, restored them
to health and beauty, and they were returned to their owner
with a warning against hemp-seed. It is said that a bullfinch
fed entirely upon this heating feed will become blind.

Nestlings.—Nestlings should be fed upon bread soaked in
water, squeezed nearly dry, and chopped up finely with rape-
seed which has been scalded by pouring boiling water upon it,
and leaving it till quite cold. Of course this food must be
made fresh every day; if it grew sour it would kill the birds at
once. About four quills full of it is enough for a meal for one
young bird; but they generally clamor for food till they have
enough, and then settle down to sleep again. They must be
fed as soon as possible in the morning after sunrise, and will
require food at intervals of from one hour and three-quarters
to two hours throughout the day, the last meal being given
about sunset, when they must be covered up for the night.
The best plan is to keep the nest in a shallow box, over which
a board can be laid to darken it, otherwise the birds will be
asking for food every quarter of an hour. As soon as they
hear a step in the room they begin to chirp; and when the box
is uncovered they will stretch out their necks, and as they grow
older jump out of the nest, and fly upon the hand or shoulder
in their impatience for food. In time they will learn to feed
themselves with the soft food, and by degrees pick up and
shell the seed put into their cage; for, of course, they must be
put into a cage as soon as they are fledged sufficiently to enable them to fly. It is best to crush the hemp-seed for them
at first, but they soon learn to shell the canary and rape-seed.

The linnets and greenfinches we brought up by hand were
very tame, and, although seed and water were always within
their reach, we accustomed them to be fed by hand, and kept
any food of which they were particularly fond—hemp-seed,

plantain, or chickweed, for instance, which all birds love—to be given them as dainties; so they always expected something nice, and would fly out of their cages and all round the room in their joy as soon as we opened the doors, returning to perch on the hand, shoulder or head when they wanted their food. The greenfinches were very bold birds, and as familiar as possible. They were great eaters, and very eager for their favorite food, so they always welcomed us very heartily; but we did not prize their affection so much as that of the linnets, which were naturally more shy and retiring, and required more courting and petting. They are very nice pets, and become very much attached to their owner, and their song is very sweet; but if kept in confinement they never acquire the red poll and breast which ought to distinguish the male bird in full plumage. They are fond of flax or linseed, but they must not have much of it or they will grow very fat. Canary and rape-seed should be the principal food both of linnets and greenfinches.

Goldfinch.—The goldfinch is a universal favorite, both from its beauty and sprightliness; it is very restless in a cage, and therefore, it hardly appears as contented as some less active birds; but it will live many years in confinement, and in an aviary is as happy as possible. It ought not to have a bell-shaped cage, as it is apt to grow giddy, twirling its beak along the wires. It is very easily tamed, and is capable of great attachment to its owner, and may generally be safely allowed a flight round the room while its cage is being cleaned. We had one which would fly across the room as soon as its cage door was opened, and perch on our shoulder for its favorite food of hemp-seed. It is rather fond of eating, and takes so much exercise that it requires plenty of food. It will not sing without a few hemp-seeds in the day, but it must not be fed solely upon this heating seed. Canary, rape, and poppy-seed should be the ordinary food of goldfinches. Lettuce, groundsel, chickweed, and water-cress, they should have frequently, and plantain in the winter; in the wild state they feed much on thistle-seed, and they should often have a thistle-head given to them, to pick the seeds out of it for themselves. They ought not to have sugar or sweet cakes, but they exceedingly enjoy a treat of biscuit, and Reading cracknels are very wholesome for them, and thoroughly appreciated by goldfinches, bullfinches, and canaries.

The goldfinch is a very tractable bird, and there are many accomplishments which he will learn, and seems to exhibit with pleasure. He may be taught to fire off a small cannon, to feign death, and stand unmoved while fireworks are let off close to him, to mount a ladder, &c.; but when these tricks are made use of by his master to exhibit in public for pay, he is often treated with cruelty to make him a proficient in them. Many very harmless accomplishments he will learn, however, merely by patience and kindness on the part of his master—to open a box for his seed, to ring a bell when he wants food, to drag a little wagon up an inclined plane into his cage, and to draw up water from a little well underneath it. All these are easily taught, and the bird really seems to find pleasure in such little tasks. "One of my birds who lived in a cage so constructed as to have the seed always in a box of which he had to lift up the lid, and the water in a well to be drawn up in a bucket, was quite unhappy when his home was undergoing repair, and he had to live for a time in an ordinary cage, and sang his merriest song when he had to go to work with his little chain and pail again. I taught him to lift the lid of the box by having it open for one day, and then gradually lowering it by means of a piece of silk put round it, fastened at the back of the cage, till it was quite shut. He very soon found out that he must lift it up with his beak in order to reach the seed; and at last he became so crafty about it, that he would take out two or three seeds at once, and put a reserve by his side between the wires while he ate one. The cage was made with a wooden back, and the box was let into this above the door, and the lid fastened to the inside with two little hinges (care should be taken that the lid is not too heavy for the bird to lift easily, and that it should fall at once when not held up); a little bow window was constructed in the front of the cage, in the floor of which was a little hole with a wire across it, to which was attached a light silver chain fastened to a silver bucket about the size of a thimble. A small colored glass tumbler was fixed below the bow window, by means of four strong wires and a ring. This was filled with water and the bucket dropped into the well, and the bird hauled up the chain

with his beak, holding each fresh haul with his feet till the
bucket came to the hole, and he could drink out of it. I taught
him this accomplishment by filling the bucket with water, and
putting it on the floor of the bow window to accustom him to
look for water there; then I let it down by means of the chain
pushed through two of the side wires by degrees, lowering it a
little more every day. At first the bird pulled up the short
bit of chain with his beak, and let it go before he could drink
out of the bucket, but he gradually found out that he must
hold the chain when he had drawn it up, and when he had
once succeeded in doing this his education was finished; he
never forgot the art, and often showed his delight in his task
by singing when he had drawn up the bucket while his chain
was under his feet, before he quenched his thirst. Of course
it is necessary to see that the machinery of the bucket, chain,
and well is always in order; any hitch preventing the bucket
from falling into the well and getting refilled with water would
cause the poor little bird to die of thirst. The bullfinch and
siskin will readily learn this accomplishment, and I had a mule
bird (whose parents were a goldfinch and canary) who learned
it very quickly; but I never succeeded in teaching a canary to
put his foot on the chain, though he would pull it up with his
beak readily enough—of course, always to be disappointed by
the falling down of the bucket. A goldfinch will learn to pull
a little wagon up an inclined plane in the same way, and
to take his seed out of it, the chain attached to the wagon
having to be hauled in and held in the same manner. The
way to teach him to ring for his food, is to suspend a little bell
in a corner of his cage, and when he has been an hour or two
without food, to ring it by means of a string attached to it, and
immediately to place some of his favorite seed in the glass. In
a few days he will discover that whenever the bell rings he gets
a meal, and will seize the string, and peal away merrily whenever he is hungry."

The goldfinch is rather subject to epileptic fits, and, whenever he is seized with one, he should be plunged head downwards into cold water, and one or two dips will restore him at
once. He is a large eater, and in all probability has indulged
his appetite too much. so that he must be kept upon a low diet

of lettuce seed and thistles, and have no hemp-seed for a few days after he has had one of these fits.

He is fond of bathing, and should have a bath every day. The goldfinch will sometimes mate with the canary, and the mules are very pretty. He must, however, be taken away from his wife as soon as she begins to lay, as he has a mischievous propensity for breaking the eggs. After the young birds are hatched he may be put back into the cage, and will help in feeding them.

Canaries.—If our readers desire to have a nursery of young birds, they will find canaries the best in every respect to rear. There is no doubt about their happiness in a cage, if proper attention be paid to them; and we would fain believe that no one who reads these pages would willingly cause them suffering from want of care, or would attempt to keep pets upon whom they are not ready to bestow all the time and trouble necessary to keep them in health and comfort. People are not worthy of their birds if they neglect them, and leave them to the care of servants, to whom they are either troublesome or indifferent. And their attention will be received with such expressive gratitude and delight—their feathered pets will welcome them so gladly, and show so plainly how much their happiness depends upon their care—that they will be sufficiently rewarded for its bestowal. They should become intimately acquainted with their birds' dispositions, too, and learn their language thoroughly, and they will find a fund of amusement in their society. This is more easily accomplished when one or two pet birds are kept in a cage alone, than when there are a number of canaries together in a very large cage or aviary, but we always like best to see them under such circumstances—they seem so thoroughly happy when they have room for flying and frolicing about; some birds, too, will sing best when they are excited by emulation with others, but occasionally a good songster is sulky when in company, and prefers being alone. One of our birds who had been accustomed to a small single cage, never seemed at ease when in a large one, and resented being jostled by others. He was an old bird, too, and did not like his saucy young companions, and showed his displeasure by total silence whenever he was placed with them; so we had to restore him to solitary grandeur.

All through the autumn and winter months, about twenty or thirty birds will live very happily together, in a cage from three to four feet long, and two feet high and wide. This should be made of tin wire, as brass is apt to corrode, and communicate its poisoned green rust to the birds, when they rub their beaks against it; the iron rust is very good for them. The wood may be either mahogany or varnished deal. The arrangements for seed and water should be carefully attended to. If the former is put into the cage, the bird-hoppers are best to use, because the seed is kept clean, and only falls down as the birds peck and scatter away the husks beneath. A good plan is to have the seed and water in long, covered boxes outside the cage, with china or glass trays to take in and out of them. These can be kept perfectly sweet and clean, and the birds cannot make the seed or water dirty. Objections are made to the old-fashioned bird-glasses, because they are sometimes carelessly put into the wires which hold them, so that they slip aside, and the poor little birds cannot get at the water; but no provision for their comfort can succeed if carelessness be allowed at all. We do not advocate their use, however, for if they are very full the seed or water often gets spilt into the cage, and, if not, the birds have to stretch their little necks painfully to reach their food. Sometimes, too, a young bird will contrive in some mysterious fashion to get into the glass, and, having got in, cannot extricate itself. Nothing looks prettier at first than a fountain in the middle of the cage; but it becomes so dirty in a few hours that it is not well to use it. A bath, wired round like the cage, should be made to hang on the doorway, and the birds will go in and out and splash about in this, with the greatest delight. It must be taken away when they have all had a good washing, in cold weather especially, as some of them will go into the bath again and again, and get completely chilled. In winter the water must have the chill taken off, and whenever the sun shines they may have a bath safely. They must always have sand spread on the board at the bottom of the cage; and the coarse gravelly sand is best for them. It is a good plan to have a second board and two sets of perches for a large cage; this gives opportunity for washing and drying them thoroughly, and when the board gets wetted by the splashing of the birds, it can be dried before it is returned to the cage. Of course the perches must be made to take in and out of the cage; they should be round and smooth like a bamboo. A swing suspended from the centre is a source of pleasure to the birds, and if the cage has a domed top, looks very pretty underneath it. They much enjoy having a pot of mignonette or of chickweed put in; and all perch eagerly about it, and soon devour every leaf and flower. No plant that would be injurious to them must be put either in or close to the cage, for they are sure to eat the leaves, and the beauty of the plant is destroyed in a few hours. A fir branch put into the cage occasionally gives them a good deal of amusement, and seems to do them no harm; but it is very soon reduced to a bare pole. Plantain is very good winter food for them, and they enjoy picking it from the stalk. Their food should have plenty of variety, to keep them in health and good humor. They must not have sugar or sweet cakes, but plain biscuits—cracknels for instance—are good for them. Their staple food should be canary and bird turnip (the small, brown summer rape) seed, a small quantity of hemp-seed each day, and occasionally, in cold weather, a pinch of maw, or poppy-seed, always to be given while the birds are moulting. When they are building they must have a mixture of hard-boiled egg and finely-crumbled stale bread, with a pinch of the same seed mixed with it every morning. It must always be made and given freshly, or it will turn sour and kill the birds. This food may be dispensed with while the hen is sitting; but as soon as she is about to hatch, it must be put in the cage for the young to feed upon.

Canaries ought to have green food three or four times a week, chickweed, groundsel, or lettuce. It is better for them to have a little constantly than a great quantity now and then, when they are apt to eat over-eagerly of it. They should have some whole oatmeal or grits every day; sometimes a little piece of bread soaked in milk, not boiled, unless it is given as medicine; a little lump of basalt to peck at, or a bit of apple, or pear, or potato, or rice pudding. All these tit-bits are, of course, to be considered as delicacies, to be given by the birds' owner, and they will help very much to win their affection.

They require warmth and nourishing food during moulting; if they seem weak, a rusty nail in the water gives them a little tonic, and a small piece of Spanish licorice is good for hoarseness. By way of physic, we have rarely found any of the many nostrums recommended as specifics of much use, excepting boiled milk. If they have been eating too freely of green food, a lump of chalk may be useful. Some bird-fanciers give ants' eggs and a spider occasionally, and it is likely that this animal food would be good for them now and then. Most birds are, to a certain extent, insectivorous in their wild state. Variety in their food is necessary for all birds; and if they have this, and the seed is good and sound, and they are not exposed to draughts or sudden changes of temperature, they will rarely have anything amiss with them which a warm bath will not cure. Whenever birds look moping, or when the hen is "egg-bound," and cannot lay her eggs, we give them a bath at $96\,^{\circ}$, holding the bird in hand while immersing all but the head in the water for three or four minutes, then taking it out and drying the feet, put it in the sunshine, or at a little distance from the fire to get dry. Sometimes, if a bird is not fond of bathing, the feet will get clogged, especially during nesting, when the claws get a bit of hair or cotton twisted around them occasionally, and the feet should be cleansed in warm water, and gently freed from their troublesome encumbrance.

An old bird's claws will sometimes grow too long, so that it cannot perch comfortably, and they must be very carefully cut, taking care not to draw blood, or to injure the bird in any way. Whenever possible, it is best to avoid catching the bird, especially if they are wild and fly about in alarm; but if taught to consider their owner as their friend, they will gradually submit; without much fluttering, to be taken hold of; and illness generally tames them sufficiently to make them quiet when they require to be taken out of the cage to be put into a bath.

Early in the spring, when the cock birds begin to fight, the hens should be taken away, and kept apart in another cage till the pairs are put together in March. Some people allow their birds to choose their own mates; but a great deal of quarrelling takes place before this, and two or three gentlemen will sometimes fix their affections on the same lady, and they will

get injured in the combats that ensue; besides which, if it be an object to secure good colored birds, it is necessary to put those together whose colors contrast well: a mealy cock with a jonque hen, or a green bird with a yellow partner. Handsomer birds are obtained by these selections than when two birds of the same color are paired; and two crested birds should never be put together, the young will probably be bald-headed. It is best to give an old wife to a young cock, and *vice versa*; and the birds of a family should never be mated together; the progeny will infallibly be weak and unhealthy if this is permitted. Two of our birds were accidentally paired, a brother and sister, and the result was that one of their children was blind and another deformed. For these reasons it is best not to leave the birds to choose for themselves, but to separate them before any attachment springs up between them. Cages sold as "breeding cages" have a wooden compartment at the top of one end for nest-boxes, and a wired-off partition underneath, into which the young birds may be put when it is desirable to separate them from their parents. There are some advantages in these cages, and the birds which are shy and like retirement prefer them to the open cages; the only objection to them is that they are inconveniently small when a large family is hatched, and that the nest-boxes are necessarily so high that the young birds sometimes fall, when they come out of the nest before they are fully fledged, and are injured thus. On this account we put nest-baskets into our cages, at a little distance from the floor, so that the young birds hop in and out easily; and if the old birds should entangle their feet in the nest (which they sometimes do if the claws are long and they fly out in a hurry), and the young birds are thrown out of it, they are not likely to be so much hurt as if they fell from the greater height. Breeding cages have compartments for the separate pairs, three in each, the centre space being kept for the young birds of each family, that they may be fed through the wires by the old birds, when they have left the nest, but cannot feed themselves. This space is necessary, too, to prevent quarrels, as the birds on each side of the wire partition will sometimes try to fight, and make furious assaults on their neighbors through the bars, or jealousies will arise to

16

break their domestic peace, if, while the hen is sitting, her husband chooses to feed his neighbor's wife through the wires.
The pairs should be kept as retired and out of sight of each
other as possible. The materials for the nest should be hung
up in the cage in a little net; fine moss and cow-hair are best;
if cotton wadding is given it is apt to get matted and clogged
round the bird's claws. The hen will generally make the nest
herself; but some birds are idle about it, and do not take the
trouble to do more than to put a little moss or wool into the
basket, and then it is as well to make a nest for her; but it
is not at all certain that she will allow it to remain in the basket. Some birds seem to prefer sitting on their eggs without
a nest, or are very capricious about its formation, and will
undo one day the work of the previous day. It is as well to
leave them to their own devices till the young are hatched, and
then they may have a little moss or cow-hair put in under
them to make their bed softer. The hen generally lays four or
five eggs, and sits thirteen or fourteen days, unless she or her
mate have a bad habit of eating the eggs. They should be left
in the nest, and not touched or interfered with at all, until a
fortnight has elapsed after the laying of the last egg; then, if
there are no signs of hatching, the eggs may be put into warm
water; if they float the probability is that they are addled, and
no young bird in the egg; if they sink, they may be replaced
for a day or two, but if not hatched then, they should be taken
away, or the hen will go on sitting uselessly (on dead birds
probably). Sometimes a violent jar, caused by the shutting of
a door near the cage, or the fall of the cage itself, will kill the
birds in the eggs, or the mother bird will cause their death by
allowing the eggs to get cold, if sitting irregularly. The egg
food must be provided in readiness for the hatching; and it is
necessary to watch the birds' proceedings at first, lest they
should not feed the young ones; but very few canaries are unnatural enough to leave them unfed, although they do not like
to be overlooked, and, if they are shy birds, will refuse to feed
their little ones when they are in sight, so that one has to
watch them without appearing to do so. If they feed them
once they will continue to do so; if not, it will be needful to
bring them up by hand, giving them the soft egg food with a

quill, as with the nestlings before mentioned. A fresh nest must be given if the first nest becomes dirty, and the young birds carefully transferred to it with no more touching than is necessary. Some parent birds will resent any interference with their young, and will desert if they are meddled with; others will appear pleased at any notice bestowed on them, and will call our attention to their children with great exultation, chirping and flying up to the nest, looking in, and then looking up in our faces as if to say, "Pray admire my lovely infants."

If our birds are as familiar with us as they ought to be, they will exhibit their confidence in our sympathy and make their wants known to us in a very pleasant and expressive manner: if they want fresh food or water they will go down to the glasses and look into them, and then look up at us and chirp; or if anything is amiss with their nestlings, they will attract our attention to the nest by signals that cannot be mistaken. One bird who wanted materials for her nest went about the cage picking up stalks, and another pulled the hair of any human head that came within her reach, to show what she wanted.

The young birds will generally be out of the nest in about a fortnight during the day, returning to it at night for warmth. The mother bird will often begin to lay again about this time, and must have a fresh nest given her; and the young ones should be put into the nursery partition, so as to be fed through the wires (or in a small cage tied on to the larger one). They are apt to tease their mother, or to break the eggs, by jumping in and out of the nest while she is sitting. We have sometimes seen three or four little heads peeping out under her wings at once, and occasionally they will sit upon her, which in hot weather is almost too much to endure. The cock bird will feed them while she is sitting, and show them how to feed themselves. They must have a supply of egg food, crushed seed, and water in their compartment, and by degrees they will become independent of their parents. The first moulting tries the young birds' strength much, and till it is over they must have the same kind of food—egg food and crushed hemp-seed, in addition to their usual provisions. The hen should not be allowed to have more than two broods in the year, for her health's sake. If she goes on laying or sitting, the nest should be taken away from her; and if that hint is not sufficient, she must be seperated from the cock till she begins to moult. The young birds should be within hearing of a good songster till after their moulting is over, when they will begin to warble feebly. If a nightingale or woodlark were to be had as music master, they would learn his notes; but we do not advise any one to keep these birds in confinement; they are not fitted for it by temperament or constitution, and their song is much more glad and sweet in their native woods. We had one canary who had learned several nightingale notes, and used to repeat the "jug, jug," continually; he would not sing in company with others, but taught the young birds very well from a little distance. They will often learn best when their singing-master is out of sight.

Cross-breeding has changed the canary of the present day from the original wild green bird of Teneriffe and the Canary Isles, and the varieties of shape and plumage are endless. There are canary societies and bird-shows now, and prizes are given for birds which excel in beauty or song. They are arranged in different divisions, and connoisseurs talk knowingly of "jonques," "spangles," "mealy birds," "flaxen," "grey," "cinnamon," and "agate-colored" canaries, all of which have their distinguishing merits. Then there is the German canary, a small, compact, smooth bird, with a sweet but not very powerful voice; and the Belgian, its opposite in every respect, very long and slender, with exceedingly high shoulders and long legs, standing so uprightly on its perch as to give one the idea that it would fall backwards. The Norwich, or London fancy, prize canary, is a large square bird, with a massive head, deep orange in plumage all over the body, excepting the wings and tail, which should be black. This, at least, used to be the prize bird, but every season has its fashion in birds as well as in dress. To our mind it is the most beautiful of all the canaries when perfect, but it is very difficult to get one without white or green feathers, or irregularly marked; and a perfect bird will become imperfect after its first two moults. This is the case also with the lizard canary, which should be of a greenish bronze throughout, excepting the crown of the head, which is yellow in the gold-spangled, and white in the silver-spangled lizard. The markings or spangles on the back are very uniform and regular, and there ought to be no yellow or white feathers in the wings or tail: but these generally come when the bird is two years old.

Virginian Nightingale.—The cardinal grosbeak, or Virginian nightingale, is a very beautiful red bird, with glossy black feathers about the head and neck. It is about eight inches long, of which the tail measures three. The song is varied and constant, and continues all through the year, except while it is moulting. The hen, which is of a reddish-brown color, is said to sing nearly as well as the cock; and perhaps that is the reason why these birds are better apart—the cock is jealous of his mate's rivalry of voice. Bird dealers have so often pronounced an unfavorable opinion of the cardinal grosbeak as regards its capabilities as a domestic pet, that we were surprised to hear of one which was so exceedingly tame that he would carry his favorite tit-bits to his mistress, and try to make her eat crushed hemp and caterpillars ! The bird is naturally very nervous and sensitive, so that it would fret and chafe in a shop surrounded by other birds, and its wild fluttering would give the idea that it could never be tamed; but patient kindness and gentleness will make it most attractive 'and pleasant pet. It should be fed chiefly on canary-seed, but should have a few hemp-seeds every day, and four or five meal-worms, or spiders, grubs, or caterpillars—some animal food, in short, to keep it well and vigorous. Spanish nuts, almonds, walnuts, and Indian corn, may be given as a treat; and a lump of basalt and a little piece of chalk should be put in the cage, and the bird should always be allowed a bath, and should be kept out of draughts. We give the directions which have been given to us by a lady whose Virginian nightingale has flourished under her judicious care many years.

Parrots.—An article on domestic pets seems scarcely complete without some notice of parrots and parakeets; but there are so many varieties of this tribe of bird, and they come from so many parts of the world, that they require a book to themselves. We can only make a few suggestions for their treatment generally. Those which are natives of tropical climates require warmth and abundance of farinaceous food and

fruit. Bread and milk should be the staple prison diet of parrots (the bread should be soaked first in boiling water, squeezed
as dry as possible, and then allowed to absorb as much fresh
boiled milk as it will hold), adding Indian corn, biscuits, nuts,
almonds (not bitter almonds), fruit (hard and soft), peach and
plum kernels, cherries, grapes, pears, &c., grain and seeds for
the larger birds; and the smaller kinds should have hemp,
canary, and millet seeds, with fruit. All should have water for
drinking and bathing within reach; and if the birds will not go
into water, it is well to sprinkle a little warm water on them
occasionally, and put them into the sunshine that they may
plume themselves and clean their feathers. Great cleanliness
is necessary to keep parrots in health, and their feet must be
frequently washed if they get dirty and they will not bathe
themselves. They are subject to diseased feet, and their
perches should be covered with flannel, and the bottom of
the cage should have a grating with a drawer underneath it
always covered with sand. Lettuce or water-cress is given
to these birds occasionally; and it is said that a chili-pod given
from time to time is useful—when they are moulting they may
have one or two cut up small once a week. If they have an
attack of asthma they should have a few grains of cayenne
pepper mixed with their bread and milk. Meat, sugar, and
sweetmeats, are all unwholesome for parrots.

Doves.—Doves are pretty, gentle, quiet birds, and easily
tamed. The stock dove, ring dove, turtle dove, and collared
turtle, are all kept in confinement, but they should all
have a great deal of air. If kept in a wicker cage, it should be
carried indoors at night (for, being natives of hot countries,
they do not bear cold well), and taken out of doors early in the
morning. The German peasants keep doves constantly in their
cottages, from a fancy that they cure colds and rheumatism by
taking the complaints themselves; and we believe it is true that
doves are subject to the diseases which people shut up in the
same room with them have, such as small-pox, swollen legs,
and tumors in the feet; but this is probably due to the close,
unwholesome condition and bad air of the room, which affects
birds and human beings alike. They are best kept in a con-
servatory or aviary, unless they are tame enough to fly in and

out of the house, and return to their cages at night or when they
want food, in which case they may be allowed their liberty.
They must have plenty of fine, dry gravel and conveniences
for bathing, and their food should be barley, wheat, peas,
vetches, hemp, and canary seed.   They like variety in it, and
are fond of bread dry or soaked, the seeds of pines and firs,
and linseed and myrtle berries.   They ought to have bay salt
mixed with old mortar or gravel.   The salt is good for their
throats, which often become diseased.   Doves generally have
two broods in the year, two young ones at a time, which they
feed from their crops.   We have been told that they are often
unnatural enough to neglect this duty; but we do not think
this is generally the case.   The young are so dependent upon
their parents, that they could hardly be reared by hand.   They
are not very interesting birds, but have great beauty of plumage,
and no disagreeable characteristics to detract from their merits
as domestic pets.

TYPICAL PLYMOUTH ROCKS.

POULTRY.

Choice varieties of fowls add a pleasant feature to the farm premises. They engage the attention and sympathy of the juvenile farmers, and the time bestowed to the poultry yard keeps them from mischief, is an agreeable and salutary relief for toil and study, and elicits the taste, the judgment, and the kindlier feelings of humanity, which are to be matured in the future accomplished breeder. When properly managed, poultry are a source of considerable profit, yielding more for the food they consume than any other stock, although their value is not often considered. The agricultural statistics of the United States, for 1839—forty-four years ago—gave its value at over $12,000,000, and the current value of the poultry in the United States is now probably thirty millions of dollars, and its annual product in eggs and flesh is much greater. It is estimated by McQueen that the poultry of England exceeds $40,000,000, and yet McCulloch says she imports 60,000,000 eggs annually from France (McQueen states it at near 70,000,000), and from other parts of the continent, 25,000,000; besides 80,000,000 imported from Ireland. The people of the United States are much larger egg and poultry consumers than the English, and thus they are a considerable object of agricultural attention, and assume an important place among the other staples of the farmer. The following are the principal breeds:

The Bantam.—The original of the Bantam is the Bankiva fowl. The small white, and also the colored Bantams, whose legs are heavily feathered, are sufficiently well-known to render a particular description unnecessary. Bantam-fanciers generally prefer those which have clean, bright legs, without any vestige of feathers. A thoroughbred cock, in their judgment, should have a rose comb; a well feathered tail, but without the sickle feathers; a proud, lively carriage; and ought not to exceed a pound in weight. The nankeen-colored and the black are general favorites.

These little creatures exhibit some peculiar habits and traits of disposition. Amongst others, the cocks are so fond of sucking the eggs laid by the hen that they will often drive her from the nest in order to 'obtain them; they have even been known to attack her, tear open the ovarium, and devour its shell-less contents. To prevent this, first a hard-boiled, and then a marble egg, may be given them to fight with, taking care, at the same time, to prevent their access either to the hen or to any real eggs. Another strange propensity is a passion for sucking each other's blood, which is chiefly exhibited when they are moulting, when they have been known to peck each other naked, by pulling out the new feathers as they appear, and squeezing with their beaks the blood from the bulbs at the base. These fowls being subject to a great heat of the skin, its surface occasionally becomes hard and tightened; in which cases the hard roots of the feathers are drawn into a position more nearly at right-angles with the body than at ordinary times, and the skin and superficial muscles are thus subjected to an unusual degree of painful irritation. The disagreeable habit is, therefore, simply a provision of nature for their relief, which may be successfully accomplished by washing with warm water, and the subsequent application of pomatum to the skin.

The Bolton Gray.—These fowls—called, also, Dutch Every-day Layers, Pencilled Dutch fowl, Chittaprats, and, in Pennsylvania, Creole fowl—were originally imported from Holland to Bolton, a town in Lancashire, England, whence they were named.

They are small sized, short in the leg and plump in the make; color of the genuine kind, invariably pure white in the whole cappel of the neck; the body white, thickly spotted with black, sometimes running into a grizzle, with one or more black bars at the extremity of the tail. A good cock of this breed may weigh from four to four and a half pounds; and a hen from three to three and a half pounds.

The superiority of a hen of this breed does not consist so much in rapid as in continued laying. She may not produce as many eggs in a month as some other kinds, but she will, it is claimed, lay more months in the year than, probably, any other variety. They are said to be very hardy; but their eggs, in the judgment of some, are rather watery and innutritious.

The Cochin China.—The Cochin China fowl are said to have been presented to Queen Victoria from the East Indies. In order to promote their propagation, her majesty made presents of them occasionally to such persons as she supposed likely to appreciate them. They differ very little in their qualities, habits and general appearance from the Shanghaes, to which they are undoubtedly nearly related. The egg is nearly the same size, shape, and color; both have an equal development of comb and wattles—the Cochins slightly differing from the Shanghaes, chiefly in being somewhat fuller and deeper in the breast, not quite so deep in the quarter, and being usually smooth-legged, while the Shanghaes, generally, are more or less heavily feathered. The plumage is much the same in both cases; and the crow in both is equally sonorous and prolonged, differing considerably from that of the Great Malay.

The cock has a large, upright, single, deeply-indented comb, very much resembling that of the Black Spanish, and, when in condition, of quite as brilliant a scarlet; like him, also, he has sometimes a very large white ear-hole on each cheek, which, if not an indispensible or even a required qualification, is, however, to be preferred, for beauty at least. The wattles are large, wide, and pendent. The legs are of a pale flesh-color; some specimens have them yellow, which is objectionable. The feathers on the breast and sides are of a bright chestnut-brown; large and well-defined, giving a scaly or imbricated appearance to those parts. The hackle of the neck is of a light yellowish brown; the lower feathers being tipped with dark brown, so as to give a spotted appearance to the neck. The tail-feathers are black, and darkly iridescent; back, scarlet-orange; back-hackle, yellow-orange. It is, in short, altogether a flame-colored bird. Both sexes are lower in the leg than either the Black Spanish or the Malay.

The hen approaches in her build more nearly to the Dorking than to any other breed, except that the tail is very small
and proportionately depressed; it is smaller and more horizontal than in any other fowl. Her comb is of moderate size,
almost small; she has, also, a small, white ear-hole. Her coloring is flat, being composed of various shades of very light
brown, with light yellow on the neck. Her appearance is
quiet, and only attracts attention by its extreme neatness,
cleanliness and compactness.

The eggs average about two ounces each. They are smooth,
of an oval shape, equally rounded at both ends, and of a rich
buff color, nearly resembling those of the Silver Pheasant. The
newly-hatched chickens appear very large in proportion to the
size of the egg. They have light, flesh-colored bills, feet, and
legs, and are thickly covered with down, of the hue commonly
called "carroty." They are not less thrifty than any other
chickens, and feather somewhat more uniformly than either
the Black Spanish or the Malay. It is, however, most desirable to hatch these—as other large-growing varieties—as early
in the spring as possible even so soon as the end of February.
A peculiarity in the cockerels is that they do not show even
the rudiments of their tail-feathers till they are nearly full-
grown. They increase so rapidly in other directions that
there is no material to spare for the production of these dec-
ora.ive appendages.

The merits of this breed are such that it may safely be
recommended to people residing in the country. For the inhabitants of towns it is less desirable as the light tone of its
plumage would show every mark of dirt and defilement; and
the readiness with which they sit would be an inconvenience,
rather than otherwise, in families with whom perpetual layers
are most in requisition. Expense apart, they are equal or
superior to any other fowl for the table; their flesh is delicate,
white, tender, and well-flavored.

The Cuckoo—The fowl so termed in Norfolk, England is,
very probably, an old and distinct variety; although they are
generally regarded as mere barn-door fowls—that is, the
merely accidental result of promiscuous crossing.

The name probably originated from its barred plumage,

which resembles that on the breast of the Cuckoo. The prevailing color is a slaty blue, undulated, and softly shaded with white all over the body, forming bands of various widths. The comb is very small; irides, bright orange; feet and legs, light flesh color. The hens are of good size; the cocks are large, approaching the heaviest breeds in weight. The chickens, at two or three months old, exhibit the barred plumage even more perfectly than the full-grown birds. The eggs average about two ounces each, are white, and of porcelain smoothness. The newly-hatched chickens are gray, much resembling those of the Silver Polands except in the color of the feet and legs.

This breed supplies an unfailing troop of good layers, good sitters, good mothers and good feeders; and is well worth promotion in the poultry-yard.

The Dominique.—This seems to be a tolerably distinct and permanent variety, about the size of the common dunghill fowl. Their combs are generally double—or rose, as it is sometimes called—and the wattles small. Their plumage presents, all over, a sort of greenish appearance, from a peculiar arrangement of blue and white feathers, which is the chief characteristic of the variety; although, in some specimens, the plumage is invariably gray in both cock and hen. They are very hardy, healthy, excellent layers, and capital incubators. No fowl have better stood the tests of mixing without deteriorating than the pure Dominique.

Their name is taken from the island of Dominica, from which they are reported to have been imported. Take all in all, they are one of the very best breeds of fowl which we have; and, although they do not come in to laying so young as the Spanish, they are far better sitters and nurses.

The Dorking.—This has been termed the Capon Fowl of England. It forms the chief supply for the London market, and is distinguished by a white or flesh-colored smooth leg, armed with five, instead of four toes, on each foot. Its flesh is extremely delicate, especially after caponization; and it has the advantage over some other fowls of feeding rapidly, and growing to a very respectable size when properly managed.

For those who wish to stock their poultry yards with fowls

of the most desirable shape and size, clothea in rich and vari‐
gated plumage, and, ⌐ t expecting perfection, are willing to
overlook one or two (⸍ r points, the Speckled Dorkings—so
called from the ⸜⸜. of Surrey, England, which brought them
into modern repute—should selected. The hens, in addi‐
tion to the gay colors, h⸗ve l⸗rge, vertically flat comb, which,
when they are in h⸗gh ⸝ ⸝⸝, adds very much to their brilliant
appearance, particularl⸝ ⸝⸝ seen in bright sunshine. The cocks
are magnificent. ⸝he ⸝ost gorg⸝ ⸝⸝ hues are lavished upon
them, which their ⸝⸝eat size and peculiarly square-built form
display to the great⸝⸝ advantage. Their legs are short; their
breast broad; there ⸝⸝ ⸝ut a small proportion of offal; and the
good, profitable flesh ⸝⸝ abundant. The ⸝⸝⸝⸝s may be brought
to considerable weight, and the flavor and appearance of their
meat are inferior to none. The ⸝ggs are produced in reason‐
able abundance; and, though not equal in size to those of
Spanish hens, may fairly be called large.

They are not everlasting layers, but at due or convenient
intervals manifest the desire of sitting. In this respect, they are
steady and good mothers when the little ⸝n⸝s appear.

With all these merits, however, they are not found to be a
profitable breed, if kept thoroughbred an u⸝mixed. Their
powers seem to fail at an early age. They are al apt to pine
away and die just at the point of r⸝⸝chin⸝ m⸝tu⸝ity. They
appear at a certain ep⸝⸝h t⸝ be seized with con⸝u⸝ption—in
the Speckled Dorkin⸝s, th⸝⸝ lung⸝ seem to b⸝ the seat of the
disease. The White Dorkings are how⸝ver hard⸝ and active
birds, and are not su⸝⸝ject to c⸝ns⸝umption or any other disease.

As mothers, an objection to the ⸝⸝⸝rkings is that they are
too heavy and clumsy to rear the chickens o⸝ any smaller and
more delicate bird than themselves.

In spite of these drawbacks the Dorkings are still in high
favor; but a cross is found to be more profitable than the true
breed. A glossy, energetic game-cock, with Dorking hens,
produces chickens in size and beauty little ⸝⸝erior to their
maternal parentage, and much more ro⸝ust. The supernu‐
merary toe on each foot almost always disap⸝ears with the first
cross; but it is a point which can very ⸝ell be spared without
much disadvantage. In other respects the appearance of the

newly hatched chickens is scarcely altered. The eggs of the Dorkings are large, pure white, very much rounded, and nearly equal in size at each end. The chickens are brownish-yellow, with a broad stripe down the middle of the back, and a narrow one on each side; feet and legs yellow.

THE BLACK DORKING.—The bodies of this variety are of a large size, with the usual proportions of the race, and of a jet black color. The neck-feathers of some of the cocks are tinged with a bright gold color, and those of some of the hens bear a silvery complexion. Their combs are usually double, and very short, though sometimes cupped, rose or single, with wattles small; and they are usually very red about the head. Their tails are rather shorter and broader than most of the race, and they feather rather slowly. Their legs are short and black, with five toes on each foot, the bottom of which is sometimes yellow. The two back toes are very distinct, starting from the foot seperately; and there is frequently a part of an extra toe between the two.

This breed commence laying when very young, and are very thrifty layers during winter. Their eggs are of a large size, and hatch well; they are perfectly hardy, as their color indicates, and for the product are considered among the most valuable of the Dorking breed.

The Game Fowl.—It is probable that these fowl, like other choice varieties, are natives of India. It is certain that in that country an original race of some fowl exists, at the present day, bearing in full perfection all the peculiar characteristics of the species. In India, as is well known, the natives are infected with a passion for cock-fighting. These fowls are carefully bred for this barbarous amusement, and the finest birds become articles of great value.

The game fowl is one of the most gracefully formed and beautifully colored of any of our domestic breeds of poultry; and in its form, aspect, and that extraordinary courage which characterizes its natural disposition, exhibits all that either the naturalist or the sportsman would at once recognize as the purest type of high blood, embodying, in short, all the most indubitable characteristics of gallinaceous aristocracy.

The flesh is beautifully white, as well as tender and delicate.

The hens are excellent layers, and, although the eggs are under the average size, they are not to be surpassed in excellence of flavor. Such being the character of this variety of fowl, it would doubtless be much more extensively cultivated than it is, were it not for the difficulty attending the rearing of the young; their pugnacity being such that a brood is scarcely feathered before at least one-half are killed or blinded by fighting.

With proper care, however, most of the difficulties to be apprehended may be avoided. It is exceedingly desirable to perpetuate the race, for uses the most important and valuable. As a cross with other breeds, they are invaluable in improving the flavor of the flesh, which is an invariable consequence. The plumage of all fowl related to them is increased in brilliancy; and they are, moreover, very prolific, and eggs are always enriched.

THE WILD INDIAN GAME.—This variety was originally imported into this country from Calcutta. The hen has a long neck, like a wild goose; neither comb nor wattles; of a dark, glossy green color; very short or fan tail; lofty in carriage, trim built, and wild in general appearance; legs very large and long, spotted with blue; ordinary weight from four and a half to six pounds. As a layer, she is equal to any other fowls of the game variety.

The cock stands as high as a large turkey, and weighs nine pounds and upward; the plumage is of a reddish cast, interspersed with spots of glossy green; comb very small; no wattles; and bill unlike any other foul, except the hen.

THE SPANISH GAME.—This variety is called the English fowl by some writers. It is more slender in the body, the neck, the bill, and the legs, than the other varieties, and the colors, particularly of the cock, are very bright and showy. The flesh is white, tender and delicate, and on this account marketable; the eggs are small and extremely delicate. . The plumage is very beautiful—a clear, dark red, very bright, extending from the back to the extremities, while the breast is beautifully black. The upper convex side of the wing is equally red and black, and the whole of the tail-feathers white. The beak and legs are black; the eyes resemble jet beads, very full and brilliant; and the whole contour of the head gives a most ferocious expression.

The Spangled Hamburgh.—The Spangled Hamburgh fowl are divided into two varieties, the distinctive characteristics being slight, almost dependent upon color; these varieties are termed the Gold and Silver Spangled.

The Golden Spangled is one of no ordinary beauty; it is well and very neatly made, has a good body, and no very great offal. On the crest, immediately above the beak, are two small, fleshy horns, resembling, to some extent, an abortive comb. Above the crest, and occupying the place of a comb, is a very large brown or yellow tuft, the feathers composing it darkening toward their extremities. Under the insertion of the lower mandible—or that portion of the neck corresponding to the chin in man—is a full, dark-colored tuft, somewhat resembling a beard. The wattles are very small; the comb, as in other high crested fowls, is very diminutive; the skin and flesh white. The hackles on the neck are of a brilliant orange, or golden yellow; and the general ground color of the body is of the same hue, but somewhat darker. The thighs are of a dark brown or blackish shade, and the legs and feet are of a bluish gray.

In the Silver Spangled variety, the only perceptible difference is that the ground color is a silvery white. The extremity and a portion of the extreme margin of each feather are black, presenting, when in a state of rest, the appearance of regular semicircular marks, or spangles — and hence the name, "Spangled Hamburgh;" the varieties being termed gold or silver, according to the prevailing color being bright yellow or silvery white.

The eggs are of moderate size, but abundant; chickens easily reared. In mere excellence of flesh and as layers, they are inferior to the Dorking or Spanish. They weigh from four and a half to five and a half pounds for the male, and three and a half for the female. The former stands some twenty inches in height, and the latter about eighteen inches.

The Malay.—This majestic bird is found on the peninsula from which it derives its name, and, in the opinion of many, forms a connecting link between the wild and domesticated

17

races of fowls. Something very like them is, indeed, still to be found in the East. This native Indian bird—the Gigantic Cock, the Kulm Cock of Europeans—often stands considerably more than two feet from the crown of the head to the ground. The comb extends backward in a line with the eyes; it is thick, a little elevated, rounded upon the top, and has almost the appearance of having been cut off. The wattles of the under mandible are comparatively small, and the throat is bare. Pale, golden-reddish hackles ornament the head, neck, and upper part of the back, and some of these spring before the bare part of the throat. The middle of the back and smaller wing-coverts are deep chestnut, the webs of the feathers disunited; pale reddish-yellow, long, drooping hackles cover the rump and base of the tail, which last is very ample, and entirely of a glossy green, of which color are the wing-coverts; the s condaries and quills are pale reddish-yellow on the outer webs. All the under parts are deep glossy blackish-green, with big reflections; the deep chestnut of the base of the feathers appears occasionally, and gives a mottled and interrupted appearance to those parts.

The weight of the Malay in general, exceeds that of the Cochin-China; the male weighing, when full-grown, from eleven to twelve, and even thirteen pounds, and the female from eight to ten pounds; height, from twenty-six to twenty-eight inches. They present no striking uniformity of plumage, being of all shades, from black to white; the more common color of the female is a light reddish-yellow, with sometimes a faint tinge of dunnish-blue, especially in the tail.

The cock is frequently of a yellowish-red color, with black intermingled in the breast, thighs and tail. H. has a small, but thick comb, generally inclined to one side i : sho. d be snake-headed, and free from the slightest tr. : f top-kno '; the wattles should be extremely small, even in ·. (bird; the legs are not feathered, as in the case of the Changhaes, but, like them and the Cochin-Chinas, his tail is small compared with his size. In the female there is scarcely any show of comb or wattles. Their legs are long and stout; their flesh is very well flavored. when they have been properly fattened; and their eggs are so large and rich that two of them are equal to three of those of our ordinary fowls,

The Malay cock, in his perfection, is a remarkable courage-ous and strong bird. His beak is very thick, and he is a for-midable antagonist when offended. His crow is loud, harsh and prolonged, as in the case of the Cochin-China, but broken off abruptly at the termination; this is quite characteristic of the bird.

The chickens are at first very strong, with yellow legs, and are thickly covered with light brown down; but, by the time they are one-third grown, the increase of their bodies has so far outstripped that of their feathers, that they are half naked about their back and shoulders, and extremely susceptible of cold and wet. The great secret of rearing them is to have them hatched very early indeed, so that they may have safely passed through this period of unclothed adolescence during the dry and sunny part of May and June, and reached nearly their full stature before the midsummer rains descend.

The Plymouth Rock.—This name has been given to a very good breed of fowls, produced by crossing a China cock with a hen, a cross between the fawn-colored Dorking, the Great Malay, and the Wild Indian.

At a little over a year old, the cocks stand from thirty-two to thirty-five inches high, and weigh about ten pounds; and the pullets from six and a half to seven pounds each. The latter commence laying when five months old, and prove themselves very superior layers. Their eggs are of a medium size, rich, and reddish-yellow in color. Their plumage is rich and varie-gated; the cocks usually red and speckled, and the pullets dark-ish brown. The have very fine flesh, and are fit for the table at an early age. The legs are very large, and usually blue or green, but occasionally yellow or white, generally having five toes upon each foot. Some have their legs feathered, but this is not usual. They have large and single combs and wattles, large cheeks, rather short tails, and small wings in proportion to their bodies.

They are domestic and not so destructive to gardens as smaller fowls. There is the same uniformity in size and gene-ral appearance, at the same age of the chickens, as in those of the pure bloods of primary races.

The Poland.—The Poland, or Polish fowl, is quite unknown in the country which would seem to have suggested the name, which originated from some fancied resemblance between its tufted crest and the square-spreading crown of the feathered caps worn by the Polish soldiers.

The Polish are chiefly suited for keeping in a small way, and in a clean and grassy place. They are certainly not so fit for the farm-yard, as they become blinded and miserable with dirt. Care should be exercised to procure them genuine, since there is no breed of fowls more disfigured by mongrelism than this. They will, without any cross-breeding, occasionally produce white stock that are very pretty, and equally good for laying. If, however, an attempt is made to establish a separate breed of them, they become puny and weak. It is, therefore, better for those who wish for them to depend upon chance; every brood almost of the black produces one white chicken, as strong and as lively as the rest.

These fowls are excellent for the table, the flesh being white, tender and juicy; but they are quite unsuitable for being reared in any numbers, or for general purposes, since they are so capricious in their growth, frequently remaining stationary in this respect for a whole month, getting no larger; and this, too, when they are about a quarter or half grown—the time of their life when they are most liable to disease. As aviary birds, they are unrivalled among fowls. Their plumage often requires a close inspection to appreciate its elaborate beauty; the confinement and fretting seem not uncongenial to their health; and their plumage improves in attractiveness with almost every month.

The great merit, however, of all the Polish fowls is that for three or four years they continue to grow and gain in size, hardiness and beauty—the male birds especially. This fact certainly points out a very wide deviation in constitution from these fowls which attain their full stature and perfect plumage in twelve or fifteen months. The similarity of coloring in the two sexes—almost a specific distinction of Polish and, perhaps, Spanish fowls—also separates them from those breeds, like the Game, in which the cocks and hens are remarkably dissimilar. Their edible qualities are as superior, compared with other fowls, as their outward apparel surpasses in elegance. They

have also the reputation of being everlasting layers, which
further fits them for keeping in small enclosures; but, in this
respect, individual exceptions are often encountered—as in the
case of the Hamburghs—however truly the habit may be
ascribed to the race.

There are four known varieties of the Polish fowl, one of
which appears to be lost to this country.

The Silver Pheasant.—This variety of fowls is remarkable
for great brilliancy of plumage and diversity   lors. On a
white ground, which is usually termed silvery, there is an
abundance of black spots. The feathers on the upper part of
the head are much longer than the rest,   d unite together in
a tuft. They have a small, d uble comb, and the wattles are
also comparatively small. A remarkable peculiarity of the cock
is that there is a spot of blue color on the cheeks, and a range
of feathers under the throat, which has the appearance of a
collar.

The hen is a smaller bird, with plumage similar to that of
the cock, and at a little distance seems to be covered with
scales. On the head is a topknot of very large size, which
droops over it on every side. The Silver Pheasants are beautiful and showy birds, and chiefly valuable as ornamental
appendages to the poultry yard.

The Spanish.—This name is said to be a misnomer, as the
breed in question was originally brought by the Spaniards from
the West Indies; and, although subsequently propagated in
Spain, it has for some time been very difficult to procure good
specimens from that country. From Spain, they were taken in
considerable numbers into Holland, where they have been carefully bred for many years; and it is from that quarter that our
best fowls of this variety come.

The Spanish is a noble race of fowls, possessing many merits; of spirited and animated appearance; of considerable size;
excellent for the table, both in whiteness of flesh and skin, and
also in flavor; and laying exceedingly large eggs in considerable numbers. Among birds of its own breed it is not deficient in courage; though it yields, without showing much fight,
to those which have a dash of game blood in their veins. It is
a general favorite in all large cities, for the additional advan-

tage that no soil of smoke or dirt is apparent on its plumage.

The thoroughbred birds should be entirely black, as far as feathers are concerned; and, when in high condition, display a greenish, metallic lustre. The combs of both cock and hen are exceedingly large, of a vivid and most brilliant scarlet; that of the hen droops over upon one side. Their most singular feature is a large, white patch, or ear-hole, on the cheek—in some specimens extending over a great part of the face—of a fleshy substance, similar to the wattle; it is small in the female, but large and very conspicuous in the male. This marked contrast of black, bright red, and white, makes the breed of the Spanish cock as handsome as that of any variety which we have; in the genuine breed the whole form is equally good.

Spanish hens are celebrated as good layers, and produce very large, quite white eggs, of a peculiar shape, being very thick at both ends, and yet tapering off a little at each. They are, by no means, good mothers of families, even when they do sit—which they will not often condescend to do—proving very careless, and frequently trampling half their brood under foot. The inconveniences of this habit are, however, easily obviated by causing the eggs to be hatched by some more motherly hen.

Fowls for Layers.—The layers must be of a breed that affords chickens easily reared, for success in the nursery department is all-important; they must be at the head of the list of prolific layers of fair-sized eggs. None but a non-sitting race will answer, for sitters make fully double the labor during half of the year; and the feathers must be light, because dark ones show badly when chickens are dressed. There is at present no breed that fulfills all these conditions so well as the White Leghorn. It may degenerate in time, as other races of fowls have done, by being bred for fancy instead of utility, but it possesses now more vigor than any other non-sitting breed. In breeding poultry, show and utility do not get on well together in the long run. To fanciers unquestionably belongs the credit of originating improved breeds, but afterwards, in fixing conventional points for the show-room, the stock is often ruined on our hands. To prevent the freezing of their combs and wattles during severe winters, they should be "dubbed" when the birds are two thirds grown. The operation is not so painful as might appear, and, if shears are used, the blood-vessels are pinched, and but little blood will flow.

The layers are relied upon to produce the principal part of the income, and, as they are chief in point of numbers, the detached stations where they are kept from the main part of the establishment, to which the breeding and sitting departments are merely tributary. Most of the layers must be kept only until the age of from fifteen to twenty months, and then killed for sale, and their places supplied by young pullets. This course is necessary, because the yield of eggs is greatest during the first laying season if the hens are of an early-maturing breed, and are fed high, and stimulated to the utmost, as they must be, to secure the highest profit. For though hens are still vigorous at two years, it will be found that after a course of forcing to their greatest capacity through the first season, they cannot be made to lay profusely during the second. If we choose not to put on the full pressure of diet the first year, but to feed moderately high for two or three years, a fair yield of eggs would be afforded during each. But such a course would not pay so well as to keep pullets only, and maintain a forcing system constantly from the time they commence to lay until they stop, and then market them before they eat up the profits in the idleness of fall and winter. Pullets grow fast during the early part of their lives, and give a return in flesh for what they eat then. After they commence laying, their eggs are prompt dividends, and, besides, their bodies increase in weight until the age of a year or more. Young hens may be killed a fortnight after ceasing to lay, and if they have been skillfully fed, their flesh will prove excellent for the table as compared with fowls that are two or three years old. It is no wonder that there is little liking for the adult fowls the markets ordinarily afford, for they comprise many that are very old and unfit for food. But regular customers will soon approve fowls a year old, which have been supplied with the cleanest food, and brought to just the proper fatness, and delivered freshly killed and neatly dressed, and our experience proves that the families upon the egg route will order all that the establishment has to dispose of. The high-pressure mode of feeding and turning off while yet young, is then the true policy. The point is, there is a certain consumption of food to enable an animal to keep alive. The ordinary vital operation, aside from laying or increase of size, demand force, obtained through food—which is money—and we should aim to support only such fowls as are all the while giving returns in either growth or eggs. The long period of moulting and recovering from its consequent exhaustion, costs, as does the maintenance of the vital fires during the cold of winter. It is a matter of quick balancing of profits and expenses with animals, which, like fowls, consume the value of their bodies in about six months. If it is urged that the stimulating diet and unnatural prolificness will subject the stock to disease, the reply is that the regimen is not continued more than six or eight months, and in that time evil effects will not ordinarily follow, for the birds are allowed freedom, sun, and air, and special provision is made for daily exercise. As none of the fowls to which this forcing system is applied leave descendants, no evil effects are accumulated and entailed upon the stock. The layers are from the eggs of fowls that have not been subjected to any such pressure, and during the period of their principal growth they have been given a nutritious but not especially stimulating food—like a colt at pasture. When they arrive at the laying age, they are kept like the horse—broken to work, and put to constant and severe labor, and fed as high as he will bear.

Fowls and Sitters.—The sitters are of a breed chosen for persistence and regularity in incubation, fidelity to their chickens, and gentleness of disposition. The Light Brahmas can not be excelled for hatching and rearing. Pure bloods, however, are not used; but to give less awkwardness and greater spread of wings, they are crossed with snow-white barn-yard fowls. The half-bloods resemble the Brahmas the most in form and other characteristics, and are almost uniformly docile. The half-blood Brahmas are extremely valuable for hatching and taking care of chickens. The results of the labors of poultry fanciers in producing two such breeds as the White Leghorns and Light Brahmas are enough to compensate for all the humbug practiced by many members of the guild. The sitters are not kept at detached stations like the layers, for several reasons. One is, they should all be near together, because of the great amount of attendance necessary in connection with hatching. Then the buildings should be large enough for the keeper to enter, in order to take care of the nests and chickens, but the size of the structure and the risk of jaring eggs will prevent moving. Nor can the system of indirect feeding and no yards be pursued, for the sitters should be fed at the attendant's feet, and tamed so as to submit quietly to the handling they receive while hatching and rearing. Their yards are sufficiently large to admit of exercise, and for the same reason their dry grain is buried in the ground or under straw. In very cold weather they are confined to their houses for warmth, and are given a stimulating diet to promote winter laying, not so much for the value of the eggs as to render it certain that there shall be a considerable number of birds ready to sit in February, and many more in March. The fowls chiefly depended upon for this, consist of the earliest pullets of the previous year, and also the old hens that have been employed much of the time the preceeding summer in hatching two or three broods. The prevention of laying by hatching and rearing, causes birds thus occupied to lay earlier the next season. By a little management there is no difficulty in procuring plenty of offers to sit from February to June. One half the sitting stock are two years old, and of the pullets of the sitting class raised yearly, some are hatched in February and March, and some in the first week of September, the better to secure sitting in various parts of the year. Except in winter, the sitters should not be fed with a view to encourage laying, but the aim should be to keep them on as moderate an allowance as possible, and not have them become poor. Their specific purpose is incubation, and they should be made to do as much of this as possible. By uniting broods, when a hen has hatched one nest full of eggs she may be given another immediately, and, if managed rightly, she will not be injured by sitting a double term. Each hen must hatch two broods per year at least, and some will hatch three. In this way the stock of 500 sitters will produce 10,000 chickens yearly, or an average of 20 apiece.

Management of Breeding Stock.—The proper management

of the breeding stock is a very important part of the scheme, for there must annually be raised a large supply of pullets of the right quality. The profits of the establishment depend largely on the excellence of the fowls, and as they can be multiplied very fast from a chosen few, no pains should be spared to secure the very best as a source from which to stock the whole farm. There is but one way to do this, and that is to keep individual birds in experimental yards in order to test their merits, recording the degree of excellence and the pedigree of the best with as much care as would be given to breeding cows or horses.

We will suppose it is designed to produce a strain of Leghorns that shall excel in prolificness, laying at an early age, and in other requisites. Procure a pullet from A and a cockerel from B, and put them in yard No. 1; purchase from C and D one bird from each, for yard No. 2, and so on, always taking care that no specimens are obtained from any locality where disease has prevailed. The smaller breeding yards are used as experimental yards, and to allow each cock a proper number of mates, two or more half-blood Brahmas pullets (whose eggs can be distinguished by their color) are added. Give each Leghorn a name or number, and enter in a book all details necessary for testing progress in improving the breed, such as weight, the age at which laying commenced, and the yield of eggs during the first year, at the expiration of which banish all but the best hens. The second year set the eggs of the reserved extra fowls, and keep the chickens produced by each pair separate from all others. At the age of five or six months, cull out the most promising pullets and cockerels, and pair them for testing and recording pedigree and prolificness as before. By mating the produce of the original birds from A and B with the produce of those from C and D, finally the four stocks will become blended in one. Proceed in this manner a number of years, and when in the course of time a very extra prolific and vigorous hen has been found, which reached full size and commenced laying early, and whose ancestry have excelled in the same respects for several generations, as shown by the book, then from her eggs cocks are raised from which to breed to replenish the main stock of layers at the itenirant stations.

These cocks are put in the large breeding yards, each with a flock of ten hens, and no further accounts are kept of the prolificness of individuals.

After new stock is introduced to the experimental yards, as must be done yearly, care is taken for a series of years to avoid breeding akin, and as purchases will be made from fanciers, who to fix the conventional points have most likely bred close and impaired strength, crossing will immediately give a decided increase of vigor. Towards the last, however, when sufficient stamina has been gained, and the stations are to be stocked, close breeding is resorted to. This is to increase the yield of eggs.

In the breeding and experimental yards, the fowls must be fed and managed in every respect with the greatest care. Over-fattening is to be deprecated above all other things, and may be avoided by burying all the grain to make the birds exercise by scratching. The supply of grain should be moderate ; meat should be given very often in very small quantities, and the allowance of fresh vegetables should be ample. Free range would be very desirable for all the breeders, but, as it is impracticable, scrupulous care must be taken to furnish artificially natural conditions. Though the birds of the laying class in the experimental yards are rated according to their prolificness, yet the test is merely a relative one, for they are not forced to profuse laying by stimulating food.

Food.—The food of hens may consist of different kinds or grain, either broken, ground or cooked; roots, and, especially, boiled potatoes, are nutritious and economical; green herbage, as clover and many of the grains; chickweed, lettuce, cabbage, etc. will supply them with much of their food, if fresh and tender. Though not absolutely essential to them, yet nothing contributes so much to their laying, as unsalted, animal food. This is a natural aliment, as is shown by the avidity with which they pounce on every fly, insect or earth worm which comes within their reach. It would not, of course, pay to supply them with valuable meat, but the blood and offal of the slaughter houses, refuse meat of all kinds, and, especially, the scraps or crackings to be had at the melter's shops, after soaking for a few hours in warm water, is one of the best and most economi-

cal kinds of food. Such, with boiled-meal, is a very fattening food. Grain is at all times best for them when ground and cooked, as they will lay more, fat quicker, and eat much less when it is fed to them in this state; and it may be thus used unground, with the same advantage to the fowls, as if first crushed, as their digestive organs are certain to extract the whole nutriment. All grain is food for them, including millet, rice, the oleaginous seeds, as the sunflower, flax, hemp, etc. It is always better to afford them a variety of grain, where they can procure them at their option, and select as their appetite craves.

They are also fond of milk, and indeed scarcely any edible escapes their notice. They carefully pick up the most of the waste garbage around the premises, and glean much of their subsistence from what would otherwise become offensive, and by their destruction of innumerable insects and worms, they render great assistance to the gardener. Of course their ever busy propensity for scratching is indiscriminately indulged just after the seeds have been planted and while the plants are young, which renders it necessary that they be confined in some close yard for a time; yet this should be as capacious as possible. Their food, if cooked, is better when given to them warm, not hot; and no more fed at a time than they will pick up clean. Besides their food, hens ought to be at all times abundantly supplied with clean water, egg or pounded oyster shells, old mortar, or slaked lime. If not allowed to run at large where they can help themselves, they must also be furnished with gravel to assist their digestion; and a box or bed of ashes, sand and dust, is equally essential to roll in for the purpose of ridding themselves of vermin.

Hen House.—The hen house may be constructed in various ways to suit the wishes of the owner, and, when tastefully built, it is an ornament to the premises. It should be perfectly dry throughout, properly lighted with glass windows in the roof, if possible, and capable of being made tight and warm in winter, yet afford all the ventilation desirable at any season. In this, arrange the nest in boxes on the sides in such a manner as to humor the instinct of the hen for concealment when she resorts to them. When desirable to set the hen, these nests may be so placed as to shut out the others, yet open into another yard or beyond the enclosure, so that they can take an occasional stroll and help themselves to food, etc. This prevents other hens laying in their nests, while sitting, and may be easily managed, by having their boxes hung on the wall of the building, with a movable door made to open on either side at pleasure. Hens will lay without a nest egg, but, when broken up, they ramble off and form new nests, if they are not confined. They will lay if kept from the cock, but it is doubtful if they will thus yield as many eggs. Hens disposed to sit at improper times, should be dismissed from the common yard, so as to be out of reach of the nests, and plentifully fed till weaned from this inclination.

The Chickens.—The chickens require to be kept warm and dry for the first few days after hatching, and they may be fed with hard boiled eggs, crumbs of bread or pudding, and milk or water, and allowed to scratch in the gravel in front of the hen, which should be confined in a coop for the first three or four weeks, after which they may be turned loose, when they will thrive on anything the older ones eat. Many use them for the table when they are but a few weeks old; but they are much less valuable for this purpose till they have attained to near or quite full maturity. The white legs are preferred by some, from the whiteness and apparent delicacy of the meat; but the yellow and dark-legged are good. The color of the feathers does not seem to affect the quality of the flesh or their character for laying. If we consider the principle of the absorption and retention of heat, we should assume the white coat to be the best, as it is coolest in summer when exposed to the sun, and warmest in winter. Yet some of the white breeds are delicate and do not bear rough usage or exposure.

The Turkey.—Unknown to the civilized world till the discovery of this Continent, it was found here both in its wild and domesticated state, and still occupies the whole range of the Western Hemisphere, though the wild turkey disappears as the country becomes settled. The wild is about the size of the domesticated bird. The color of the male is generally of a greenish brown, approaching to black, and of a rich, changeable, metallic lustre. The hen is marked somewhat like the cock, but with duller hues. Domestication through successive generations has changed the color of their plumage, and produced a variety of colors—black, buff, pure white, or speckled. They give evidence to the comparative recency of their domestication in the instinct which frequently impels the cock to brood and take care of the young. Nothing is more common than for the male bird to supply the place of the hen, when any accident befalls her, and bring up the family of young chicks with an equally instinctive regard for their helplessness and safety. The flesh of this bird, both wild and tame, is exceedingly delicate and palatable; and, though not possessing the high game flavor of some of the smaller wild fowl, and especially of the aquatic, as the canvas-back duck, etc., it exceeds them in its digestibility and healthfulness. The turkey is useful principally for its flesh, as it seldom lays over a nest full of eggs at one clutch, when they brood on these and bring up their young. If full fed, and their first eggs are withdrawn from them, they frequently lay a second time. We have had them lay throughout the summer and into late autumn.

BREEDING.—Those intended for breeders should be compact, vigorous, and large, without being long-legged. They should be daily, yet lightly, fed, through the winter, on grain and roots, and some animal food is always acceptable and beneficial to them. They are small-eaters, and without caution will soon get too fat. One vigorous male will suffice for a flock of ten or twelve hens, and a single connection is sufficient for each. They begin to lay on approach of warm weather, laying once a day, or every other day, till they have completed their clutch, which, in the young or indifferently fed, may be ten or twelve, and, in the older ones, sometimes reaches twenty. The hen is sly in secreting its nest, but usually selects a dry, well protected place. She is an inveterate sitter, and carefully hatches most of her eggs. The young may be allowed to remain for twenty-four hours without eating, then fed with hard boiled eggs, made fine, or crumbs of wheat bread. Boiled milk, curds, buttermilk, etc., are food for them. As they get older, oats or barley meal is suitable, but Indian meal, uncooked, is hurtful to them when quite young. They are very tender, and will bear neither cold nor wet, and it is of course necessary to confine the old one for the first few weeks. When able to shift for themselves, they may wander over the fields at pleasure; and, from their great fondness for insects, they will rid the meadows from innumerable grasshoppers, etc., which often do incalculable damage to the farmer. Early chickens are sufficiently grown to fatten the latter part of autumn or the beginning of winter, which is easily done on any of the grains or boiled roots. The grain is better for cooking. They require a higher roosting place than hens, and are impatient of too close confinement, preferring the ridge of a barn, or a lofty tree, to the circumscribed limits of the ordinary poultry house. When rightly managed and fed, turkeys are subject to few maladies, and even these careful attention will soon remove.

The Peacock and Guinea Hen.—The peacock is undoubtedly the most showy of the feathered race. It is a native of the southern part of Asia, and is still found wild in the islands of Java and Ceylon, and some parts of the interior of Africa. They are an ornament to the farm premises, and are useful in destroying reptiles, insects and garbage, but they are quarrelsome in the poultry yard and destructive in the garden. Their flesh is coarse and dark, and they are worthless as layers. The brilliant silvery green, and their ever-varying colors give place to an entire white in one of the varieties.

The Guinea hen is a native of Africa and the southern part of Asia, where it abounds in its wild state. Most of them are beautifully and uniformly speckled, but occasionally they are white on the breast, like the Pintados of the West India Islands, and some are entirely white. They are unceasingly garrulous, and their excessively pugnacious character renders them uncomfortable inmates with the other poultry. Their flesh, though high colored, is delicate and palatable, but, like the peacock, they are indifferent layers. Both are natives of a warm climate, and the young are tender and rather difficult to rear. Neither of these birds is a general favorite, and we omit further notice of them.

The Goose.—There are many varieties of the goose. Main enumerates twenty-two, most of which are wild; and the tame are again variously subdivided. The common white and gray are the most numerous and profitable. The white Bremen is much larger, often weighing over twenty pounds net. It is of a beautiful snowy plumage, is domestic, and reared without difficulty, though not as prolific and hardy as the former. The China goose is smaller than the gray, and one of the most beautiful of the family, possessing much of the gracefulness and general appearance of the swan. There are three varieties of these in the United States; the small brown, with black bill and legs; the larger gray, with black bill and reddish legs; and the pure white, with orange bill and legs. It is prolific and tolerably hardy, but has thus far not been a successful rival with the first. The Guinea or African goose is the largest of the species. It is a majestic and graceful bird, and very ornamental to water scenery. Several other varieties are domesticated in the United States. The finest goslings we have ever reared or seen were a cross from the China gander and common gray goose. They are very hardy and easy to raise.

BREEDING.—Geese pair frequently at one year old, and rear their young; but with some kinds, especially of the wild, this is deferred till two and sometimes three. They require a warm, dry place for their nests, and when undisturbed they will sit steadily, and if their eggs have not been previously chilled or addled, they will generally hatch them all, if kept on the nest. To insure this, it is sometimes necessary to withdraw the first hatched, to prevent the old ones wandering before all are out. They should be kept in a warm, sheltered place till two or three weeks old, if the weather be cold or unsettled. The best food for the goslings is barley or oats, or Indian meal boiled, and bread. Milk is also good for them. They require green food, and are fond of lettuce, young clover, and fresh, tender grass, and after a few weeks, if they have a free range on this, they will forage for themselves. Geese are not a profitable bird to raise, except in places where they can procure their own subsistence, or at least during the greater part of the year. This they are enabled to do wherever there are extensive commons of unpastured lands, or where there are streams or ponds, lakes or marshes, with shoal, sedgy banks. In these they will live and fatten throughout the year, if unobstructed by ice and snow.

They may be fattened on all kinds of grain and edible roots, but it is more economical to give them their food cooked. The well-fattened gosling affords one of the most savory dishes for the table. Geese live to a great age. They have been known to exceed forty years. When allowed a free range on good food and clean water, they will seldom get diseased. When well fed, they yield nearly a pound of good feathers in a season, at three or four pluckings, and the largest varieties even exceed this. But plucking is a cruel business, and should not be done closely, and only between the months of May and October. Goslings intended for eating should not be plucked at all until fatted and killed

Ducks—Are more hardy and independent of attention than the goose, and they are generally the most profitable. They are omnivorous, and greedily devour everything which will afford them nourishment, though they seldom forage on the grass. They are peculiarily carnivorous, and devour all kinds of meat, putrid or fresh, and are especially fond of fish and such insects, worms, etc., as they can find imbeded in the mud or elsewhere. They will often distend their crop with young frogs, almost to the ordinary size of their bodies. Their indiscriminate appetites often render them unfit for the table, unless fattened out of the reach of garbage and offensive matters. An English admiral used to resort to well fattened rats for his fresh meat, when at sea, and justified his taste by saying they were more cleanly feeders than ducks, which were general favorites.

The varieties of ducks are almost innumerable. Main describes thirty-one, and some naturalists number many more. The most profitable for domestic use, aside from the common one, are the Black Cayuga, the Aylesbury, and Rouen, all being of much larger size, and richer and more delicate flavor of flesh. They lay profusely in the spring, when well fed, often producing forty or fifty eggs, and sometimes a greater number, if kept from sitting. They are much larger than those of the hen, and equally rich and nourishing, but less delicate. They are careless in their habits, and generally drop their eggs wherever they happen to be through the night, whether in the water, the road, or farm-yard; and, as might be expected from

18

such prodigality of character, they are indifferent sitters and nurses. The ducklings are better reared by sitting the eggs under a sedate, experienced hen, as the longer time necessary for hatching requires patience in the foster-mother to develop the young chicks. They should be confined for a few days, and away from the water. At first they may be fed with bread, or pudding made from boiled oat barley, or Indian meal; and they soon acquire strength and enterprise enough to shift for themselves, if afterwards supplied with pond or river water. They are fit for the table when fully grown, and well fattened on clean grain. This is more economically accomplished by feeding it cooked. We omit further notice of other varieties, and of the swan, brant, pigeons, etc., as not profitable for general rearing, and only suited to ornamental grounds.

DISEASES AND REMEDIES.

Most of the diseasos to which fowls are subject are the results of errors in diet or management, and should have been prevented, or may be removed by a change, and the adoption of a suitable regimen. When an individual is attacked, it should be forthwith removed, to prevent the contamination of the rest of the flock. Nature, who proves a guardian to fowls in health, will nurse them in their weakness, and act as a most efficient physician to the sick; and the aim of all medical treatment should be to follow the indications which Nature holds out, and assist in the effort which she constantly makes for the restoration of health.

Asthma.—This common disease seems to differ sufficiently in its characteristics to warrant a distinction into two species. In one it appears to be caused by an obstruction of the air-cells, by an accumulation of phlegm, which interferes with the exercise of their functions. The fowl labors for breath, in consequence of not being able to take in the usual quantity of air at an inspiration. The capacity of the lungs is thereby diminished, the lining membrane of the windpipe becomes thickened, and its minute branches are more or less affected.

Another variety of asthma is induced by fright, or undue excitement. It is sometimes produced by chasing fowls to catch them, by seizing them suddenly, or by their fighting with each other. In these cases, a blood-vessel is often ruptured, and sometimes one or more of the air-cells. The symptoms are short breathing; opening of the beak often, and for quite a time; heaving and panting of the chest; and, in case of a rupture of a blood-vessel, a drop of blood appearing on the beak.

TREATMENT.—Confirmed asthma is difficult to cure. For the disease in its incipient state, the fowl should be kept warm, and treated with repeated doses of hippo-powder and sulphur, mixed with butter, with the addition of a small quantity of cayenne pepper.

Costiveness.—The existence of this disorder will become apparent by observing the unsuccessful attempts of the fowl to relieve itself. It frequently results from continued feeding on dry diet, without access to green vegetables. Indeed, without the use of these, or some substitute—such as mashed potatoes—costiveness is certain to ensue. The want of a sufficient supply of good water will also occasion the disease, on account of that peculiar structure of the fowl, which renders them unable to void their urine, except in connection with the fæces of solid food, and through the same channel.

TREATMENT.—Soaked bread, with warm skimmed milk, is a mild remedial agent, and will usually suffice. Boiled carrots or cabbage are more efficient. A meal of earth-worms is sometimes advisable; and hot potatoes, mixed with bacon-fat, are said to be excellent. Castor-oil and burned butter will remove the most obstinate cases; though a clyster of oil, in addition, may sometimes be required in order to effect a cure.

Diarrhœa.—There are times when fowls dung more losely than at others, especially when they have been fed on green or soft food; but this may occur without the presence of disease. Should this state, however, deteriorate into a confirmed and continued laxity, immediate attention is required to guard against fatal effects. The causes of diarrhœa are dampness, undue acidity in the bowels, or the presence of irritating matter there.

SYMPTOMS.—The symptoms are lassitude and emaciation; and, in very severe cases, the voiding of calcareous matter, white, streaked with yellow. This resembles the yolk of a stale egg, and clings to the feathers near the vent. It becomes acrid, from the presence of ammonia, and causes inflammation, which speedily extends throughout the intestines.

TREATMENT.—This, of course, depends upon the cause. If the disease is brought on by a diet of green or soft food, the food must be changed, and water sparingly given; if it arises from undue acidity, chalk mixed with meal is advantageous, but rice-flour boluses are most reliable. Alum water, of moderate strength, is also beneficial. In cases of bloody flux, boiled rice and milk, given warm with a little magnesia, or chalk, may be successfully used.

Fever.—The most decided species of fever to which fowls are subject, occurs at the period of hatching, when the animal heat is often so increased as to be perceptible to the touch. A state of fever may also be observed when they are about to lay. This is, generally, of small consequence, when the birds are otherwise healthy; but it is of moment, if any other disorder is present, since, in such case, the original malady will be aggravated. Fighting also frequently occasions fever, which sometimes proves fatal.

SYMPTOMS.—The symptoms are an increased circulation of the blood; excessive heat; and restlessness

TREATMENT.—Light food and change of air; and, if necessary, aperient medicine, such as castor oil, with a little burned butter.

Indigestion.—Cases of indigestion among fowls are common, and deserve attention according to the causes from which they proceed. A change of food will often produce crop-sickness, as it is called, when the fowl takes but little food, and suddenly loses flesh. Such disease is of little consequence, and shortly disappears. When it requires attention at all, all the symptoms will be removed by giving their diet in a warm state.

Sometimes, however, a fit of indigestion threatens severe consequences, especially if long continued. Every effort should be made to ascertain the cause, and the remedy must be governed by the circumstances of the case.

SYMPTOMS.—The symptoms are heaviness, moping, keeping away from the nest, and want of appetite.

TREATMENT.—Lessen the quantity of food, and oblige the fowl to exercise in an open walk. Give some powdered cayenne and gentian, mixed with the usual food. Iron-rust, mixed with soft food, or diffused in water, is an excellent tonic, and is indicated when there is atrophy, or diminution of the flesh. It may be combined with oats or grain. Milk-warm ale has also a good effect, when added to the diet of diseased fowls.

Lice.—The whole feathered tribe seem to be peculiarly liable to be infested with lice; and there have been instances when fowls have been so covered in this loathsome manner that the natural color of the feathers has been undistinguishable. The presence of virmin is not only annoying to poultry, but materially interferes with their growth, and prevents their fattening. They are, indeed, the greatest drawback to the success and pleasure of the poultry fanciers; and nothing but unremitting vigilance will exterminate them, and keep them exterminated.

TREATMENT.—To attain this, whitewash frequently all the parts adjacent to the roosting-pole, take the poles down and run them slowly through a fire made of wood shavings, dry weeds, or other light waste combustibles. Flour of sulphur, placed in a vessel, and set on fire in a close poultry house, will penetrate every crevice, and effectually exterminate the vermin. When a hen comes off with her brood, the old nest should be cleaned out, and a new one placed; and dry tobacco leaves, rubbed to a powder between the hands, and mixed with the hay of the nest, will add much to the health of the poultry.

Flour of sulphur may also be mixed with Indian meal and water, and fed in the proportion of one pound of sulphur to two dozen fowls, in two parcels, two days apart. Almost any kind of grease, or unctuous matter, is also certain death to the vermin of domestic poultry. In the case of very young chickens, it should only be used in a warm, sunny day, when they should be put into a coop with their mother, the coop darkened for an hour or two, and everything made quiet, that they may secure a good rest and nap after the fatigue occasioned by greasing them. They should be handled with great care, and greased thoroughly; the hen, also. After resting, they may be permitted to come out and bask in the sun; and in a few days they will look sprightly enough.

To guard against vermin, however, it should not be forgotten that cleanliness is of vital importance, and there must always be plenty of slacked lime, dry ashes, and sand, easy of access to the fowls, in which they can roll and dust themselves.

Loss of Feathers.—This disease, common to confined fowls, should not be confounded with the natural process of moulting. In this diseased state, no new feathers come to replace the old, but the fowl is left bald and naked; a sort of roughness also appears on the skin; there is a falling off in appetite, as well as moping and inactivity.

TREATMENT.—As this affection is, in all probability, constitutional rather than local, external remedies may not always prove sufficient. Stimulants, however, applied externally, will serve to assist the operation of whatever medicine may be given. Sulphur may be thus applied, mixed with lard. Sulphur and cayenne, in the proportion of one quarter each, mixed with fresh butter, is good to be given internally, and will act as a powerful alterative. The diet should be changed: and cleanliness and fresh air are indispensable.

Pip.—This disorder, known also as the gapes, is the most common ailment of poultry and all domestic birds. It is especially the disease of young fowls, and is most prevalent in the hottest months being not only troublesome but frequently fatal.

SYMPTOMS.—The common symptoms of this malady are the thickened state of the membrane of the tongue, particularly toward the tip, the breathing is impeded, and the beak is frequently held open, as if the creature were gasping for breath; the beak becomes yellow at its base; and the feathers on the head appear ruffled and disordered; the tongue is very dry; the appetite is not always impaired; but yet the fowl cannot eat, probably on account of the difficulty which the act involves, and sits in a corner, pining in solitude.

TREATMENT.—Most recommend the immediate removal of the thickened membrane, which can be effected by anointing the part with butter or fresh cream. If necessary, the scab may be pricked with a needle. It will also be found beneficial to use a pill, composed of equal parts of scraped garlic and horse-radish, with as much cayenne pepper as will outweigh a grain of wheat; to be mixed with fresh butter, and given every morning; the fowl to be kept warm.

If the disease is in an advanced state, shown by the chicken's holding up its head and gaping for want of breath, the fowl should be thrown on its back, and while the neck is held straight, the bill should be opened, and a quill inserted into the windpipe, with a little turpentine. This being round, will loosen and destroy a number of small, red worms, some of which will be drawn up by the feather, and others will be coughed up by the chicken. The operation should be repeated the following day, if the gaping continues. If it ceases, the cure is effected.

It is stated, also, that the disease has been entirely prevented by mixing a small quantity of spirits of turpentine with the food of fowls, from five to ten drops to a pint of meal, to be made into a dough. Another specific recommended is to keep iron standing in vinegar, and put a little of the liquid in the food every few days.

Roup.—This disease is caused mainly by cold and moisture, but it is often ascribed to improper feeding and want of cleanliness and exercise. It affects fowls of all ages, and is either acute or chronic; sometimes commencing suddenly, on exposure; at others gradually, as the consequence of neglected colds, or damp weather or lodging. Chronic roup has been known to extend through two years.

SYMPTOMS.—The most prominent symptoms are difficult and noisy breathing and gaping, terminating in a rattling in the throat; the head swells, and is feverish; the eyes are swollen, and the eyelids appear livid; the sight decays, and sometimes total blindness ensues; there are discharges from the nostrils and mouth, at first thin and limpid, afterwards thick, purulent and fetid. In this stage, which resembles the glanders in horses, the disease becomes infectious. As secondary symptoms, it may be noticed that the appetite fails, except for drink; the crop feels hard; the feathers are staring, ruffled, and without the gloss that appears in health; the fowl mopes by itself, and seems to suffer much pain.

TREATMENT.—The fowls should be kept warm, and have plenty of water and scalded bran, or other light food. When chronic, change of food and air is advisable. The ordinary remedies—such as salt dissolved in water—are inefficacious. A solution of sulphate of zinc, as an eye-water, is a valuable cleansing application. Rue-pills, and a decoction of rue, as a tonic, have been administered with apparent benefit.

The following is recommended: of powdered gentian and Jamaica ginger, each one part; Epsom salts, one and a half parts; and flour of sulphur, one part; to be made up with butter, and given every morning.

The following method of treatment is practiced by some of the most successful poulterers in the country: As soon as discovered, if in warm weather, remove the infected fowls to some well-ventilated apartment or yard; if in winter, to some warm place; then give a dessert-spoonful of castor-oil; wash their heads with warm Castile-soap suds, and let them remain till next morning fasting. Scald for them Indian-meal, adding two and a half ounces of Epsom salts for ten hens, or in proportion for a less or larger number; give it warm, and repeat the dose in a day or two, if they do not recover.

Perhaps, however, the best mode of dealing with roup and all putrid affections is as follows: Take of finely pulverized fresh-burnt charcoal, and of new yeast, each three parts; of pulverized sulphur, two parts; of flour, one part; of water, a sufficient quantity; mix well, and make into two doses, of the size of a hazel nut, and give one three times a day. Cleanliness is no less necessary than warmth; and it will sometimes be desirable to bathe the eyes and nostrils with warm milk and water, or suds, as convenient.

Wounds and Sores.—Fowls are exposed to wounds from many sources. In their frequent encounters with each other, they often result; the poultry house is beseiged by enemies at night, and, in spite of all precaution, rats, weasels and other animals will assault the occupants of the roost, or nest, to their damage. These wounds, if neglected, often degenerate into painful and dangerous ulcers.

When such injuries occur, cleanliness is the first step towards a cure. The wound should be cleansed from all foreign matter, washed with tepid milk and water, and excluded as far as possible from the air. The fowl should be removed from its companions, which, in such cases, seldom or never show any sympathy, but on the contary, are always ready to assault the invalid, and aggravate the injury. Should the wound not heal, but ulcerate, it may be bathed with alum-water. The ointment of creosote is said to be effectual, even when the ulcer exhibits a fungous character, or proud flesh is present. Ulcers may also be kept clean, if dressed with a little lard, or washed with a weak solution of sugar of lead. If they are indolent, they may be touched with blue-stone.

When severe fractures occur to the limbs of fowls, the best course, undoubtedly, to pursue—unless they are very valuable —is to kill them at once, as an act of humanity. When, however, it is deemed worth while to preserve them, splints may be used, when practicable. Great cleanliness must be observed; the diet should be reduced; and every precaution taken against the inflammation, which is sure to supervene. When it is established, cooling lotions—such as warm milk and water—may be applied.

MEDICINAL.

The Management of the Sick-Room.—The arrangements of the sick-room require attention, and demand special notice. They influence very much the result, and may, indeed, where faulty, baffle the efforts of medicine. We would lay down the following brief rules:—

1. FRESH AIR.—Secure a full and free change of air without chilling the patient. According to the state of the weather, have the door, or window, or both open. In the summer time the upper part of the window of a sick-room should always be opened; in cold weather, a fire burning acts as suction-pump to draw off the vitiated air of the room, at the same time that it diffuses sufficient warmth. To secure purity of air, as well as the quiet so necessary for a sick-room, no more persons than are required should be in the room. A crowd of people leads to gossiping, and often exciting talk.

2. The temperature of a sick-room should, if possible, be maintained as near to 60° as possible. In the winter season, unless great care is taken, it will easily fall below this. At other times of the year it is more readily overheated.

In some affections of the respiratory organs there is a great advantage in cold weather in keeping the air of the room warm and moist by the steam from the spout of a kettle. If a piece of tin or lead pipe be attached to the spout, the steam can be brought further into the room. This plan has the additional advantage of securing a tolerably even temperature in the room—an important point in the treatment of croup and other inflammatory affections of the chest.

3. LIGHT.—The light should be so adjusted as to be moderate, according to the sensibility of the patient. Some

persons when ill like a dark room. This is more particularly the case when the head is at all affected. In delirium, a darkened chamber has often a very soothing effect. The bed should not be so placed that the strong lights fall upon the face of the patient. During convalescence, the bright and cheerful light of the sun exerts a beneficial restorative influence.

4. CLEANLINESS.—A well-known proverb expresses the importance of cleanliness; and, if the proverb apply anywhere, it applies still more forcibly in the sick-room. A common error is that in eruptive fevers the clothes should not be changed for fear of exposure of the surface of the body to a chill. Nothing can be more mistaken; the body linen should not only be changed daily, but the bed-linen should also be changed with advantage at least every two or three days, and removed from the room as quickly as possible. The body should also be washed daily. Children suffering from a scarlet fever, measles, or typhoid, derive comfort and benefit from their bodies being sponged all over daily with warm vinegar and water.

LOTIONS.—These may be applied simply by frequently washing the surface with them. In scarlet fever the sponging with warm vinegar and water allays the irritation and heat of the surface, and promotes the healthy functions of the skin. A more efficient method for an evaporating lotion is to soak one or two layers of soft linen or lint, wet with the lotion, and laying them on the surface, wet them again when they become dry. The drying takes place through the heat of the surface, the more rapidly, the higher the temperature of the part. An evaporating lotion is readily made by a wineglassful of gin or whisky in a pint of cold water.

SEDATIVE LOTIONS.—When the lotion is intended to act more by its sedative than by its evaporating effects, it will suffice to lay lint or linen soaked in it upon the surface, and cover it with oil silk or guttapercha tissue. Spongio-piline is a convenient medium for the application of sedative or other than evaporative lotions. Care, however, must be taken that it is not put on too wet, or the lotion will drain out and wet the clothing or bedding. A sedative lotion is made by boiling half a pound of fresh hemlock-leaves, or half a dozen poppy heads, in three pints of water down to a pint and a half.

ICE.—A greater degree of cold is sometimes required to be applied to a small   part of the surface, as in the case of a rupture or in fever when the headache and heat of the head are extreme. A convenient mode of reducing the temperature of a part by ice is to pound some small and enclose it in a bladder, taking care first to squeeze out the superabundant air, and then tie the neck of the bladder very tightly. The water in the bladder will continue at the temperature of the ice until every, particle of it is melted.

FOMENTATIONS.—Fomentations are of a very great value in the relief of pain of internal organs and of large joints when inflamed. They are part of the nurse's duties which require promptitude and judgment. If a large joint—a knee, for instance—be inflamed, much benefit is derived from swathing the joint in flannels wrung out of hot water, and wrapping these in dry outer flannels. Fomentations likewise are of great use in inflammation of the chest or of the bowels. The hot, wet flannels should be put on quickly, and changed quickly, about every five minutes, so as to avoid exposure to the cold air. They may be continued half an hour or more if they do not fatigue the patient.

WET SHEET.—In fevers with great neat of skin, wrapping the whole body in a wet sheet, and then enclosing in a blanket for an hour or more, will sometimes cause the skin to break into a profuse perspiration, reduce the heat of the skin, and moderate the pulse. In some affections of the kidney, attended with dryness of the skin and absence of perspiration, the wet sheet has been known to restore the action of the skin, and relieve the kidneys. The wet sheet is, however, so much a part of the hydropathic treatment of disease that it can scarcely be safely or properly used apart from the medical supervision with all the means and appliances of a hydropathic establishment.

POULTICING.—So common a thing as a poultice might seem beneath notice in such a treatise as the present, but some hints may be given thereon to the nurse. Thus, in making a linseed-meal poultice, most persons pour hot water upon the meal. To make a smooth, firm poultice, however, the reverse should be the plan—viz., to stir the meal into the water. A poultice should not be too heavy especially if to be applied on the abdomen. It need not be changed oftener than when it gets cold. There are various kinds of poultices—e. g, mustard, yeast, carrot, bran, charcoal, bread.

Bread poultice may be used alone, for most small purposes, such as a boil. It will be the basis also of the charcoal and carrot poultices.

Charcoal, bruised or powdered coarsely, and mixed with bread poultice, is useful for absorbing offensive odors.

Scraped carrot, mixed with bread poultice, is used to stimulate a sluggish and sloughing or mortifying surface.

Yeast, mixed with bread-crumb, forms also a good poultice for sluggish and offensive ulcers.

Mustard poultice, or sinapism, may be made several ways; sometimes equal parts of bread-crumb or flour, and mustard are used, but the best way is to make a tolerably thick paste of mustard and water, spread it on stiff brown paper, and cover with thin muslin. This poultice is stronger, but requires to be kept on the part a less time than the others. When removed, the surface is easily cleansed by a soft towel. A handy way of making a mustard plaster is to soak a slice of bread in water, and sprikle it with flour of mustard. A ready and efficient sinapism is afforded by Rigollot's "mustard leaves."

BLISTERING PLASTER AND LIQUID.—Blistering a surface with cantharides may be effected in two ways; one, by the application of the ordinary blister plaster, the other by painting with blistering liquid. When the plaster is used it is usual to leave it on the skin of an adult for eight or ten hours; when, if it has raised a blister, this is to be cut, and the fluid having run out, the surface is then to be covered with a piece of fine dry wadding or carded wool. This dressing being left on for two or three days, the skin will be found healed underneath. This plan is simple and less painful than dressing with lard or spermaceti ointment. If desirable to "keep the blister open" —i. e., its surface discharging—it may be dressed with savine ointment spread on lint or linen.

In the cases of young children, the blister plaster should not be allowed to remain longer than two hours, after which period a muslin bagful of warm bread-and-water poultice should be laid on, and the blister will form under that. After the blister has been cut, the surface can either be dressed with continuation of the poultice, or with dry wool. A warm poultice is a most suitable dressing for blisters, when applied for quinsy or other sore throat.

BLISTERING LIQUID.—As this is intended to be swift in its actions, it should be of the strongest kind that can be purchased. After it has been painted on for a few minutes the skin will be seen to turn white; that is a sign that enough has been painted on. In the course of half an hour blisters will begin to form. These can be dressed as above directed. This mode of raising a blister has many advantages over the plastering. It is speedy in its operation, it is cleaner, and it is more manageable for children and persons in a state of delerium. For cases of apoplexy or paralysis, where a speedy impression upon the nervous centres is desirable, the blistering liquid possesses great advantage, as it does also in acute rheumatism, in which affection the pain is often quickly relieved by having a strip of the liquid painted round the limb near to the swollen joint.

Counter-irritation acts by derivation or diversion of a morbid action from one part by setting up another equally or more powerful influence on the nerves of another part. It places in our hands a very powerful means of acting upon diseases of internal organs that are not absolutely close to the part acted upon, as well as when applied near to the seat of the malady. An example of the latter is afforded by the influence of belladonna or aconite on rheumatic or neuralgic pains; of the former, in the beneficial effects produced on the brain by a blister plaster applied to the nape of the neck.

COUNTER-IRRITANTS AND EXTERNAL STIMULANTS.—The following are the chief agents of this class mentioned:—

Blistering plaster.

Tincture, liniment, and ointment of iodine.

Compound camphor liniment and turpentine liniment.

Soap liniment (opodeldoc).

Nitrate of silver

Basilicon ointment.
Citrine ointment.
Belladonna liniment.

The Nurse.—It is not always possible to meet with a well trained nurse, even in a large town, while for those who are likely to consult the pages of this book it may be an impossibility to meet with a professional nurse of any kind. The hints here given are therefore addressed to those who may be compelled to be both nurse and doctor, and who in either capacity may be beyond the reach of professional or other aid. Cheerfulness and forgetfulness of self are prime requisites in the character of the women who undertakes the duties of a nurse. Illness makes people selfish, therefore it is the more necessary that there should be unselfishness to cope with this weakness.

A nurse should secure quietness in the sick room, and should permit only cheerful conversation—if possible, not too much of that. In acute affections of the brain this is a point of the highest importance. In hæmoptysis, or "spitting of blood," strict silence must be enjoined upon the patient, who should make use of a pencil for questions or answers. The nurse should carefully avoid the narration of doleful tales of fearful cases she has seen or heard of, as these depress the patient and interfere with recovery.

Directions for the management of the patient, given by those who are responsible for the well-doing of each case should be strictly attended to by the nurse. In all severe cases of illness, such as fevers, inflammations, accidents, etc., a written memorandum should be kept of each time of taking food, wine, medicine, etc., with their precise quantities. Without a check of this kind it is very easy to give too much or two little, or to transgress directions as to time. It need hardly be remarked that sobriety is absolutely indispensable in a nurse. This requisite is at once admitted; but many persons do, through false kindness' their very best to banish temperance from the sick room. They will leave wine and spirit bottles open in the room, and expect that they shall not be touched. Until nurses in general have gained a much higher character than is at present the case, it is safer not to put temptation in the way.

CAUTION IN USE OF STIMULANTS.—Another point in reference to this same subject may be mentioned. When stimulants are advisable for illness, great care must be taken not only that they are judiciously administered as to present quantity, but that they are discontinued with regard to future consequences, when no longer wanted for immediate requirements.

Lying-in Room.—LABOR.—We assume for the purposes of the present work that there is no medical attendant at hand. This state of things may and often does occur even in populous towns; it is, therefore, more likely to happen in new and distant places beyond the reach of medical aid. The possession, therefore, of the knowledge what to do on such occasions may be the source of the greatest possible comfort in an emergency, and possibly the means of saving life. Influenced by this conviction, then, we shall endeavor to lay down such simple rules as shall be found applicable by any one who may find him or herself by imperious necessity called upon to act the midwife's part. Happily, in healthy, well-made women, the process of childbirth rarely terminates otherwise than safely.

The principal point during the progress of labor is to keep the patient cheerful, and, as far as may be, divert her attention from the lapse of time. A light, but not starvation, diet should be taken. A first labor is generally far longer in duration than subsequent ones. Indeed, second and third and subsequent labors are often finished in a few minutes by two or three pains. Twenty-four hours is not too long a time for a natural first labor. It is not requisite here to describe all the stages of labor; suffice it to say, that there are certain promonitory symptoms, such as increased irritability of the bladder, a sinking of the weight and bulk of the abdomen, and the occurrence of pains "such as have not been felt before," as they are usually graphically and not incorrectly described. At this period it is as well to administer a dose of castor-oil if the bowels have not acted freely previously.

The "promonitory" pains, which at first are somewhat irregular in their character, become sooner or later changed into more severe and more irregular periodical pains, at intervals varying from five to ten minutes between, and are at some uncertain time followed by a gush of "the waters." These pains which occur generally in the back at first, gradually become longer, and are seated more to the front in the abdomen, and are more expulsive in character. Moderate allowance of stimulants should be administered from time to time. A straining effort to expel becomes unavoidable. The woman should then lie on her left side on a bed properly guarded by a piece of waterproof. A pillow placed between the knees will facilitate the passage of the head into the world. The feet should be fixed against the bedpost or footboard, to which, above the feet, a rope or jack-towel has been affixed, so that with each pain of the expulsive sort the patient may be enabled to bear down the more effectively. This towel or rope should not be used before expelling pains set in

MANAGEMENT OF THE NEW-BORN INFANT.—As soon as the child is born, it should be turned with its face upward, so that it shall be insured breathing room. Care must be taken to pass the navel-string over the child's head, if it be twisted round its neck, otherwise it may be strangled thereby. It should then be separated from its mother by first tying and then dividing the navel-string. The first step, the tying, may be done by any strong ligature. Usually half a dozen brown threads are used to tie the cord with, but a piece of twine or tape will do just as well. The cord or navel-string must be tied firmly in two places—first, about two inches from the child, and then two inches further, and then by a sharp pair of scissors divided between the ligatures.

In the preceding remarks it has been assumed that medical attendance is not to be had. If it be expected in a reasonable time, and the child is born before the arrival of the medical man, all that will be required will be to secure its being able to breathe freely. An infant may be left alone for an hour or two under these circumstances without its incurring harm.

When the child has been expelled and separated, firm pressure should be made on the lower part of the abdomen, the hand grasping the large tumor of the emptied womb. Steady pressure being made firmly in a direction downward and backward, the tumor will be felt to decrease in size, and at the same time the after-birth will be expelled. When this has taken place the labor is finished, and the best thing for the woman is then to let her alone to rest for a couple of hours. She should on no account be suffered to rise up quickly in bed, as by reason of the recent diminution of the contents of the abdomen, she is peculiarly liable to faint on sitting up. If the labor has been long and exhaustive, a moderate stimulant, such as a glass of wine, or of brandy and water, should be given.

At the end of two hours after the labor, the patient's clothes, etc., should be changed, and a broad binder or bandage pinned round the abdomen, not tightly, but only so as to give the feeling of a comfortable degree of support.

TREATMENT OF THE LYING-IN WOMAN.—It has been too much the custom to regard a woman after childbirth as an invalid, or to speak of her as a patient, whereas she is the very reverse. She is in the most natural and healthy of all conditions for a woman, but one requiring more than common care to prevent her falling into diseases, to which she is prone from the great strain that has been put upon her constitution for months past, capped with the climax of hours of pain and strong muscular effort. Under the influence of erroneous views, lying-in women have been kept for days together upon gruel, tea, etc. This treatment has, however, of late years given way to a plan more consistent with common sense, and better calculated to restore the nervous energies after the fatigues of perhaps many weary hours of labor, superadded to months of gestation.

DIET.—Light, but nutritious, food should be given. Beef-tea, milk, eggs, etc., may be freely allowed the first day, and meat on the second day, with wine or malt liquor, according to previous usage, and with strict moderation. After months of gestation and hours of suffering, with absolute loss of bulk, the constitution certainly requires restoration rather than depletion or further pulling down. It should be borne in mind, moreover, that a source of weakness is going on for many days afterwards.

By a strange perversity the contradictory practice of nearly absolute starvation was formerly followed too often by that of inordinate stimulation. It was deemed necessary for the due performance of maternal functions that a large quantity of strong beer should be taken daily. The quantities consumed

19

under this plea would have seemed incredible to persons of moderate habits. The writer has the still heavier charge to lay against the practice—that it has made many women drunkards.

It may be laid down as a rule that healthy women require no larger quantities of stimulants when nursing than at other times. What serves the purpose, of health before childbirth will serve them afterwards. The secretion of milk, instead of being promoted, is retarded by over stimulation. A pint or a pint and a half of malt liquor daily, is ample allowance for any healthy mother. Those who have been water-drinkers before they were mothers, may safely remain so afterwards.

REST AND NURSING.—Next to care in diet, is care as to rest and quietness. There is no need for absolute silence or total darkness in the room. The cheerful conversation of the nearest relatives may be allowed without fear of ill effects. The room should be kept light and airy. Ventilation should be carefully attended to. There is a popular notion—erroneous, like a good many old nurses' fables—that the eyes of lying-in women are especially intolerant of light. Such is not a fact. The reading of light literature is peculiarly grateful and suitable for this time. The recumbent posture must be preserved for at least a week. After that time, if all be going on well, sitting up in an easy-chair may be permitted. Walking about or standing had better not be attempted earlier than ten or twelve days, as the womb has not yet returned to its normal size, and is consequently heavy and prone to lay the foundation of future maladies if left to its own gravity too early.

SUCKLING.—The period at which milk is secreted varies in almost every case. Some women will have milk in the breast for weeks before the child is born, others will not have it for several days after. In most instances it comes quietly into the breasts on the second or third day. In some there is a slight degree of febrile disturbance attending its appearance. This, however, quickly subsides under a small reduction of diet— the low-diet system is not to be put in force on account of this trifling disturbance. The infant should be put to the breast about every two hours—not less frequently, lest the breast get painfully distended; not more frequently, lest it disturb the rest of both itself and mother by its much importunity.

SORE NIPPLES.—The nursing of the first child is often attended with extremely sore nipples, so that it becomes an excruciatingly painful proceeding, calling for all the firmness of a woman and all the strongest feelings of the mother to enable her to persevere. Perseverance, however, is the great remedy for sore nipples.

A host of drugs and many other means have been recom· mended for the cure of this distressing affection, but we know of none that in our experience we have known really deserving of confidence. The only serviceable means next to, or in aid of, the perseverance we have spoken of, is the use of Wansbor- row's metal shields. These being worn in the intervals of suckling, keep the nipples soft and promote the healing of their cracks.

To GIVE MEDICINE TO AN INFANT.—Put a portion of the dose in a teaspoon, then, holding the child on the lap in a half-sitting and half-lying posture, place the spoon on the tongue and slide it gently back towards the throat; when it has reached quite to the root of the tongue, tilt it up and hold it still on the tongue until the child swallows. Repeat the rest of the dose in the same way. It is better to give the dose in portions, so that there is less risk of choking by too large a dose

DISEASES AND REMEDIES.

Ague.—Ague is a periodic fever, occurring in three distinct stages, with an interval of distinct remission, or freedom, from fever—viz., a cold stage, a hot stage, and a sweating stage, occupying about eight hours. The attack recurs with more or less regularity, giving rise to types according to the period of their recurrence. 1. The quotidian, recurring once in twenty-four hours. 2. Tertian, every forty-eight hours. 3. Quartan, every seventy-two hours.

The quotidian ague is the most common form; an inter-change, or irregularity of the periods of return, is sometimes seen, giving to it modifications which greatly obscure the type of the disease. The term, "intermittent fever," which is given to ague, is derived from the entire remission which occurs between the paroxysms, leaving the patient apparently in his ordinary health.

SYMPTOMS.—The disease is ushered in, for a few days, by indefinite malaise, such as slight feverishness, and a feeling of fatigue and debility. On these premonitory symptoms there follows somewhat suddenly the cold stage, in which the patient becomes cold, pale, and "goosey," the teeth chatter. Severe headache occurs, the pulse is rapid, and breathing hurried. The cold stage continues for a period varying up to two or three hours, and then gives way to the hot stage, in which the headache becomes more severe; the whole surface of the body is flushed, hot, and dry, the features appear swollen, the eyes bloodshot, the pulse full and strong; thirst is very urgent, appetite lost, the urine scanty and high-colored. The febrile excitement is so great that sometimes delerium occurs in this stage, and may mislead as to the real nature of the fever. The hot stage may last for six hours or upwards, and is then replaced by the sweating stage, in which relief comes by, at first, a moisture appearing on the forehead and face, gradually increasing until it breaks out all over the body as a profuse sweat, followed by a general relief of symptoms, and, with the exception of a feeling of exhaustion, the patient is apparently quite well, until another paroxysm occurs, which it is very prone to do. A degree of sallowness of the complexion, however, usually remains, sometimes even after the entire subsidence of the disease. The preceding set of symptoms constitute an "attack" of intermittent fever, or ague, but their subsidence, unfortunately, is not always the complete restoration of health. The subjects of ague, in marshy districts, may almost always be recognized by their muddy or sallow complexion, indicative of a "cachectic" or impaired state of general health. The extent to which this depreciation of health and vigor may reach depends upon the length of the duration of the fever and the severity of the paroxysms. When these are severe and long-continued, serious congestion and disorders of the internal organs is very prone to follow. The spleen is more especially obnoxious to this congested condition, with consequent enlargement known as "ague cake." The enlarged condition of the organ may even be perceptible to pressure beneath the lower border of the ribs on the left side.

CAUSES.—The cause of ague is usually marsh miasm. It is not absolutely essential that a marsh shall yield the poison, as we occasionally meet with the disease in London and other places, in the presence of malaria arising from the decomposition of dead vegetable matter. It was formerly very common in London, but has disappeared from that city since sanitary regulations have very much cleared away the vegetable refuse which in bygone times disfigured the streets.

TREATMENT.—The treatment of ague resolves itself into

two principal indications, of getting rid of the cause—i. e., the malarious poison in the blood, and diminishing the violence of the paroxysms. The cold stage is that part of the paroxysm which, more particularly in hot climates, most urgently requires aid, and is that from which injurious effects may follow on the congestion of internal organs. As soon as the shivering begins the patient should go to bed, be well covered with blankets, and have hot bottles to the feet, bags of hot bran, salt, etc., together with a free supply of hot drinks. If these means do not succeed in arresting the rigor, an emetic of mustard and hot water will often be effectual to bring on the sweating stage. As this comes on, the quantity of clothing should be gradually decreased, taking care to avoid a sudden chill. The sweating may be promoted if it do not come on too freely; it may be promoted by the administration of stimulants, such as brandy and arrowroot, or wine and egg, etc. After the paroxysm has passed off, an aperient dose is often of service.

In order to ensure the full benefit of medical treatment, a change from the malarious to a purer air is desirable, and should not be omitted where it can be put in practice. The medical treatment in the remission, or the endeavor to eliminate the poison, must be put in practice in the intervals. For this purpose the most valuable remedy is the Peruvian bark, or quinine, the essentially active principle of bark.

In this country it is seldom necessary to give the quinine in so large or so continued doses as in some tropical climates, where it is essential not only as a curative, but also as a preventive means. Two, three, or five grains, taken every morning, has been found of the greatest service in keeping Europeans free, not only from ague, but also from other endemic fevers of the African continent.

In the ordinary treatment of ague in temperate climates it is usual to give two or three grains of quinine three times, or one large dose of five to ten grains given as nearly as possible before the expected access of the paroxysm. This will often anticipate or cut short the paroxysm.

The quinine may be given simply mixed in water, or added to a glass of sherry wine. It is usual, but entirely superflous, to render the sulphate of quinine solvent by the addition of a few drops of diluted sulphuric acid.

Apoplexy.—SYMPTOMS.—The Greek etymology of this word, —viz.: to strike or knock down with violence—expresses the leading symptoms of the attack. In the severest form of the disease, the patient is suddenly struck down, deprived of voluntary motion, sensation, and intellect, it may be, with convulsions of one side of the body, and lies as one in deep sleep from which he cannot be roused, with snoring, puffing breathing, dilated pupils, a flushed face, and full, slow pulse, and, possibly, with vomiting.

In another class of cases, the patient does not, perhaps, fall suddenly to the ground, but turns pale, and feels faint, or experiences an attack of giddiness or headache, with sickness or vomiting, and occasionally with slight convulsive movements, the pupils natural, or but slightly dilated, the pulse weak and irregular. The pain in the head may be attended with loss of memory, loss of power in the limbs, passing into entire apoplexy or paralysis. The symptoms will vary in their intensity, and in their duration—the attack may last for a few minutes only, or be extended over several days, and at last the patient sinks into a state of coma, or profound stupor, from which he never recovers.

TREATMENT.—At the time of the fit the first thing to be done is to loosen all articles of clothing about the neck and chest, so as to favor the return of the blood from the head—to place the patient in a reclining posture, not flat down. If the pulse be feeble or irregular, a small quantity of brandy and water may be given; cautiously, on account of difficulty of swallowing. Mustard plasters, or rags soaked in turpentine, should be applied to the calves of the legs. If the person be of a full habit, and have a strong, slow pulse, a strong purge should be given as soon as possible. One drop of croton oil placed on the tongue, is at once convenient to give and effective in action. Should this fail to act, in two or three hours a clyster of castor oil and turpentine should be administered.

Bleeding in any form is seldom required in these cases, and is never safe in non-professional hands. It is very easy, under circumstances of alarm and excitement, to do too much. The after effects of an apoplectic seizure require very judicious management; and here, again, we would warn the reader against expecting too much from mere medical means, and to be careful not by over-anxiety for stimulation, to accelerate a dangerous reaction. As the insensibility passes off, and the patient wakes up to what is passing around him (supposing that he has been unconscious), great care must be taken to secure quietness and rest. As little conversation as possible should be carried on; the room should be well aired and moderately lighted. Complete rest of body and mind are essential to recovery. As the limbs recover their muscular power, they must be carefully and only gradually brought into use. Caution must also be exercised in the administration of food of a light and nutritious character. The muscles of the throat having probably suffered in the attack, will require time to resume their power, and hence there will be danger of choking if care be not taken. The food must be light and easy of digestion, since the functions of the stomach will also be impaired, and, if too solid or indigestible food be given, it may cause vomiting and serious disturbance. Should the pulse be feeble, a little brandy or wine may be allowed to be taken with light food. All this precaution is required to guard against inflammation of the brain, which may follow on reaction indicated by increased rapidity of pulse, heat of skin, thirst, and headache.

Should the bowels be costive, some simple saline purgative, such as Epsom salts or Seidlitz powder, should be taken. If there be persistent headache, blistering behind the neck will relieve it. If these means fail to subdue the inflammatory and febrile symptoms, the case must be treated as one of inflammation of the brain. Paralysis, or permanent loss of power on one side of the body, or of some muscles or portion of the surface on one side, is not unfrequently left after an apoplectic attack. (See Paralysis.)

Asthma.—This is sometimes called "Spasmodic Bronchitis," and consists of a sudden attack of tightness across the chest, with difficulty of breathing, of a most urgent and distressing kind—so much so, that in the course of less than an hour immediate suffocation seems to be impending. The patient is fighting and struggling for very life, gasping for air, speech nearly impracticable, the eye protruding, the countenance anxious, flushed, or of a blue discoloration. The skin becomes bedewed with cold clammy sweat, the hands and fingers blue; altogether forming as distressing a scene as can be witnessed, but happily not one that is often fatal, as it passes off generally with a restoration of the bronchial secretion which has been suspended. This favorable occurrence varies in its advent. The paroxysm, however, seldom lasts more than a few hours at the utmost, but the bronchitis which follows lasts sometimes for several days. The attack is liable to return at uncertain periods.

Treatment.—The treatment of this affection is guided by its essentially spasmodic character during the paroxysm. Hot and stimulating fomentations should be applied to the chest, and sedative and nauseant medicines given at short intervals, thus:—

Ipecacuanha wine, 2 drachms; paregoric, 2 drachms; tincture of henbane, 4 drachms. Add water to eight ounces, and give one tablespoonful every hour, until the breathing is easier. Or an emetic of mustard and water may be given previously.

As the paroxysm subsides, give the following: Compound tincture of cardamoms, 1 drachm; chloric ether, 20 minims; fœtid spirits of ammonia, 30 minims; water, a wineglassful; every four hours for some hours and then either treat as for

acute bronchitis, if cough, etc., continue, or withdraw all
medicine, and leave nature to complete the cure.

Biliousness, Billiary Derangements, Congestion of the Liver.
—These are known under various names, confounding together
stomach and liver disorder; thus we have them spoken of as
"sick-headache," "bowel complaint," "jaundice," etc.

SYMPTOMS.—They may be classed under the two heads of
"diminished secretion," and "excessive secretion." The latter
produces English cholera, or diarrhœa, of a troublesome character, attended with griping pains, and more or less sickness,
the attack being of an acute character.

A diminution in the secretion of bile generally manifests
itself by symptoms of a more chronic type. They are more
tardy in their approach, and do not pass off so quickly as those
of an excessive flow of bile. This form of deranged functions of the liver is indicated by irregularity in the intestinal
functions; the bowels act with sluggishness, and become constipated; the evacuations are pale or slate-colored; the stomach
begins to show its participation in the disorder by dyspepsia,
flatulence, nausea. A well-known pain under the right shoulder-blade is one of the commonest attendants of this disorder.
Headache occurs. The sight is impaired or interrupted by
dark specks or films, termed "muscæ volitantes," floating, as it
were, before the eyes. The complexion becomes sallow, or of
a muddy, yellowish color. The patient becomes a sufferer
from piles, and, as an almost inevitable consequence of such
varied derangement of functions, depression of spirits follows.
This latter is a very common attendant upon disorders of the
liver, the word hypochondrical having an etymological reference to the liver as the seat of the disorder. Jaundice is not
an unfrequent occurrence to children suffering from bilious
derangement, but has not then a serious import. Jaundice is
a very frequent occurrence with new-born infants, and arises
from an alteration in the course and quantity of blood that
passes through the liver after birth. It cannot be called a disease under such circumstances, nor does it require medicinal
treatment. In the former condition—that of an excessive
flow of bile—the liver is said to be in a state of active congestion; in the latter, of passive congestion. The former may
pass into inflammation. This, however, is rarely seen in this
country, but is only too frequently met with in hot climates.
The pain that is felt in the right side with the above described
symptoms, and not uncommonly regarded as an indication of
inflammation of the liver, is the result of congestion of the
organ. Acute inflammation of the liver is attended with great
pain in the right side, extending to the right shoulder-blade,

and tenderness on pressure over the region of the organ, aggravated by lying on the left side. The pain in the region of the
liver may be so acute as to make it difficult to distinguish from
that of plurisy, while, on the other hand, the mistake is often
made of regarding a limited extent of plurisy in the lower part
of the chest as an attack of inflammation of the liver. With
the pain there is, in inflammation of the liver, a varying degree
of fever, thirst, loss of appetite, nausea, vomiting, hiccup. The
urine becomes scanty and is high-colored. The bowels are
frequently costive, the evacuations very pale, even white, showing a deficiency in the flow of bile. The same defect of flow
of bile by the intestines causes its absorption into the circulation, giving rise to yellowness of the complexion and coats of
the eye—jaundice. If the inflammation is not subdued, the
pain will probably become of a throbbing character, severe
shivering will occur, and an abscess form. This may burst
into the chest and the matter be expectorated, or it may become the cause of serious mischief in the cavity of the chest,
or it may find its way by opening into the stomach and be vomited, or it may escape externally by opening into the surface
of the body; which of these shall occur we cannot determine.

In chronic inflammation of the liver the preceding symptoms are present in a milder degree, but are slower in their
progress—they are attended with less feverishness. There is
present depression of spirits amounting sometimes to melancholy. As the disease progresses, diarrhœa, debility, wasting,
and dropsy are pretty sure to make their appearance, followed
by death from exhaustion.

TREATMENT.—Bilious derangement, "congestion of the
liver," or jaundice, is prone to occur in overfed children, and
produce sickness and diarrhœa, with light-colored, slimy
stools. This derangement (English cholera), under judicious
dietary, generally corrects itself by carrying off excess of bile
or badly-digested food. If, however, it continues more than a
day or two in spite of careful dieting and abstinence from
stimulative food, a mild mercurial will be of service, such as,
(for a child over three years of age):

Gray powder (mercury with chalk), 1 grain; prepared
chalk, 3 grains; magnesia, 1 grain. Given night and morning. Or: — Rhubarb powder, 3 grains; ipecacuanha powder,
one-fourth grain; nitre powder, 2 grains. Mix and give twice
a day.

In biliousness occurring to adults, and attended with sickness, the first thing is to give the stomach as nearly as possible
entire rest by putting almost nothing into it while the vomiting
lasts. This may moreover be checked sometimes by small
pieces of ice taken into the mouth, and swallowed when par-

tially melted. Soda-water in small quantities frequently taken is also serviceable. A mustard plaster on the pit of the stomach assists also in checking sickness. When the sickness has passed off, the greatest care in diet is required. Fish, poultry, boiled mutton, with a moderate allowance of well-cooked green vegetables, such as cauliflower, asparagus, marrows. Light wine, such as claret, may be allowed.

The diarrhœa that occurs in these disorders of the liver may be checked by mineral acids—e. g.,

Diluted muriatic acid, 2 drachms. Compound tincture of cardamoms, 1 ounce.

Cinnamon water, to 8 ounces. Mix, and give an eighth part every three or four hours.

In chronic biliary derangements occurring in "bilious habits," more may be done by abstemious living than by physic. The habit of taking so-called "anti-bilious" pills, calomel, blue pill, etc., to correct disorders of the liver, that may be avoided by avoiding there causes, is simply absurd. But where, in spite of care, the liver is habitually sluggish, an occasional small dose of blue pill at bedtime, followed by a simple aperient in the morning, may safely be taken. In some persons, however careful they may be, the proneness to biliary derangement is greater than can always be managed by even great care in dieting. In such cases the repeated use of small doses of mineral acids, with extract of dandelion or sarsaparilla, is believed to be useful. Fresh air and outdoor exercise are also important means—horse exercise, if possible.

Acute inflammation of the liver is, as already remarked, rarely met with in temperate climates. In parts of India and other hot climates, it is not unfrequently met with, owing partly to the solar heat and partly, it is said, to imprudence in dieting and exposure. An active treatment is required, such as free leeching over the region of the liver, or cupping if there be any skilled person to perform it. At the same time full doses of calomel are to be given (five to ten grains), and repeated every six hours, followed up by saline purgatives, such as Epsom salts and senna. While these are taking effect, mercurial ointment should be rubbed into the armpits and groin night and morning. This would be the treatment for a case of acute inflammation of the liver occurring in a tropical climate, in an adult person. There is, however, some reason to believe that calomel has been somewhat too liberally given in such cases.

Bite of a Venomous Serpent.—Suck the wound immediately, if you can, yourself; if not, get a friend to do so (it can be done without danger, if there be no abrasure—scratch, that is—or sore on the tongue or lips), and then tie a string, if possible, tightly round the part, finger or limb, that has been bitten, be-

tween the wound and the body; wash well with warm water, and
apply liquor ammoniæ diluted to the wound, and take fifteen
to twenty drops in a wine-glass of water internally, every three
or four hours; keep the patient from going to sleep.

Bite from a Dog Suspected to be Mad.—Soak immediately
in, and wash with, water as hot as you can bear it; then apply
salt to it freely, and send for a doctor to cut out the part, if
practicable, or to burn it with lunar caustic, and if you cannot
get one, do it yourself, only do not overdo it. If you have no
lunar caustic at hand, use a good, strong solution of carbolic
acid to the place. Take a Turkish bath at once if possible; it
is one more chance in your favor.

In all cases, if possible, send for a medical man, but if one
cannot be had, the above remedies are applicable.

N. B.—The wound may be sucked with impunity either by
the person himself who is bitten, or by a friend for him, if he
has no abrasion, that is, scratch, or sore place, or sore on his
mouth, or lips. Do not cauterise the wound yourself, if you
can help it; leave that to a medical man, if one can possibly be
got within a short time. Sad results have been known to occur
from unskillful cauterization.

A bite from a dog not mad gives rise to great inflammation;
linseed poultice, sprinkled with from fifteen to twenty drops of
laudanum, is the best application for this; it may be continued
about a week.

Bleeding at the Nose.—Lay the patient immediately at his
full length upon the floor, or on a table, or on a bench, and
stretch out his arms behind his head, to their full length, on a
level with his body; unloose the collar, and apply wet towels
to the back of his neck. I have always found this posture,
that is, laying the patient flat on the back, answer best; but
many excellent doctors do not consider the posture of the body
of importance, and as sitting or reclining back in an arm chair
is more convenient and less fussy, it will probably be sufficient
to place the arms in a vertical position, that is, straight up above
the head. If the bleeding continue obstinate, use ice if you
can get it, instead of water, and put a plug of lint in the nostril,
steeped in a strong solution of alum and water. If you can
get it, snuff up the nose a solution of gallic acid, or, better still,
of tannic acid, or even inject it up the nose. It is the most
powerful astringent of all. For a child's nose when bleeding,
a large, cold door key laid behind the neck and between the
shoulders, will often suffice, compressing at the same time the
nostril with the finger firmly for a few minutes. When the
above treatment fails, snuff up a few drops of tincture of saffron
(**crocus sativus**) in a little water. This is almost sure to
answer.

Bladder, Inflammation of.—SYMPTOMS.—This affection is indicated by acute pain of a burning character at the lower part of the stomach, or, more strictly speaking, abdomen, and of the body, and down the thighs. The pain is augmented by pressure, and by passing water, occasion for which is frequent, its voidance difficult, and in small quantities. A considerable degree of fever is present, attended with restlessness, heat of skin, and increased frequency of the pulse. The urine that is passed is turbid, cloudy, and high-colored, and sometimes bloody.

TREATMENT.—In the treatment of acute inflammation of the bladder the patient must be kept to his bed, and have a dozen leeches applied to the lowest part of the body or just in front of the fundament—the bleeding to be encouraged by hot fomentation and poultices or a hot hip bath. At the same time free purgation should be promoted by epsom salts or Glauber's salts; full doses of opium, either as pill or tincture, should be administered to relieve the pain and urgency to evacuate the bladder. After these measures have been put in force, and have somewhat relieved the suffering, the following mixture may be given:—

Bicarbonate of potash, 15 grains; tincture of henbane, 1 drachm. And repeated every four or six hours, according as the symptoms yield or not.

The diet must be of the mildest and most unstimulating character.

Bleeding from the Lungs, Spitting of Blood, Expectoration of Blood, Hæmoptymis.—SYMPTOMS.—Occurr usually with the presence of cough, and a tickling feeling at the back of the throat, preceded frequently by sense of oppression or of weight in the chest: the blood is expectorated in very varying quantities, generally exciting a well-founded alarm. The blood may be brought up pure, or mixed with the mucus of the air passages. In some instances, the mouth fills with blood, unattended with cough. A saltish taste in the mouth is very often experienced. Its florid color, frothy character, and attendant cough, will assist in its distinction from vomiting of blood.

TREATMENT.— Bleeding from the lungs is not always attended with the danger that is generally apprehended. Although its occurence excites alarm in reference to the existence of consumptive disease, it is sometimes beneficial rather than otherwise, as it tends to relieve congestion in the weak part of the lung. Very few cases prove fatal from the bleeding alone.

The strictest rest and quiet, and absolute silence, should be enforced; the chamber be cool and airy, admitting of free ventilation. The patient should be placed half-sitting. Only cold drinks, or pieces of ice should be allowed at first. All food should be given cold. Only in case of extreme faintness should stimulants be given.

The medical treatment required, is the administration of astringents internally, e. g.: Gallic acid, 30 grains; epsom salts, one-half ounce; diluted sulphuric acid, 1 drachm; water, to 6 ounces. Mix. Give a sixth part every three hours, unless the medicine purge too freely, then the epsom salts may be omitted.

Cloths dipped in cold water, or spirit and water, should be kept applied on the chest. The rest and quiet should be observed for several days after the hemorrhage has ceased, which it will do, probably, only gradually, the expectoration being streaked for a variable time.

Bleeding from the Stomach and Bowels.—Hæmatemesis or Vomiting of Blood—Is usually a result of some internal disease causing obstruction of the circulation of blood through the liver, spleen, or stomach; or it may be a result of the derangement of more distant organs. Ulceration of the mucous surface of the stomach itself may lead to the opening of a vessel therein. It is preceded by a sense of nausea or sickness, or faintness, and by a feeling of heaviness or of oppression at the pit of the stomach. The blood vomited is generally of a dark color, and is mixed with food, and differs in color from the frothy fluid blood that is coughed up from the air passages.

Treatment.—If the bleeding be traced to some derangement or congestion of the liver, it should be treated according to the directions laid down for vomiting in bilious disorders, and the treatment directed for chronic biliary disorders. If it have been preceded by dyspepsia, pain in the pit of the stomach, or other signs of disorder of that organ alone, without much general derangement of the health, it is to be feared that the bleeding, may proceed from an ulcer within the stomach perforating a blood-vessel. In this case, ice should be given, and very little else, at the time, except it be some astringent medium—e. g., five or six grains or gallic acid or tannin every four hours, with a drachm of epsom salts, since an aperient may be useful to clear away what blood may have passed into the bowels. In these cases of bleeding from the stomach the curative treatment is dietic. Milk alone should be allowed for a few days. After four or five days, some white of egg may be stirred up in the milk, and this should constitute the sole diet for two or three weeks. At the end of this time, small quantities of whiting, or some other white fish, may be allowed. The longer this diet can be maintained, the more sure the result. A return to ordinary diet must be very gradual, and by taking carefully of poultry or well-cooked mutton.

Boils and Carbuncles.—Symptoms.—Boils are distinguishable from carbuncles by their smaller size, by their conical shape, inflamed base, and tendency to form matter at the point. Beneath the matter is a portion of dead tissue or " core."

Carbuncle is a large and flattened compound boil, without the tendency to present a conical point. A carbuncle tends to form matter, and opens at various parts of its surface. At these points the skin gives way, presenting a riddled aspect, gradually running into one sore. The inflamed base of a carbuncle extends wider than that of a boil, and has a harder feel, resembling, indeed, the consistence of brawn.

Treatment.—A small boil requires no treatment beyond protection from friction, by diachylon or soap plaster. If, however, it be large, inflamed, and painful, water dressing or warm poultices should be applied, until the core has sloughed out. It should then be dressed with zinc ointment. A carbuncle should, in the first instance, be kept well covered with the water dressing protected by oil silk, until the surface begins to give way, and presents numerous small, yellow points of matter; it should then be dressed with strips of lint smeared with the yellow basilicon ointment, covered outside with linen, moistened with Condy's fluid or carbolic oil, if there be any offensive odor. After the slough of dead tissue beneath the skin has separated, the sore may be dressed with zinc ointment. The diet should be full and nutritious, with a moderate allowance of stimulants. The medicines that will be useful will be quinine, compound tincture of bark, muriated tincture of iron, etc.

Bowels, Inammflation of.— This is often ushered in by slight shivering fit, a degree of nausea with thirst, and a white, furred tongue with a red tip or red spots. There will be pain or tenderness of some parts of the abdomen, more commonly in the lower part or about the middle region. The pain is of a dull sort, except in the part that is most tender on pressure, where it will become acute and increased by bodily movements. The knees are generally drawn up in order to take off the pressure of the muscles of the abdomen. There is loss of appetite, sickness, sometimes vomiting, with increasing thirst, a coated tongue, and a hot, dry skin. The bowels are often obstinately constipated at the commencement of an attack of inflammation, and afterwards they become relieved even to diarrhœa. The character of the motions will vary—they are usually thin and watery, consisting of mucus and fœces, and are occasionally tinged with blood.

These symptoms are generally attended with a feverish condition of the system, as shown by a rapid, sharp pulse, thirst, heat of surface, &c. Inflammation of the bowels may originate in indigestible or undigested food; the action of irritant poisons, or of too active purgation.

TREATMENT.—Complete rest of body, and, as far as is possible, of the intestines, is the first and most essential point of treatment. The patient must be confined to the bed, and warm fomentations and poultices should be applied over the abdomen. Pain and diarrhœa may be relieved by Dover's powder—five grains every four or six hours, according to the severity of the symptoms, in cases of adults; for children, smaller doses may be cautiously given. If the pain be very acute, one grain of plain opium may be given every six hours. Turpentine stupes will be found useful. The constipation that sometimes ushers in an attack of inflammation of the bowels is often relieved by a few doses of opium. It depends upon spasm or cramp of the intestinal fibres. The diet should be of the simplest kind, soft and nutritious—e. g., milk, beef tea, mutton broth, eggs, arrowroot, etc., in small quantities frequently.

Breast, Inflammation of (acute).—MILK ABSCESS.—SYMPTOMS.

—A portion of the breast becoming harder than the rest, and having a throbbing pain, with slight redness of the skin. The hardness and pain extending, a degree of fever is set up. Shivering takes place, the throbbing increases—at last some one spot on the surface becomes softer as the matter which has been formed comes to the surface—the skin is thinned and gives way, if not opened by a lancet, and allows of the escape of matter, sometimes in large quantities.

Abscess of the breast occurs during the early weeks of nursing, and sometimes during weaning, sometimes through neglect in drawing off the milk when it is required to be done, and often without any known cause, and despite every care that may have been taken.

TREATMENT.—When only a small portion of the gland is affected, the application of cold lotion will sometimes disperse the inflammation, especially if at the same time the breast be drawn by breast-pump or drawing glass, and the breast be carefully supported by a sling made of a pocket-handkerchief, or band of any convenient kind. Should these means not have the desired effect of checking the course of the abscess, then warm poultices should be applied, or some folds of soft linen dipped in warm water and covered with oil-silk. From the first, a full diet, with wine or beer, is preferable to low diet, and any depleting or weakening treatment should be avoided.

After the matter has come to the surface, the continued application of poultices will cause the abscess to burst; and, if it points at one depending point, it is better left to take its course. If, however, it should not point freely at one spot, but at several, the opening of the most depending should be done by the lancet.

CHRONIC INFLAMMATION OF THE BREAST.—Sometimes at the time of weaning, a portion of the breast becomes tender and hard, but does not give the pain or produce the redness of "milk abscess." It occurs sometimes to young girls after mumps, and at the period of puberty. In women, at the change of life it also occurs. It readily follows also on a blow.

TREATMENT.—The treatment consists in improving or keeping up the general health. The less that is done to the breast in the way of local applications the better. The hardened lump often rapidly disappears of itself.

Bright's Disease.—Degeneration of the Kidneys.—SYMPTOMS.—This is a disease of a very grave nature, and one which is seldom recovered from; but it is one of which it would be difficult to give an intelligent description to non-professional persons. Only the physician can treat it properly.

Bruises.—The variation of the colors of bruises is owing to changes going on in the blood which has been effused under the skin by violence. A bruise generally goes through all the various tints from black to green and yellowish-green. Bruises sometimes, from the large quantities of blood effused, become inflamed and form abscesses.

TREATMENT.—To prevent or diminish discoloration from bruises, it is well to apply cold or warm water as soon after the violence has been done as possible. To allay the swelling or inflammation which may follow, cooling lotions should be used. A mixture of tincture of arnica and water has been strongly recommended, but a mixture of spirit and water, or spirit, vinegar and water, will be found quite as efficacious. Spirits of wine, 1 oz; vinegar, 1 oz; water, to 4 oz.

GRAZE, OR ABRASION.—An abrasion of the skin, or what is commonly termed "barked skin," is the simplest form of a wound. It consists in the superficial skin being rubbed off by violence. This form of injury of course varies in severity as the amount of violence varies.

TREATMENT.—For a slight abrasion a piece of linen or linen wetted with cold water and covered with oil-silk or gutta-percha tissue, will generally be sufficient dressing. Or it may be covered with gold-beater's skin.

For a graze or bruised wound of considerable extent or

depth, a dressing of carbolic acid and oil will be found a serviceable application. Take of carbolic acid, 1 part; best olive oil, 28 parts; apply on lint or soft linen.

In a majority of cases any simple application that will protect the denuded surface, while it is being skinned over, is enough—e. g., spermaceti ointment, spread on linen, will be all that is required. One method of treatment for abrasions, is to apply a piece of dry lint, and let the blood soak into it. This may be allowed to dry on the sore, and thus form an artificial scab; or the lint may first be soaked into compound tincture of Benzoin, known as Friar's Balsam.

Burns and Scalds.—The effect of these will vary with the extent of surface, or the depth of skin injured or destroyed. Recovery, moreover, must depend greatly upon the state of health at the time of the accident. Under ordinary states of health a superficial scald or burn, not destroying the skin below the surface, and not involving more than half the superfices, may be recovered from. Less than half of this extent of burn may, however, be fatal, if it extend to the true skin and the muscles below.

Burns as a rule destroy more than scalds. Scalds usually form blisters and go no deeper, but burns may char the deeper skin and the muscles beneath; they are, therefore, the more dangerous of the two. Should the burn have resulted from the clothes catching fire, they should carefully be removed, so as not to break the blisters, which may be forming or formed, lest violence be done to the raw skin beneath, and, for the same reason, pieces of the clothing that stick to the surface should not be removed at the time. If the burn or scald be extensive, some stimulant, wine and water, should be given at once to diminish the effect of "shock."

TREATMENT.—The principle to be observed in the treatment of burns and scalds, is to cause a gradual diminution of heat in the part, not to allow it to cool too quickly. This is effected by protecting the burnt or scalded part from the air, by immediately dredging with flour, or covering with cotton-wool or oil. If the case is a slight one, these dressings may be left on for a day or two; but, if it be more severe, the damaged parts should be dressed with lint, spread with basilicon or resin ointment, or a mixture of equal parts of that ointment and spirits of turpentine. Another useful lotion for application to burns and scalds of slight extent, consists of "carron-oil," or, lime-water, 1 part; linseed-oil, 2 parts; well shaken together, and applied by means of strips of lint, or soft linen rag, soaked in it, and changed twice a day.

THE BLISTERS.—How TO BE TREATED.—It is generally

advisable not to cut the blisters which may be formed, as they
protect the true skin under them; but, if the base of the blister
shows symptoms of inflammation, it is as well to evacuate the
contents, but, even then, to do it by means of a small prick,
and to leave the skin on, so that it may protect the raw surface
from the air.   The black char of skin that is sometimes left
should be poulticed with bread, or linseed meal and bread, till
the slough separates.   When this has taken place, there is left
a surface of what appear to be little mounds of flesh, and these
give out a discharge of matter.   They are called granulations,
and are the commencements of the process of healing.   At
times these granulations grow very rapidly and abundantly,
rising above the level of the adjacent skin.   This is what is
commonly meant by "proud flesh."   Their growth may be
checked by gently touching them with stick of nitrate of silver,
and dressing the surface with oxide of zinc ointment.   Burns
between the fingers, or in any place where two contiguous sur‑
faces are likely to come in contact, should be separately dressed,
and great care should be taken to keep the granulating surfaces
apart, or they may grow together and produce deformity.

OPIATES.—If there be much pain, it will be advisable to
give opium, in the form of the tincture, as it will also allay ner‑
vous excitement.   Tincture of opium, 10 minims; water, one
teaspoonful every four hours.   This dose, it should be borne
in mind, is for an adult person.

· BURNS FROM CHEMICALS.—The destructive chemicals most
likely to produce these accidents are sulphuric acid, or oil of
vitrol; nitric acid, or aqua fortis; ammonia, and hydrofluoric
acid; strong carbolic acid, and chloride of zinc.   In cases of
burns from any of these the parts should be well washed with
water, in which a little bicarbonate of soda is dissolved, or soap
and water in the case of the acids.   Afterwards treat as in a
case of inflammatory ulcer or ordinary burn.

GUNPOWDER BURNS.—Explosions of gunpowder cause de‑
struction of skin, and resemble burns or scalds in their effects.
They should be treated in the same manner as burns, first re‑
moving particles of carbon by means of a soft sponge and warm
water.

The diet, in severe burns, should be supporting.   Some
stimulant is usually advisable.

Cold.—Either one or other of the following remedies is
likely to succeed.   Put twenty to thirty, or even thirty-five,
according to age and strength, drops of laudanum in a tumbler
of cold water.   You can add a few drops of peppermint or
half a glass of sherry to take away the nasty taste; but the effect
of the laudanum is just the same.   Sip it slowly for an hour or

an hour and a half before going to bed, as if it were wine, and as if you liked it. Do not go out again the same night, but go to bed pretty early. The chances are you will be perfectly well in the morning.

In case you are afraid to take laudanum, though it is but an idle fear, adopt the following recipe:—Before going to bed, put the feet in hot water, and have a warm bed. As you step into bed, or just after it, take either a Dover's powder in a little preserve, or a teaspoonful of sweet spirits of nitre in a teacupful of hot milk; cover up with extra blankets or rugs. Either one or other of the remedies will produce violent perspiration, which will probably bring about the desired effect. If all else fails, try a Turkish bath.

Another remedy—whose value is as yet unknown to the medical profession—for colds, viz. aconite, either in tincture or pilules, one every four hours, often produces an excellent effect; and gives relief as soon as, or sooner than anything else.

Chapped Hands.—After washing the hand, and before drying them, pour over the backs of them some glycerine and water (equal proportions), smear it over them, and then quickly dip it into water and dry the hands gently, so as not entirely to wipe off the glycerine.

Chest, Inflammation of.—VARIETIES.—This term would include pneumonia, or inflammation of the substance of the lungs; bronchitis, or inflammation of the air tubes going to the lungs; and pleurisy, or inflammation of the thin membrane which covers the lungs and lines the chest. It requires medical knowledge to distinguish these one from the other, but as they have many symptoms in common they are here, for facility or domestic treatment, classed together. The following principal distinctive features of each may, however, be of some use:

SYMPTOMS.—In pneumonia, or inflammation of the lungs, there is a dull aching, or more severe, pain at some parts (usually the lower part) of the chest; difficulty of breathing, with a frequent short cough with very little expectoration, which will probably be of a rusty color or slightly streaked with blood. There is also a difference in the two sides as to the ease or discomfort of lying down. The skin dry or pungently hot, and in feverish state.

In bronchitis the pain is more extended but less acute, and the fever runs less high, the tightness of breath less; expectoration is looser, and frothy.

In pleurisy there may be no cough at all, the fever less active; but the pain is cutting and acute, and usually referable to a spot or limited part, and increased by coughing, etc. The pulse will be accelerated in each, the tongue furred, the bowels disturbed in their functions, the urine high colored and depos· iting a red sediment.

Inflammation of the chest generally begins with the symp- tioms of catarrh, or of a severe cold; when the inflammation, however, affects the substance of the lung or its covering, the previous catarrhal stage is often short or entirely absent. The pain and feverish symptoms appear at once. The tendency of these forms of inflammation of the chest is to recover under ordinary care; but pneumonia sometimes goes on to absces, bronchitis may run on into a chronic form, and cause suffoca- tion by the profuse quantity of phlegm secreted. Pleurisy may terminate in the pouring out of a quantity of fluid into the chest.

BRONCHITIS.—This is the form of inflammation of the chest that is most prone to become chronic, and to recur as "winter cough" periodically, attended with profuse expectoration and shortness of breath. In aged people, the winter cough is prone to become seriously aggravated by severe weather, under which circumstances debility rapidly becomes extreme, and the patient becoming drowsy, and unable to relieve himself of the phlegm, dies from suffocation.

TREATMENT.—In the mildest form of bronchitis, or simple catarrhal fever, the treatment need be little more than what is practiced for a common cold, such as, for an adult: Ten grains of Dover's powder, taken at bedtime, and followed by some simple aperient early the next morning; or, three or four grains of James' powder at bedtime, together with warm bath or warm footbath, and warm drinks—such as tea, wine, whey, &c. If the cough persists, take of ipecacuanha wine, two drachms; oxymel of squills, 10 drachms. Mix. Take a tea- spoonful three or four times a day. Apply also mustard plas- ter to the chest at bedtime. In the feverish colds to which children are very liable, the above plan of treatment may be pursued, reducing the doses to suit the ages of the little patients, avoiding the use of the opiate (Dover's powder) in their cases.

TREATMENT OF ACUTE BRONCHITIS.—If the skin be hot, the cough urgent, and the breathing accelerated or oppressed and attended with pain, the surface of the chest should be en- veloped with hot fomentations, or turpentine stupes, or mustard plasters. Should the pain be very acute in breathing, the painfal part might be painted with the blistering liquid and afterwards covered with wadding, or with spongiopiline, soaked in warm water. If the pulse be full and rapid, an emitic of antimonial wine may be given—viz., a teaspoonful every five minutes until vomiting occurs, which is to be encouraged with draughts of warm water. If the fever be not very high, or if the patient be not very robust and strong, an emetic of ipecacuanha wine, given in the same way, should be preferred, as the antimonial emetic sometimes proves very depressing. After these first measures have been carried out, the expectorant effects of the medicines may be kept up by repeated small doses—e. g., ten drops of ipecacuanha or antimonial wine every three hours.

Acute bronchitis occurring in children is to be treated on the same plan. The following powder is useful for a child about two or three years of age, where there is much cough and fever; Take of powdered ipecacuanha, 1 grain; calomel, 3 grains; nitre, 12 grains; white sugar, 12 grains. Mix, and divide into six or eight powders, according to the age of the child, and the strength and severity of the disease. If the bowels are relaxed by the powders, the calomel should be omitted. A warm bath should be given morning and evening.

TREATMENT.—Chronic bronchitis, occurring mostly in constitutions impaired either by age or previous illness, requires a different treatment as regards diet and regimen, as also it demands more stimulant and tonic medicines. The frequent application of external irritants and stimulating liniments is more useful here than even in acute bronchitis. This may be effected by friction with compound camphor liniment, or hartshorn and oil, or spirits of turpentine, or the use of repeated mustard plasters, and occasionally blistering the chest.

Chicken Pock.—In the majority of cases this is a mere trifling malady, with little or no febrile symptoms. In many others it is preceded with a four-and-twenty or six-and-thirty hours' feverish disturbance. These symptoms usually subside on the appearance of an eruption of pimples on the body, face, and head. On the second day the pimples present small vesicles or bladders, containing a clear fluid like water. On the third or fourth day the vesicles contain opaque yellowish fluid; these dry and fall off in scabs during the next two or three days, leaving, generally, no trace behind. Sometimes, however, the skin is slightly pitted, especially if the spots have been scratched or picked.

TREATMENT.—This consists in a light diet, and the mildest aperient medicine, if even any be required at all. The disease is sometimes mistaken for modified small-pox, and vice versa. But it will be noticed that the vesicles of chicken pock stand on the pimple like a small bubble or bladder of water, and that they have little or no inflammation around their bases. In small-pox, even when modified, there is always an inflamed base to the vesicles, which are flattened instead of globular. Chicken pock runs a much shorter course than modified small-pox. The latter seldom, even when most distinctly modified, lasting less than ten or twelve days; chicken pock seldom exceeding six or seven, and being mature on the fourth day.

Chilblains.—The best remedy for these, when not broken, is to paint them twice a day with strong tincture of iodine.

A liniment of equal parts of extract of lead and spirits of turpentine is also very useful.

If inflamed and broken, they should be poulticed and dressed with some simple ointment.

Cholera:—English or Autumnal Diarrhœa.—Symptoms.— In the heat of autumn it is very common that diarrhœa sets in suddenly, without any signs of previous bilious disorder. It is frequently accompanied by cramps of the legs, with nausea or vomiting; the tongue is furred, and great thirst is caused; the pulse is feeble; the loose motions are numerous—bilious at first—becoming more and more watery until they contain little more than mucus.

Treatment.—If there has been no indiscretion in diet to excite the attack, some warm and astringent medicine may be given at once; as, creasote, or chalk mixture, or tincture of catechu. (See Table of Medicines for the doses). If these fail to relieve the symptoms, a pill of one grain of opium will sometimes stop the looseness and relieve pain and sickness. This dose, however, should not be given to children. Should the attack be traceable to indigestible or improper food, a dose of castor oil should be given in the first instance. Opium or astringents may be given afterwards. The simplest diet should be taken, such as beef-tea, arrowroot, etc. Brandy may be given if there be signs of prostration or faintness.

Cholera:—Spasmodic, Malignant, or Asiatic.—Symptoms. —This is usually preceded by a variable period of promonitory looseness of the bowels and a feeling of general indisposition, although there are many cases on record of its sudden acces-sion without any warning. Such cases have generally been met with in hot climates. In the severe form of cholera the previous choleratic diarrhœa becomes altered in character; before this takes place, recovery is not unfrequent. The stools b ·come watery, having a peculiar odor and "rice-water" appear-ance. The vomiting assumes the same character. There is a feeling of sinking and prostration, rapidly increasing. Cramps occur, beginning in the feet and hands, extending to the limbs and body. The features assume a sunken, contracted aspect, with a look of indifference in the countenance. The surface of the body becomes cold and blue, or leaden-hued, and has a clammy sweat. The tongue partakes of the coldness of the surface. There is great thirst. The pulse feeble, soon altogether fails to be felt. The voice also acquires a feeble tone, being sometimes scarcely audible. The kidneys cease to act, and urine is suppressed, and complete collapse and death rapidly supervine, at periods varying up to two days on the average. Notwithstanding the feeling of coldness of the surface, the patient himself suffers from a sensation of burning heat internally, and craves for cold drinks. After the cold stage has lasted an uncertain time—it may be as long as forty-eight hours, if recovery takes place—it is followed by reaction and a febrile stage, which may run into a typhus condition, in which stage many cases prove fatal.

TREATMENT.—Everything here depends upon early treatment; half an hour's delay may determine a fatal ending. When cholera is prevalent a mere loose motion should immediately be attended to.

FOR THE PRELIMINARY DIARRHŒA.—Immediately on the occurrence of diarrhœa, if there be any suspicion of its having been excited either by indiscretion in diet or impurity of water, half an ounce of castor oil should be given, and in three hours after its action it should be followed up with some astringent and sedative, as: For an adult, one grain of opium in the form of a pill every four hours, until the diarrhœa begins to decline. Or, chalk mixture, 1 ounce; tincture of catechu, 2 drachms every three hours. Or, creasote, 20 drops; spirits of salvolatile, 4 drachms; paregoric, 4 drachms; water, to 6 ounces. Mix. Give a fourth every three or four hours. Or, dilute sulphuric acid, 30 mins; tincture of opium, 10 mins; water, 2 ounces. Every four hours.

Mustard plasters on the pit of the stomach help to check sickness.

A light diet, consisting mainly of beef-tea, with small occasional doses of brandy. If these means fail, and the case go into the stage of collapse, external warmth in every possible way should be promoted. Bottles of hot water, heated bricks, bags of hot salt, etc., should be placed about the body and limbs, over which warm blankets should be covered. Copious draughts of cold water should be allowed to allay the thirst, notwithstanding that these may be rejected by vomiting. At the same time half a drachm of spirits of salvolatile should be given every two hours. The cramps are to be relieved by friction, or by pressure on the muscles that are cramped. When reaction takes place, the treatment must be gradually modified, with greater caution in the use of stimulants. If the febrile reaction go into the typhus state, the case then requires the treatment of typhoid fever. (Which see.)

Clergyman's Sore Throat.—SYMPTOMS.—An affection of the organs of the voice, to which public speakers are liable. It is not a sore throat in the ordinary sense of the term, but is an affection of the vocal organs extending to the surface of the throat. There is a relaxed and elongated state of the uvula. The surface of the back part of the throat has a reddish-purple and congested appearance. The throat becomes dry and the mucus tenacious, so that a constant hawking is occasioned. Hoarseness and difficulty in speaking follow. There is some pain felt in the seat of the organs of voice, and the voice becomes so altered that it is scarcely audible, or is harsh and discordant.

TREATMENT.—As this affection depends partly upon the state of the general health, its condition should be carefully looked to. There is, however, much to be done by the careful management of the respiration in public speaking, so as not to admit a rush of cold air upon the organs at the instant of using them. The lungs should be filled as much as possible through the nostrils, by which means the air is warmed and the force of its entry in inspiration is moderated.

There are two remedies which have considerable power over the parts, viz.: the nitrate of silver, and sulphurous acid. The nitrate of silver may be freely applied with a mop of sponge on the end of a stick or piece of whalebone. Nitrate of silver, 40 grains; distilled water, 3 ounces. The sponge dipped in this solution should be applied to the congested surface of the throat. As, however, this does not effectually apply the remedy to the deeper seat of the affection, the organs of voice, a " spray apparatus " will be found much more effectual. Several convenient forms of the apparatus can be had of the surgical instrument makers, with directions for their use. The sulphurous acid solution is a very valuable means in these cases, when thus applied, twice a day, the inspiration of the spray being repeated for about twenty minutes each time.

Colic.—SYMPTOMS AND DIAGNOSIS.—A severe twisting and griping pain in the bowels, accompanied with flatulence, sometimes with vomiting, and always attended with constipation. The pain is paroxysmal and comes on suddenly, and is rather relieved than aggravated by pressure, as would be the case in inflammation of the bowels, in which also the manner of the attack is different, being in general less sudden in the onset, and constant. In colic the tongue is not necessarily furred, nor is the pulse quickened, both of which conditions will be found in inflammation of the bowels. In one obstinate form of colic the action of the bowels becomes reversed, and vomiting of the motions may take place. In such a case it should be clearly made out that no rupture or internal strangulation of the intestines exists. It is to be observed that a mere muscular pain may be mistaken for colic or for inflammation—the latter, it may be added, more likelv than the former to be the error that is committed

TREATMENT.—The cause of this painful maiady being generally the irritation of some indigestible or acrid food—such as unripe fruit, poisonous fungi, uncooked vegetables, sour drinks, etc.,—these should be removed as quickly as possible, by a full dose of castor oil, with from twenty to forty drops of laudanum for an adult, repeated every three or four hours if need be. At the same time hot fomentations or turpentine stupes should be applied over the belly. A hot bath will often relieve pain and relax the spasm which causes both the pain and the constipation. If flatulence be a predominant symptom, it is very likely the cause of the spasm of the bowel. In that case, the following will probably give relief:

Rhubarb powder, 20 grains; carbonate of magnesia, 30 grains; spirits of nutmeg (or peppermint), 1 drachm; spirits of salvolatile, 1 drachm; water, 2 ounces. Taken as a draught, and repeated in four or five hours if the colic continue. A dose of laudanum may be added. This same mixture, in reduced doses (omitting the laudanum), will serve well for the flatulent griping to which infants are liable.

PAINTERS' COLIC—Being caused by the poisonous influence of white lead (used in their trade), the treatment varies somewhat. White lead (carbonate of lead) being the poisonous pigment that forms the basis of most paint, is rendered inert by being converted into sulphate of lead.

TREATMENT.—This consists in the administration of sulphate of magnesia (Epsom salts) with alum and laudanum. Thus—Epsom salts, 2 ounces; alum, 1 drachm; laudanum, 80 minims; water, 8 ounces. Mix. Give an eighth part every three or four hours, until the bowels are purged and the pain relieved; other local means, as above mentioned, being also employed. Painters may almost entirely avoid the occurrence of colic by making it a point always to wash their hands before meals.

STRANGULATION OF THE BOWEL.—Closely allied to colic, and sometimes following upon it, is this accident, although it may occur from several conditions independent of colic. It is more frequently met with in young children than in adults, as an independent affection. Extreme obstruction of the intestines, from an overloaded condition, may give rise to the same set of symptoms. It may be scarcely possible to distinguish between them, except by the result. Fortunately the treatment may be the same.

SYMPTOMS.—The symptoms are: Frequent desire to empty the bowel, without success; severe pain, usually at some one spot, with extreme tenderness in that part.

TREATMENT.—As soon as the fruitless nature of the attempts to evacuate the intestines are apparent, all purgatives should be withheld. Clysters of large quantities of warm water, or of warm olive oil, should be passed gently into the bowel. By persevering with these, the obstruction is sometimes overcome, and if the cause of the obstruction be loaded bowels, relief will pretty surely follow. The obstruction may last for several days, and yet give way to this simple and unirritating mode of treatment. Vomiting and nausea generally attend these cases, which may be relieved by pieces of ice and small quantities of champagne, or soda-water and brandy.

Concussion of the Brain.—SYMPTOMS.—This condition may be the result of either a fall, or blow on the head, or it may be occasioned by a violent jerk to the body, especially to the lower part of the spine. After one or other of these accidents, the symptoms of concussion will be: Unconsciousness, and loss of power of moving; a small and feeble pulse; the pupil of the eye insensible to the light; the complexion pallid; skin cold, and there may be vomiting. Convulsions, also, are likely to occur if a child is the subject of concussion.

TREATMENT.—Small quantities of stimulants, such as wine, brandy, ether, or salvolatile in water, should be given every half hour, if the patient can swallow, until signs of reaction begin to show themselves. This will be known by the restoration of warmth and color to the surface of the body, together with increased force in the pulse, and gradually reviving consciousness.

Congestion of the Brain.—SYMPTOMS.—Many very different sets of symptoms are often included under this one term. Thus, a "fit" is said to be caused by congestion of the brain, and so is a feverish condition with "head symptoms," so with a "stroke," so also with delirium.

It is indicated by headache, giddiness, unusual dullness of the mind, and of the senses of sight and hearing, or preternatural excitability, impairment of memory, noises in the ears, and a flushed countenance. There is feebleness or sluggishness of movement. The dullness may pass on into apoplexy, or paralysis, or convulsions; or the morbid excitability may be but the precursor of inflammation of the brain.

TREATMENT.—The treatment must be modified very much by its causes. If from over use of the brain, change of scene, fresh air, and bodily exercise may be sufficient to dispel it. Shower-baths, with tonic medicines and mild aperients, will suffice. Sea-bathing, or plunging-bath, should be avoided, so long as there are any symptoms referable to the brain. If the dullness and heaviness persist, more active purgatives may be employed, and a rather more abstemious diet followed.

Constipation.—Costiveness of the bowels is a relative condition—with most persons in health the daily evacuation of the intestines is a habit, while others will allow several days to pass without experiencing any discomfort from sluggishness of the bowels. When this is prolonged beyond the ordinary period, various functional derangements occur—e. g., headache, dyspepsia, nausea, flatulent distention, etc.

TREATMENT.—The graver cases of obstinate obstruction, if they can be made out to be the result of neglected constipation, may be relieved sometimes by hot baths, with repeated small doses of castor oil (a quarter or half an ounce every two hours), or by a pill composed of two grains of extract of aloes and two grains of hard soap, given also every two hours. At the same time clysters of warm soap and water with castor oil (two ounces of oil to a pint of warm soap and water) may be thrown into the bowels every two or three hours. The sickness meanwhile may be relieved by soda-water or champagne, or by swallowing small pieces of ice. The pain should at the same time be relieved by repeated small doses of laudanum (fifteen or twenty drops). It is to be noted that opium should not be given to infants or young children.

Consumption.—The approach of this disease is, as is well known, often most insidious and gradual, so that its real existence may be masked and overlooked in its early stage.

SYMPTOMS.—The first symptom that will generally excite fear is cough. If a young person, a member of a family wherein consumption has been known to occur, has a dry, irritable, ringing cough, or a short, moist cough every morning, and lasting for some time, suspicion should be excited. The cough continuing, some " tightness " in breathing is expressed, and a general derangement of the health follows, with some loss of flesh and strength, disinclination to exertion, dyspepsia, costiveness. Irregular mensturation commonly attends the approach of consumption. The cough occasionally, but not commonly in this early stage, is accompanied with a slight expectoration of blood, and with "stitches" in the side, or partial attacks of pleurisy. These early symptoms may last a variable time, and their true import be overlooked until on some one occasion a profuse bleeding from the lungs, or "breaking a blood-vessel" in popular language, occurs and draws attention to the real cause of all the previous ill health. An attack of inflammation of the lungs, or of pleurisy, may also occur. Or, as is the more common course of the disease, the cough becomes more frequent, and is attended with thick, copious expectorations; the emaciation becomes more striking; the pulse increases in frequency, and is more feeble; the patient suffers from chills, and flushes of the face and hands.

As the disease advances these symptoms become more pronounced as hectic fever; diarrhœa becomes a troublesome symptom; there are profuse night sweats, and rapidly increasing debility. In the face of all these signs of an approaching fatal termination, the patient indulges himself with fales hopes of recovery, and dies sometimes with projects and schemes for the future on his lips.

TREATMENT.—So far as the causes are under control, all prejudicial habits or conditions should be avoided by the patient; all dissipation or excessive work, either bodily or mental. Regular outdoor exercise, with due protection of the surface of the body, and of the lungs also, by respirators in cold weather, avoiding especially sudden change from heated rooms to cold air. Cold sponging and friction of the surface of the body will tend to promote the general health. A nourishing full diet should be taken, consisting of meat, eggs, milk; and, if there be wasting of the body, malt liquor and wine. Residence at the seaside will often so far improve the health as to retard the progress of disease; but change of climate is of little use unless adopted early in the course of the disease. It will then sometimes save or prolong a life. Temperate or cold climates are more suitable for consumptive patients than hot climates.

Of medicines, tonics are those which are most useful. In the early stages of the disease, iodide of potass is useful—e. g., five grains thrice a day with a drachm of tincture of bark. Cod-liver oil, with some mineral acid, thus: Dilute nitric acid, 20 drops; tincture of gentian, 1 drachm; water, a wine glass full, with cod-liver oil, one teaspoonful. Pain in the chest may be relieved by mustard plasters, or painting with blistering liquid. Tincture of iodine painted under the collar bones, in the earliest stages, diminishes cough and relieves pain.

Convulsions, or Fits, are, strictly speaking, symptoms, not a disease; thus they are seen in the low weak state of the termination of disease of various kinds; they are seen in hysterical excitement, and are caused by the disturbance of parturition, and of dentition. They occur in apoplexy, in epilepsy. and other diseases of the nervous system.

TREATMENT.—At the time of the convulsions but little can really be done—cold water may be dashed on the face, and mustard plasters applied to the soles of the feet and calves of the legs. In the fits of children—the child's body being immersed in a hot bath—cold water should be poured on the head from a jug held at a good height. The hot bath, however, cannot be repeated if the fits recur with frequency; the cold water can always with safety be poured on the head.

Corns.—Repeated soaking of the feet in hot water and paring down the corn with a sharp knife, then applying nitrate of silver, and afterwards paring off the hardened black skin. Corn-plasters, having a hole in the center, give great relief also in wearing. Soft corns are relieved by soaking in warm water, and the subsequent application of nitrate of silver. A thick plaster to take off unequal pressure, is extremely serviceable.

Cough.—See Bronchitis, Consumption, etc.; also List of Medicines, Expectorants.

Croup.—This is a disease which is alarming, from the suddenness of its attack and the rapidity with which its runs its fatal course if unchecked; but, on the other hand, in the majority of cases, it is easily checked if the treatment begins immediately it occurs.

SYMPTOMS.—The following is generally the course of the disease: A child is put to bed in its ordinary health, apparently, or it may have a slight cold, and a cough a trifle rough, but not enough to excite attention to it. After a variable time the child wakes up with a hoarse, ringing, rasping cough and difficulty in breathing, and countenance expressive of its trouble; each inspiration and expiration being attended with a rough metallic tubular sound, and the voice masked or obliterated by a harsh, hoarse, croaking vocalization. The cough is dry, harassing, and unattended with expectoration in the outset, but after awhile some portions of a membrane-like mucus may be coughed up. The pulse becomes rapid, the skin hot, the countenance more and more distressed, and if relief be not afforded, the patient becomes drowsy, the complexion becomes blue, and the little patient may die from suffocation within forty-eight hours. Happily, however, this is not the most common course of the disease, if the treatment be prompt and active.

The first thing to be done is to give a teaspoonful of ipecacuanha wine every ten minutes until vomiting occurs. Ipecacuanha wine is preferable to antimonial wine, as the latter is too depressing. (Where children are subject to croup, ipecacuanha wine should always be at hand.) Meanwhile, a hot bath should be prepared, and used as quickly as possible; and while

in the hot bath a wet sponge, sprinkled with mustard, should
be held on the upper part of the chest and front of the neck.
After the vomiting has subsided, small doses of the ipecacuanha
wine (from five to fifteen drops, according to the age of the
child) should be continued every three hours, until the hoarseness in the breathing and voice ceases and the cough becomes
loose. The atmosphere of the bedroom should be kept warm
and moist by steam from a pipe or spout of a kettle. The
temperature should not be allowed to fall below 60 degrees, if
possible. The diet light and simple.

As a last resource, supposing these remedies are not at hand
or obtainable, and the disease is making rapid strides, life may
be saved by applying scalding water to the neck, holding it
there on a sponge or flannel for a minute at least. This is a
most extreme and violent means, but it is one by which the
writer has seen a life saved.

Dandriff.—SYMPTOMS.—Scurf, or dandriff, consists in an
exuberant exfoliation of the minute scales of the outer skin
and sometimes forms an obstinate and annoying effection of
the hairy scalp.

TREATMENT.—Rub in some mild ointment or pomatum,
over night, and wash it out in the morning with soap. Or apply the following ointment at bedtime: Ointment of red precipitate, 2 ounces; balsam of Peru, 1 drachm, and wash it out
the next morning with juniper tar soap.   ·

Delirium Tremens.—SYMPTOMS.—Although one of the
medical terms for the affection, *Mania a potu* (drunkard's mad-
ness) expresses its most common source, yet there are conditions of a very different nature to which occasionally its origin
may be traced. Thus a predisposition to it is engendered by
excessive mental anxiety or exertion, while it may also be excited by any cause of debility operating secretly and suddenly,
such as loss of blood, a serious wound or injury, a severe mental shock. Symptoms sometimes follow on these, precisely resembling those seen in the ordinary delirium tremens, and it
would be incorrect morally and medically to attribute them in
such instances to the vice of intemp   ce. The symptoms
generally appear suddenly, sometimes ..cr a premonitory state
of nervous restlessness, with disturbed sleep, loss of appetite.
and general derangement of the bodily health

TREATMENT.—Where the cause has clearly been intemperance, the first, and, indeed, the cardinal point in the treatment,
is to get the alcohol that has caused the disease withdrawn from
the system. It is usual to administer freely of stimulants;
which plan possibly arose out of the proverbial treatment of
hydrophobia—"a hair out of the tail of the dog that bit you,"

The practice is contrary to reason, and has not the results of experience in its support. The system being already more than saturated with alcohol, it is surely heaping Pelion on Ossa to administer more. The practice further places the victim of his own bad habits at a disadvantage, by robbing him of the opportunity of breaking them off. Too often, indeed, whatever pains may be taken to restrain him, "the sow that was washed will return to her wallowing in the mire;" but no reason is thereby supplied for holding the poor beast down in the mire.

If the patient be preserved as much as possible from the sources of excitement, by being kept in a quiet and darkened chamber, protected by strong attendants from injuring himself or others, and fed with light nourishing diet, such as beef-tea, arrowroot, milk, eggs, etc., the delirium will gradually subside, and sleep will follow. This plan of treatment, which has been advocated by Dr. Wilks, of Guy's Hospital, has the great advantage over the usual systematic administration of heroic doses of opium, that it is safer. In the hands of non-professional persons, the attempt to cure delirium tremens by large doses of opium, must succeed only by the death of many patients. If, as the delirium subsides, the pulse be found feeble, ammonia may be given, or steel and quinine. In what has now been laid down in regard to the delirium of *mania a potu*, it is not intended to forbid the moderate use of stim lants and opiates in delirium arising out of other causes of delirium than drink. In the sleepless delirium of a brain exhausted by overwork, from shock, or by other debilitating causes, small quantities of wine or brandy, and doses of Dover's powder, may be advisable.

Dentition, Teething Fever, Irritation of the Brain.—The febrile disturbance attending the cutting of the first set of teeth, which process is not complete until the end of two years, is often very considerable, and, inasmuch as the symptoms produced by it not seldom resemble to a certain extent those of inflammation of the brain, they have been collectively termed "irritation" of the brain, although it would not be easy for those who employ the term to define it.

A febrile condition appears, the infant becomes restless and fretful, its rest is disturbed, its head becomes hot. The gums are swollen and hot. Sometimes there is sickness and diarrhœa, in other cases the bowels are found to be costive. One point of distinction between the disturbance of teething and that caused by inflammation of the brain, is that the soft space on the top of the head, if it still remain open, is not full and raised, but depressed and cupped. Another point to be noticed is the age of the infant. Dentition commences at very varying periods—from the ages of three or four to upwards of twelve months—and is usually completed on or about two years of age, so that these symptoms occurring sooner or later must be regarded as depending upon some other morbid condition of the brain or its membranes. Before the teeth appear, their growth is often indicated by dribbling, which may appear as early as two months of age. Over-feeding or indiscreet dieting will sometimes produce the symptoms of brain disturbance. It should be borne in mind that the period of dentition is one of febrile disturbance in the constitution, and is calculated, in the event of the existence of any lurking taint of constitutional disorder, to be the occasion of its being brought out into activity. This being the case, and dentition frequently following near to the operation of vaccination, the latter has to bear the discredit of what probably neither the one nor the other alone would produce.

TREATMENT.—In the first place, use warm baths and mild aperients, such as magnesia or grey powder, with a light, careful diet. This will generally suffice to assist in removing the symptoms, which, however, generally quickly subside if the gum can be lanced.

Diabetes.—Considerable misapprehension of the meaning of this word exists in the minds of many persons. It is not every excessive secretion of urine that constitutes diabetes. In the sense of a disease, as here intended, it includes the voiding of sugar therewith persistently.

SYMPTOMS.—This condition comes on very gradually and insidiously. The patient gets out of health, is weak, has a general feeling of malaise, why or how he does not know This state of things continuing for some time, he begins to notice that he voids more urine than usual, and at last perceives that very large quantites are voided. Then loss of flesh to emaciation becomes observable, as also thirst, with dryness of the tongue, which exhibits great fissures in its length. The breath acquires a smell like fresh hay. The skin becomes harsh, the bowels constipated. There may be some pain in the loins.

TREATMENT.—The principal part of the treatment resolves itself into rigid dieting, which should consist in the exclusion of sugar in all its forms, and in the use of animal food, mainly —e. g., meat, eggs, milk. "What to eat, drink, and avoid," becomes almost the business of life, in some cases of diabetes. We may briefly enumerate some rules for the guidance of choice in diet.

WHAT TO EAT AND DRINK.—Bran bread, gluten-bread; mutton or beef; poultry, game; ham, sausages, brawn; whitefish, shell-fish—e. g., oysters, lobsters, crabs; green vegetables and sa ads; water, milk, tea, coffee; claret, sherry, brandy and water. Condiments, e. g., vinegar, pickles, mustard, salt.

WHAT TO AVOID.—Ordinary bread, potatoes, farinaceous substances generally; sweet fruits and pastry of any kind; malt liquors and sweet wines. These rules of dieting should be rigidly observed by young subjects of diabetes; they may be somewhat relaxed in the cases of aged persons. The surface of the body should be protected by warm flannel undergarments; the sponge bath, with brisk friction, should also be employed to promote the circulation in the skin.

MEDICINES.—The only medicine that can be administered with any certainty of benefit is opium. This may be given in the form of pills, half a grain three times a day, or as Dover's powder, five grains three times a day. The dose may be safely, if very cautiously, augmented.

Diarrhœa.—As a symptom of bilious disorder, and as constituting the prominent feature of English or Asiatic cholera, this complaint will be found treated of under those heads. There is, however, a common form of the disorder, which appears very often in hot weather, without any other indication, and which, if neglected, will lead to fully-developed cholera, if that disease or its causes be at the time prevalent; while, on the other hand, it is easily arrested if taken in time.

TREATMENT.—For an ordinary attack of diarrhœa—not arising from any known cause, such as irregularity of diet—a dose of the common chalk mixture (one ounce), with a drachm of tincture of catechu, repeated every three or four hours, will generally prove sufficient. If otherwise, three or four drops of creasote, mixed with a teaspoonful of spirits of salvolatile in a wineglass of water, will check it.

. If the diarrhœa be profuse, and attended with much pain, a single dose of one grain of opium (taken as a pill) will often be sufficient for the purpose of relieving pain and arresting the purging. This dose is for an adult only. Diarrhœa occurring in infants and young children is best controlled by one or two teaspoonfuls of chalk mixture, given after each loose purge. If it prove obstinate, the following will most probably be efficacious: Take a few chips of logwood and boil half an hour in half a pint of water. Mix two ounces of this decoction with half a drachm of powdered alum, and enough powdered sugar to sweeten it, and give a teaspoonful after each action of the bowel

Diseases of the Eye.—Ophthalmia (inflammation of the eye). There are several forms of this disease, named according to the exciting cause of the inflammation. They are seen

21

in the following forms: Catarrhal; Purulent in children; Purulent in adults; Strumous, or Scrofulous; Rheumatic.

CATARRHAL OPHTHALMIA (MILD OR CATARRHAL INFLAMMATION OF THE EYE).—SYMPTOMS.— There is a redness or bloodshot appearance of the eye, an itching and smarting pain in it such as might be caused by a grain of sand or dust. There is a certain feeling of stiffness in moving the ball of the eye, and some difficulty is experienced in looking at the light. There is also a profuse discharge of tears from the eye, which causes the lids to be glued together in the morning, when the patient wakes. If the disease becomes more acute, there is a discharge of thicker matter. Sometimes this form of ophthalmia terminates in the formation of vesicles on the eye.

TREATMENT.—The following lotion will be found useful: Sulphate of zinc, 3 grains, dissolved in distilled water, one and a half ounces. A drop or two of this lotion should be carefully dropped into the corner of the eye, the lids being then parted, the lotion will run into the eye. If a small notch be cut along each side of the phial cork, the lotion can be allowed to pour out only a drop or two at a time. A dose of compound ipecacuanha powder (Dover's powder) at bedtime, and a few doses of saline aperient will generally set this form of inflammation to rights. If, however, the discharge should become thick, and the pain more severe, blistering should be applied to the temple

PURULENT OPHTHALMIA OF CHILDREN.—SYMPTOMS.—This generally commences on the second or third day after birth, and extends over the entire surface of the eye. There is swelling of the lids, which are glued together by a copious discharge of pus or matter, which, when the lids are separated, pours out from between them. On opening them, the inside of the lid is found to be of a bright scarlet color. The discharge from the eyes is generally yellow, but it becomes sometimes green, or tinged with blood. Should the inflammation not be properly and early attended to, it causes ulceration of the cornea or transparent circle in the centre of the front of the eye, and, if this occur, blindness follows.

PURULENT OPHTHALMIA OF ADULTS.—EGYPTIAN OPHTHALMIA.—SYMPTOMS.—This disease is very similar to the above, with these exceptions, that it generally attacks both eyes at once, and there is but little intolerance of light. In this disease also the inflammation sometimes spreads into the ball of the eye, causing thereby intense intermittent pain

TREATMENT.—Purulent ophthalmia requires very much the same treatment, both for adults and for infants. It must be stated, however, that this form of the disease in infants is catching. Great care should therefore be taken to wipe the discharge with pieces of rag which can be burnt directly. After applying the various remedies recommended, the hands should always be carefully washed.

The following lotion should be dropped into the eye as above directed: Nitrate of silver, 3 grains, dissolved in distilled rain water, one and a half ounce. (The solution of nitrate of silver will stain like marking ink anything it falls upon.) Blisters should be applied behind the ear on the affected side, or on the temples. For adults the following mixture should be taken: Epsom salts, 4 drachms; powdered nitrate of potash, tartar emetic, 1 grain; nitre, 30 grains; infusion of senna, 2 ounces; water to 6 ounces; a sixth part every four hours. The first dose or two may produce sickness; this will subside with subsequent doses, and is calculated to check the inflammation. To infants, a teaspoonful of fluid magnesia should be given every day, or more frequently if the bowels be confined. Should the pain be very severe, ten grains of Dover's powder may be given, but only to adults, as it contains opium.

RHEUMATIC OPHTHALMIA.—SYMPTOMS.—A form of inflammation which attacks the thick white coat of the eye. The eye becomes of a dusky red, but not so much blood-shot as in the other forms. The fully distended blood-vessels can be distinguished radiating in straight lines from the edge of the cornea or transparent circular membrane in the front of the eye, which also becomes duller. There is excessive flow of tears, and great intolerance of light. In this form of inflammation the pain is more intense, and is not confined to the ball of the eye, but is felt in the surrounding bones of the forehead and cheek.

TREATMENT.—If the inflammation be very acute, it will be advisable to apply three or four leeches on the temples, and then to blister either in that situation, or behind the ear. The following aperient should be given at once, and repeated until it acts: Sulphate of Magnesia (Epsom salts), 2 drachms; powdered nitrate of potash (nitre), 10 grains; infusion of senna, one-half ounce; peppermint water, one-half ounce.

The following mixture should be taken three times a day, after the above draught has acted upon the bowels: Iodide of potassium, 40 grains; bicarbonate of potash, 80 grains; colchicum wine, 2 drachms; water to make 8 ounces. Two tablespoonfuls for a dose three times a day.

The following ointment should be applied round the eye, avoiding the raw or tender surface of a blister or leech-bites: Extract of belladonna, 80 grains; prepared lard, 1 ounce. Rub together.

INFLAMMATION OF THE CORNEA, OR TRANSPARENT CIRCU-
LAR MEMBRANE IN FRONT OF THE EYE.—SYMPTOMS.—This
membrane first appears slightly hazy. This haziness increases,
and the membrane becomes slightly opaque. Minute white
specks may be observed on the membrane; these, after a time,
prove to be ulcers. Sometimes a yellow spot appears. This
is a small quantity of matter which is contained between the
layers of the membrane. If this is discharged inside the
cornea, it falls to the lower edge, and may be seen there like a
yellow crescent. It may, however, ulcerate through in front,
and be thus discharged. Ulcers of the cornea, when healed,
always leaves an opaque white spot. Sometimes they perfor-
ate the membrane, and thus allow of the escape of the fluid
which is contained at the back of it. The eye all round the
cornea is bloodshot; there is a bright scarlet ring close round
the edge of the cornea.

TREATMENT.—This should be much the same as recommended for rheumatic ophthalmia, with this exception—instead
of the iodide of potassium mixture, recommended for that
disorder, the following will be found more useful in this case:
Sulphate of quinine, 16 grains; dilute sulphuric acid, 1
drachm; syrup of orange peel, 1 ounce; water to make 8
ounces. Mix. Two tablespoonfuls should be taken three
times a day.

INFLAMMATION OF THE IRIS, OR COLORED BAND ROUND
THE PUPIL OF THE EYE.—The iris is a muscle, and is largely
supplied with blood by numbers of minute vessels, and therefore very liable to inflammation. The forms of inflammation
which attack the iris may by divided into two kinds. 1st, that
from which arises after injuries, over-exertion of the eyes,
cold, and other common causes of inflammation. This is
called Idiopathic Iritis. 2nd, those forms which are caused by
the poison of constitutional diseases. This is called Specific
Iritis.

SYMPTOMS.—The symptoms be o. diopathic and specific
iritis are mainly the same, with exception—the symptoms
of the latter kind show themselves rather more slowly than
those of the former. There is a change of color in the iris
itself, causing it to lose its brilliant appearance; it becomes
muddy, or acquires a tint which is f rr :d by the mixture of
red with the original color. There is loss of power of motion,
whereby the sharp outline forming the pupil is destroyed and
becomes irregular. The substance of the iris is swollen, there
appear little brown lumps or nodules on the surface of it,
and these sometimes increase in size, so much as to block up
the pupil. There is severe pain all ound the ball of the eye,

affecting the cheek and temple. This pain becomes worse at night.

TREATMENT.—Idiopathic iritis: Three or four leeches should be applied to the temple; the light should be carefully excluded by means of a shade covering the eye; perfect rest of the eye is important. The patient should take for some little time a low diet of .broth, bread, and gruel, or barley water.

The eyebrow should be painted with extract or ointment of belladonna.

One of the following pills should be taken every six hours by adults: Calomel, 3 grains; powdered opium, 3 grains; confection of roses, a sufficient quantity to make a small mass, to be divided into six pills. The effect of these pills on the gums should be carefully watched.

Dislocations.—The difference between dislocations and fractures is that in fracture the bone is broken, while in dislocation it is, as a consequence of some violence, forced from its connection with the neighboring bones. As we speak of compound fractures, or those which are accompanied by a wound, simple fractures, or those in which there is no wound of the skin, so in dislocations, these may be either simple or compound.

It is not always an easy matter to distinguish between a fracture and a dislocation. In certain forms of fracture, there is no crepitation or grating of the ends of the bones to be detected, as the same violence which breaks the bone drives the fragments forcibly together, and causes them to become impacted, or fixed together. In fractures about the region of a joint, the crepitation would be a main symptom by which to distinguish this injury from dislocation. Where it is absent, it is almost impossible for a non-professional person to come to a decision as to the real nature of the accident. Should, however, surgical assistance not be obtainable, the best plan to pursue will be to pull steadily at the injured limb until it resumes its shape and length. By this means, if the bones be dislocated, it may be possible to reduce the dislocation, and if fractured, it may, by loosening the bones, cause the distinctive sound of crepitation, and other signs of fracture, to be distinguished.

DISLOCATION OF THE JAW.—This may readily be detected by the imbecile appearance it gives the patient. The mouth is fixed wide open, and the saliva runs out at the corners. It is impossible to close the mouth, the patient making ineffectual efforts to articulate.

TREATMENT.—The patient should be seated in a high-backed chair, or against a wall, in such a manner that his head may lean against the back of the chair, or the wall. The operator should then wrap a couple of napkins round his thumbs, one on each, and when by this means they are well protected, he should place them as far back along the jaw inside the mouth as he can reach. He should then press with his thumbs downward and backwards, and at the same time raise the chin with his fingers. The bone will return to its place with a snap. The advantage of having wrapped the thumbs well round with napkins will then be experienced; for the teeth come together very sharply, and, were the thumbs not well protected, bites of a severe character might be suffered. Another method pursued for the reduction of this dislocation is to place a couple of corks between the back teeth, raising the chin, and making the corks act as a fulcrum between the jaws.

DISLOCATION OF THE SHOULDER JOINT.—Th' may be distinguished by the evident lengthening of the arm and flattening of the shoulder. If compared with the other side there will be found a dent, or depression, just under the point of the shoulder. Frequently the round head of the arm-bone may be felt in the armpit.

TREATMENT.—The patient should sit on the ground and lean his shoulder against a sofa or couch; the operator should mount the couch, and, having removed his boot, should place his foot gently on the patient's injured shoulder; at the same time he should raise the dislocated arm upwards, gently increasing the pressure made by his foot on the shoulder. By these means the bone may soon be felt to slip into the socket with a jerk. When this is effected, the arm should be gradually restored to its original position, and there fastened by bandaging for about a week.

HIP JOINT.—This dislocation may be recognized by the deformity of the limb, the inability to stand on the injured extremity, and, perhaps, the head of the bone may be detected out of its place under the skin.

TREATMENT.—The plan to be pursued is to place the patient on his back, the operator taking off his boot, and placing his heel between the patient's thighs, to make a steady pull at the foot till the bone slips into the socket. The great obstacle to success in this kind of proceeding, is the muscular resistance offered by the patient involuntarily. To overcome, or rather to divert this, the patient's attention should, if possible, be called away to something else, or, if this is of no avail, ipecacuanha should be given in doses of one-fourth to one grain every quarter of an hour. By its nauseating pro- perties it debilitates the patient and relaxes the muscles.

COMPOUND DISLOCATIONS.—These, consisting of fractures also, are, of course, more dangerous than simple dislocations, and are rendered very serious if complicated with fracture.

TREATMENT.—The bones should be replaced as nearly as possible in their natural position, as in the case of simple dislo- cation. Any bleeding should be stopped, either by the appli- cation of cold water, or, if that is insufficient, bleeding arteries should be sought and tied. (See Hæmorrhage.) When the bleeding has been checked, the wound should be searched for splinters of bone, which should be removed by the forceps. The wound should then be dressed and splints applied, as recommended under Compound Fractures.

Dog Bites.—These are very much, though somewhat un- necessarily, dreaded, on account of the fear which exists that they may be followed by hydrophobia. When it is considered how many people are bitten by dogs, and how few people have hydrophobia, it will be seen of what groundless nature is that fear.

The best method of treatment which can be pursued in dog bites is to make a free application of lunar caustic to the bite.

HYDROPHOBIA.—Although, as above stated, hydrophobia is excessively rare, its occasional occurrence cannot be doubted; it will therefore be advisable not to neglect the above remedies, as there is no doubt that the confidence inspired by their adop- tion soothes alarm, and prevents nervous excitement conse- quent on fright alone.

TREATMENT.—Should hydrophobia come on, chloroform, Indian hemp, and opium are the only means that offer any chance of allaying the symptoms. These drugs may, in such a case, be given in larger doses and at shorter intervals than under other circumstances, watching carefully their effects. (For doses, see List of Medicines.)

Dropsy.—This is purely a symptom of disease of some internal organ, or is the result of the debility and deterioration of the blood in certain eruptive fevers. As its nature and treatment occur in speaking of the diseases of various organs, it is unnecessary to speak here what is said under those several headings.

Drowning, or Suspended Animation.—The following in- structions, compiled by the Royal National Lifeboat Institu- tion, are the result of a wide field of experience:

RESTORATIVE TREATMENT.—Send immediately for medi-

cal assistance, blankets and dry clothing, but proceed to treat
the patient instantly, on the spot, in the open air, with the face
downwards, whether on shore or afloat; exposing the face,
neck, and chest to the wind, except in severe weather, and
removing all tight clothing from the neck and chest, especially
the braces. The points to be aimed at are—first, and immediately, the restoration of breathing; and, secondly, after
breathing is restored, the promotion of warmth and circulation. The efforts to restore breathing must be commenced
immediately and energetically, and persevered in for one or
two hours, or until a medical man has pronounced that life is
extinct. Efforts to promote warmth and circulation, beyond
removing the wet clothes and drying the skin, must not be
made until the first appearance of natural breathing. For if
the circulation of the blood be induced before breathing has
commenced, the restoration of life will be endangered.

To Restore Breathing.—Place the patient on the floor
or ground, with the face downwards, and one of the arms
under the forehead, in which position all fluids will more readily
escape by the mouth, and the tongue itself will fall forward,
leaving the entrance into the windpipe free. Assist the operation by wiping and cleansing the mouth.

If satisfactory breathing commences, use the treatment prescribed below to promote warmth. If there be only slight
breathing, or no breathing, or if the breathing fail, then, to excite breathing, turn the patient well and instantly on the side,
supporting the head; and excite the nostrils with snuff, hartshorn, and smelling-salts, or tickle the throat with a feather, if
they are at hand. Rub the chest and face warm, and dash
cold water, or cold and hot water alternately, on them. If
there be no success, lose not a moment, but instantly—to imitate breathing—replace the patient on the face, raising and
supporting the chest well on folded coat or other article of
dress. Turn the body very gently on the side and a little
beyond, and then briskly on the face, back again; repeating
these measures cautiously, efficiently, and perseveringly, about
fifteen times in a minute, or once every four or five seconds,
occasionally varying the side. On each occasion that the body
is replaced on the face, make uniform, but efficient, pressure,
with brisk movement on the back between and below the
shoulder-blades or bones on each side, removing the pressure
immediately before turning the body on the side. During the
whole operation, let one person attend solely to the movements
of the head and of the arm placed under it. Whilst the above
operations are being proceeded with, dry the hands and feet,
and as soon as dry clothing or blankets can be procured, strip
the body, and cover, or gradually reclothe, it, but **taking care
not to interfere** with the efforts to restore **breathing.**

Should these efforts not prove successful, in the course of from two to five minutes, proceed to imitate breathing by Dr. Silvester's method, recommended by the Royal Humane Society, as follows: Place the patient on the back on a flat surface, inclined a little upwards from the feet; raise and support the head and shoulders on a small, firm cushion or folding article of dress placed under the shoulder-blades. Draw forward the patient's tongue, and keep it projecting beyond the lips—an elastic band over the tongue and under the chin will answer this purpose, or a piece of string or tape may be tied round them, or by raising the lower jaw the teeth may be made to retain the tongue in that position. Remove all tight clothing from above the neck and chest, especially the braces. To imitate the movement of breathing: Standing at the patient's head, grasp the arms just above the elbows, and draw the arms gently and steadily upwards above the head, and keep them stretched upwards for two seconds. (By this means air is drawn into the lungs). Then turn down the patient's arms and press them gently and firmly for two seconds against the sides of the chest. (By this means air is pressed out of the lungs.) Repeat these measures alternately, deliberately, and perseveringly, about fifteen times a minute until a spontaneous effort to respire is perceived, immediately upon which cease to imitate the movements of breathing, and proceed to induce circulation and warmth.

TREATMENT AFTER NATURAL BREATHING HAS BEEN RESTORED.—Commence rubbing the limbs upward, with firm, grasping pressure and energy, using handkerchiefs, flannels, etc. (By this measure the blood is propelled along the veins towards the heart.) The friction must be continued under the body by the application of hot flannels, bottles, or bladders of hot water, heated bricks, etc., to the pit of the stomach, the armpits, between the thighs, and to the soles of the feet. If the patient has been carried to a house after respiration has been restored, be careful to let the air play freely about the room. On the restoration of life, a teaspoonful of warm water should be given; and then, if the power of swallowing have returned, small quantities of wine, warm brandy and water, or coffee, should be administered. The patient should be kept in bed, and a disposition to sleep encouraged.

APPEARANCES WHICH GENERALLY ACCOMPANY DEATH.— Breathing and heart's action cease entirely; the eyelids are generally half closed, the pupils dilated, the jaws clinched, the fingers semi-contracted, the tongue approaches to the under edges of the lips, and these, as well as the nostrils, are covered with a frothy mucus. Coldness and pallor of surface increases.

CAUTIONS.—Prevent unnecessary crowding of persons round the body, especially if in an apartment. Avoid rough usage, and do not allow the body to remain on the back, unless the tongue is secured. Under no circumstances hold the body up by the feet. On no account place the body in a warm bath unless under medical direction, and even then it should only be employed as a momentary excitant.

Dysentery, Bloody Flux.—This is an inflammation of the larger and lower intestine, more commonly met with in hot and unhealthy climates, and on board of ships. It is ushered in with almost incessant desire to go to stool. The motions, hard and lumpy at first, become little more than blood and mucus, and are voided with painful straining. The pulse is rapid and feeble, the skin hot, the countenance anxious, the patient restless. In the worst cases the disease becomes chronic, and the patient is worn out by the pain and fever, or sinks rapidly into a state of collapse.

TREATMENT.—A condition essential to the success of treatment is the removal of the patient, if possible, from the sphere of morbid influences that have predisposed him to the disease. Hence the importance of removal to a healthy situation, at the same time that the strictest care and temperance in mode of life be observed, and the protection of the surface of the body by warm flannel clothing. The early and acute symptoms may be subdued by hot baths, hot fomentations, and turpentine stupes to the abdomen. Half an ounce of castor oil should be given, and after it has acted and cleared away any hard motions, five grains of Dover's powder should be taken every four or six hours, according to the urgency of the case; with two grains of mercury and chalk if the motions still contain lumps of hardened fæces. The painful straining at stool is relieved by the injection into the bowel of twenty drops of laudanum mixed in a wineglassful of cold gruel or starch. A gentle aperient at the end of a few days will assist the above remedies by removing morbid secretion and bloody mucus. A nourishing but light diet should be taken, avoiding all hard substances, and for sometime avoiding solids of any kind until the healthy action of the intestines is restored.

The chronic form of the disease requires the continual use of metallic astringents with opium—e. g., Sulphate of copper, 3 grains; powdered opium, 2 grains; bread crumbs, sufficient to form a small mass. To be divided into six pills, one to be taken every six hours. Or: Acetate of lead, 12 grains; powdered opium, 2 grains. Made into pills in the same way, and one to be taken every six hours.

Ear-ache.—SYMPTOMS.— Deafness, pain and noise in the

ear, are often produced by the mere accumulation of wax in the ear.

TREATMENT.—It will generally suffice to clear out the passage by syringing. A large syringe and plenty of water should be used. If not relieved in this way, the application of repeated mustard plasters behind the ears will have a good effect.

Ear, Inflammation in.—IN INTERNAL EAR.—Inflammation in the ear will be inferred from the occurrence of a severe, dull pain in the head, where the ear is placed, accompanied with confusion or loss of hearing, a considerable degree of fever, and even of delirium, if the inflammation be seated in the internal ear.

TREATMENT.—This, in the first case, should be active— e. g., six or eight leeches should be applied behind the ear, followed by hot poultices or fomentations. Brisk purgation should be adopted, while at the same time pain may be relieved by opiates taken internally.

Inflammation in the passage should be treated by poulticing, and a few drops of laudanum in the passage.

Epilepsy—Consists in the concurrence of the sudden loss of consciousness, with more or less convulsive movement of the limbs. In proportion as the two are slight, and the convulsion wanting, the disease has been divided into two forms, called by French writers the petit mal and the grand mal.

The grand mal, the full epileptic fit, is the sudden loss of consciousness and of muscular power, so that, with a shriek, the patient falls to the ground senseless, and is violently convulsed in the limbs, with great distortion of the countenance, lividity of the face, frothing at the mouth, the eyes staring and pupils large, and not answering to the stimulus of light, the breathing labored, appears even to be suspended, while the heart beating so tumultuously that the pulse cannot be counted. In consequence of the tongue being protruded, it is bitten in the violent, convulsive movements of the jaws. The excretions often pass involuntarily. This, the full fit, seldom lasts longer than a few minutes. When it passes off it leaves the patient in a drowsy state, in which he may remain for several hours. The fit may recur during this sleeping state.

The slighter form frequently consists of little more than a slight and rapidly passing condition of unconsciousness or mental confusion, with a varying degree of want of muscular power, so that there may be some unsteadiness of gait or imperfection of vision, and numbness of parts of the limbs. This form usually passes away in a few seconds, and may not well be perceptible to those around, the patient himself being scarcely aware that anything has been amiss with him.

SYMPTOMS.—There are certain, or rather they should be called uncertain, premonitory symptoms that sometimes usher in an attack of epilepsy. The most known of these is a peculiar and indescribable sensation, originating in the extremities and passing up towards the head; this has been termed the "epileptic aura," or vapor. Other indefinite derangements, referred to the nervous system, frequently precede the fit; but, in by far the majority of cases, the fit is sudden and without warning of any kind. A great many fits may occur daily.

Epileptic fits are somewhat difficult sometimes to distinguish from hysterical fits, and from the convulsive movements of apoplexy. In the former case the diagnosis may be made by considering the history of the case, and the absence or presence of hysterical laughing and crying. From apoplexy it may be distinguished sometimes by the dilated state of the pupils in epilepsy, and by the profound snoring and paralysis that commonly attend apoplexy.

TREATMENT.—Protect the patient during the fit from injuring himself. Loosen the dress around the neck and waist, and place him on a bed or couch, with the head and shoulders slightly raised. Sprinkle the head and face with cold water. It is in the intervals of the fits that curative or preventive treatment must be pursued. The exciting causes of dentition, worms, constipation, intemperance, indulgence of passions, etc., should be sedulously avoided or remedied. Tonics may be given, and every measure that can improve the general health should be put in force.

Fainting.—Swooning occurs generally from sudden shock, or from large and sudden loss of blood, or any other cause of depression, mental or bodily, such as profuse diarrhœa and affections of the heart.

TREATMENT.—The patient should be laid flat on a couch or on the ground, with the head as low as possible; the face should be sprinkled or dashed with cold water, free access of fresh air being secured. If able to swallow, let some stimulants be given, such as a small quantity of wine, brandy, or spirits of salvolatile, and apply strong smelling salts to the nostrils.

Fractures.— These are, for convenience of description, divided into several kinds.

1. SIMPLE FRACTURE.—The bone being merely broken in one place, without any wound of the skin at the seat of the fracture.

2. COMPOUND FRACTURES—In which, over and above the fracture of the bone, there is a wound in the skin, through which, perhaps, a portion of the broken bone may be forced.

3. COMMINUTED FRACTURE.—The bone being broken into several pieces.

4. COMPOUND COMMINUTED FRACTURES.—The bone not only being broken into several pieces, but a wound also existing in connection with the fracture.

When a severe accident happens to a limb, it is often difficult to say what is its exact nature—whether a bone is broken or bent, the joint sprained, or the bone dislocated. The following few points may assist in the detection of fracture, if it exist:

DEFORMITY.—This, with shortening of the limb, is sometimes so obvious that there can be no mistake, as, when the arm is so broken that its firmness is lost and the broken portions move on each other. Or when the leg is broken, the fracture is generally rendered evident by the outline of the shin bone. In the latter case, also, as in the case of the fracture of the thigh-bone, if the patient be laid on his back the foot of the broken limb will be seen to be wanting its support, and will fall to one side or the other. The loss of power over the limb will also be some guide, though this will be noticed also in dislocations.

If, however, the limb supposed to have sustained a fracture be carefully taken hold of by both hands and gently moved about, it will, if broken, be found to give way at some one point, where also what is technically termed crepitus, or grating, of the broken ends of the bone may be felt.

GENERAL TREATMENT OF FRACTURES.—The one most important point in the treatment of broken bones is to secure absolute rest of the member to which the fracture may have happened. The utmost care is required in removing the patient from the spot where the accident has occurred to his bed, or more harm may be done in the removal than was done in the first instance. From a simple fracture the injury may become compound, or even comminuted, if care and gentle handling be overlooked. In all cases the bones should be brought as nearly as possible into their natural relative positions. This is called "setting" the bone. "Setting" the bone is effected by one person steadying the portion of the limb attached to the body, while a second person firmly but gently pulls on the other end until it resumes its proper position. The difficulty of effecting this will depend much upon the direction in which the bone is broken, whether transversely or obliquely.

SPLINTS.—This being done, the next thing is to take means

for keeping them in position. This is to be effected by a "splint" of some kind. Where proper splints, made by surgical instrument makers, cannot be procured, there are many things often at hand which may be improvised into what is wanted. Thus, long, straight straws, placed and bandaged on, side by side, will form a clean and handy splint. Pieces of straight wood, cut to proper length and shape, and covered with a soft pad; pasteboard, or any other stiff material, fastened on with bandages, not too tightly. When the ends of the bone in a simple fracture are easily set into their normal positions, a good and ready splint may be made out of plaster of Paris, or gum and chalk, or white of egg and flour. Either of these two last being spread upon strips of rag, and several strips laid one over the other, will soon dry into a case as hard as board, and from which it may not be necessary to remove the limb until the cure is complete. Before putting this or any other form of splint on the broken limb, the skin should be well washed with warm soap and water.

If the fracture be compound, a portion of the bandage must be so arranged as to allow of water dressing and the drainage of discharges. In the case of comminuted compound fractures, if any pieces of loose broken bone be visible, they should at once be removed by the help of forceps. Diluted Condy's fluid, or carbolic acid and oil (one part of acid to twenty-eight of oil), will be found of great use in dressing compound fractures, as they destroy the injurious effects and fœtid odor of the discharge.

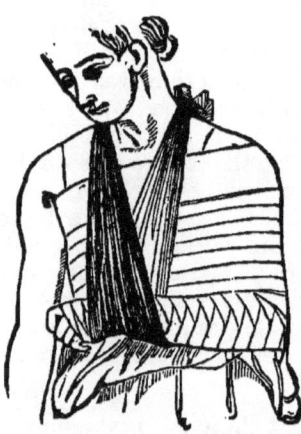

ARM BONES.—If both bones be broken, a splint and bandage as follows: Care must be taken that the palm of the hand is flat to the chest, with the thumb uppermost. Or it may be put up in strips of linen thickly smeared with a paint of chalk and gum, or eggs and flour. Unless severe pain occur the bandage need not be removed under four weeks. A handkerchief, adjusted as a sling, should support the arm.

If one bone of the arm only be broken, the other bone will act, in some measure, as a splint to keep the broken bone in its position.

If the upper or large bone of the arm be broken, the lower arm, from the elbow, should be supported in a sling; or the shaft of the bone being bound by two or four splints, may be bandaged to the side of the body, as shown in the cut.

FRACTURE OF ARM ABOVE THE ELBOW.—This can generally be recognized by the deformity which it produces. The bone should be placed in its proper position in the following manner: One person should steady the shoulder while another person should firmly draw the elbow downwards, until the arm is straightened. When this result is obtained, the bones should be kept in their proper position by means of four splints, which should be well padded and applied round the arm; these should be firmly fastened with a couple of straps, or bands of adhesive plaster. Before the splints are applied, the arm should be well washed with soap and water, and dusted with powdered starch or oxide of zinc. It is advisable not to put the splints on too tight at first, in order to allow for swelling. They may be tightened after a day or so. Fractures of this bone require the splints to be kept on for six weeks.

FRACTURE OF THE ARM BELOW THE ELBOW, OR FOREARM. —Both the bones of the forearm are generally broken together; but it sometimes happens that only one of them is broken. In this case it is not always easy to discern the nature of the accident, as the uninjured bone will act as a splint to the other, and help to disguise the ordinary symptoms of fracture. Crepitation, may, however, generally be detected by taking in one hand the arm at or below the elbow, and gently rotating the hand on the arm. The bones, if displaced, should be set, that is, replaced in their proper position, by gently drawing the hand in a straight line from the elbow, which, for that purpose, should be held by an assistant. When the bones are set, the arm should be well washed with soap and water, and dusted with powdered starch or oxide of zinc. Two well padded splints should then be applied on each side of the arm, and strapped down with plaster. After this, the whole arm should e placed in a sling, taking that it is always carried with the palm of the hand towards the buiy, that is, with the thumb uppermost. The reason of this is that, in that position the two bones are furthest apart, and there is no danger of the wrong bones uniting. The splints should not be too tight to begin with, as the arm will swell a little at first; they should, however, be gradually tightened as the swelling subsides. The most common fracture in this region occurs just above the wrist, and in this the deformity is very great.

The splints in fractures of both bones of the forearm should not be removed under five weeks; if, however, only one bone is broken, four weeks will suffice.

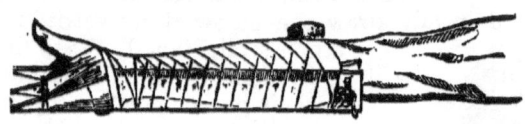

FRACTURES OF THE FINGERS AND HANDS.—When any of the bones of the fingers are broken, they are best treated by placing the whole hand, sandwich fashion, between two well padded splints, strapping them together by means of leather straps or adhesive plaster. When the bones in the middle of the palm of the hand are broken, the patient should be made to grasp a ball of tow, or cotton-wool, and the hand should be bandaged in that position; but if either of the outside bones are broken, the hand should be put up as described under "Broken Fingers."

FRACTURES OF THE THIGH.—These may be recognized by the great deformity, the limb being generally shortened, the inability of the patient to stand on the injured leg, and the unnatural mobility of the limb. The proper treatment of fracture of this bone can scarcely be efficiently applied by a non-professional person.

FRACTURE OF LEG BELOW THE KNEE.—In this region there are two bones; one, which is commonly called the shin-bone, may be distinctly felt down the front of the leg, and for about an inch on the inside of the leg. The other, which is much smaller, is on the outside of the leg, and forms the outer ankle. It can only be felt distinctly in two spots, the one where it forms the prominence of the ankle, and the other where it is attached, just below the knee-joint. In the intermediate space it is embedded in the muscles, and, except with persons of exceptionally small calves, cannot be detected. For the above reasons it will be seen that fractures of this bone are far more difficult to detect than are fractures of the shin bone, whilst fractures of both bones are comparatively easy or detection from the deformity they cause. In fractures of both bones, or of the shin-bone alone, the patient should be placed in bed on his back, with the broken leg supported upon a pillow, and should remain so until any swelling of the leg has gone down. If only the outer, or smaller, bone is broken, a few days rest will allow of the application of egg and flour, or gum and chalk bandage.

The larger bone, or both, being broken, a well padded splint may be applied up each side of the leg, extending to the foot, and bound on with a calico bandage, or by leather straps. The splint on the outer side must be cut away so as not to exert undue pressure on the ankle bone. A cross-piece may be fixed so as to support the sole of the foot at a right angle to the leg, by means of a few turns of bandage. Before the splints are finally bandaged on, care must be taken that the bones of the leg are placed in a straight position, and as nearly as possible to their natural position. This may be judged of by comparing the relative positions of the great toes. The setting of the bones may be effected by an assistant holding the thigh steady, while firm but gentle extension is made from the foot. If there be no displacement of the broken bones, the use of starch and egg, or gum and chalk bandages will give a firm support to the limb.

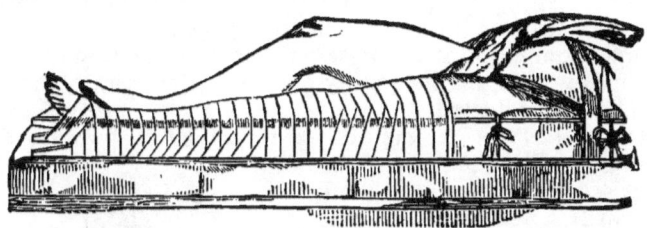

FRACTURE OF THE KNEE CAP.—This may be distinctly felt over the knee joint by the space between the broken edges, and by the loss of power in extending the leg.

TREATMENT.—The limb should be put quite straight, and raised on a pillow. The patient should keep on his back. By these means the two portions of the bones will be brought as near to each other as possible. There will be great swelling of the part, which should be treated with cold water dressing. When this has subsided, two handkerchiefs should be placed round the leg, one above the upper fragment, and the other below the lower one, and these should be connected by pieces of tape. The handkerchiefs may be gradually drawn nearer and nearer together. The nearer they approach each other, the nearer the two fragments will come together, and the pieces will be firmly knit together. This position and bandaging should be maintained for a month, at the end of which time the patient should be allowed to move the limb gently until he regains the use of the limb.

BROKEN RIBS.—The best method of detection of this injury is to place the hand over the painful spot, and to make the patient breathe as deeply as possible. By this means crepitation or grating caused by the rubbing of the fractured ends of the bone together, may be sometimes detected; but as it is by no means certain that this can be always detected, and as it is the only sign by which a broken rib can absolutely be detected, it will be advisable to treat in all cases of doubt as if there were a fracture.

TREATMENT.—The treatment of broken ribs consists mainly in procuring rest for the ribs. This is done by firmly bandaging with a calico bandage, three or four inches wide, the entire chest, so as to diminish the movement of the ribs in breathing. The patient should be kept in bed quietly on his back for a few days after the accident. Any pain should be allayed by Dover's powder or tincture of opium. If severe pain or distress of breathing come on, it probably results from pleurisy.

BROKEN COLLAR-BONE.—When this bone is broken the patient cannot raise his arm without pain. The arm drops, and the patient supports it with the other hand; the shoulder also drops forward and inwards. On feeling gently along the collar-bone, comparing it at the same time with the same bone on the opposite side, the inequality of line at the point of fracture may often be detected.

TREATMENT.—The method of treatment to be pursued is as follows: The shoulder should be raised and pressed gently backward; a pad should be placed in the armpit. This pad should be about two inches thick, and is best made with a pair of stockings rolled up. A figure-of-eight bandage should then be applied, as in the figure. The arm on the injured side should he bound to the side with another bandage, and the hand and forearm placed in a sling. This bone should be kept in this position for four weeks, the bandage not being moved during that time, unless they slip or loosen, in which case they should be carefully tightened

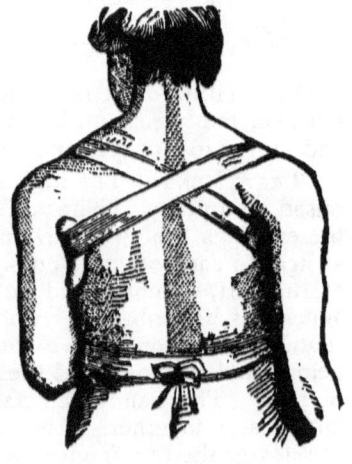

BONES OF THE NOSE.—The broken fragments should be replaced as near as possible in their proper position. This may be conveniently done by raising them from the inside by means of a probe. If the fracture is compound—that is to say, if there is a wound communicating with the broken bones—this should be searched for splinters of bone, which should be removed by means of the forceps. Then apply water dressing.

COMPOUND FRACTURES.—These are fractures in which there is a wound communicating with the broken bone. In cases of this kind the fractured limb after being set should not be encased entirely with splints, but a space should be left for dressing the wound, which should be done as follows: If there are any pieces of bone loose, or nearly so, in the wound, they should be removed by means of the forceps. The wound should then be dressed with a piece of soft linen rag steeped in the following mixture: Carbolic acid, liquified by heat, 50 minims; olive oil to 4 fluid ounces; shake up, and mix thoroughly. This rag should be applied in such a manner as to exclude all bubbles of air; the best way to do this is to cut the rag square and large enough to cover the entire wound—it does not signify if it overlaps the edges of the wound; soak it in oil, and then take hold of two of the corners of it and draw it slowly over the wound until it is covered. Any stray bubbles of air which may remain from the inequality of the surface of the wound should be gently pressed out by the fingers. This dressing should be changed every four or six hours. The limb should be kept cool.

The patient's health should be carefully watched, as in these cases fever very often comes on. Should there be any shivering, an aperient should be given. Thirst should be relieved by iced lemonade or soda-water, and a saline draught should be taken about three times a day. The following will be found most useful: Take of solution of acetate of ammonia, 1 drachm; sweet spirits of nitre, 20 minims: water to 1 fluid ounce. Mix. A compound fracture is always longer in recovering than a simple one, the process of restoration sometimes extending over many months, through the frequent falling off of small fragments of bone, each of which will keep up a discharge of matter until it is removed, either by the use of the forceps, or by the extrusion of the pus.

Ganglion.—SYMPTOMS.—A swelling upon one of the joints, most frequently met with on the back of the wrist. Its seat is the sheath of the tendons.

TREATMENT.—Hard, steady pressure should be made upon it with the thumb of the operator's hand, that holds the arm firmly at the same time. If the pressure be made hard enough, and kept up long enough, the tumor will generally burst and the fluid be dispersed. A tight bandage should be applied immediately afterwards and kept on a few days. Sometimes, if the ganglion be small, it will give way under a smart, sharp blow with a book.

Goitre.—Derbyshire Neck. — Bronchocele. — Symptoms.—

Peculiar enlargement of a gland that is situated at the front and sides of the neck. The swelling, at first slight, and only amounting to a trifling degree of fulness, is prone to increase rapidly, and to cause inconvenience in breathing, as well as considerable disfigurement by its bulk.

Treatment.—The treatment consists in the amendment of the general health, by removal from any locality where the malady is known to prevail, or by remedies directed to correct irregularities of menstruation, to which also it is sometimes attributable. The best medicinal agents are iodine and steel, alone, or in their various forms of combination, with the external application of iodine as tincture, painted on the enlargement night and morning, until the skin becomes too irritable to bear it. The application can be resumed when the skin has recovered, or the iodine may be applied as ointment thus: Ointment of iodine of potash, 1 ounce; ointment of idoine of mercury, one half drachm. Mix. Apply night and morning.

Gout.—Symptoms.—

An attack of gout is generally preceded by disturbed digestive functions, broken sleep and feverishness. The symptoms of an attack generally come on in the course of the night. Severe throbbing pain in some joint, generally in the joint at the ball of the great toe, accompanied with great tenderness, sufficient to prevent the patient from bearing the least movement of the bedclothes over the joint affected. With these symptoms there is a feverish condition, with thirst, rapid pulse and furred tongue. The joint affected is red and swollen, the pains become more and more acute, extending sometimes up the leg, and the fever becomes more severe. This goes on until morning, when a perspiration breaks out, and the paroxysm is over. It, however, probably occurs again the next night, subsides, and recurs at intervals. The hands are liable to attacks of gout, and, after repeated recurrences, the finger joints become the seat of deposits of a white concretion, called "chalk stones," and are thus rendered stiff and useless. The disease may become chronic if not guarded against by careful dieting.

· The heart or brain are either of them liable to suffer in this disease. In the event of the heart becoming the seat of an attack, there is pain, with severe palpitation and difficulty of breathing. Nervous symptoms, such as headache, and sometimes paralysis, or even apoplexy, may attend an attack of gout, and show that the brain is affected by the disease. Gout and rheumatism are often confounded. To distinguish between them the following points should be borne in mind: Acute gout is generally confined to one joint, and the pain is more acute. The constitutional antecedents differ. Gout is an hereditary disease. In the chronic form, these diseases are intermingled with each other, are not easy to distinguish in their acute form. There is a disease called rheumatic gout which combines the two so closely as to render necessary the name applied to it. To distinguish chronic gout from chronic rheumatism, it is necessary to remember that gout is hereditary, rheumatism is not generally so. The history of the attacks, the habits of life of the patient, must also be taken into account. If the patient is indolent, self-indulgent, and given to what are called the "pleasures of the table," the chances are that what he is suffering from is an attack of the gout.

TREATMENT.—In a person of the above habits, the premonitory attacks of indigestion, want of sleep, and feverishness, should be treated with three or four grains of mercurial pill (blue pill) at bed-time, and the following draught early the next morning: Powdered rhubarb, 40 grains; tartrate of potash, 1 drachm; compound spirits of ammonia (salvolatile), one-half drachm; water to one and one-half ounce. Mix.

The attack of gout should be treated as follows: If the pain be severe, and redness of the joint be excessive, a few leeches should be applied to the inflamed surface, but it will not always be necessary to apply them, as hot fomentations or poultices will be sufficient. A small blister raised near the inflamed joint, either by plaster or the "blistering liquid," will sometimes give speedy relief to the pain. When the pill and draught above advised have been taken, and the bowels are thoroughly cleansed, the following medicine may be given: Iodide of potassium, 40 grs; bicarbonate of potash, 2 drachms; colchicum wine, 2 drachms; water to make 8 ounces. Mix. Take two tablespoonfuls three times a day.

If there be want of sleep, compound ipecacuanha powder (Dover's powder) should be given in ten grain doses at bedtime; if the fever be great, antimonial powder (James's powder), combined as follows, will allay it, and relieve pain: Compound ipecacuanha powder, two and one-half grains; antimonial powder, three grains. Mix. Take one every four hours.

Warm baths should be given every day while the attack lasts. At bed-time, a foot-bath of mustard and hot water gives comfort, especially if the feet be afterwards wrapped in cotton-wool, and kept so until the swelling abates.

If the stomach become the seat of the attack, a mustard plaster should be applied on its region, and some narcotic and stimulant given—e. g., tincture of henbane and ammonia. If there be persistent severe headache, a plaster may be placed on the back of the neck, and may ward off more serious symptoms. The diet should be carefully regulated during and after an attack of gout. Stimulating drinks and rich food should be avoided as much as the constitutional power will permit.

The curative treatment of gout, if to be attained at all, must be aimed at during the intervals of the attack. To this end, careful and abstemious living, with exercise in the open air, are important means.

Gravel.—SYMPTOMS.—Pain in voiding urine, sometimes very severe in character, and extending from the loins down the front and inside of the thighs. A small portion of gravel, passing from the bladder, will often cause great difficulty in voiding the urine. A sediment, or small fragment of gravel, may be found deposited in the vessel after a paroxysm.

TREATMENT.—During the paroxysm of pain, a hot bath will give relief, an opiate being taken at the same time.

After the paroxysm is past, the morbid condition of the urine that gave rise to gravel should be corrected. If the sediment be red, alkaline medicines may be taken. (See List of Medicines.)

Hæmorrhage from the Bladder.—SYMPTOMS.—The occurrence of blood in the urine is readily perceived, and therefore requires no description; but as a symptom it is desirable that its several sources should be pointed out. If there be pains in the loins and a feeling of general illness, and the blood be equally diffused through the urine, or be accompanied with minute worm-like clots, the blood proceeds from the kidneys. Should the stream of urine be at first free from, or only slightly tinged with, blood, and the flow become more and more deeply colored, the inner surface of the bladder is most probably the source of the blood. If blood flows drop by drop without urine, the passage external to the bladder will be its source.

TREATMENT.—If the blood be believed to come from the kidney, it will probably be the result of inflammation of that organ, or of some injury inflicted on the loins, or from the existence of a calculus or stone in the kidney. In either case absolute rest in bed must be enforced. Leeches, from eight to twelve, should be applied on the loins; or, if practicable, cupping on the same region to the extent of eight or ten ounces will be preferable. The bowels should be freely opened by saline purgatives, such as Epsom salts, Glauber salts, or Rochelle salts, at the same time, if there be pains in the loins, it may be relieved by five grains of Dover's powder, or extract of henbane, every four hours.

If from the previous condition of the urine—i. e., if it has deposited gravel for some time—it is to be inferred that the bleeding is caused by a stone in the kidney, some alkali should be combined with the sedative, thus: Bicarbonate of potash, 1 drachm; tincture of henbane, one-half ounce; water to 6 ounces. Mix, and give a sixth part every four hours while the pain lasts.

If from the symptoms, before described, the hæmorrhage appears to have occurred in the bladder itself, it will in all probability partake of the character of debility. In such cases the tincture of perchloride of iron or gallic acid or acetate of lead may be tried.

Hæmorrhoids (Piles).—SYMPTOMS.—There are tender and painful swellings of the extremity of the bowels, the inconvenience and troublesome irritation of which are aggravated by walking or riding. They are commonly caused or accompanied by constipation, at the same time the action of the bowels increase their soreness, and often cause them to bleed freely, while the subject of them is at stool. The color of the blood is usually of a bright red.

TREATMENT.—As they originate usually in some defective state of the circulation in the liver and intestines, so they are to be relieved by correcting the state of those organs. This is most surely done, if the piles are of recent appearance, by a light diet, abstinence from stimulants, and the use of enemata of cold water. Simpl. aperients, such as castor oil, or lenitive electuary, by diminishing fulness of the vessels of the lower bowel, are of great use. Bathing the parts with cold water affords relief. Considerable comfort is derived from the application of ointment of galls or any unirritating ointment, as these diminish the friction and pressure that cause sometimes much distress and discomfort. These latter applications are almost the only palliatives within reach of the non-professional for piles of long standing, and which assume to all intents and purposes the characters of tumors.

Headache.—There are few more distressing complaints than a severe headache, few more puzzling to account for in point of suddenness and intensity and in the rapidity of their disappearance. A "nervous" headache, for instance, comes suddenly upon one, and disables us from our duties, and may perhaps be dispelled, as it were magically, by a cup of tea, or a spoonful of spirits of salvolatile. This, however, is rarely the extent of headache. It is not a disease of itself essentially, but is the indication of some morbid condition, it may be only temporary, of the brain or of its coverings. As such it is often a persistent symptom, and the source of inexpressible suffering, more especially if it be the result of some structural disease within the brain or skull. There are, therefore, various kinds of headache—the nervous,' congestive, neuralgic, rheumatic, bilious, etc.

The nervous headache, arising from various causes of debility, may, as already mentioned, be very short lived, and yields rapidly to stimulants and antispasmodics. Congestive headache is of a character distinct from the preceding, as it does not generally come suddenly, is not amenable to the same treatment, but requires the reverse—viz., purgatives and low diet. This form proceeds from constipation, from over-use and exertion of the brain. Bilious headache, or sick headache, differs very little either in origin or treatment from the preceding and requires similar treatment. Neuralgic and rheumatic headache are so closely allied in their nature that they must be spoken of together in relation to treatment. This kind of headache is prone to assume a periodic form. It is to be relived by the remedies for rheumatism—e. g., quinine, or iodide of potassium. Neuralgic headache is sometimes also much relieved by the external application of sedatives. The Belladonna liniment of the British Pharmacopœia applied freely over the surface of the forehead, or on the back of the neck, frequently gives great relief. Care must be taken that the skin is entire. It would not do, for instance, to apply any sedative or narcotic if the skin be tender from a blister, or leechbites.

Whooping Cough (Chin Cough).—SYMPTOMS.—A contagious or infectious disease, beginning as a common cold, and, after a few days, when the febrile symptoms have disappeared, showing a spasmodic or paroxysmal character. The cough comes in distinct fits, each of which consists of a series of forcible expirations or cough noises, followed by an inspiration, or hard drawing in of the breath, with a sound almost exactly like the word "whoop," hence the name. The fits are accompanied with great distress to the patient—the face becomes red, the eyes bloodshot, and at times bleeding from the nose and mouth takes place. These fits are terminated generally by vomiting. During an attack, a child will exhibit great fear, and will run to its nurse or mother, to whom it will cling tightly for protection as it were against the cough.

TREATMENT.—For children of two years old and upwards, the following mixture may be given: Tincture of cantharides, 1 drachm; compound tincture of camphor (Paregoric), one and one-half drachms· compound tincture of bark, 3 drachms;

syrup of Tolu, to make 2 ounces.· Mix. One teaspoonful to
be given three times a day. The chest should be rubbed freely
with compound camphor liniment, or oil of turpentine, or
Roche's embrocation.

If the cough is very troublesome, and prevents sleep at
night, the following will be found useful for children above one
year of age: Hydrate of chloral, 24 grains; syrup of orange
peel, one-half ounce; water to make 2 ounces. Mix. One teaspoonful to be taken at bedtime. The patient should be confined to one room if the disease comes on during the latter end
of autumn, or the beginning of winter, or whenever the weather
is cold. If, however, it comes on in the summer, or when the
weather is warm, the restriction is less necessary.

Hysteria.—SYMPTOMS.—The following are among common
indications of hysteria: Flatulency; the feeling of a lump or
ball at the front of the throat, causing a sense of choking; a
pain in the left side, just below the ribs, as of something sharp,
like a nail, running in; and uncomfortable impulse to laugh or
cry without sufficient provocation, this going on until it becomes
what is known as an "hysterical fit," in which the patient tosses
herself about violently, and, unless protected, would injure
herself.

The causes of hysteria are manifold; constitutional peculiarity, irregular menstruation, luxurious living, or want of something to occupy the mind and body, or mental troubles. A
condition very similar to hysteria sometimes attacks persons
of the male sex; when this is the case, the chances are that the
nervous system is in a weakened state, and will, before long,
manifest more serious signs of its condition.

TREATMENT.—No other disease is more obstinate or more
difficult to treat than hysteria. The general health should be
looked to in the first instance. The following medicine, taken
regularly, may have considerable influence over the symptoms:
Compound tincture of valerian, one-half ounce; fœtid spirits
of ammonia, 2 drachms; spirits of nitrous ether (sweet spirits
of nitre), one-half ounce; water, to make 8 ounces. Mix.
Two tablespoonfuls to be taken three times a day. An attack
of hysterical fit cannot be better treated than by a liberal
application of cold water to the face and chest. The water
should be applied in large quantities, and should be dashed
from a height on the patient. The various antispasmodic medicines, such as ammonia, valerian, assafœtida, camphor, are all
useful for hysteria. They exert still more power if combined
with tonics, such as steel, quinine, zinc, etc. (See **List of
Medicines.**)

Incontinence of Urine occurs most commonly in **young**
children, partly from the effects of habit, partly from the

effects of muscular weakness or spasm of the bladder. When it is met with in elder persons it is doubtless a symptom of some disease of, or injury to, the bladder.

TREATMENT.—When it can be traced to spasm, sedatives are useful; when, however, as is more frequently the case, it is the result of weakness of the muscular fibres of the bladder, the following should be tried: Tincture of perchloride of iron, 10 minims; water, 1 ounce. Mix. To be given twice a day. This dose is for a child of five years and upwards; for a younger child half the quantities will suffice.

Indigestion (Dyspepsia).—SYMPTOMS.—Various kinds of

pains in the region of the stomach, which occur soon after meals. These pains are also sometimes felt between the shoulders and in the back, flatulency causing some distention of the bowels; pain that is called "heartburn," nausea, and sometimes vomiting, headache, disturbed sleep, palpitation of the heart, and other sympathetic inconveniences also occur. Among the chief causes of this disorder of the stomach is the abuse of stimulating liquors, or of narcotics, such as tobacco and opium, the use of too highly seasoned or rich food, sedentary habits, and want of proper exercise. Mere weakness of the system, in which the stomach will partake, is often a cause of indigestion.

TREATMENT.—The main object in the treatment of indigestion is to find out what is the cause of the disorder. This being done, care should be taken to avoid those causes, as above named. Urgent symptoms, such as acrid eructations, heartburn, flatulency, and pain, may be relieved by bicarbonate of soda or potash, or by carbonate of magnesia, e. g.: Bicarbonate of soda, 120 grains; tincture of rhubarb, 3 drachms; peppermint water, 3 ounces; infusion of gentian, to make 6 ounces. Mix. One tablespoonful after every meal; or two tablespoonfuls morning and evening will probably prove curative. If not, the mineral acids should be tried, taken with bitters, such as gentian or calumbia. (See List of Medicines.) The diet should consist of light and easily-digested substances. Care should be taken to avoid those articles which experience has shown the sufferers to be excitants of indigestion.

Infantile Remittent Fever.—(Low fever of children, worm

fever). A non-infectious fever, generally due to some irritation in the stomach or intestines.

SYMPTOMS.—The symptoms of this fever come generally at night, passing off in the morning. They are, shivering, heat of skin, thirst, furred tongue, frequent pulse, sometimes pain and tenderness of the abdomen, sickness. The sleep is disturbed by starting and moaning, the little patient is fretful and restless. Superadded to these, is a short, dry, hacking cough. The bowels are out of order, the appetite at times is good, at others fails altogether, the urine is scanty and high colored. The symptoms vary greatly in different cases; at times the brain seems to be affected, and there may be convulsions; this form is, of course, dangerous. In other cases there is profuse diarrhœa, and, in some, inflammation of the bowels, or lungs, occurs. This fever has been called "worm fever," from a mistaken idea that it is always caused by worms. Though undoubtedly intestinal worms may accompany the other symptoms, they are far from being its cause. Teething is much more frequently a cause; bad feeding, or over-feeding, excessive cold, may one and all produce the disease.

TREATMENT.—Having removed all causes of irritation from the stomach and bowels, by means of castor oil, or a dose of syrup of senna, the patient should be placed on a light diet. As long as vomiting or diarrhœa continues, milk or milk gruel, or arrowroot, or both, should be given; if there be no diarrhœa, rice milk, bread pudding, and jellies may be given in addition to the above; no animal food should be allowed. In young infants, a still stricter diet is required, as the stomach is often very irritable, and will not bear the lightest farniaceous food. In such cases a tablespoonful of cream or new milk should be given every hour or hour and a half. A warm bath should be given for a few nights, and the patient should be kept in bed during the commencement of the illness and its acute periods. The thirst should be met with small pieces of ice or cold water.

The following powder will be found useful to regulate the bowels, if they are disordered, if given at bed-time occasionally: Mercury, with chalk, 3 grains; powdered rhubarb, 5 grains; bicarbonate of soda, 2 grains. The following medicine may be taken when the fever is acute, the doses being apportioned according to age: Powdered nitre, 3 grains; ipecacuanha wine, 2 drachms; syrup, 3 drachms; water to make one and a half ounces. Take one teaspoonful three times a day. As signs of amendment begin to appear quinine wine or steel wine with quinine should be given.

Inflammation.—SYMPTOMS.—Inflammation, while it is certainly the commonest form of disease, and the most frequent cause of both functional and structural maladies, is at the same time a condition much more frequently assumed than ascertained. There exists a common apprehension that any internal pain, especially if it be attended with functional derangement, proceeds from inflammation of some internal organ. It is important that this misapprehension should be corrected if

possible, inasmuch as the treatment must differ widely, accordingly as inflammation is present, or mere congestion, or
neuralgic pain.

TREATMENT OF INFLAMMATION AND ITS RESULTS.—The
general principles of the treatment consist in—1st, moderating
the force of the circulation; 2nd, in reducing the temperature,
and causing contraction of the loaded small vessels; and, 3rd,
in removing the effects of inflammation. The first indication
is effected by depletion, or by medicines which affect the force
of the heart's action. Depletion is effected by bleeding from
a vein, by cupping and by leeching. The last of these is the
only means of depletion that can be employed by a non-professional person; and is, indeed, almost the only means that is
adopted even by professional persons. Venesection, or bleeding from the arm, is now so nearly exploded that there are
medical men who have been many years in practice, who have
never performed this operation. Even leeching is seldom
required. The occasions under which they may be advisable
will be found under the instructions for the treatment of
respective diseases. (See also Leeching.) With the view of
moderating the force of the circul… on, the employment of the
warm bath will be found serviceable, although it would seem
that during the bath the pulse may at first be quickened, faintness may be induced by its prolonged use. Short of this, however, the profuse perspiration that often follows its use reduces
both the rate of the pulse and the temperature of the surface.

The next means for fulfilling this indication will be found in
lowering medicines—such as tartar-emetic, ipecacuanha, calomel, and various purgatives. An important means also to the
same end will be the relief of pain by the use of henbane, etc.
The second indication in the general treatment of inflammation,
viz., the reduction of the temperature and contraction of the
loaded vessels, will, in a great measure, follow on the successful
employment of the means above named for the first indication.
These will be aided by local application of cold, either by
evaporating lotions, or by the use of ice, or by the astringent
action of certain medicines applied externally, such as nitrate
of silver, extract of lead, tannin, etc. If the inflammation be
seated in an internal organ, blistering and external irritants are
serviceable. The last indication, viz., the removal of the
effects of inflammation, such as thickening of parts by deposi-
tion of material into their structure, is to be fulfilled by the use
of stimulants, internal and external, and by tonic medicines,
aided by a full diet.

Inflammation of the Brain, or Brain Fever.—SYMPTOMS.
—This affection, which is also known as water on the brain, or

Hydrocephalus, is of two forms, acute, and chronic. **In the** acute form, symptoms will vary with age.

IN CHILDREN.—In infants, the first symptoms that will be noticed will probably be simple restlessness or fretfulness. The head will become hot, and there may be sickness, which will soon become a predominant symptom. The bowels are for the most part relaxed; the flow of urine notably diminished. If old enough to express its feelings, the child will complain of pain in the head; if too young for that, the same will be indicated by its constantly putting its hand to its head, and rolling its head about. An early symptom is the bending of the thumb inwards on the palm of the hand, and downward flexion of the toes. The eye will be bloodshot, and the brows knitted The sleep of the child is disturbed with starts, or it will wake up as if alarmed. In young infants, the soft part on the top of the head will be full and throbbing. These symptoms are followed in fatal cases by a bending backward of the neck, with convulsions and stupor. It will be seen also that one side of the body is more convulsed than the other, which may be paralyzed. This disease may last for several weeks; during this time the child is constantly uttering a peculiar sharp cry, or moaning, or screaming.

IN ADULTS.—In the adult, the symptoms of inflammation of the brain constitute what is generally called " brain fever;" in which there is a great mental excitement giving rise to delirium. The senses become morbidly acute, so that the ordinary amount of light is not bearable, and noise of any kind is intolerable. The inflammation is attended with great pain in the head, hot skin, and fever. The eyes are bright and bloodshot, the pupils readily contract. The bowels are costive, the urine scanty and high colored. If the disease do not yield to treatment, twitching of the limbs, convulsions, collapse and stupor precede death.

The chronic form is seen exclusively in children, and is often born with them. Its predominant sign in that case is the enlargement of the head, and retarded development of the mental powers, or their premature development. The body is badly nourished, and the digestive functions are disordered.

TREATMENT OF ACUTE INFLAMMATION OF THE BRAIN.— In infants, difficult dentition is one of the exciting causes, the condition of the gums therefore should be looked to in the outset of the symptoms, and, if full and swollen, should be freely lanced, as the pressure of the gum upon the growing teeth and their nerves keeps up irritation of the nervous centres. This operation is simple enough, and requires only one precaution—viz., to cut parallel with the edge of the jaw, **toward**

the front of the gums. The incision should be made downward until it comes in contact with the tooth. If it be made
behind the middle lines of the gums, there is a risk of cutting
through the sac of the second set, which are being developed
behind the first. The operation is better performed with a
proper-shaped gum-lancet, but as this instrument is not often
in the hands of the non-professional, a sharp pen-knife will
serve the purpose. The child's head should be steadily held
between the operator's knees, while its hands are held by some
one else.

Cold applications, such as spirit lotions—e. g., one part of
gin to ten of water, should be kept constantly applied on a rag;
or ice-cold water may be used.

If the symptoms be very acute, two or three leeches may be
applied on the bony prominence behind the ears, as pressure
can efficiently be made there to stop the bleeding as soon as
they come off.

Calomel should be given in repeated small doses, unless it
produces diarrhœa; it should be then changed to grey powder,
with a little powdered nitre. Thus: Calomel, 2 grains; nitre,
6 grains; white sugar, 6 grains. Mix, and divide into six powders. Give one every four or six hours. Or, take of grey
powder, 6 grains; nitre, 12 grains; white sugar, 6 grains. Mix,
and divide into six powders. Give one every six hours. The
diet should be of the lightest kind, consisting mainly of milk
and water. A hot bath should be given at least once a day;
and the body of the infant may with great advantage be
sponged over with warm vinegar and water, equal parts.

If, in about eight-and-forty hours after the adoption of the
above means, the symptoms do not abate, a blister-plaster
should be applied to the nap of the neck. This, in case of
infants, should not be allowed to remain on longer than two
hours. It should then be taken off, even if it has not
raised a blister. A muslin bag filled with bread and water
poultice should be applied to the surface, where the plaster has
been; the skin will then shortly begin to blister. The poultice
should be repeated every four hours, or when it becomes cold.

In most cases the preceding means will have succeeded in
subduing the malady; if, however, as is very frequently the
case, there is a scrofulous constitution, the remedies will not
have so favorable an effect. The symptoms may continue for
many days in a milder degree, and the little patient will then
require the withdrawal of all mercurial medicines and the sub-
stitution of a fuller diet for the milk. Beef-tea may then be
given several times a day, and if the sickness and diarrhœa
should continue, small doses of brandy (from ten to twenty
or thirty drops, according to age) may be given every three or
four hours.

Mouth, Inflammation of.—SYMPTOMS.—Pain in moving the tongue, and sometimes in moving the cheeks, the insides of which are swollen and red; the gums and the tongue also are often much swollen. There appear numerous white patches, which are in reality superficial ulcers, covered with a white false membrane. The tongue is cracked, and scored with a whitish-brown fur, the breath is very offensive, and there is general feverish disturbance, with irregularity of the bowels, and sometimes extreme prostration. This affection may almost invariably be traced to the injuriou influence of sewage air.

TREATMENT.—The first thing therefore to be done is, if possible, to remove the patient to a purer atmosphere. If the bowels be confined, some mild aperient should be given, such as castor oil; or, in the case of a child or infant, the carbonate of magnesia. The following medicine should be given three times a day: Chlorate of potash, 80 grains; water, 4 ounces. A tablespoonful for a dose for an adult, a teaspoonful for a child. In the latter case some sugar may be added for the sake of flavoring it. The following lotion will also be found useful: Chlorate of potash, 40 grains; water, 4 ounces. The mouth being repeatedly washed with it. For children it will be as well to add a little honey, or for infants it will often suffice to smear borax and honey upon the tongue, whence it will be unconsciously applied in the mouth. With adults, some tonic will promote convalescence when the acute soreness has subsided.

Itch.—SYMPTOMS.—An eruption of small pimples, which excite intense itching. They occur most frequently, to begin with, between the fingers, and on the backs of the hands. After a few days, the pimples may also be detected in the bends of the joints—e. g., on the wrist, on the feet, and it may even spread all over the body. The itching is constant, though it is worse at night, when warm in bed, and after violent exercise. If the disease be neglected, and if cleanliness be not sufficiently attended to, the spots become inflamed and fill with matter.

This disease is caused by a minute microscopical insect, called the "Acarus scabies," which burrows beneath the skin.

TREATMENT.—The following lotion should be applied: Quicklime, 1 ounce; sulphur, 4 ounces; water, 1 pint (imperial measure). These should be boiled together slowly for about four hours, and then allowed to stand till the clear yellow fluid can be poured off. Water should be added to this to make the quantity up to two pints.

The manner of applying this lotion is to wasn the affected part with warm water, and then to apply the lotion for half an hour. After twelve hours, the body should be well washed with soap and water, and the skin carefully examined, to see if any spot remain unacted upon by the lotion. Its sufficient action must be judged by the aspect of the vesicles or pimples, those on which it has taken effect will present an opaque yellow white head. This application, well applied once, will generally be found efficient, but it may require a second, and even a third, application. If the pimples be inflamed, and have heads filled with matter, or be ulcerated, the lotion will aggravate them and give pain. Under these circumstances, it must either be considerably diluted with water, or the common sulphur ointment may be substituted for it. When the ointment is applied, it should be allowed to remain on the skin for two or three days, fresh quantities being applied if it is rubbed off. After the second or third day, the whole skin should be well washed with soft soap and water.

Measles.—This is an infectious, eruptive fever, having an incubative period of about fourteen days, commencing with marked catarrhal symptoms, and belonging more especially to the ages of infancy and childhood. The little patient appears to have a severe cold; he has sneezing and running at the nose, "watering at the eyes," and a short, hard cough. This condition, in the course of a day or two, or it may be in a few hours, becomes one of a distinct febrile state. A general heat of the skin comes on, the pulse is quickened, and on the third or fourth day, on the face, chest and body a mottled rash begins to show itself. The rash consists of distinct spots slightly raised above the surface of the skin, and clustered in groups, often having an indistinctly crescentic arrangement. It begins to disappear again in about three or four days, and is usually all gone by the end of a week.

TREATMENT.—The catarrhal symptoms which usher in the measles require only the simplest treatment of nursing, warm baths, and low diet. When the eruption appears and makes it clear that the case is one of measles, the same plan of treatment is still applicable. There is a very large proportion of cases of measles that are in themselves so slight that they really amount to little more than an attack of common cold, and require no other treatment. If, however, there be fever, rather more severe, with a troublesome dry cough (which is very commonly an attendant), a simple saline mixture, as follows, will be found of service: Powdered nitre, 1-2 drachm; ipecacuanha, 1 drachm; paregoric, 1-2 drachm; water (sweetened with sugar), 2 ounces. Mix. A teaspoonful to be given every four hours, to an infant about two or three years of age; the doses for older children should be increased, on the scale given in the list of medicines. For an infant under one year old it may be as well to omit paregoric. If there be constipation of the bowels, some simple aperient should be administered, such as castor oil or grey powder. The body should be sponged over every day with warm vinegar and water.

Should the eruption suddenly disappear, and difficulty of breathing or other symptoms of congestion of the lungs, as shown by du ..ess of the skin and coldness of the surface, come on, a hot bath, with mustard in it, should be had. At the same time stimulants, such as compound spirits of ammonia, wine, or brandy should be administered—e. g., for an adult, a drachm of spirits of salvolatile in a wine-glass of water, every two or three hours. Wine, to the extent of four ounces in six hours, may be given: or brandy in proportion, allowing for its greater strength.

MEASLES IN ADULTS.—When the disease occurs in adults it is usually more severe, and calls for more active treatment. The doses prescribed above should be augmented on the scale given in the list of medicines. There is a popular notion that measles leave behind them something that requires clearing away, and acting thereupon it is not uncommonly the case that the unfortunate child is actively physicked for a few days. The whole proceeding is based on error. When the child is well, better let well alone.

Milk Fever.—SYMPTOMS.—A light form of puerperal fever is that which is commonly known as "milk fever." This is simply a passing febrile condition attending the establishment of the secretion of the milk, if not drawn off freely enough, when the breasts sometimes become painfully distended, and the fever is rather smart for a few days, and then rapidly subsides, with simple aperient salines and abstinence as far as may be from fluids, taking care that the breast is emptied as thoroughly and frequently as possible.

Miscarriage, or Abortion.—SYMPTOMS.—It occurs very often without any warning, but commonly it is preceded by slight pains in the back and abdomen, and by a slightly colored discharge. These symptoms occurring in the early months or weeks of pregnancy, are sometimes mistaken for the return of the ordinary period, which may have been supposed to have been suppressed from some other cause. These warnings may end as such, or the abortion becomes completed by the sudden expulsion of the contents of the womb, attended with more or less hæmorrhage. In some cases considerable hæmorrhage will continue for several days before miscarriage is complete.

TREATMENT.—Rest, with the administration of opiates to allay pain. If the hæmorrhage be profuse, napkins wetted with cold water, or cold vinegar and water, should be applied to the lower parts of the body. The patient should be kept as cool as the season will admit, and some mild aperient should be given, if the bowels have been costive. A light diet should be taken. The following pill should also be given every four hours, if the bleeding continue: Acetate of lead, 2 grains; opium, 1-4 grain; conserve, or moist bread crumb, enough to make a pill. Prevention is an important point in these cases, as when the accident has happened once, it is very prone to recur at the same period of future pregnancies. The third month is a very usual period for abortion to occur.

Nervous Shock.—On the occurrence of a severe accident, such as a fracture of a limb, or a fall from a height, the sufferer is generally found pale, fainting, and perhaps half unconscious, with a small and irregular pulse. This condition of shock to the system may go into a state of collapse from which the patient may never recover. Under such circumstances, however, what is termed "reaction" takes place, attended either with complete recovery in a few minutes, or the complete reaction may be prolonged for a day or two.

TREATMENT.—First and foremost, see that the patient has a good supply of fresh air; let him be placed in the recumbent posture, with the head on a line with the body. Small quantities of stimulants should be given, such as about a tablespoonful of brandy in a wine-glass of water, or a teaspoonful of compound spirits of ammonia (spirits of salvolatile) should be given in a wine-glass of water. Warmth should be secured to the surface of the body by blankets and hot bottles to the feet and legs.

Paralysis.—SYMPTOMS.—After the immediate symptoms of an attack of apoplexy have passed away, more permanent effects are often left in the form of palsy of some of the muscles, or of insensibility of parts of the surface of the body. The body may be palsied vertically, that is, one-half of the body from head to foot, may have lost its sensibility to external impressions, or the muscles on the side of the body may have lost their power of moving the limbs. When the right side of the body is paralyzed, there is very often a defect in the power of speech, by which the patient uses wrong words to express his ideas. Or, the palsy may effect the body transversely, the trunk and limbs below a certain line having lost their power. Another more restricted loss of power may occur, as local paralysis. Thus, one hand, or one foot, may be palsied, or the muscles of one side of the face alone may suffer; or, again, the tongue and palate, etc., may have lost their free movement without impairment of the muscular power of other parts of the body.

TREATMENT.—If the case come under treatment soon after the attack of apoplexy, the symptoms more readily yield to treatment; but the result too commonly is that some degree of paralytic impairment is commonly left behind. In the early phases of this affection, the careful administration of small doses of mercurials—e. g., two grains of blue pill, night and morning, continued for a week or ten days, unless it produce tenderness of the gums and flow of saliva, when it should immediately be stopped. This effect should be carefully watched against day after day. The effects of the mercurial will be assisted by some form of counter irritation, such as blistering the nape of the neck, and keeping the blister open by dressing it with savine ointment, or by rubbing the following ointment on the nape of the neck, night and morning, until an eruption of pimples appears: Tartar emetic, 1 drachm; lard, or spermaceti ointment, 1 ounce. Mix.

After the mercurial has been discontinued, tonic medicines will be found of service, such as steel, quinine, and cod-liver oil.

Pregnancy.—SIGNS OF.—It is sometimes a difficult matter to determine the fact of pregnancy. There is, however, strong ground for belief in its existence, if under possible conditions menstruation becomes suspended in a healthy woman, previously regular in her periods. If to this sign be added, after about four or five weeks, the occurrence of morning sickness, with enlargement of the breasts and development of the glands around the nipple, which begins to be encircled by an areola of darkening skin, the suspicion becomes strengthened, and, generally speaking, time confirms it.

MANAGEMENT OF.—Of the management of the period of pregnancy there is not much to be said, as each woman may act according to her ordinary mode of life and circumstances when in good health.

THE DISORDERS of pregnancy will, however, require notice as to their prevention as well as treatment. The stomach being, through sympathetic irritation, prone to derangement, care should be taken to avoid what is known by individual experience to be indigestible, avoiding the frequent recourse to stimulants to relieve the slight ailments incidental to a natural condition. Indigestion is one of these, and may generally be relieved by bicarbonate of soda or magnesia, or by a rigidly abstemious diet for a few days. Costiveness is also a common attendant upon pregnancy, and leads to a troublesome affection—piles, and should be prevented by dieting, or by occasional doses of some mild aperient, such as castor oil, or rhubarb and magnesia, or citrate of magnesia. Piles, if present, will also be relieved by the action of the aperients. We would warn against the senseless practice of taking frequent doses of oil as a matter of course. There is no call in nature for anything of the kind, and no need for such gratuitous physicking.

VOMITING.—The morning sickness that attends the early weeks of pregnancy amounts in general to little beyond annoyance every morning. Sometimes, however, it becomes so constant and persistent as to be a real illness of itself, preventing the retention of food of any kind, so that the sufferer becomes enfeebled, emaciated, and as if bloodless. The ordinary morning sickness may be moderated by a teaspoonful or two of Noyau, or cherry-brandy in milk, taken quite early in the morning before rising. It should be swallowed, the patient merely turning on her side and raising only on to her elbow—not getting up into the upright or sitting posture. Then lying quietly for an hour, and taking after that time a small cup of strong coffee and dry biscuit; again resting for half an hour after this breakfast.

Quickening is very frequently attended with faintness and palpitation of the heart, but these soon pass away, and are relieved by simple means. These symptoms, however, are apt to recur at any period, under circumstances that disturb health, such as over-fatigue, either in pursuit of pleasure or of duty.

Enlargement and distension of the veins of the legs are apt to occur during the latter months of pregnancy, when the womb, being large and heavy, presses upon the veins in the lower part of the body, and retards the return of the blood from the limbs. Hence, varicose veins are established, and become a fixed trouble. The recumbent posture, by taking off some of the pressure from the internal vessels, is calculated to diminish the distention of the veins of the legs; additional support may be afforded to these by wearing elastic-web stockings.

CUTANEOUS IRRITATION of the private parts often occurs in the early months of pregnancy, and, indeed, in some persons forms the first indication of the pregnant condition. A lotion of carbolic acid applied to the parts several times a day affords considerable comfort. Take of goulard water, one-half pint; saturated solution of carbolic acid, 10 drops. Mix and use as lotion.

IRRITABILITY OF THE BLADDER, giving occasion for constant calls to micturition, is another excessively troublesome affection that often attends pregnancy, especially during the later weeks. The following mixture will be found useful: Muriated tincture of iron, 1 drachm; tincture of henbane, one-half ounce; water to 6 ounces. Mix. Take a sixth part every four or six hours.

Protrusion of the Navel.—This frequently occurs in the early weeks of infantile life.

TREATMENT.—The best method of treating it is to cut a piece of cork or ivory, in the form of a half sphere, and place the rounded side on the protruded navel. Adhesive plaster should then be used to retain it in its place. It is generally necessary to pursue this treatment for some months, particularly in female children. The plaster should be changed every morning, and the skin washed before the cork is replaced.

PUERPERAL FEVERS.—SYMPTOMS.—When a labor has been protracted, a degree of fever sometimes occurs and passes off in the course of a few days. This passing febrile state is, however, very different from the condition commonly known as "puerperal," or "child-fever," which does not make its appearance generally until several days, and is indeed a very grave malady. It is ushered in by indefinite symptoms referable to the nervous system, such as headache and sleeplessness. If night after night passes in disturbed sleep, with or without dreams of a distressing character, and restless indefinite discomfort by day, suspicion should be aroused, and attention drawn to the probable approach of fever. After this indefinite illness has lasted for seven or eight days, it will be found that there is a degree of tenderness on pressure at the lower part of the abdomen, with some pain in moving or on taking a long breath. There will also be a degree of flatulent distention of the bowels. The ordinary discharge will have diminished, as will also the secretion of milk. Shivering will occur alternately with flushing and heat of surface, as detectable by the thermometer. The pulse becomes rapid, but wanting in force.

TREATMENT.—While the symptoms are mild, a few doses of Dover's powder, with mild saline aperient and careful dieting, will generally suffice to insure their disappearance. If there be pain in the abdomen, hot fomentation or turpentine stupes will give relief. Should these simple means prove ineffective, and the symptoms become aggravated, with increase of pain, reliance may be placed in small repeated doses of opium, either as Dover's powder or in form of pill,—e. g., Dover's powder, 5 grains every six hours; opium, in form of pill, half a grain every six hours; turpentine stupes repeated every morning and night. If the bowels should be confined, a dose of castor oil or a rhubarb draught should be given. In most cases this treatment will suffice, with a light nutritious diet. In those cases, however, in which there is a feeling of sinking and prostration, stimulants may be cautiously given. Should there be sickness or vomiting, champagne may be taken, or small and frequent doses of soda-water and brandy.

This form of fever will sometimes last two or tnree weeks, and requires the greatest care in nursing, and in diet, etc., during convalesence.

Purpura.—(THE PURPLES.)—SYMPTOMS.—Patches or spots of a purple color, resembling bruises, their colors also going through the various shades shown in bruises. They are sometimes accompanied by a tendency to bleeding at the nose. There may be some febrile disturbance, but usually the general health shows no sign of derangement.

TREATMENT.—Tonics are required in this disorder. The muriated tincture of iron, with the addition of quinine, forms a very useful medicine. If the bowels be confined, sulphate of magnesia should also be added. For children, steel wine will generally be sufficient, together with a careful nutritious diet of beef tea, meat, etc.

Remittent Fever.—ENDEMIC FEVER.—This fever is not infectious, and it differs from ague in there being no distinct intermissions, but frequently recurring attacks, generally taking place in the morning.

SYMPTOMS.—The face is flushed, there is headache, and occasionally delirium; there is great tenderness in the stomach, accompanied with vomiting of a bilious nature; the bowels are confined, and the urine is scanty. If the bowels are relieved, the motions are of a dark, greenish color, and very offensive. The skin is hot, the pulse rapid, the tongue has a brownish fur. The fever becomes less as the skin becomes moist, and as the patient goes into a sweat, the remission occurs. The remission generally lasts from one to three hours, when the fever again comes on, and gradually increases in severity till it attains the intensity of the former attack, and perhaps exceeds it. During the remissions of the attacks, the patient remains in a state of mild fever, accompanied by giddiness or lassitude. The fever may last from five days to five weeks. A patient may be said to have the fever in a favorable manner as the remissions are more distinct.

TREATMENT.—If the bowels are constipated, the following aperient mixture should be taken: Epsom salts, one-half ounce; tincture of rhubarb, 1 drachm; water to make one and a half ounces. Mix. When the remissions have clearly set in, the patient should take the following draught three times a day: Sulphate of quinine, 3 grains; syrup of orange peel, 1 drachm; dilute sulphuric acid, 10 minims; water, 1 ounce. Mix. Quinine is not only of value as a curative agent in the endemic fever, but it is also a preventive. Travelers in the low and marshy districts of tropical climates do well to take two or three grains of quinine every morning.

Rheumatism—Is an inflammation or febrile affection that attacks the joints and muscles, or their coverings and sheaths, in various parts of the body. When the large joints are the seat of the disease, in its most active form, it is known as rheumatic fever, on account of the feverish condition that accompanies it. It is often, however, met with in a less active form, as subacute, chronic, or neuralgic rheumatism.

GENERAL SYMPTOMS.—In the acute form the pain in the joints is so acute, and they are so sensitive to the slightest movement, that the patient dreads even a shaking of the bed he lies on. The joints are swollen, and red as well as painful. A high degree of fever attends the inflammatory affection of the joints; the pulse is full, strong and fast; the tongue is furred; the bowels generally costive; the urine scanty and high colored. The seat of the inflammation is rapidly changed from one joint to another, the pain subsiding to return perhaps as severely as before.

SUBACUTE RHEUMATISM.—In this form the pain is less severe, and there is a slighter amount of fever. It affects more the muscles than the joints. Of this kind are "lumbago," "rheumatic headache," etc.

RHEUMATIC AFFECTION OF THE HEART.—In the acute form, or "rheumatic fever," the coverings and interior of the heart are prone to become inflamed. The occurrence of this complication may be inferred if pain be felt in the region of the heart, attended with palpitation and difficulty of breathing.

TREATMENT.—The several joints as they are affected should be wrapped round in cotton-wool, covered with gutta-percha tissue or oil-silk, the joint being previously gently rubbed with belladonna liniment. When the pain and inflammation first come on, the patient should, at bed-time, take the following powder: Calomel, 2 grains; Dover's powder, 10 grains. Mix. Next morning the patient should take the following draught: Infusion of senna, 2 ounces; tartrate of potash, 2 drachms; compound spirits of ammonia (salvolatile), one-half drachm. After the bowels have been freely open, the following medicine should be commenced: Bicarbonate of potash, 2 drachms; water, 6 ounces. Mix. Two tablespoonfuls to be taken, either alone or effervescing, with a tablespoonful of lemon juice, three times a day. The addition of ten minims of colchicum wine sometimes aids the effects of this mixture, but it is apt to produce sickness and purging.

If there is great pain and want of sleep, or if the bowels are open too much, a grain of opium, or twenty minims of laudanum should be taken every night. The above alkaline mixture should not be continued too long, as it is apt to cause irritation of the intestines. As soon as the pain begins to subside, and the urine to assume its usual appearance, it should be stopped, and the following medicine substituted: Sulphate of quinine, 16 grains; dilute sulphuric acid, 1 drachm; water, 8 ounces. Mix. Two tablespoonfuls three times a day. If there be reason to suspect that the coverings of the heart are affected, a blister should be applied on the front of the chest, over the seat of the heart.

A low diet of milk, arrowroot, rice or sage, or beef tea, should be continued throughout the acute stage, with a change to a more liberal diet as the symptoms subside.

CHRONIC RHEUMATISM.—SYMPTOMS.—The pain of this form of rheumatism is less acute, and is more frequently situated in the muscles or their tendons than in the joints. The parts affected become stiff and painful on movement. There is not often much swelling or inflammation of the joints —except of the small joints, as of the fingers—after the disease has lasted long.

TREATMENT.—The parts affected should be rubbed with a mixture of equal parts of belladonna and soap liniment, or with compound camphor liniment (see External Applications), and if the pain and inflammation be very acute, as sometimes they are, turpentine fomentations should be applied.

The following medicine should be taken: Iodide of potassium, 40 grains; bicarbonate of potash, 2 drachms; water to make 8 ounces. Mix. Two tablespoonfuls three times a day.

SCIATICA.—It sometimes attacks the leg, beginning at the upper part of the back of the thigh, and extending downwards to the foot. The pain of this-form of rheumatism is very acute, and it is by far the most troublesome to treat.

TREATMENT.—The application of strong stimulating liniments over the seat of the pain. If the pain be severe, it may sometimes be allayed with half-grain doses of opium every six hours. Iodide of potassium and tincture of bark should also be given. (See Medicines.)

Scarlatina. Scarlet Fever.—SYMPTOMS.—This is a highly infectious eruptive fever, common to all ages, which makes its appearance sometimes almost suddenly, but generally after a day or two of general indisposition, in which vomiting almost always occurs. The rash consists of minute scarlet spots, which are scattered over the entire body. They are not raised above the surface of the skin, over which a diffuse redness commonly prevails. The characteristic appearance is presented by the tongue, which is of a bright scarlet color round the edges, the middle being furred with the papillæ of a bright scarlet color, standing out, and giving it the appearance of a strawberry. The throat is sore and scarlet, with difficulty in swallowing. On examining the throat it will be found that the tonsils are often swollen and ulcerated. The glands in the neck are swollen also. The pulse is rapid and small. There is great thirst, with entire loss of appetite for food. The rash lasts from five to seven days, when it gradually fades away. The skin, after a variable period, begins to peel off as fine dust or scales; sometimes large flakes come off. The entire skin of the fingers or toes sometimes comes off in one piece like the finger of a glove. The itching caused by the eruption is sometimes a source of great irritation and sleeplessness. In the active febrile stage of the disease it often happens that delirium occurs during night, which subsides with the fever.

TREATMENT.—A hot bath should be given night and morning, so as to promote the functions of the skin and bring the rash out fully. This is an important point, as when the rash is not out plenteously, the specific poison of the disease has a tendency to affect internal organs, the brain especially. The bowels should be kept open by means of saline aperients. The following mixture is useful during eruptions: Carbonate of ammonia, 40 grains; simple syrup, 1 ounce; water to make 8 ounces. Two tablespoonfuls to be taken three times a day, one tablespoonful by children less than ten years of age, and less for infants; but it is not easy to get young children to swallow medicine or food, in consequence of the soreness of the throat. If the throat be ulcerated, small blisters should be applied outside, on the neck, under the angles of the lower jaw bone. (See Blistering). The throat and tonsils should be painted inside with the following: Nitrate of silver, 20 grains; dissolved in distilled water, 1 ounce. The best way of painting or mopping this on the throat, is to tie a small piece of sponge very tightly on the end of a piece of whalebone, taking care to touch the tonsils at each application. The diet should be light. Free ventilation is an essential point in the treatment of scarlet fever. It must be secured so as not to expose the patient to sudden cold or chill. Disinfection should be carefully attended to.

Scarlet fever sometimes assumes a malignant form. From the very beginning there is a depression of nervous power, the eruption is dusky, and the ulceration of the throat very acute. In this case, stimulants must be given, as wine or brandy and water; but in other forms of the disease, these are seldom needed.

Small-pox. Variola.—CHARACTER.—This is an infectious eruptive fever, having, in its natural form, a definite course from the moment of infection to its termination. We shall in the first place describe the disease as unmodified, in which its course is divisible into the several phases, or stages, of incubation, invasion, eruption, decline.

INCUBATION.—The stage of incubation, or period during which the disease is being developed in the system, covers a lapse of twelve days from the date of infection, and passes usually without any manifest sign of disease.

INVASION.—At the end of twelve days, the symptoms of invasion make their appearance in indefinite febrile illness, principally marked by pain in the back, and at the pit of the stomach. These premonitory symptoms last for forty-eight hours, and vary greatly in degrees of severity—some cases assuming the character of very severe illness, the exact nature of which is not clear. The use of the clinical thermometer will here be found a help in diagnosis. If the temperature of the body be as high as 100 degrees, or above that, there will be no room for doubt that a fever is impending. Other circumstances, such as possibility of infection, etc., will further assist in arriving at an opinion. The severity of the premonitory symptoms has usually a direct relation to the severity of the subsequent eruptive fever.

STAGE OF ERUPTION.—The premonitory illness having existed for forty-eight hours, begins to decline simultaneously with the outbreak of the eruption, in the shape of minute, red pimples, which feel like millet-seeds beneath the skin. They appear first on the upper parts of the body, and last on the legs and feet. In from twenty to thirty hours the eruption is nearly as fully out as it will be.

VARIETIES.—The number and character of the pimples give rise to varieties, which have been recognized and designated as: 1. Distinct, or discrete; the spots not being very numerous, and clear spaces of skin being left among them. The fever is slight in these cases. 2. Confluent: in many cases the eruption is more copious, the pimples running together and forming large clusters. In this form the fever runs high, and the danger is greater in proportion to the number of pustules. There may be an intermediate variety. 3. The semi-confluent, in which the clusters occur in patches, leaving other portions of skin free from the eruption. The febrile symptoms are neither so mild, nor so severe, as in the above varieties.

TYPES.—Any one or all of these varieties of the disease may run through their course, ending in perfect recovery; or the symptoms may be characterized by extreme severity or prostration from the beginning. This is the "malignant" type of the disease; the others are the "mild" or "benignant."

COURSE OF THE ERUPTION.—In the ordinary course of the disease, the pimples are red and inflamed by the end of the second day; after this, they gradually begin to show a conical apex, filled with a colorless fluid, and, by the fifth day, they present a small vesicle of this fluid with flattened instead of a conical top. The vesicles from this date alter in appearance, and become pustules, being filled with matter which is "mature" by the eighth day. In this state of the eruption the surrounding skin is red and swollen, and it is at this point that the eyelids swell considerably from the looseness of their texture. The patient is then commonly spoken of as being blind, but in truth he is only blinded for a time. Some pimples appear also in the mouth, and throat, in most cases causing hoarseness and cough.

STAGE OF DECLINE.—After the maturation of the pustules on the eighth day, up to the eleventh day, the pustules begin to dry up and form scabs. This scabbing process, however, does not proceed equally over the body, and may last for several weeks on the extremities. It is accompanied by a return of febrile symptoms, often rather severe, and attended with excitement of the brain. This has been termed the "secondary fever." It generally begins to subside after the eleventh day, which has been regarded by some observers as a "critical day." Pitting is pretty sure to follow on unprotected or natural small-pox. Such is the ordinary course of natural small-pox, in its non-malignant form.

MODIFIED SMALL-POX.—If the subject of small-pox has been vaccinated, the disease may be cut short at any one of its stages, and disarmed of its dangers. The eruption is rendered slighter, and less likely to leave pits. The fever is slighter, so much so as often to exceed very little that of chicken-pox. It may be affirmed that as a rule vaccinated cases of small-pox recover with very little of ill effects of any kind, beyond discolored traces of the pustules, which gradually fade away.

MALIGNANT SMALL-POX.—This form of disease is marked from its outset by signs of nervous depression, and deterioration of the blood. The pulse indicates loss of strength, while the blood shows grave alterations in its composition, such as blood spots on the skin, resembling bruises and flea-bites. The pimples scarcely go into the vesicular or pustular stage, but becomes filled with extravasated blood, giving them a purple hue. When vesicles of this character are seen, even if it be among others of a healthier aspect, they betoken more than usual danger. Hæmorrhage from internal organs most commonly follows, and the patient succumbs in the course of a few days.

The conditions most favorable to recovery from small-pox are youth, previous good health, and vaccination. The unfavorable circumstances are infancy and old age, the supervention of other diseases, such as erysipelas, boils, abscesses, congestion of internal organs, and pregnancy. This last is almost always attended with abortion in small-pox.

Inflammation of the coats of the eye is very prone to occur during an attack of small-pox—in severe cases running on sometimes to the total destruction of the globe of the eye.

PROPAGATION.—Small-pox may be propagated by infection, or by inoculation. The latter is now never practiced, since it has been made to be, in law, a felony, punished by heavy fine or imprisonment. The incurrence of the disease by infection is called "taking it in the natural way." How long after the subsidence of all the symptoms of small-pox an individual may be able to communicate it "in the natural way" is not known. Probably no risk exists of its propagation from the person after all the scabs have fallen off, and the patient has had repeated baths. To prevent its propagation the thorough disinfection of all clothing and bedding should be effected as early as possible.

TREATMENT.—For the disease itself the treatment consists more in watching its course and relieving complications than in the administration of remedies with any view to cure. Small-pox having a definite course cannot be interfered with by active treatment without fear of causing mischief:—all that need be done is to administer some mild aperient in the outset, and then some simple saline mixture if the fever run high. A mild distinct case is far better left to run its natural course. Separation of the sick from the healthy, and a plentiful supply of pure air, are of greater importance, almost, than the adoption of curative measures. The sleeplessness and delirium which often attends the febrile state that accompanies maturation of the vesicles, are readily allayed by Dover's powder. If the entire surface of the body be sponged daily with warm water, or vinegar and water, the irritation of the skin is much allayed thereby. Inflammation of the eyes should be immediately attended to. A small piece of linen rag, dipped in cold water, or Goulard water, should be laid over the eyelids and be kept constantly wetted. The main treatment of mild or simple small-pox resolves itself into nursing and dieting. During the early febrile stages, diet of bread and milk is the best. Light slops, such as broths, may be allowed also, and ripe fruits, such as grapes, oranges, etc., to allay thirst. When the process of scabbing has advanced a few days, and the secondary fever is on the decline, meat should be given, and if the pulse becomes feeble some wine in addition will prove beneficial. In the severer or malignant small-pox, wine or brandy will be required earlier. The indication will be a sense of sinking expressed by the patient, and feebleness of the pulse. In the malignant or hæmorrhage form wine should be given to begin with, and doses of the muriated tincture of iron.

PREVENTION OF PITTING.—A point in treatment to which great importance is attached is to prevent pitting or scarring. Countless have been the schemes that have been put forward with great boast and pretention as infallible preventives of the disfigurement. Having tried a great many of the plans, and seen them tried on a great scale, we cannot advise our readers to rely upon any one that has yet been put forward, except previous vaccination. This exerts such a controlling power over the disease that it, even in severe cases, may pass away without pitting. The separation of the scabs is promoted by painting them with sweet oil as soon as they are formed.

Spasm, or Cramp, may be a symptom of some nervous affection, or of inflammation of some internal organ. Essentially they are the same thing, but a distinction is generally made to the effect that spasm affects internal muscular parts, as of the stomach or intestines, while cramp affects the muscles of the limbs. Internal cramp or spasm may be distinguished from inflammation by pressing on the part. Steady pressure gradually affords some relief in spasm, whereas the pain is increased thereby if its cause be inflammation.

TREATMENT.—For immediate relief of spasms or cramp, an adult may take laudanum, 20 minims; ether, 30 minims; or, chloric ether, 30 minims, in a wineglass of water. And repeat every three or four hours.

Splinters, Thorns, etc.—These should be removed, if possible, by the use of forceps. If they are left in they may cause inflammation, and the formation of abscesses, or gatherings. If the foreign body cannot be extracted, a linseed-meal or bread-poultice should be applied. Matter will probably form, and may be required to be let out by a puncture, in which case most probably the thorn or splinter will be evacuated at the same time. The inflammation will begin to subside as soon as this has occurred.

Stings of Insects, etc.—SYMPTOMS.—The stings of wasps or ants, or bees, as, indeed, do most of the bites of insects, present very much the appearance of what are called poisoned wounds. The history of the case will generally be that the patient has suddenly felt a very sharp pain in the part affected, though, perhaps, he has not noticed any unusual appearance about it. Within a short, but variable period, there is a feeling of irritation about the spot, which rapidly becomes red and swollen, and sometimes acutely painful. On close examination, it will be found that there is a small speck about the centre of the inflamed part, and in this the sting of the insect is sometimes found. The severity of the symptoms will of course vary, according to the state of health, or constitution of the patient. The inflammation may be confined to a small circumscribed spot, or it may spread over a whole limb, and be attended with signs of prostration.

TREATMENT.—If the sting have been left in, as it usually is by wasps, it should be carefully extracted, if it can be got hold of, by forceps or tweezers. If there be simply a small red irritable spot, it will be sufficient to dress it with a cold evaporating lotion, such as the following:

Vinegar, 1 ounce; spirits of wine, 1 ounce; water, 4 ounces. Mix. This should be kept constantly applied by means of a piece of lint, or soft linen rag.

Spirits of salvolatile is also very useful for local application in slight cases of stings. Should, however, the inflammation spread much, poultices of linseed-meal should be applied.

Should the wound have been inflicted by a snake or other venomous insect, and the system be at all affected, if the patient seem faint or prostrated, stimulants should be given freely, thus: Spirits of salvolatile, 1 drachm; water to 1 ounce; every hour; or brandy and water, if the ammonia be not at hand. If the bite proceed from some animal, whose bite is known to be of a dangerous nature, nitrate of silver should be freely applied to the wound as quickly as possible. If the wound be on a limb, it will be as well to tie a handkerchief or other ligature tightly round it above the part bitten.

The venomous effect of certain snake bites, as that of the cobra di capello, are so rapid in their development that, unless speedy or immediate aid be rendered, the patient will stand but little chance of recovery. The bite of the adder is occasionally followed by very serious symptoms. The bite, or rather the stings, of certain scorpions are often of a severe nature. In nearly all cases of snake-bite, the symptoms consist in a fearful state of depression, during which, unless the strength be supported, the patient will sink.

If the wound be inflicted on one of the limbs, a ligature should be very tightly tied round it above the wound.

The object of the treatment, as above stated, is to support the strength of the patient until the poison shall have passed out of the system.

Stomach-Ache: 1. IN CHILDREN; 2. IN ADULTS.—1. To begin with this very "common heritage" of infantine and childish "woe," first and foremost show your sense, as far as a fond (and foolish?) papa or mamma can be supposed to show it, by preventing the "little ones" from eating and drinking what you know, and they don't know, to be a likely *fons et origo malorum.* For instance, prevent their eating raw and unripe fruit; going into the garden and picking and swallowing green peas, sour gooseberries, and so on; in short, keep them on their proper diet, eggs and milk, in especial, the only two perfect *per se* kinds of food; good brown bread, made at home of whole-ground wheat, infinitely more nourishing than the fine white bread, too often adulterated, for the sake of the color, with alum, to the ruin of the teeth and confinement of the bowels; Scotch oatmeal porridge, with plenty of milk, not odious salt and the like. N. B.—Do not expect your young child to thrive on tea and white bread and butter only; still less on buttered toast. A growing child needs something better at breakfast than that. If you yourself know nothing about the proper diet for a child, then buy one of the London Hospital Pharmacopœias, particularly one of the "Children's Hospital Pharmacopœias," at the end of which a proper dietary for a child, according to its age, is given.

If stomach-ache does come, in spite of all reasonable precautions, then, if you have no doctor at hand, or in case you don't, in your wisdom, think fit to call one in, or in case you cannot pay him if you do—then, *faute de mieux,* give from a quarter of an ounce of tincture of rhubarb to half an ounce, according to age and strength, with from two to four drops of laudanum, and four or five drops of essence of ginger in about a wineglass or a little more of water. A little sugar and grated nutmeg in it will do no harm, and make it more palatable. Cut him, or her, as the case may be, a bit of thin fresh lemon-peel, and give it to set the little teeth into as soon as the *succus amarus* is swallowed, to take the taste away; or, if you cannot get this, then a thin slice of a ripe apple, or a small suck at an orange. A child won't take medicine any the better another time, for having had the nasty taste in its mouth for minutes after it has swallowed its first dose. Put the child to bed, warm and comfortable; and, if the pain continues, repeat the dose, and apply warm fomentations, flannels wrung out in hot water, with a few drops of spirits of turpentine sprinkled on them to the pit of the stomach.

Better still, if you are near and have access to a hospital dispensary; or, failing that, to a good chemist's, then have the following recipe made up, and give it: Ten grains of carbonate of magnesia; 10 grains of aromatic powdered chalk; 15 to 20 drops of the tincture of rhubarb; 1 ounce of peppermint water. Repeat the dose in half an hour if the pain be not quieted. This will suit a child of eight or ten years of age.

For pain in the stomach in infants, try, before you give Dill or any other medicine, gentle pressure with the palm of the warm hand on the abdomen, quietly and steadily applied. The pain, probably owing to wind only, will pass away.

N. B.—Have woolen clothing (as soft flannel) worn next the skin. Whole-meal bread, but not bran bread for little children, and fine oatmeal only should be used. Avoid newly-baked bread too. Second day bread is the best, well-fired, and not raw and doughy.

If pain be aggravated by pressure and rubbing, the stomach-ache may be more serious, and advice should be sought. Warm light poultices and one dose only of castor-oil. The directions for the use of laudanum must be regulated according to the age of the child; viz., one drop for every year of its age. For adults, the castor oil and peppermint draught should be advised too.

2. IN AN ADULT.—Act much in the same manner as with this complaint in a child, if you have nothing better within reach than tincture of rhubarb; only, of course, use a stronger dose, say from half an ounce to an ounce of the tincture, and from five to ten drops of laudanum. In case you can get it made up, probably no better prescription can be given than that which bears in Hospital Pharmacopœias the barbarous Latin name of *Haustus carminativus*, the draught, that is, that acts like a charm, viz: Five grains of rhubarb powder, with the same quantity of powdered ginger; 10 grains of bicarbonate of soda; 20 drops of the aromatic spirits of ammonia, and 1 ounce of cinnamon water; or, if you cannot get that, plain water will do.

Stone-Pock.—SYMPTOMS.—This troublesome and disfiuring affection of the skin has the synonyms of "Acne," "Carbuncle-face," and "Rosy drop." It consists in scattered pimples, occurring usually on the face, chest, back, and shoulders. They appear first as small hard pimples, with minute black points, consisting of obstructed openings of the glands of the skin. After an uncertain period, the pimples increase in size, become inflamed at their base, pus forms, presenting yellow heads, then scabbing off in the course of a week or ten days. This is the form in which the eruption makes its appearance in the young and healthy, about the period of puberty, to their great annoyance and discomfort. In advanced life the eruption assumes a congestive character, and is of a dark or fiery red hue, often very obstinate and chronic in its nature. It is this form which has acquired the rather approbrious synonym of "Carbuncle-face."

TREATMENT.—However anxious young people may be to

get rid of what they feel to be a very disfiguring eruption, they must make up their minds to endure it with as much patience as may be, since it will often last for a year or two, and then gradually disappear. We would, therefore, warn our readers against taking strong medicines with a view of getting rid of it. A more important point is attention to diet and the general state of health. A nutritious, unstimulating diet should be taken. A simple aperient of an alkaline character, taken occasionally, together with the use of mild lotions, are the utmost that should be attempted. Thus, for aperient mixture: Bicarbonate of potash (or soda), 2 drachms; infusion of senna, 2 ounces; infusion of gentian, 6 ounces. Mix. Take an eighth part twice a day. For lotion: Corrosive sublimate, 2 grains; rose-water, or pure water, 8 ounces. Mix, and mark "poisonous." Apply to the skin night and morning. Or, common washing soda, 1 drachm, to a pint of water, and apply freely, drying the skin again with a soft towel. Or, half an ounce of bicarbonate of soda, or potash, added to the water of a sponge bath.

The chronic form of acne may be taken as a type for the treatment of chronic diseases of a pustular order generally.

In all these, attention to diet is equally important, but it may be fuller, and some stimulant should be taken in the cases of adults. The internal use of arsenic, and of mineral acids, according to the age and state of constitution, will be found most serviceable, due attention being paid also to the functions of the liver and kidneys. The following prescriptions may be tried. Diluted nitric acid, 2 drachms; compound tincture of bark, 10 drachms. Mix. Take a teaspoonful three times a day in a wineglass of water. Or, Fowler's solution of arsenic, 1 drachm; solution of potash, 3 drachms; tincture of gentian, to 2 ounces. Given as above. The dose of solution of arsenic should be cautiously increased by 30 drops to the bottle at end of each ten days, for about three times. The dose will then be as large as it will be safe to entrust to nonprofessional hands.

If, during the administration of arsenic in these small medicine doses, there should occur griping sickness and itching of the eyelids, the medicine should be stopped. Its use should also be discontinued if it seems to exert a depressing influence on the system.

For outward application, in chronic acne and other pustular affections, there are several ointments and lotions. Thus: Sulphate of zinc, 20 grains; glycerine, 1-2 ounce; water, to 6 ounces. Mix.

Stranguary (Difficult Micturition). — SYMPTOMS. — This spasmodic affection may be caused by the application of a blister-plaster or of blistering liquid to any part of the body; or by inflammation of the bladder or other disorder of the urinary organs; by hysteria or by pregnancy. The spasm causes great distress by the ineffectual efforts that are made to empty the bladder, which, the more it is distended, the more severe the pain becomes, so that the slightest movement or pressure becomes intolerable.

TREATMENT.—It is caused by the irritation of a blister-plaster, a sedative (as tincture of henbane, or laudanum) and warm drinks, with time, will relieve the suffering.

When it proceeds from internal causes it will depend also on these for its treatment; when, however, it occurs in hysterical states, the tincture of perchloride of iron, with tincture of valerian, or assafœtida, may be tried. (See List of Medicines.)

Struma, or Scrofula.—This is an unhealthy state of constitution, which gives a character to the diseases or disorders of those who possess it. Thus it is regarded as the basis of glandular swellings in the neck, and is somewhat loosely spoken of as "scorbutic habit of body."

All diseases occurring in strumous habits require a supporting and tonic treatment.

Sunstroke.—SYMPTOMS.—These resemble the symptoms of congestion of the brain, and come on occasionally with great suddenness after exposure to the direct heat of the sun. In other cases the symptoms are slower in their approach, and in children resemble those of affection of the brain from teething.

TREATMENT.—Apply cold to the head, and mustard-plasters to the soles of the feet and calves of the legs, giving repeated moderate doses of stimulants at the same time.

Swallowing Foreign Bodies.—It often happens that children swallow money, or other hard substances, such as pins, etc. In these cases, if the substance be completely swallowed, it should be left to take its course through the stomach and intestines. The custom of giving purgatives in such cases is altogether contrary to physiological principles, as the intestinal movements will more safely carry them through than if violently urged by physic.

Toothache, How to Treat.—To alleviate the wretched pain —for nothing probably short of "cold steel," that is, extraction, can work a perfect cure—take at once a tolerably strong dose of opening medicine; as soon as this operates, in all probability the pain will be gone for a week or two. Meanwhile, apply a small mustard poultice outside, just over the place where the pain is most violent, and rub the gum and the tooth with chloroform and laudanum. It will ease tne dreadful pain. A little bit of cotton dipped in a solution of shellac, or of gum mastic and spirits of wine, makes a good temporary stopping for bad teeth. Avoid the ordinary vaunted "nostrums," that is, the quack medicines said instantly to remove toothache. Kreasote is the safest domestic remedy to employ, if the pain be very bad; only get a friend to employ it, by putting a little bit of cotton-wool dipped in it into the hollow of the tooth for you, and do not try to put it in yourself, or you will scarify your tongue and gums.

Vomiting, Obstinate.—WHEN THE STOMACH WILL RETAIN NOTHING.—GENERAL DIRECTIONS, WHEN A DOCTOR CANNOT BE GOT.—Keep the patient perfectly quiet, in a bed, if possible, and on his back. Give no food for some time, and then only teaspoonful doses at a time, with long intervals; leave him to himself for an hour or two; then give five drops of chlorodyne in a little water, and, after an interval, a little chicken-broth or beef-tea. Milk, pure and simple, or milk with lime-water, in very small quantities at a time, is often useful. If you cannot keep these down lay a piece of lint soaked in a teaspoonful of brandy and a teaspoonful of laudanum mixed, on the pit of the stomach, cover it with a bit of oiled silk or guttapercha twice the size of the lint, and renew it every four or five hours. A mustard plaster will answer the same purpose, and is, probably, more easily procured. Either application will help to quiet the stomach. A teaspoonful of lime-water in a teacupful of milk or of cold beef-tea (I have found that the stomach will always keep down the white of an egg, well beaten up with a teaspoonful of brandy, and given a very little at a time, when it would retain nothing else), or of arrowroot, will often abate the vomiting and enable the stomach to retain a small quantity of food.

Thirty drops of wood naphtha and as much of the tincture of cardamoms, in a tablespoonful or two of water is sometimes used in this distressing complaint, and with success. It is very useful in preventing the vomiting of consumptive patients. Other experienced doctors say, use one drop of ipecacuanha wine every half hour.

Typhoid Fever.—Intestinal, or Enteric, Fever.—SYMPTOMS. —This fever generally begins with slight premonitory symptoms, such as chilliness, loss of appetite, and heat of skin; sometimes vomiting, and generally diarrhœa, which seems to defy remedies. The patient becomes weaker, and, from about the seventh to the tenth day from the seizure, there appear on different parts of the body—generally on the back and front of the chest and abdomen—rose-colored spots, which are slightly raised above the surface, but which disappear on pressure, and quickly return when the finger is removed.   At first, only two or three make their appearance, and are liable to be over-looked.   More come out, but they are very variable in number; in ordinary cases, about a dozen.   In forty-eight hours these spots fade out, and are replaced by fresh ones; this crop also fades as the former, and is replaced by another, and so on. The probable severity and danger bear some relation to the number of the spots; the abdomen feels hard, and is tender, but more particularly just above the right groin.   The tongue is furred in the centre and red at the tip, as the diarrhœa con-tinues, the motions being loose, sometimes quite black, at other times light-colored.. If this continue, the tongue becomes ulcerated, brown, and dry. The teeth become caked over with a brown matter called "sordes," and there is great thirst.   The pulse ranges between 90 and 120.   The temperature will reach 102 degrees to 104 degrees.   The patient may become deliri-ous, but this does not always denote that the disease will assume a serious form.   In favorable cases the improvement is gener-ally slow.   It is indicated by the number of stools diminishing and becoming more and more solid.   The spots disappear, the skin becomes cooler and moist, the appetite returns, and, as convalesence progresses, sometimes becomes ravenous.   The appetite requires to be carefully controlled during convalescence. Ulceration of the bowels being the dangerous tendency of the fever, indiscretion in diet will easily induce a relapse.

TREATMENT.—The diet is an important point in the treat-ment of the disease.   It should consist of light fluid food, easy of digestion; nothing solid should on any account be given.   The patient should have milk and beef tea, coffee or tea; arrowroot or gruel are both useful.   The staple article of diet should be milk during the first ten or twelve days, unless symptoms of extreme debility should occur, in which case beef tea and port wine may be given.   Soups also may be given, but care must be taken that they are clear from indi-gestible fibres of meat and vegetable.

The administration of wine is often a most difficult problem in the treatment of fever.   If the signs of debility are so evi-dent as to render prostration imminent, an ounce of port wine, or even brandy, may be given every four or six hours; but it is necessary to caution the reader not to mistake the feeling of weakness, which is an inseparable attendant on fever, for dan-gerous debility.   A vastly larger proportion of cases would do well without stimulants than is generally believed.   It may be a help to the determination of the question if we point out some symptoms that will call for the use of alcoholic stimu-lants.   These are great fluctuations in the number of the pulse and in the degrees of temperature of the body, and a want of muscular power to maintain a comfortable posture in bed, accompanied with sighing and irregular breathing. It may be stated broadly that it is not the number of the pulse that is so important as its steadiness. A pulse of a hundred and fifty— if it continue day after day at that number—affords a better sign than a pulse that beats a hundred at one time, and a hundred and twenty at another, and a hundred and something else at another time. The same remark applies to the readings of the clinical thermometer. If these are steady, the case will, in all probability, do well without the use of alcohol.

For medicinal means, but little is required in the shape of drugs. Some simple effervescing saline, or soda-water, which will serve to allay thirst and fever, will suffice in mild cases. Dilute hydrochloric acid, in small doses, is often of some service. Diarrhœa may be checked by chalk mixture, to which, if there be pain in the bowels, small doses of Dover's powder may be added. If there be tenderness on pressure of the abdomen, a mustard plaster may be applied, or a linseed poultice should be kept on day and night. When convalescence begins it may be assisted by the administration of quinine.

Typhoid fever has a specific duration, viz.: either twenty-one or twenty-eight days; this, the ordinary duration, may, however, be interfered with by the complication of inflammation of any internal organ, and convalesence may be prolonged through many weeks by the occurrence of mischief in the intestines. The termination of the disease, if not in health, is in exhaustion; or sometimes by inflammation in the cavity of the abdomen, through the perforation of an ulcer in the intestines. In this last case, pain of a most intense character sets in suddenly, and is rapidly followed by collapse and death.

Typhoid fever is not, as supposed, a milder form of typhus; it is distinctly different. Typhus is infectious; typhoid is not. The prominent symptom of typhus fever is the disturbance it causes in the brain. Diarrhœa is the prominent symptom of typhoid.

The above distinctions are sufficient reasons with some authorities for dispensing with the name "typhoid," as that, from its similarity to "typhus," is liable to mislead, hence the name "Enteric" as the more appropriate distinctive designation of this fever is frequently employed.

Typhus.—This is an infectious fever of a very grave character, known under various names as jail-fever, camp-fever, etc. It begins like most other fevers with indefinite symptoms of malaise, lasting an uncertain period. The incursion of the fever is sometimes sudden, commencing with a shivering fit, headache, and feeling of extreme debility. As the fever becomes more pronounced, the pulse is rapid, the temperature of the skin above 100 degrees; thirst becomes urgent, the tongue furred; vomiting sometimes occurs. Severe headache and delirium occur early in the course of this fever. With the advance of the disease, the tongue becomes coated with fur, the eyes bloodshot, the skin hot and dry, the urine scanty, and the skin assumes a dusky hue.

A characteristic eruption, distinctive of symptoms, appears on the chest and body, usually after the fifth day. By the peculiar features of this eruption, the disease may be identified and distinguished from typhoid. The appearance of the eruption somewhat resembles that of measles, but has mixed with it numerous minute spots like flea-bites. The stress of typhus is on the brain, as manifested by the early occurrence of severe headache, delirium, painful dreams, sleeplessness, twitching of the muscles, and, lastly, coma. The bowels, usually, are confined, a condition the reverse of what is observed in typhoid. Cough and shortness of breathing direct attention to the organs of respiration, inflammation of the lungs of a low and insidious character, being one of the most frequent and most dangerous complications of this fever.

Typhus fever has no definite duration, like typhoid, but generally declines in fourteen days, although some cases last many days longer.

TREATMENT.—.. well ventilated apartment is essential to the success of treatment, and should by any means be secured. In the winter time a fire should be kept burning, as it not only supplies warmth, but it secures a change of air in the apartment. The tendency of typhus being towards depression and prostration of the nervous energies, the point in treatment is to support the vital powers by beef tea, milk, port wine, or brandy. The dose and the frequency of the repetition of the stimulants must be guided by their effects on the pulse.

In cases where the debility is extreme and the pulse very rapid, a judiciously administered dose of alcohol will give it force and reduce its frequency. In this case the dose should be repeated at intervals of two or three hours, closely watching the effect on the pulse. In cases in which the debility is not so intensely marked, wine may be omitted, and the patient supported on milk, beef tea, soups, etc. Mild aperients should be given if the bowels be costive, and for medicine, four or five grains of carbonate of ammonia, dissolved in water, should be given every four hours.

The head symptoms—e. g., headache, delirium and sleep-lessness—will be relieved by blistering the back of the neck. (See Blistering.) If the head be hot, ice-cold water should be constantly applied. If the excitement of the brain prevent sleep, a small dose of Dover's powder at bed-time will have a soothing effect, and perhaps favor perspiration. If there is cough and symptoms signifying that the chest is becoming affected, mustard-plasters should be applied. We repeat, however, that the most important of all measures is good nursing and careful dieting.

The infection of typhus may be guarded against by the free use of disinfectants, such as carbolic acid or Condy's fluid (see Disinfection), and by free ventilation, which is of the first importance, and goes a long way to prevent the spread of all sorts of infectious diseases.

Vaccination.—Vaccination is the insertion into the human system of the infectious matter of a mild disease called cowpox. Cow-pox is really small-pox, which, having been acted on by the system of the cow, has been thus rendered innocuous to the human body, at the same time that it is protective of a second attack. Thus, in vaccination we have a mild and harmless form of small-pox, which is voluntarily accepted in the place of the more malignant form of small-pox, which seizes its victims against their will.

Vaccination is the only real protector we have against the ravages of small-pox. This is proved by the following facts, among many others: In proportion as vaccination is properly and efficiently performed, so the mortality of small-pox is reduced. Secnodly, by the freedom from infection which is enjoyed by properly re-vaccinated persons, in constant attendance upon, and actual contact with, small-pox patients. There has never been a case of small-pox among the nurses or the attendants at the Small-pox Hospital, Highgate, within a period of considerably over thirty years. This is simply because they are all properly re-vaccinated before they enter upon their duties.

MODE OF VACCINATION.—The operation of vaccination is simple, but so highly important that no care bestowed upon its performance is thrown away.

The following instructions will be sufficient, if carefully followed: Select an arm of a vaccinated infant that has good vesicles on the eighth day, i. e., the day week on which the lymph was inserted. Then, with a perfectly clean lancet, make several punctures in the clear part of the vesicles, avoiding the red border of the inflamed skin, so as not to draw blood. A clear watery fluid will ooze out in beads. Take off some of this clear fluid on the point of the lancet, and then, taking the arm of the infant, or person to be vaccinated, draw the skin tense and insert the point of the lancet nearly horizontally

into the skin to an extent of about one-tenth of an inch (-);
then give the lancet a turn round, withdraw it, and press it
down upon the puncture.   Five such punctures, to the distance
of about half an inch apart, should be made on one arm.

Supposing that an arm with mature vesicles should not be
available, lymph may be procur-
ed from any vaccine station.   It
will be received in that case,
preserved either in tubes, or on
small points of ivory. If in tubes,
the point at each end of one
must be broken off, and the contained lymph be gently breathed
on to the point of the lancet,
and inserted as above directed.
If the lymph have been preserved
dry on "points," one of these
should be used for each puncture. Dip the point quickly into

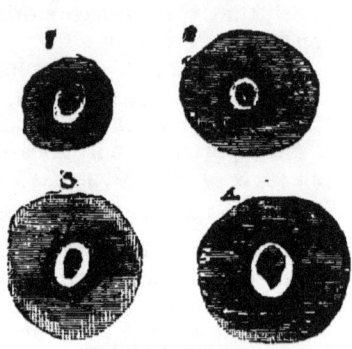

VACCINE VEISICLES.

cold water, and shake off any excess of water.   The object is
just sufficiently to moisten the lymph, that it will be easily
scraped off on to the point of the lancet, and inserted as before
directed.

Some degree of inflammation occasionally occurs on the
vaccinated arm.   This will generally disappear quickly under
the application of simple water-dressing.   A slight eruption of
small, colorless pimples on various parts of the body also
occasionally follows vaccination, and disappears in the course
of a few days.

To ensure the success of vaccination, the infant to be vaccinated should be in good health, and free from any eruption
of the skin, and the child from whom the lymph is taken should
also be in perfectly good health.   With these precautions, there
is no ground for the fear that other diseases than cow-pox will
be transmitted by the operation.   Very great exaggerations
and misrepresentations have been put forth on this point in
order to excite prejudice against vaccination.

RE-VACCINATION.—The primary vaccination of infancy, if
well and thoroughly performed, as shown by the existence of
several well-marked cicatrices, affords protection for life from
severe small-pox—protection, however, not so complete but
that modified small-pox shall not occur.   It is shown by a vast
accumulation of statistics that there is a greater tendency in
vaccinated persons to take the small-pox between the ages of
fifteen and twenty-five than at all other ages put together.   It
is, therefore, advisable, in order to obtain complete protection,
the operation of vaccination should be performed at puberty,

or when growth is completed. The insertion of lymph by three punctures is sufficient for re-vaccination. The lymph from a re-vaccinated vesicle should never be used for primary vaccination.

Voice, Loss of.—Sometimes without the existence of catarrh, or inflammation of the larynx, the voice suddenly becomes reduced to the faintest possible whisper, or without great difficulty even this is not achieved. It occurs sometimes after long continued speaking, but it is most frequently met with in hysterical females. The same thing may, however, happen as the result of a cold, or from a more serious cause some form of paralysis of the organs of the voice.

TREATMENT.—When the affection is the result of catarrh, it may be relieved by the inhalation of the steam of hot water, with a few drops of creasote, or a teaspoonful of spirits of salvolatile. When it proceeds from hysteria or paralysis, the treatment must be sought under the heads of those diseases.

Wounds, Cuts, Stabs.—These are of several kinds—e. g., incised, contused, lacerated, punctured—requiring each a modified treatment.

INCISED WOUNDS.—These are clean cuts or wounds, with smooth defined edges.

CONTUSED WOUNDS—Are wounds attended with bruising of the parts, such as seen in gunshot injuries.

LACERATED WOUNDS—Are pretty much the same as bruised wounds—the edges are rough and jagged.

PUNCTURED WOUNDS—Are where the orifice of the cut is small, but its extent deep, such as in stabs.

TREATMENT.—INCISED WOUNDS.—In the case of incised wound or clean cut, if not large in extent, it will heal readily by the edges being brought together by means of some simple unirritating plaster, such as " adhesive plaster," or " isinglass plaster," or goldbeater's skin. It may be advisable to bring the edges of a wound together with stitches. The most convenient needle for this purpose is a glover's needle, and white silk is the best material for the sewing. If the wound has been inflicted by broken glass, etc., the surfaces should be carefully searched for any fragments or foreign bodies, before the edges are brought together. If the bleeding be profuse, the wound should be left exposed to the air for a while, or the ordinary means used to stop the bleeding. If the cut be a long one, there should be small intervals left between the strips of plaster, in order to allow blood or other fluids to escape. This strapping plaster need not be removed for three or four days, unless there be pain and throbbing in the wound; in this case they should be loosened, or even removed, as these symptoms indicate inflammation. If it be necessary to remove the strapping before union has taken place, the wound should then be dressed with water and lint, covered with oil-silk or gutta-percha.

SCALP WOUNDS.—Cuts on the scalp should be carefully cleansed from hair, which should also be removed for about half an inch around the wound. If small, the edges can be brought together with plaster. If the wound be large, it is better simply treated with cold water dressing. No stitches should be put in these wounds, unless they are very ragged and gaping, as they are prone to excite erysipelas in this part of the skin.

BRUISED, CONTUSED, AND LACERATED WOUNDS. — In consequence of the tearing or bruising of the edges of a lacerated wound, the vitality of those parts is more or less impaired; hence these wounds do not heal as readily as a clean cut. In treating a contused wound, the surface should first be carefully sponged clean of clotted blood, or foreign bodies of any kind, such as portions of clothing, small shot, etc. The simple water dressing, or wet lint, covered with oil-silk, is the most suitable for this kind of injury. If the soft parts be much torn, they may be bound down by a roller and water dressing applied. After a time, the surface of a wound of this kind becomes sluggish in its healing, and resembles an ulcer. It should then be treated with zinc ointment or yellow basilicon.

STABS, OR PUNCTURED WOUNDS—Require special treatment, varying with their depth, and the part in which they occur. A slight wound of this sort, not penetrating deeply, may be dressed with isinglass-plaster, adhesive-plaster, or gold-beater's skin. If, however, deeper, but not entering a cavity, the simple water dressing should be applied, and the part wounded be so placed that blood may escape freely. For this reason it is not advisable to endeavor to heal a punctured wound quickly. If the bleeding from the wound does not stop from the exposure to cold, the wound may be plugged with lint or soft linen, soaked in tincture of perchloride of iron, diluted with an equal quantity of water, or with tincture of matico. The plugging may be allowed to remain in twelve hours. After its removal, if the bleeding be checked, dress as above directed with water. A deeply punctured wound is prone to heal at the surface. This should be prevented by inserting a strip of linen between the lips of the wound, so as to allow of the escape of matter. The healing from the bottom is sometimes to be promoted by injecting with a weak solution of Condy's fluid (a teaspoonful to a pint of water).

STABS, OR PUNCTURED WOUNDS OF THE CHEST.—The dan-
ger of these will depend upon the fact and extent of penetration.
Those wounds that do not pene-
trate the cavity of the chest may
be treated as ordinary stabs. (See
previous directions.) Penetration
of the chest is probably attended
with a wound in the lung. This
may be inferred if there be difficulty in breathing, or spitting of
blood, with distress and anxiety
of countenance.

The first indication of treatment in wounds of the chest is to
give remedies to stop the bleeding.
Should this proceed from a vessel
in the wall of the chest, it should
be sought for, and, if possible,
tied; should it, however, proceed
from the lungs, ice and cold drinks
should be given.

For the organs within the chest,
see diagram, which will point out
the parts probably wounded.

A draught as follows: Tincture of opium, 20 minims;
infusion of oak-bark, to make one ounce. This should be
given every hour until the patient sleeps, and then discontinued.
The sleeping is important, as it diminishes the force of breathing, and so insures a certain amount of rest to the wounded
lung. The wound in the wall of the chest should then be
accurately closed with stitches, or plaster, and the patient
kept as quiet as possible.

Should there be any heat, swelling, or pain in the part, or
should the patient have any shivering fits, small doses of opium
should be continued at frequent intervals; thus: Compound
ipecacuanha powder (Dover's powder), two and a half grains.
Every two hours. It will be as well, when these symptoms
show themselves, to give the patient also half an ounce of
Epsom salts, in order to open the bowels. He should be
allowed a light, cool diet.

Pleurisy is often a consequence of wounds in the walls of
the chest. For its treatment, see under the name "Pleurisy."

PUNCTURED WOUNDS OF THE ABDOMEN.—These may be
slight and easily repaired, or they may be so serious as to end
fatally in the course of a few hours. The gravity will depend
upon the amount of injury inflicted upon the intestines. The
following divisions of the subject will illustrate this point:

1st. NON-PERFORATING WOUNDS.—A simple wound of the walls of the abdomen, not passing through into the abdominal cavity, is not more serious than an incised or punctured wound elsewhere, and should be treated in the same way. A probe, or the finger, will readily detect the fact of a perforation; besides that, in the event of such an occurrence, there will probably be more severe pain in the part.

2d. PERFORATING WOUNDS.—In the event of a stab of the abdomen passing through its walls, either the intestines, or some other organ, may be wounded. Which of these may be injured, it may be difficult even for a surgeon to determine exactly. As, however, this treatise will be of more service to those who are beyond the reach of surgical aid, we shall endeavor to assist their diagnosis by referring to the positions of the principal internal organs relatively one to the other. A perforating wound, reaching to any one of the organs in the abdomen cavity, is attended with symptoms of alarming prostration. Means should be taken to stanch the bleeding of the external wound, and the patient must be supported by stimulants and light diet. Opium must be given freely to relieve pain. It acts beneficially also by moderating the muscular movements of the intestines. If there be vomiting of blood, it may be feared that the stomach is wounded. There is every inducement and hope that by rigidly enforcing rest and quietness, with the above means, life may be saved. Wounds even of the liver and spleen have been known to heal.

The next most serious effects of stabs in the abdomen, and those which give rise to great fear for the 'results, are those attended with protrusion of the intestines. If, however, the latter be not wounded, it may be returned, and the wound closed as directed above. Wounds of the walls of the abdomen, through which the intestines protrude, and are themselves wounded, call for particular treatment.

The wounds in the intestines should first be attended to. The edges of these should be united by means of a continuous or glover's stitch, similar to the stitch used in hemming. It should be so done that the exterior surface of the bowel, on either side of the cut, shall be in contact; and then the bowel having been carefully washed in luke-warm water, should be returned, stitches and all. If all goes on well, the silk will be removed by the bowel when the wound is healed. The after treatment is to be conducted as for a simple punctured wound. The general treatment of the perforated wound of the intestines will be the same as that of wounds of other organs in the abdomen—viz., rest of the parts secured by opiates, and support of the system by stimulants and light food.

GUNSHOT WOUNDS are perforated, bruised wounds, complicated with nervous shock. These wounds do not bleed so much as cuts, but they are more troublesome to heal on account of the large amount of destruction of tissue they occasion. This varies on account of the size of bullet. Another cause for their being more dangerous than cuts is that it sometimes happens a piece of the wad becomes lodged in the wound, and being difficult to detect, is sometimes left behind when the bullet is extracted, causing mischief by its presence until removed or thrown off in the sloughing of the wound. Inflammation generally sets in about the wound within twenty-four hours. The external parts become swollen and red, the patient complains of pain in the wound. After another day or so a discharge of pus and matter appears. The bruised parts, or rather those parts with which the ball in its passage has come in contact, will now begin to be cast off by sloughing, though this process may occupy several weeks before all the dead parts or foreign substances are cast off. Mortification may follow a gunshot wound if the destruction of tissue be considerable, or if much bone be included in it; if the patient be in a bad state of health, or if the atmosphere is confined and of an unhealthy character.

TREATMENT.—Stimulants, such as brandy or wine, should be given to relieve the depression; then, if the bullet has completely passed through, the surface should be cleaned, and a piece of wet lint should be applied. This should be continued for three or four days, and then the patient treated as for a bruised wound. Bullets are frequently lodged in the wound. If visible at the orifice, they should be removed, but if not, there should be no attempt made by a non-professional person to find them, as much injury may be inflicted in the attempt to explore for them. Their removal must be postponed until surgical aid can be obtained.

Wounds and Bruises. Dressings for.—CARDED OAKUM STYPIUM.—A convenient dressing for confused and lacerated wounds. Oakum has this advantage, that where old rope is to be found, this substance can be made. It can, however, be obtained "carded" for surgical purposes, and in this shape, known as "stypium," it is a clean and useful means of arresting hæmorrhage from wounds by causing coagulation of the blood in its meshes, as well as absorbing discharges. The creasote, which is one of the constituents of tar, has preservative properties, stimulates a sluggish surface, and destroys unpleasant odors. It will be found very useful in the wounds of compound and comminuted fracture.

CARBOLATED OIL.—Solid carbolic acid liquefied by heat, 48 minims; olive oil to 4 fluid ounces. Mix. This is an admirable dressing for the suppurating surface of open wounds. It should be applied as follows: A piece of soft linen rag, rather larger than the surface to be covered, should be steeped in the mixture, and carefully drawn from the edge of the wound right across it until it is completely covered. Care should be taken to exclude all bubbles of air, which should be pressed gently out, in order that the oil may be in contact with the whole surface.

ISINGLASS PLASTER.—A very clean, simple and useful kind of plaster can be home-made—that is isinglass plaster. What is called "Persian" silk, is to be firmly stretched and painted with a moderately thick solution of isinglass, which is then suffered to dry. This plaster has the advantage of allowing the state of a cut beneath it to be pretty clearly seen—it is besides readily removed, when required, by the application of warm water.

Wounds, Hæmorrhage or Bleeding from.—MEANING OF THE WORD "TRAUMATIC."

—We have elsewhere spoken of the various forms of hæmorrhage that arise out of the disease of the internal organs, and require what is, more strictly speaking, called "medical treatment." By "traumatic" bleeding is meant the consequence of wounding of the blood vessels, calling for surgical means to its arrest. Traumatic or surgical bleeding may be either arterial or venous, and require different treatment accordingly.

ARTERIAL HÆMORRHAGE.—When a wound or other injury causes bleeding of a bright or vermillion red color, the blood flows from an artery. This is rendered clearer still if the blood flow in spirts or intermittent jets corresponding with the beats of the pulse.

VENOUS HÆMORRHAGE is known by the even flow of the blood and its darker color.

TREATMENT.—VENOUS BLEEDING.—If the bleeding from a wound be of the dark venous character, or being, as is often the case, partly arterial also, but not very profuse, gentle pressure will sometimes suffice to check the flow; or the application of cold water or ice, or exposure to cold air, may stop the bleeding. A slight flow of blood can be arrested by matico, or by a piece of linen lint soaked in Friar's balsam or tincture of perchloride of iron.

ARTERIAL BLEEDING.—If the bleeding be arterial, as indicated by its flowing in jets, firm pressure should be made over the wounded vessel, if in such a position as to admit of it. Supposing that the pressure of the hand does not suffice to stanch the bleeding, then pressure should be made by tying a handkerchief or bandage so that the knot shall press over the wound. If the wound has been inflicted on one of the extremities, the bleeding may be arrested by tying a ligature round the limb, so as to press a pad of lint upon the artery. If the pad be soaked in Friar's balsam, or tincture of matico, it will be of more service.

ARRÉSTING BLEEDING FROM THE ARM.—Pressure by the fingers on the main artery of the arm, as it passes in the arm-pit along the inner side of the arm under the shoulder joint, will assist in checking the hæmorrhage from a wound of the forearm or hand. The artery may also be firmly compressed at the elbow-joint by bending the arm firmly, and laying the hand of the same side on the point of the shoulder.

ARTERY OF THE THIGH.—In cases of obstinate arterial bleeding from any part of the lower extremity, firm pressure should be made in the groin, where the large artery of the limb may be easily felt beating as it passes down the thigh. When, by the means above described, the bleeding has been arrested, we should proceed to examine the wound with the help of a sponge, and search for the bleeding vessel.

OF TYING AN ARTERY.—Supposing that all these means have been tried, and the bleeding still continues or returns when the pressure is taken off, the wound should be carefully washed with a sponge and cold water, and pressure being applied, the cut end of the wounded vessel sought for and tied, thus: When found, the bleeding end of the vessel should be taken hold of with a pair of fine-pointed forceps and held up, so that an assistant may pass a piece of silk or thread round it, which should then be tied into a double knot, taking care that the thread be not tied too tightly, as by doing so the artery may again be divided. One end of the thread should then be cut off and the other left hanging out of the wound, which should then be dressed with lint or linen dipped in cold water. The ligature will generally come away in about a week. There are other means of checking bleeding, if the vessel wounded is not very large, of which the following are the most handy:

A piece of lint or cotton wool soaked in the tincture of the perchloride of iron or tincture of matico may be pressed down into the wound in contact with the bleeding vessel. Or, the vessel should be lightly and rapidly touched with a piece of iron ware heated red hot. This is, perhaps, the most effective way of checking the bleeding, and is by no means so painful as it might seem. Another plan is to touch the orifice of the bleeding vessel with a stick of nitrate of silver.

LEECH BITES.—The bleeding from these is often very troublesome more especially when the leeches have been inadvertently applied at some part of the body where, from the absence of bone, there is a difficulty in applying firm pressure. For this reason leeches, when applied, should always be placed over some bone or other hard part upon which the necessary pressure can be applied and continued for some minutes. If pressure cannot, for the reason above stated, be applied, the bites may be touched with the point of a camel's hair brush steeped in tincture of the perchloride of iron, or they may be touched with a stick of nitrate of silver, and, as this is generally at hand, it is a convenient means. A ready method is to cut a small piece of glazed visiting card, and, having pressed with a dry handkerchief for a short time on the bites, then quickly, before the blood comes again, press the glazed surface of the card on the bite, and fasten it there with plaster or a bandage.

MATICO, AND TINCTURE OF MATICO.—A valuable styptic may be kept readily at hand by steeping a few matico leaves in a phial with gin, brandy or proof spirit. A piece of lint soaked in this will stay the bleeding of slight cuts. Matico leaf itself laid on a bleeding surface, or a slight cut, or a leech bite, will also stanch the bleeding.

FAINTING.—The faintness that often occurs in cases of bleeding, from whatever cause, favors the stanching of the blood. All that is required is to place the patient on his back with his head low, and administer some slight stimulant.

Worms, Intestinal.—SYMPTOMS.—Variable and vitiated appetite, fœtid breath, feverishness, grinding of teeth, picking at the nose, itching at the seat, disordered bowels, and pains in the stomach. There are three varieties of worms voided from the intestines, viz.: 1st, the round worm, resembling the common earthworm; 2d, the threadworm—some short white worms, some of a larger variety; 3d, tapeworm, the length of which extends to many feet, and which consists of small square joints.

TREATMENT.—The first two of these varieties may be expelled by doses of calomel and scammony, or of santonine. The third (tapeworm) requires either the oil of male fern (one drachm in an ounce of water), taken fasting early in the morning; or: Castor oil, one-half ounce; spirits of turpentine, one-half ounce; cinnamon water or peppermint water, 2 ounces. Mixed, and taken fasting.

It is seldom necessary to repeat this dose. The tapeworm when voided should be carefully examined in order to ascertain that the head is expelled, since, if this be not the case the worm quickly grows again. The head may be recognized by means of a common pocket lens. It is very minute, but is rounded, on a narrow neck, and presents on its surface sucking discs, by which it attaches itself to the inner surface of the bowel.

Remedy for Diphtheria.—The treatment consists in thoroughly swabbing the back of the mouth and throat with a wash made thus: Table salt, 2 drachms; black pepper, golden seal, nitrate of potash, alum, 1 drachm each; mix and pulverize; put into a teacup half full of water; stir well and then fill up with good vinegar. Use every half hour, one, two, and four hours, as recovery progresses. The patient may swallow a little each time. Apply 1 ounce each of spirits of turpentine, sweet oil, and aqua ammonia, mixed, every hour, to the whole of the throat, and to the breast bone every four hours, keeping flannel to the part.

Worm Lozenges.—Powdered lump sugar, 10 ounces; starch, 5 ounces; mix with mucilage; and to every ounce add 12 grains calomel, divided into 20 grain lozenges. Dose, two to six.

Soothing Syrup.—Take 1 pound of honey; add 2 table-spoonfuls of paregoric, and the same of oil of anise seed; add enough water to make a thick syrup, and bottle. For children teething, dose, teaspoonful occasionally.

Infants' Syrup.—This syrup is made thus: 1 pound best box raisins; 1-2 ounce anise seed; 2 sticks licorice; split the raisins, pound the anise seed, and cut the licorice fine; add to it 3 quarts of rain water, and boil down to two quarts. Feed three or four times a day, as much as the child will willingly drink. The raisins are to strengthen, the anise is to expel the wind, and the licorice as a physic.

Swaim's Vermifuge.—Wormseed, 2 ounces; valerian, rhubarb, pink-root, white agaric, of each 1 1-2 ounces; boil in sufficient water to yield 3 quarts of decoction; add to it 30 drops of tansy and 45 drops of oil of cloves, dissolved in a quart of rectified spirits. Dose, 1 tablespoonful at night.

Ayer's Cherry Pectoral.—Take 4 grains of the acetate of morphia; 2 fluid drachms of tincture of bloodroot; a fluid drachm each of antimonial wine and wine of ipecacuanha, and 3 fluid ounces of syrup of wild cherry. Mix.

Brown's Bronchial Troches.—Take 1 pound of pulverized extract of licorice; 1 1-2 pounds of pulverized sugar; 4 ounces of pulverized cubebs; 4 ounces of pulverized gum arabic, and 1 ounce of pulverized extract of conium. Mix.

Russia Salve.—Take equal parts of yellow wax and sweet oil; melt slowly, carefully stirring; when cooling, stir in a small quantity of glycerine. Good for all kinds of wounds, etc.

To Extract Teeth with Little or no Pain.—Tincture of

aconite, chloroform, and alcohol, of each 1 ounce. Mix.
Moisten two pledgets of cotton with the liquid, and apply to
the gums on each side of the tooth to be extracted, holding
them in their place with pliers or other instruments for from
five to ten minutes, rubbing the gum freely inside and out.

Tooth Wash.—To REMOVE BLACKNESS.—Pure muriatic
acid, 1 ounce; water, 1 ounce; honey, 2 ounces. Mix. Take
a tooth brush and wet it freely with the preparation, and briskly
rub the black teeth, and in a moment's time they will be perfectly white; then immediately wash out the mouth with water,
that the acid may not act upon the enamel of the teeth.

Compound Extract of Buchu.—Buchu leaves, 1 pound;
boiling distilled water, 3 gallons; boil the leaves in 2 gallons of
the water down to 6 quarts; then boil it again in the remaining
water till reduced to 2 quarts. Evaporate the mixed liquors
down to 6 pints, and add 1 quart strong sage tea, 2 drachms
bicarbonate of potassa, 2 drachms tincture of cannabis Indica,
5 ounces rectified spirits, 2 ounces balsam of copabia, and
Harlem oil. Bottle.

New Method of Embalming.—Mix together 5 pounds of
dry sulphate of alumine, 1 quart of warm water, and 100 grains
of arsenious acid. Inject three or four quarts of this mixture
into all the vessels of the human body. This applies as well to
all animals, birds, fishes, etc. This process supercedes the old
and revolting mode, and has been introduced into the great
anatomical schools of Paris.

Hair Dye.—No. 1.—Take galic acid, 1-2 ounce; alcohol, 8
ounces; soft water, 16 ounces. Put the acid in the alcohol,
then add the water.

No. 2.—Crystalized nitrate of silver, 1 ounce; strongest
ammonia, 3 ounces; gum arabic, 1-2 ounce; soft water, 6
ounces. Put the silver in the ammonia; do not cork till it is
dissolved; dissolve the gum in the water, then mix, and it is
ready for use.

Keep Nos. 1 and 2 in separate bottles, and apply each alternately to the hair. Be particular to cleanse the hair before
applying the dye.

ANOTHER.—Nitrate of silver, 11 drachms; nitric acid, 1
drachm; distilled water, 1 pint; sap green, 3 drachms; gum
arabic, 1 drachm. Mix.

ANOTHER.—Nitric acid, 1 drachm; nitrate of silver, 10
drachms; sap green, 9 drachms; mucilage, 5 drachms; distilled
water, 37 1-2 fluid ounces,

Hair Invigorator—Bay rum, 2 pints; alcohol, 1 pint; castor-oil, 1 ounce; carbonate of ammonia, 1-2 ounce; tincture of cantharides, 1 ounce. Mix them well. This compound will promote the growth of the hair and prevent it from falling out.

Razor-Strop Paste.—Wet the strop with a little sweet oil, and apply a little flour of emery evenly over the surface.

Oriental Cold Cream.—Oil of almonds, 4 ounces; white wax and spermaceti, of each, 2 drachms; melt and add rose water, 4 ounces; orange-flower water, 1 ounce. Used to soften the skin. Apply as the last.

Shaving Cream.—White wax, spermaceti, and almond oil, of each, 1-4 ounce; melt, and while warm beat in two squares of Windsor soap, previously reduced to a paste with rose water.

Circassian Cream.—Take 2 ounces of perfectly fresh suet, either of mutton or venison; 3 ounces of olive oil; 1 ounce of gum benzoin in powder; and 1-4 ounce of alkanet root. Put the whole into a jam jar, which, if without a lid, must be tied over with bladder, and place the jar in a sauce pan containing boiling water, at the side of the fire. Digest for a whole day, then strain away all that is fluid through fine muslin, and stir till nearly cold. Add, say 1 drachm of essence of almonds roses, bergamot, or any other perfume desired.

Yankee Shaving Soap.—Take 3 pounds of white bar soap, 1 pound of Castile soap, 1 quart of rain water, 1-2 pint of beef's gall, 1 gill spirits of turpentine. Cut the soap into thin slices, and boil five minutes after the soap is dissolved; stir while boiling; scent with oil of rose or almonds. If wished to color it, use 1-2 ounce vermillion.

Freckle Cure.—Take 2 ounces of lemon juice, or 1-2 drachm of powdered borax, and 1 drachm of sugar; mix together, and let them stand in a glass bottle for a few days, then rub on the face occasionally.

Hair Restorative.—Sugar of lead, borax, and lac-sulphur, of each, 1 ounce; aqua ammonia, 1-2 ounce; alcohol, 1 gill. These articles are to stand mixed for 14 hours; then add bay rum, 1 gill; fine table salt, 1 tablespoonful; soft water, 3 pints; essence of bergamot, 1 ounce. This preparation gives a splendid glossy appearance to the hair, turns gray hair to a dark color, and restores the hair when common baldness sets in. When the hair is thin or bald, apply twice a day with a hard brush, working into the roots of the hair. For gray hair, once a day is sufficient.

Barber's Shampoo Mixture.—Soft water, 1 pint; sal soda, 1 ounce; cream tartar, 1-4 ounce. Apply thoroughly to the hair.

Febrifuge Wine.—Quinine, 25 grains; water, 1 pint; sulphuric acid, 15 drops; epsom salts, 2 ounces; color with tincture of red sanders. Dose, a wine glass, three times a day. This is a world-renowned medicine.

Barrell's Indian Liniment.—Alcohol, 1 quart; tincture of capsicum, 1 ounce; oils of origanum, sassafras, pennyroyal, and hemlock, of each, 1-2 ounce. Mix. More than $70,000 have been cleared by the sale of this medicine during the last twelve years in the Western States.

Paregoric.—Best opium, 1-2 drachm; dissolve it in about 2 tablespoonfuls of boiling water; then add benzoic acid, 1-2 drachm; oil of anise, 1-2 a fluid drachm; clarified honey, 1 ounce; camphor gum, 1 scruple; alcohol, 76 per cent., 11 fluid ounces; distilled water, 4 fluid ounces. Macerate (keep warm) for two weeks. Dose, for children, 5 to 20 drops; adults, 1 to 2 teaspoonfuls.

Cough Syrup.—Syrup of squills, 2 ounces; tartarized antimony, 8 grains; sulphate of morphine, 5 grains; pulverized gum arabic, 1-4 ounce; honey, 1 ounce; water, 1 ounce. Mix. Dose for an adult, one small teaspoonful; repeat in half an hour if it does not relieve. Child in proportion.

Camphor Ice.—Spermaceti, 1 1-2 ounce; gum camphor, 3-4 ounce; oil of sweet almonds, 4 teaspoonfuls. Set on stove in an earthen dish till dissolved; heat just enough to dissolve it. While warm, put into small moulds, if desired to sell; then paper, and put into tinfoil. Used for chaps on hands or lips.

Imperial Drops for Gravel and Kidney Complaints.—Oil of origanum, 1 ounce; oil of hemlock, 1-4 ounce; oil of sassafras, 1-4 ounce; oil of anise, 1-2 ounce; alcohol, 1 pint. Mix. Dose, from 1-2 to 1 teaspoonful three times a day in sweetened water, will soon give relief when constant weakness is felt across the small of the back, as well as gravelly affections causing pain about the kidneys.

Positive Cure for Gonorrohœa.—Liquor of potass, 1-2 ounce; bitter apple, 1-2 ounce; spirits of sweet nitre, 1-2 ounce; balsam of copabia, 1-2 ounce; best gum, 1-4 ounce. To use, mix with peppermint water. Take 1-2 teaspoonful three times a day. Cure certain in nine days.

Celebrated Pile Ointment.—Take carbonate of lead, 1-2 ounce; sulphate of morphia, 15 grains; stramonium ointment, 1 ounce; olive oil, 20 drops. Mix, and apply three times a day, or as the pain may require.

Sweating Drops.—Ipecac, saffron, boneset and champhor gum, of each, 3 ounces; opium, 1 ounce; alcohol, 2 quarts. Let stand two weeks and filter. A teaspoonful in a cup of hot sage or catnip tea every hour until free perspiration is induced; excellent in colds, fevers, inflammations, etc. Bathe the feet in hot water at the same time.

Syrup for Consumptives.—Of tamarac bark, take from the tree without rossing, 1 peck; spikenard root, 1-2 pound; dandelion root 1-4 pound; hops, 2 ounces. Boil these sufficient to get the strength in two or three gallons of water; strain and boil down to one gallon; when blood warm, add three pounds of best honey, and 3 pints of best brandy; bottle and keep in a cool place. Dose, drink freely of it three times per day before meals, at least a gill or more; cure very certain.

Female Complaints.—PILLS TO PROMOTE MENSTRUAL SECRETION.—Take pills of aloes and myrrh, 4 drachms; compound iron pills, 280 grains. Mix, and form into 100 pills. Dose 2, twice a day.

FOR OBSTRUCTED MENSTRUATION.—Sulphate of iron, 60 grains; potassa (sub. carb.), 60 grains; myrrh, 2 drachms. Make them into three and one-half-grain pills; two to be taken three times a day, in the absence of fever. For painful menstruation, take pulverized rhei, 2 drachms; pulverized jalap, 2 drachms; pulverized opium, 2 drachms; syrup of poppies to mix. Divide into 200 pills, and take night and morning. To check immoderate flow: Tincture of ergot, 1 ounce; liquor of ammonia, 3 drachms. Mix. Dose teaspoonful in water three times a day.

STIMULANT.—IN LOW FEVERS AND AFTER UTERINE HÆMORRHAGES.—Best brandy and cinnamon water, of each 4 fluid ounces; the yolks of 2 eggs, well beaten; loaf sugar, 1-2 ounce; oil of cinnamon, 2 drops. Mix. Dose, from one-half to one (fluid) ounce, as often as required. This makes both meat and drink. Of course, any other flavoring oils can be used, if preferred, in place of the cinnamon.

FOR FEMALE COMPLAINTS.—One of the best laxative pills for female complaints is macrotin and rhubarb, each 10 grains; extract of hyoscyamus, 10 grains; Castile soap, 40 grains. Scrape the soap, and mix well together, forming into common sized pills with gum solution. Dose, one pill at bedtime, or sufficiently often to keep the bowels in a laxative state.

ANODYNE FOR PAINFUL MENSTRUATION.—Extract of stramonium and sulphate of quinine, each 16 grains; macrotin, 8 grains; morphine, 1 grain. Make into 8 pills. Dose, one pill, repeating once or twice only, forty to fifty minutes apart, if the pain does not subside before this time. Pain must subside under the use of this pill, and costiveness is not increased.

POWDER FOR EXCESSIVE FLOODING.—Gums kino and cate-chu, each 1 drachm; sugar of lead and alum, each 1-2 drachm. Pulverize all and thoroughly mix, then divide into 7 to 10 grain powders. Dose, one every two or three hours until checked, then less often merely to control the flow.

INJECTION FOR LEUCORRHEA.—When the glairy mucus dis-charge is present, prepare a tea of hemlock inner bark and witch hazel (often called spotted alder) leaves and bark, have a female syringe large enough to fill the vagina, and inject the tea, twice daily; and occasionally in bad cases, say twice a week, inject a syringe of the following composition:

FOR CHRONIC FEMALE COMPLAINTS.—White vitriol and sugar of lead, each 1-8 ounce; common salt, pulverized alum, and loaf sugar, of each, 1-2 drachm; soft water, 1 pint. Inject as above.

FOR PROLAPSUS UTERI, OR FALLING OF THE WOMB.—Not only the cheapest but the best support will be found to be a piece of firm sponge, cut to a proper size to admit, when damp, of being pressed up the vagina to hold the womb in its place. The sponge should have a stout piece of small cord sewed two or three times through its centre up and down, and left suffic-iently long to allow its being taken hold of to remove the sponge once a day, or every other day at the farthest, for the purpose of washing, cleaning, and using the necessary injec-tions; and this must be done while the patient is lying down, to prevent the womb from again falling or prolapsing. After having injected some of the above tea, wet the sponge in the same, and introduce it sufficiently high to hold the womb in its place. If pain is felt about the head, back, or loins, for a few days before the menses appear, prepare and use the fol-lowing:

UTERINE HÆMORRHAGES.—Unfailing cure. Sugar of lead, 10 grains; ergot, 10 grains; opium, 3 grains; epicac, 1 grain; All pulverized and well mixed. Dose, 10 to 12 grains, given in a little honey or syrup. In very bad cases after childbirth, it might be repeated in thirty minutes, or the dose increased to 15 or 18 grains; but in cases of rather profuse masting, repeat it once at the end of three hours, or as the urgency of the case may require.

In every case of female debility make a liberal use of iron, as the want of iron in the system is often the cause of the trouble. Mix fine iron filings with as much ground ginger.

Dose, half of a teaspoonful three times daily in a little honey or molasses; increase or lessen the dose to produce a blackness of the stools. Continue this course until well.

Nerve and Bone Liniment.—Beef's gall, 1 quart; alcohol, 1 pint; volatile liniment, 1 pound; spirits of turpentine, 1 pound; oil origanum, 4 ounces; aqua ammonia, 4 ounces; tincture of cayenne, 1-2 pint; oil of amber, 3 ounces; tincture of Spanish flies, 6 ounces. Mix well.

Positive Cure for Ague Without Quinine.—Peruvian bark, 2 ounces; wild cherry tree bark, 1 ounce; cinnamon, 1 drachm; capsicum, 1 teaspoonful; sulphur, 1 ounce; port wine, 2 quarts. Let it stand two days. Buy your Peruvian bark and pulverize it yourself, as it is often adulterated otherwise. Dose, a wine-glass full every two or three hours after fever is off, then two or three per day till all is used. A certain cure. Before taking the above, cleanse the bowels with a dose of epsom salts, or other purgative.

Green Mountain Salve.—For rheumatism, burns, pains in the back or side, &c. Take 2 pounds of rosin; burgundy pitch, 1-4 pound; beeswax, 1-4 pound; mutton tallow, 1-4 pound. Melt slowly. When not too warm, add oil hemlock, 1 ounce; balsam fir, 1 ounce; oil of origanum, 1 ounce; oil of red cedar, 1 ounce; Venice turpentine, 1 ounce; oil of worm-wood, 1 ounce; verdigris, 1-2 ounce. The verdigris must be finely pulverized and mixed with the oils; then add as above, and work in cold water like wax till cold enough to roll; rolls five inches long, one inch in diameter, sell for 25 cents.

English Remedy for Cancer.—Take chloride of zinc, blood root pulverized, and flour, equal quantities of each, worked into a paste and applied. First spread a common sticking-plaster, much larger than the cancer, cutting a circular piece from the centre of it a little larger than the cancer, applying it, which exposes a narrow rim of healthy skin; then apply the cancer plaster, and keep it on 24 hours. On removing it, the cancer will be found to have been burned into, and appears the color of an old shoe sole, and the rim outside will appear white and parboiled, as if burned by steam. Dress with slippery-elm poultice until suppuration takes place, then heal with any common salve.

Charcoal, a Cure for Sick Headache.—It is stated that two teaspoonfuls of finely powdered charcoal, drank in half a tumbler of water will, in less than fifteen minutes, give relief to the sick headache, when caused, as in most cases it is, by superabundance of acid on the stomach.

Felons.—If Recent, to Cure in Six Hours.—Venice turpentine, 1 ounce; and put it into half a teaspoonful of water, and stir with a rough stick until the mass looks like a candied honey; then spread a good coat on a cloth, and wrap around the finger. If the case is only recent it will remove the pain in 6 hours.

Felon Salve.—A salve made by burning one tablespoonful of copperas, then pulverizing it and mixing with the yolk of an egg, is said to relieve the pain, and cure the felon in 24 hours; then heal with cream two parts, and soft soap one part. Apply the healing salve daily after soaking the part in warm water.

Felon Ointment.—Take sweet oil, 1-2 pint, and stew a three-cent plug of tobacco in it until the tobacco is crisped; then squeeze it out and add red lead, 1 ounce; and boil until black; when a little cool add pulverized camphor gum, 1 ounce.

Warts and Corns.—To CURE IN TEN MINUTES.—Take a small piece of potash, and let it stand in the open air until it slacks, then thicken it to a paste with pulverized gum arabic, which prevents it from spreading where it is not wanted.

Liniment for Old Sores.—Alcohol, 1 quart; aqua ammonia, 4 ounces; oil of origanum, 2 ounces; camphor gum, 2 ounces; opium, 2 ounces; gum myrch, 2 ounces; common salt, 2 tablespoonfuls. Mix, and shake occasionally for a week.

Liniment.—GOOD SAMARITAN.—Take 98 per cent. alcohol, 2 quarts, and add to it the following articles: Oil of sassafras, hemlock, spirits of turpentine, tincture of cayenne, catechu, guaiac, (guac) and laudanum, of each 1 ounce; tincture of myrrh, 4 ounces; oil of origanum, 2 ounces; oil of wintergreen, 1-2 ounce; gum camphor, 2 ounces; and chloroform, 1 1-2 ounces. This is one of the best applications for internal pains known; it is superior to any other enumerated in this work.

Electro-Magnetic Liniment.—Best alcohol, 1 gallon; oil of amber, 8 ounces; gum camphor, 8 ounces; Castile soap, shaved fine, 2 ounces; beef's gall, 4 ounces; ammonia, 3 F's strong, 12 ounces. Mix, and shake occasionally for 12 hours, and it is fit for use. This will be found a strong and valuable liniment.

Great London Liniment.—Take chloroform, olive oil, and aqua ammonia, of each 1 ounce; acetate of morphia, 10 grains. Mix and use as other liniments. Very valuable.

Ointments.—FOR OLD SORES.—Red precipitate, 1-2 ounce; sugar of lead, 1-2 ounce; burnt alum, 1 ounce; white vitriol, 1-4 ounce, or a little less; all to be very finely pulverized; have mutton tallow made warm, 1-2 pound; stir all in, and stir until cool.

Judkins Ointment.—Linseed oil, 1 pint; sweet oil, 1 ounce; and boil them in a kettle on coals for nearly 4 hours, as warm as you can; then have pulverized and mixed borax, 1-2 ounce; red lead, 4 ounces; and sugar of lead, 1 1-2 ounce; remove the kettle from the fire, and thicken in the powder; continue the stirring until cooled to blood-heat, then stir in 1 ounce of spirits of turpentine; and now take out a little, letting it get cold, and, if not then sufficiently thick to spread upon thin, soft linen, as a salve, you will boil again until this point is reached. It is good for all kinds of wounds, bruises, sores, burns, white swellings, rheumatisms, ulcers, sore breasts; and, even when there are wounds on the inside, it has been used with advantage by applying a plaster over the part.

Green Ointment.—Honey and bees-wax, each 1-2 pound; spirits of turpentine, 1 ounce; wintergreen oil and laudanum, each 2 ounces; verdigris, finely pulverized, 1-4 ounce; lard, 1 1-2 pounds; mix by a stove fire, in a copper kettle, heating slowly.

Mead's Salt-Rheum Ointment.—Aqua fortis, 1 ounce; quicksilver, 1 ounce; good hard soap dissolved so as to mix readily, 1 ounce; prepared chalk, 1 ounce; mixed with 1 pound of lard; incorporate the above by putting the aqua fortis and quicksilver into an earthen vessel, and, when done effervescing, mix with the other ingredients, putting the chalk in last, add a little spirits of turpentine, say 1-2 tablespoonful.

Itch Ointment.—Unsalted butter, 1 pound; burgundy pitch, 2 ounces; spirits of turpentine, 2 ounces; red precipitate, pulverized, 1 1-4 ounces; melt the pitch and add the butter; stirring well together; then remove from the fire, and, when a little cool, add the spirits of turpentine, and lastly the precipitate, and stir until cold.

Jaundice.—Dr. PEABODY'S CURE.—IN ITS WORST FORMS.—Red iodide of mercury, 7 grains; iodide of potassium, 9 grains; aqua dis (distilled water) 1 ounce; mix. Commence by giving 6 drops three or four times a day, increasing 1 drop a day until 12 or 15 drops are given at a dose. Give in a little water, immediately after meals. If it causes a griping sensation in the bowels, and fullness in the head, when you get up to 12 or 15 drops, go back to 6 drops, and up again as before.

Inflammatory Rheumatism. — WRIGHT'S CURE.—Sulphur and salt-petre, of each 1 ounce; gum guaiac, 1-2 ounce; colchicum root, or seed, and nutmegs, of each 1-4 ounce; all to be pulverized and mixed with simple syrup, or molasses, 2 ounces. Dose, 1 teaspoonful every two hours until it moves the bowels rather freely; then 3 or 4 times daily until cured.

Asthma Remedies.—Elecampane, angelica, confrey, and spikenard roots with hoarhound tops, of each 1 ounce; bruise and steep in honey, 1 pint. Dose, a tablespoonful, taken hot every few minutes until a cure is affected.

ANOTHER.—Oil of tar, 1 drachm; tincture of veratum viride, 2 drachms; simple syrup, 2 drachms; mix. Dose, for adults, 15 drops 3 or 4 times daily. Iodide of potassium has cured a bad case of asthma by taking 5 grain doses, 3 times daily. Take 1-3 ounce, and put into a phial, and add 32 teaspoonful of water; then 1 teaspoonful of it will contain the 5 grains, in which put 1-2 gill more water, and drink before meals.

Dropsy Pills.—Jalap, 50 grains; gamboge, 30 grains; podophyllin, 20 grains; clatarium, 12 grains; aloes, 30 grains; cayenne, 35 grains; Castile soap, shaved and pulverized, 20 grains; croton oil, 90 drops; powder all finely, and mix thoroughly; then form into a pill mass, by using a thick mucilage made of equal parts of gum arabic and gum tragacanth, and divide in 3 grain pills. Dose: 1 pill every 2 days for the first week; then every 3 or 4 days, until the water is evacuated by the combined aid of the pill with the alum syrup. This is a powerful medicine, and will thoroughly accomplish its work.

Eclectic Liver Pills.—Podophyllin, 10 grains; leptandrin, 20 grains; sanguinarian, 10 grains; extract of dandelion, 20 grains; formed into 20 pills by being moistened a little with some essential oil, as cinnamon, peppermint, etc. Dose: In chronic diseases of the liver, take a pill at night for several days, or 2 may be taken at first to move the bowels; then 1 daily.

Positive Cure for Hydrophobia.—The dried root of elecampane, pulverize it, and measure out 9 heaping tablespoonfuls, and mix it with 2 or 3 teaspoonfuls of pulverized gum arabic; then divide into 9 equal portions. When a person is bitten by a rabid animal, take one of these portions, and steep it in 1 pint of new milk, until nearly half the quantity of milk is evaporated; then strain, and drink it in the morning, fasting for four or five hours after. The same dose is to be repeated three mornings in succession, then skip three, and so on till the 9 doses are taken.

The patient must avoid getting wet, or the heat of the sun, and abstain from high-seasoned diet, or hard exercise, and, if costive, take a dose of salts. The above quantity is for an adult; children will take less according to age.

Eye Preparations.—EYE WATER.—Table salt and white vitriol, of each 1 tablespoonful; heat them up on copper or earthen until dry; the heating drives off the acrid or biting water, called the water of crystalization, making them much milder in their action; now add them to soft water, 1-2 pint; putting in white sugar, 1 tablespoonful; blue vitriol, a piece the size of a common pea. If it should prove too strong in any case, add a little more soft water to a phial of it. Apply it to the eyes three or four times daily.

INDIA PRESCRIPTION FOR SORE EYES.—Sulphate of zinc, 3 grains; tincture of opium (laudanum) 1 drachm; rose water, 2 ounces; mix. Put a drop or two in the eye, two or three times daily.

ANOTHER.—Sulphate of zinc, acetate of lead, and rock salt, of each, 1-2 ounce; loaf sugar, 1 ounce; soft water, 12 ounces; mix without heat, and use as other eye waters.

If sore eyes shed much water, put a little of the oxide of zinc into a phial of water; and use it rather freely. It will soon cure that difficulty.

Copperas and water has cured sore eyes of long standing; and used quite strong, it makes an excellent application in erysipelas.

INDIAN EYE WATER.—Soft water, 1 pint; gum arabic, 1 ounce; white vitriol, 1 ounce; fine salt, 1-2 teaspoonful; put all into a bottle, and shake until dissolved. Put into the eye just as you retire to bed.

Egyptian Cure for Cholera.—Best Jamaica ginger root bruised, 1 ounce; cayenne, 2 teaspoonfuls. Boil all in one quart of water to one-half pint, and add loaf sugar to form a thick syrup. Dose: One tablespoonful every fifteen minutes, until vomiting and purging ceases; then follow up with a blackberry tea.

King of Oils, for Neuralgia and Rheumatism.—Burning fluid, 1 pint; oils of cedar, hemlock, sassafras and origanum, of each, 2 ounces; carbonate of ammonia, pulverized, 1 ounce. Mix. DIRECTIONS.—Apply freely to the nerve and gums around the tooth; and to the face in neuralgic pains, by wetting brown paper and laying on the parts, not too long, for fear of blistering. To the nerves of teeth by lint.

Neuralgia. — INTERNAL REMEDY. — Sal-ammoniac, 1-2 drachm; dissolve in water, 1 ounce. Dose, one tablespoonful every 3 minutes for 20 minutes, at the end of which time, if not before, the pain will have disappeared.

Wens.—To CURE.—Dissolve copperas in water to make it very strong; now take a pin, needle, or sharp knife, and prick or cut the wen in about a dozen places, just sufficient to cause it to bleed; then wet it thoroughly with the copperas water daily.

Animal Poisons.—In the first class is poisoning from certain shellfish, such as mussels, lobsters, etc., the eating of which is sometimes followed by an eruption of nettle-rash over the whole body, which causes it to have a swollen, bloated appearance, and produces difficulty of breathing, accompanied with giddiness, nausea, stomach-ache, and great thirst.

TREATMENT.—If commenced within two or three hours after the appearance of the symptoms, an emetic of mustard, salt, and warm water, should be given. The emetic should be compounded thus:

Mustard, 1 teaspoonful.
Common salt, 1 teaspoonful.
Warm water, 1 tumblerful.
Mix, and take as a draught.

Should, however, a longer time have elapsed, purgatives, such as a teaspoonful of castor-oil, or half an ounce of epsom salts, should be administered and repeated until full action is obtained. Stimulants, such as salvolatile, or aromatic spirits of ammonia, and ether, may also be administered if there be much depression.

The following form would be a useful draught: Take of nitrous spirits of ether, 30 minims; spirits of salvolatile, 30 minims; water, to make up 1 1-2 ounces. Repeat the dose every two or three hours until the system rallies.

Vegetable Poisons.—Of these, the most commonly met with are the aconite or monkshood, belladonna or deadly nightshade; the hellebore, hemlock, henbane, foxglove, laburnum, yew, colchicum, or meadow saffron, and mushrooms, all of which are indigeneous to this country. Others, such as opium, Indian hemp, nux vomica, and gamboge, are not native here.

Among vegetable poisons should be included oxalic acid, and that most deadly of all poisons, prussic acid, which is found in undiluted " almond flavoring," used for culinary purposes.

SYMPTOMS.—Vegetable poisons have many features in common, thus they are strongly acrid and narcotic, or depressing, causing drowsiness, feebleness of pulse, vomiting, purging, griping.

Under the following enumeration, the symptoms peculiar to each will be found, together with their appropriate treatment:

Aconite (*Monkshood*).—SYMPTOMS.—A sensation of burning, tingling or numbness, in the mouth and throat. Giddiness, loss of power to stand firmly, pain in the region of the stomach, frothing at the mouth, vomiting and purging. The pupils are

dilated, the skin cold and livid, the breathing becomes difficult. In some cases delirium and paralysis follow.

TREATMENT.—An emetic should immediately be given, such as a mixture of mustard, salt, and warm water, thus: Mustard, 1 teaspoonful; common salt, 1 teaspoonful; warm water, a tumblerful. Or, sulphate of zinc, 20 grains; water, 1 ounce. Given every half hour until the stomach has been emptied of the poison. Acidulous fluids, such as vinegar and water, and cordials should be given freely. External warmth should be kept up by mustard plasters, hot water bottles to the feet and friction to the surface.

DISTINCTION.—The root of this plant is often mistaken for horseradish which it closely resembles; therefore great care should be taken not to allow the two plants to grow in the same garden. The leaves and seeds of the plant are also poisonous.

Belladonna (*Deadly Nightshade*).—The leaves, berries, stalks—or extract or tincture made from these—are most commonly met with as a cause of poison.

SYMPTOMS.—Heat and dryness of mouth, a feeling of tightness in the throat. Nausea, vomiting, giddiness, indistinct or double sight, intense excitement, delirium of a peculiar kind, the patient twists himself round and round, butts against the wall with his head, and performs various other antics. These are followed by heaviness and lethargy.

TREATMENT.—Begin by giving freely a mixture of about one part of vinegar to two of water. Then cause evacuation of the stomach by means of emetics, such as mustard, 1 teaspoonful; common salt, 1 ditto; warm water, a tumblerful. Taken at a draught. Or, sulphate of zinc, 20 grains; water, 1 ounce. Dissolved, and taken as a draught. Promote vomiting by warm water slightly acidulated with vinegar. The bowels should be emptied by injections of castor oil.

Digitalis Purpurea (*Foxglove*).—SYMPTOMS. — Vomiting, purging, accompanied with severe pain in the stomach. This is followed by a state of lethargy, during which the patient will sleep for hours; this, again, is followed by convulsions. The pupils are dilated and insensible to the stimulating effect of light; the pulse becomes small and irregular; and, should the dose have been large, and the proper measures not adopted, coma or insensibility of a severe kind will rapidly set in, and be followed by death.

TREATMENT.—A free use of emetics (see under Hemlock) should be pursued. Drinks containing tannic acid, such as strong tea and infusion of gall-nuts, should be given; if the prostration be great, brandy should be given freely.

All the parts of this plant are poisonous. They owe their poisonous properties to an active principle called *digitalin*. This, in combination with tannic acid, is rendered innocuous; hence the reason for its administration in cases of poisoning.

Gamboge (*Cambogia*).—SYMPTOMS.—Violent vomiting, severe pain in the stomach and excessive purging, followed by great prostration of strength.

TREATMENT.—Carbonate of potash should be given as follows: Carbonate of potash, 20 grains; mucilage, or solution of gum, 1-2 ounce; water to make up 1 ounce. Mix, and take every hour until the purging has stopped. When this is the case, and the poison is supposed to have been evacuated, give the following every half hour: Tincture of opium, 10 drops; water, 1 ounce. Mix. Gamboge is a gum resin obtained from the Garcinia Morella, a native of Spain. It is but little used in legitimate medicine, on account of its violent and uncertain action. Quack pills contain it in very variable quantities.

Hellebores, the.—The Green Hellebore (*Helleborus virids*). The White Hellebore (*Veratrum album*). The Black Hellebore, or Christmas rose (*Helleborus niger*). The Fœtid Hellebore (*Helleborus Fœtida*). All of these are powerful poisons, the white hellebore especially so.

SYMPTOMS.—Vomiting, purging, giddiness, dilation of the pupils, convulsions, insensibility, great heat of the throat, and tightness, with severe pain in the stomach.

TREATMENT.—Vomiting should be excited by large doses of solution of gum, and other mucilaginous fluids, such as milk, white of egg, etc., and injections of the same materials should be thrown up into the bowel. Coffee should then be given freely, and acidulous fluids and camphor-water. The roots and leaves of this plant are both poisonous, the roots especially.

Hemlock (*Conium Maculatum*).—SYMPTOMS.—This plant attacks the muscular power, and causes paralysis of the limbs, sickness, pain in the head, drowsiness, and sometimes it so affects the muscles of respiration as to cause death.

TREATMENT.—The stomach should be evacuated by some powerful emetic, such as the following: Sulphate of zinc, 20 grains; dissolved in water, a wineglassful. Or, mustard, 1 teaspoonful; common salt, 1 teaspoonful; water, a tumblerful. After this cold water should be applied to the head. Vinegar and water (see under Deadly Nightshade) should be administered. The poisonous properties of this plant reside in the leaves, which somewhat resemble parsley, for which they have occasionally been mistaken. The seeds and the root are also poisonous.

Henbane (*Hyoscyamus*).—SYMPTOMS.— Vomiting, double vision, dilatation of the pupils, sleepiness, loss of muscular power, a peculiar tremulous motion of the limbs, flushing of the countenance, heat and weight of head, giddiness, fullness of the pulse and general excitement. If the dose has been a large one, the symptoms will be aggravated; there will be loss of speech, delirium, coma, coldness of the surface, and jerkings of the muscles.

TREATMENT.—As soon as possible empty the stomach by emetics, and give acidulous drinks; if, however, the poison has entered the system, purgatives must be given. The seeds are the most poisonous, the leaves next, and the roots last.

Indian Hemp (*Cannabis Indica*). — HASCHISCH. — SYMPTOMS.—Much the same as those of opium, but are of a much more pleasant nature to the patient, being associated with delightful dreams and visions.

TREATMENT.—Much the same as in the case of poisoning by opium.

Cases of poisoning by this plant are very rarely met with in America. In hot climates, however, it is frequently met with, especially in India.

Laburnum (*Cyitalisus Laburnum*).—SYMPTOMS.—Pain in the stomach, followed by vomiting and severe convulsions if the dose has been a large one. There is also shivering, great feebleness, and severe purging.

TREATMENT.—The vomiting should be encouraged by mucilage, milk, white of an egg, flour and water. Should the feebleness be very great, cordials and brandy should be given in repeated and small doses. The bark and seeds of this plant are poisonous, and owe their deleterious properties to an active principle called Cytisine.

Meadow Saffron (*Colchicum autumnale*).— SYMPTOMS.— A burning pain in the gullet and stomach, violent vomiting, and sometimes bilious purging.

TREATMENT.—Give some mild emetic, thus: Ipecacuanha wine, one-half ounce; honey, 1 tablespoonful; milk, a teacupful. Stir up and mix thoroughly, and let the patient take it at a draught. This should be repeated every quarter of an hour till vomiting sets in. Of course the dose of ipecacuanha wine should be smaller for children, one-half or one-fourth of the above quantity being ample for a child under five years old.

Then give opium as follows (to adults only): Powdered opium, 3 grains; confection of dog rose, sufficient to make a small mass with the opium. Divide this into six pills, and let the patient have one every four hours, until the symptoms of poisoning abate. Or, tincture of opium, 1 fluid drachm; water, to six fluid ounces. Mix. Two tablespoonfuls to be taken every two hours.

Mushrooms (*Fungi*).—Symptoms.—Pain in the stomach accompanied with vomiting, giddiness, drowsiness, dimness of sight, and debility. The patient appears to be intoxicated.

Treatment.—This cannot be better expressed than in the terse and plain terms of Professor Taylor. They are: "The free use of emetics and castor oil."

Nux Vomica (*Strychnine*). — Symptoms. — An intensely bitter taste in the mouth. Tipsy manner, sickness, headache, jerking of the arms and legs, and twitching of the body; lock-jaw, great difficulty in breathing, with intense pain in the chest, and a sense of suffocation.

Treatment.—Evacuate the stomach and bowels. Give vinegar (see Deadly Nightshade) and other acidulous drinks. If the spasm be very severe and constant, and do not yield to the emetics, etc., then try injections of infusions of tobacco, as follows: Tobacco (shag), 30 grains; water, 8 fluid ounces. Mix, and allow to stand for half an hour, occasionally shaking. Then strain and inject into the bowel in the intervals of the spasms.

Strychnia is one of the most deadly poisons, a very small quantity being capable of killing a strong man.

Opium.—*An extract from the poppy.* (*Papaver Somnifera*). —Symptoms.— Drowsiness, stupor, delirium, pallid counte-nance, contracted pupil, sighing, loud or snoring respiration, cold sweats, coma, and death.

Treatment.—Emetics of the sulphated zinc (see under Hemlock), or, if the patient be too far gone to take these, the stomach pump should be applied. The patient should on no account be allowed to sleep, but his attention should be con-stantly aroused. A good plan is to walk the patient rapidly and incessantly about. A tepid bath is useful for arousing the sleeping energies, and cold water should be dashed over the head at the same time. Opium is the juice of the poppy, which runs from the incisions made in the unripe fruit. Its principal properties are due to an active principle contained in it, which is called morphia. In cases of overdoses of this drug, the same treatment should be adopted.

Oxalic Acid.—Symptoms.—If the dose be a large one, while it is being swallowed a hot, burning, acid taste is experienced, extending downward to the stomach; vomiting then occurs, or within a few minutes. There is a severe feeling of tightness in the throat, and sometimes delirium. When the dose is smaller the pain is less, and vomiting does not set in so soon. At times there is no vomiting, at others it alone causes death by causing exhaustion.

Treatment.—Some chalk and water should be immediately administered, and a quantity of water drunk to encourage vomiting. This is not often administered with a criminal intent, the taste is too strong; but it is taken sometimes in mistake for epsom salts, which it somewhat resembles.

Prussic Acid (*Hydrocyanic Acid*). — Symptoms. — Pallid appearance, giddiness, great nervous prostration, loss of sight more or less complete, faintness, labored and hard respiration, loss of power of motion.

Treatment.—The stomach pump should be applied; or, if this is not handy, emetics, such as mustard, salt and water. (See under Hemlock). Dash cold water over the head and chest. Give salvolatile as follows: Spirits of salvolatile, 1 drachm; water, to 1 ounce. Mix. Every quarter of an hour until there is some signs of revival. Prussic acid is the most powerful poison known. This poison is often met with in the essential oil of almonds, and great care should therefore be taken in the use of this pleasant flavoring.

Yew (*Taxus baccata*).— Symptoms.— Professor Taylor gives the symptoms of poisoning by this plant as follows: "Convulsions, insensibility, coma, dilated pupils, pale countenance, small pulse, and cold extremities are the most prominent; vomiting and purging are also observed among the symptoms."

Treatment.—As in many other vegetable, indeed it might safely be said in all poisons, vomiting should be excited, and this is best done, and perhaps in the quickest, safest manner, by an emetic of mustard, salt and water. Should the convulsions be very acute, and there be great heat of head, cold should be applied. If the pulse is very small, and the prostration of the patient is great, as soon as the stomach is thoroughly emptied, brandy should be given.

It is commonly supposed that the leaves of this plant are not poisonous when fresh, but this is erroneous. They are at all times poisonous. The berries also are very dangerous, more especially to children, as they have an agreeable taste, and look tempting. The danger of the leaves is not so much for the human race as it is for cattle, who are fond of eating them.

MINERAL POISONS.—The mineral poisons are perhaps the most commonly used for criminal and suicidal purposes, and they are certainly more easily detected by chemical means than are either the vegetable or animal poisons. Science has yet found out but few certain tests for the vegetable poisons compared with the large number of accurate and easily available tests for the mineral poisons.

Perhaps the most important of this class of poisons is arsenic, as it is certainly the most fatal; others, such as antimony, copper, lead, mercury, and the acids, are in many cases very fatal, but few of these possess the power of destroying life to anything like the extent that is possessed by arsenic.

Acid, Carbolic.—The powerful odor of this acid prevents its being frequently taken accidentally, but it has been taken with suicidal intent.

SYMPTOMS.—These are much the same as the other powerful irritant poisons. There is an intense burning in the mouth and gullet, accompanied with a feeling of tightness in the throat, vomiting of shreds of mucus, griping pain in the stomach, the lips and insides of the cheeks present a charred appearance, and, if its action be not checked, the nervous system suffers, and the organs of the senses are impaired, and death rapidly follows.

TREATMENT.—Albuminous fluids should be given in large doses, such as white of egg, flour and water, gruel and milk. Magnesia, and chalk and water, is used in these cases. Emetics of mustard should also be freely administered.

Acid, Hydrochloric (*Muriatic Acid. Spirits of Salt*).— Both the symptoms and treatment of a case of poisoning by this acid are given under Sulphuric Acid.

Acid, Nitric (*Aqua Fortis*).—SYMPTOMS.—(See Sulphuric Acid.) The only difference is that nitric acid does not cause such a dark discoloration of the lips and mouth.

TREATMENT.—Precisely the same as under case of Sulphuric Acid.

Acid, Sulphuric (*Oil of Vitriol*).—This acts as a poison by its powerful corrosive powers. It seldom causes death by its absorption into the system, but rather by the excessive irritation and inflammation which it causes to the lining of the mouth, the gullet, and the stomach. It immediately causes the skin to have a charred appearance of a whitish hue, which gradually becomes darker and browner; it causes pain in the stomach, vomiting, and eructations of a gaseous character; great nervous depression, which is also shared by the pulse; convulsions, and death.

Treatment.—Give magnesia and water, or lime-water; or, should neither of these be at hand, give soap and water freely.

Antimony (*Tartar Emetic Butter of Antimony*).—Symptoms.—These are very much the same as those of arsenic, with the exception that the depression, vomiting, and collapse are much more rapid, owing to the immediate action of the poison the heart.

Treatment.—Should the vomiting not occur freely, it will be as well to give an emetic, and afterwards a dose of tannic acid and water, thus: Tannic acid, 10 grains; water, 1 ounce. Mix. Or, a dose of very strong tea, or infusion of gall-nuts, mixed with magnesia.

Arsenic (*Realgar or Red Arsenic, White Arsenic, Scheele's Green, Orpiment, or Yellow Arsenic*).—Symptoms.—An unpleasantly strong metallic taste, a tightness in the throat, vomiting of a brown mucus character, mixed with blood, fainting, great thirst, excessive pain in the stomach, with shivering purging, the stools being very offensive and of a dark character, pulse small and rapid, great nervous prostration and delirium. Arsenic is sometimes administered in repeated small doses, and by this means is produced a state which is called "chronic arsenical poisoning." In this case, disorder of the stomach and bowels exists, but does not form such a prominent symptom as in the more acute form of this poisoning. There will be redness and smarting in the eyes, great sensibility of the skin, at times accompanied either by a rash, which consists of minute vesicles or blisters, or else by nettle-rash. There is also local paralysis—that is to say, paralysis of one particular set of muscles, accompanied, or rather preceded, by numbness and tingling in the fingers and toes. The patient loses flesh and becomes exhausted. Sometimes the skin peels off, and loss of hair occurs.

Treatment.—A substance termed hydrated peroxide of iron has been strongly vaunted as an antidote to arsenic. The best way to give it is to mix a tablespoonful with water, and give every five or ten minutes. Should this not be procurable, it is best to use the stomach-pump or emetics. (See under Hemlock.) Large quantities of mucilage should be given to drink, or eggs, or milk. When the worst symptoms have subsided, and the patient is out of immediate danger, he should be kept in bed, with warm poultices applied to the pit of the stomach. Small pills of one grain of opium should be given every four hours while pain continues, but no violent aperient. Arsenic is one of those poisons which, begun with very small doses, and gradually increasing them, may become almost harmless. One form of arsenic ("Scheele's green") is largely used as a coloring for room papers. In this form it often does insidious mischief, as it separates from the paper in minute particles, and circulates freely in the air of the room as dust. This fact may be proved by submitting some of the dust which collects on bookshelves, etc., in a room thus ornamented to a few simple chemical tests, or by causing some expert to analyze it. By so doing, the inquirer will often receive satisfactory evidence of the existence of this poison, if he has not previously had some practical experience of its effects.

Copper (*Blue Vitriol. Mineral Green. Verdigris*).—SYMPTOMS.—These, again, are much the same as in arsenic, but rather less acute. It may here be stated that many alleged cases of poison by verdigris, from cooking vessels, etc., are in reality owing to bad or decomposed food. A poisonous dose of salts of copper is always followed (if the patient recovers from the first effects) by inflammation of the bowels.

TREATMENT.—Begin with the stomach-pump, or an emetic. When the stomach has been evacuated, give white of egg, flour and water, milk. The subsequent inflammation of the bowels should be treated as described under arsenic.

Lead (*White Lead. Sugar of Lead*).—SYMPTOMS.—This also causes many of the symptoms described under arsenic, when taken in a large quantity; but there is a particular form of disease called lead colic, which particularly affects workers in lead (see colic); these people are also subject to a form of paralysis (see paralysis).

TREATMENT.—When taken in a large dose, give an emetic of sulphur of zinc or copper (see hemlock). If the pain in the stomach be severe, small doses of tincture of opium, about 10 minims, should be given at short intervals, combined with sulphate of magnesia.

Mercury (*Corrosive Sublimate. Calomel. White Precipitate*).—SYMPTOMS.—Intense metallic taste in the mouth, pain in the stomach, purging, vomiting, etc.; in fact, the symptoms of nearly all metallic poisons are similar. There are, of course, certain peculiarities belonging to each, and that belonging to mercury is the largely increased flow of saliva, commonly called "salivation," which almost invariably follows a poisonous dose of mercury in any of its forms. The period which elapses between the taking of the poison and appearance of the salivation, varies from a few hours to some days.

TREATMENT.—An emetic of sulphate of zinc or copper (as under hemlock) should be given in white of egg, mixed with milk or water, milk, and flour and water in large draughts. When the salivation sets in, the following will be found useful when in conjunction with astringent gargles: Iodide of potassium, 24 grains; tincture of bark, 1 ounce; water, to 8 ounces. Mix, and take two tablespoonfuls three times a day. A good form of an astringent gargle is as follows: Alum, 30 grains; water, to 4 ounces. Mix, and use about a tablespoonful as a gargle every three or four hours.

Ammonia.—SYMPTOMS.—Pungent acrid odor, hot taste, stomach-ache, followed by convulsions, delirium, and death.

TREATMENT.—Vinegar and water in large doses, lemon juice and olive oil. For any other of the alkalies, soda or potash, in their caustic forms, the same treatment should be pursued.

Chloride of Zinc.—SYMPTOMS.—Pain of a burning kind in the throat, nausea and vomiting, griping pains in the stomach, pallor and coldness, the legs are drawn up, and there are appearances of collapse.

Alkalies.—The strong or concentrated preparation acts with extreme corrosive violence on the mouth, gullet, and stomach. Should the action of this poison be further continued, it will be found that it affects the nervous system. This will be demonstrated by the patient's sight becoming dim, and the power of taste and smell less acute than it is normally—by extreme depression, syncope, and death.

TREATMENT.—Milk and white of egg should be given freely. and emetics of mustard and warm water, combined with flour or oatmeal.

Baths and Bathing.—In infancy, bathing or washing at least twice a day is necessary to preserve the skin in a healthy condition. In so doing, however, care must be taken that the surface of the body be not chilled; a judicious warmth (avoiding too great heat) should be studied. In the early weeks of life the body does not readily maintain its own temperature; hence the reason that the young of animals remain a certain time constantly near their mother. It is the same with our infants; no warmth is so equable or so good for them during the few first days or weeks of life as the warmth of their mother; hence, also, the necessity for a warm bath as the means of cleanliness.

A fallacy lurks in the notion of hardening children. The argument in favor of the attempt so to do, drawn from the "state of nature," is altogether a dangerous fallacy. All that can really be said in its favor is that it is not possible to kill all the children submitted to the system. The delicate ones will be sifted out, and the hardy ones will survive in spite of "system." It is an error in reasoning to quote the savage state as that of nature, and, therefore, worthy of imitation. It may be urged with greater force that the nature of man's mental endowments tends to raise him from the savage to the civilized state. The natural state of man is that of civilization, with its attendant fostering care of infantile existence.

SPONGE BATH.—In after-life the daily sponge bath contributes greatly to the preservation of health, by the promotion of cleanliness, and by the exhilarating influence in stimulating the circulation of the blood on the surface of the body. The warmth of reaction is more sure to follow if the bath be used on rising, while the body is still warm, and before the surface is chilled by exposure in dressing In using this, a due regard to the feelings should be observed. Some persons are extremly sensitive to cold, while others enjoy its reaction and bracing influence. The temperature of the water should, therefore, be regulated by the climate, weather, and individual susceptibility. After sponging, the whole body should be briskly dried with a rough towel, and a glow of warmth will follow.

COLD BATH.—(Temperature 50° to 60°.)—A cold bath will vary in its effects according as it is taken in a small bath, or in a river, the sea, or a quantity of water large enough for swimming, and according to the temperature of the air. The benefit to be derived from a cold bath is governed also pretty much by the state of the bather, or on the greater or less vigor of the heart's action, and of the circulation in the skin. A cold bath should not be taken with a cold skin; the best preparation is the warm glow of exercise. A plunge (head first) into cold water, even when hot and perspiring after exercise, and a good swim for a few minutes, is more surely followed by healthful reaction than the waiting until the body is dry and cool, or perhaps chilled by evaporation of perspiration. A cold bath without the active exercise of swimming should not be prolonged beyond three or four minutes; even the good swimmer must be warned that prolonged action of cold incurs the risk of cramp.

Persons in impaired state of health should take little more than a single immersion, and this should be followed by friction of the surface with towels or dry flannels. Such persons should avoid bathing on an empty stomach; it is better not to take a cold bath immediately after a meal.

The answer to questions on the advisability of cold bathing, whether in the sea or otherwise, is to be found in the state of the pulse and of the skin. With a feeble pulse and a disposition to palpitation of the heart, the flow of blood through the skin is sure to be tardy, as compared with that of health, and reaction will consequently be slowly established at the risk of congestion of internal organs. Hence, in persons disposed towards head, or heart, or lung affections, great caution should be exercised. Persons who are subject to palpitation of the heart, giddiness, etc., had better avoid the cold bath.

Generally, it may be laid down as a rule that if cold bathing be not followed by a glow of warmth on the skin, it should not be repeated.

About two or three hours after a meal is the best time for cold bathing.

THE TEPID BATH (temperature 70° to 80°) is suitable for those whose health, or sensitiveness to cold, forbid the use of the cold bath. The same rules, however, apply especially as regards the delicate in health.

THE HOT BATH (temperature 98° to 110°) differs from the cold or tepid bath, inasmuch as they are preservative of health, while this is curative of disease.

It opens the pores of the skin, relaxes the muscles, soothes the nervous system, and (after its first stimulation of the heart's action is past) is a valuable agent in reducing fever and inflammatory action by the profuse perspiration that it induces—so much so, that it is often an efficacious remedy in the treatment of inflammation.

In the convulsions of infancy, the hot bath, continued from five to ten minutes, is an important part of the treatment.

In order to avoid any possible risk of the sudden immersion in hot water, it is a safe plan to have the bath at about 95° to begin with, and gradually raise the temperature to 100°, or even 105°, if profuse perspiration afterwards be desired; in this case, the bath may be continued by an adult twenty minutes or half an hour. On coming out of the bath, after rapidly wiping the surface of the body, a warm blanket should be wrapped round before getting into a warm bed.

When it is desirable to give a hot bath to a child for any febrile malady, or in any case where the child would be frightened at being put into the water, its fears may be disarmed by covering the bath with a blanket, and letting the little patient down gently into the bath.

VAPOR BATH (temperature 100° to 120°) is of great use in exciting perspiration in catarrh, in simple fever, and in rheumatism. It may be extemporized by sitting on a chair enclosed in a blanket, and having a pail of hot water placed under the chair, adding to the water some red-hot stones, or brick, or iron chain. If a long pipe can be connected with the spout of a large kettle, and made to pass within the blanket, it affords a ready means of making a vapor bath.

HOT-AIR BATH.—(Temperature 100° to 120°.)—This acts in the same way as a vapor bath. It is readily made by burn-

ing some spirits of wine under the canopy of blanket. A convenient mode is, after the patient is seated and covered up to
the throat with blankets, to place an ounce of spirits of wine in
a cup, the cup standing in a basin with some water, then light
the spirit and let it burn out.

THE TURKISH BATH, a combination of these, is useful in
rheumatic and other chronic diseases, but requires to be used
for medical purposes only under medical advice.

HYDROPATHY professes the cure of disease by baths of
various kinds. It can only be properly practiced in establishments especially devoted thereto. It is expensive and, therefore, only within the reach of comparatively few.

SLEEP.

No rule can be observed with regard to the proportion of
time that should be given to sleep. Much depends upon individual habit and disposition. The active mind and cheerful
disposition that is never more happy than when busily employed, and finds its recreation in change of work, will generally sleep soundly and be refreshed, by six or seven hours'
sleep. Less than this cannot be safely devoted to sleep by any
one who does a good day's work, either bodily or mentally.
There have been those who could abridge their hours of sleep
to four, three, or even two, hours out of the twenty-four, but
they paid the penalty of such an infringement of nature's laws
by shortening the number of their days, and embittering them
by the impairment of health.

The daily wear and tear of life needs the restoration of
sleep to ensure healthy balance of nervous power, and that
equanimity of mind so desirable in this world's strife and tur-
moil.

Infants and children require more sleep than grown-up
persons. In fact the early days of infancy are passed in
sleeping, to the infant's great gain. If otherwise its health
soon suffers, and shows the want of "balmy sleep." Warmth,
sleep, and food are all that are wanted in early infancy. For
the first three or four years the mid-day "nap" contributes to
the vigor and activity of the young child.

Throughout childhood up to puberty from twelve to fourteen hours' sleep is not an undue allowance. At all events, if
less time be accorded for sleep, "early to bed" is a golden
maxim. The practice of allowing infants and young children
to be awake and up until ten or eleven o'clock at night, amid
the glare of lights, and perhaps the noise and excitement of
festivity, is the most injudicious sort of kindness to which they
can be exposed.

CLIMATE.

This word embraces the consideration of many topics which our limits forbid our touching upon; but, as the present work will doubtless be read in all parts of the country (at least such is our hope), it would be incomplete without a few remarks thereon in relation to the causation and treatment of disease.

"The climate of a country or district," Dr. Copland remarks, "depends, 1st, upon its position in respect of distance from the equator, and upon its elevation above the level of the sea, and its proximity to the shores of the ocean, or the beds of large rivers, etc.; 2nd, upon the geological and mineralogical formations constituting the basis of its soil; 3rd. upon the nature of the soil itself, its cultivation, and the evgetable productions by which it is covered; and, 4th, upon the prevailing winds or currents of the air."

THE EFFECT OF CHANGE OF CLIMATE.—An inhabitant of a temperate climate going to a tropical country will suffer from excitement of the nervous and vascular systems, by the heat and moisture of the air. The respiratory functions become less active; while there is a decrease of the ordinary action of the kidneys in carrying off the refuse matters of the circulation. The consequence is that the skin and the liver have an excess of work thrown upon them (to speak metaphorically, and also exactly), in order to rid the system of certain effete elements which the lungs cannot throw off.

Hence the "seasoning fevers," as they are called, and the disorders of the liver to which Europeans are specially liable on arrival in a hot climate, and to which full often they render themselves the more obnoxious by injudicious diet. An eminent English authority says that:

Europeans visiting hot climates should live abstemiously, taking every means to promote the functions of the skin by moderate exercise, and by daily free ablutions. Exposure of the head to the heat of the sun should be carefully avoided, as well as the risk of contracting fever by exposure to dews, the cold, and the malaria of the night air. Warm clothing should be worn at night by new-comers, as the extremes of day and night temperature in tropical regions often pass through a very wide range.

The effects of a warm and moist climate upon the inhabitants of colder regions, in decreasing the functional activity of the lungs, and increasing that of the liver and skin, has formed the basis of the recommendation of a change from a cold to a warm climate in pulmonary affections. It is, however, very doubtful whether the relaxing and enervating influence of the heat on the nervous system does not more than counterbalance this functional compensation. Certainly, when disease in the lungs has advanced much, more harm than good generally comes of the migration. On the other hand, the tonic and bracing effect of a cold climate more frequently checks the advance of consumption, if care is taken to protect the surface from sudden chills, and so to protect it as to ensure a free circulation of the blood in the skin by out-door exercise. The British Hippocrates, Sydenham, was wont to call horse exercise the " palmarium remedy " for consumption, so strongly was he convinced of the importance of out-door exercise. A confirmation of this opinion is to be found in the fact that coachmen (if temperate men) are among the healthiest classes. In the days when locomotion was performed more on horseback than is now the case, it was said that " bagmen," or commercial travelers, enjoyed a singular freedom from consumption. Unfortunately, however, these men, then as now, too often threw away their better health by their irregularities in other directions.

While the stress of the effects of removal to warm climates upon the inhabitants of temperate regions is thus seen to fall upon the liver and skin, the reverse is seen to occur when the natives of hot climates migrate to colder countries. The negro, brought direct from Africa to England, will almost surely be the victim of consumption.

The change of climate must therefore be guided by these several conditions, both of place and person, and may further have to be altered according to the changes of the seasons, and according to the special character of the season itself. Thus, it not unfrequently happens that the south coast of England is not suitable for invalids, even so late as June, if easterly winds prevail. The air is then almost as keen as that of the directly eastern coast, and a return inland becomes inevitable.

CONSUMPTION.—In this disease, change of climate, to be productive of real benefit, must be tried at a much earlier period than is generally done, as it is often delayed a year or two after the period that any good can be expected, and the result is that more harm than good is done thereby. Hence the trial is often not made through the discredit that arises out of its misapplication. It should be borne in mind that consumption is not merely a disease of the lungs, but a general morbid constitutional condition, of which the disease in the lungs is but a manifestation. The early treatment must, therefore, be directed to invigorating the system and improving the quality of the blood. With these objects, the climate most suitable for winter residence are those of our southern coast, Madeira, Nice, Pisa, and Rome, with removal during summer months to the drier situations of our own islands.

CHRONIC BRONCHITIS.—This is an affection that is often mistaken for consumption, and one which, through its persistence and its debilitating and emaciating effects, constitutes a veritable decline. The change from a cold and moist to a mild and dry air relieves the morbid conditions of the mucous surfaces. The same climates that are of service in consumption are beneficial in chronic bronchitis. When asthma is combined with chronic bronchitis, it is also relieved by the same climate as is found useful in chronic consumption. Torquay and Undercliff, for example, are most adapted to irritable states of the mucous membrane without much secretion; Clifton or Brighton for those in which expectoration is profuse and the system debilitated; Rome, Pisa, Madeira, are suited for the latter class of cases; Nice to the former.

CHRONIC RHEUMATISM.—This is benefitted by residence in a warm climate, such as the southwestern coast of England, the south of France, Rome, and Pisa.

GOUT.—This also derives benefit by a warm climate. The West India Islands are especially marked in this respect.

DYSPEPSIA and nervous affections connected therewith are aggravated by a cold and damp atmosphere, and are greatly relieved by change to a drier and warmer climate; but great care in dieting is needful in order to ensure the full benefit of the change. The use of stimulants must be very carefully watched. The nervous symptoms associated with dyspepsia are prone to take on the form of hypochondriasis; the change of climate should therefore be accompanied with change of occupation and of amusement. This class of cases rapidly improve under change of scene, and the relinquishment of the cares of business, to say nothing of "throwing physic to the dogs."

DIET IN RELATION TO DISEASE.

In acute diseases, the diet should generally be of the simplest and lightest kind, such as beef-tea or mutton-broth, sago, tapioca, arrowroot, or gruel, with, at the same time, some little respect paid to the palate. Due regard, however, must be paid to the general character and condition of the constitution. For instance, acute diseases may occur in a very debilitated state of the health, and then may require the addition to the above of some alcoholic stimulant. The stomach in such cases would not be able to digest solid food. The absence of this must be supplied by soups, broths, eggs, etc.

In the feeding of invalids, even children, some attention may be paid to their cravings after different articles. It will often be found that the thing longed for is not injurious, and may be often called for in obedience to some indication by nature. The following incident may serve to illustrate this observation: A child of about four or five years old was suffering under diphtheria, and had got to refuse the port wine and beef-tea that had been ordered it. It seemed that there was nothing for it but that the child must die from starvation and diphtheria together. One day she woke up from a nap and saw a glass of ale, which was being drunk by its mother with her luncheon. This ale the child cried for, but the mother feared to allow her to drink. When appealed to, the medical attendant said, "By all means let the child have it; and even put it in her way that she may take it herself without let or hindrance." The next time the child woke up she eagerly clutched at the malt liquor and drank off a tumblerful. From that moment she began to mend, and for the next forty-eight hours persistently refused everything else, either as food or medicine, and eventually made a good recovery. When the disease, though acute, is of a less severe character, and is not stamped with extreme debility, the stomach will tolerate light solids, such as white fish, fowls, bread, rice, light puddings, and ripe, pulpy fruit and vegetables may be taken with advantage, as the acids allay thirst. In chronic disease a fuller diet is required, comprising meat with some stimulant.

MILK.—Milk is the most important article of diet in infancy, and is also both nutritious and digestible in diseases of adult life. A prejudice exists in the minds of many persons to the effect that milk is not easily digested. The opinion is, however, refuted by the fact that it forms the nourishment of infants and of young animals of all kinds. Cow's milk, however, is sometimes unsuited to the stomachs of infants brought up by hand; or, from its richness in oil and curd, to the stomachs of persons enfeebled by disease. The best substitute that can be used is asses' or goat's milk. The latter, however, is richer than the former.

For the first three or four months of an infant's life the best food is breast-milk alone. If for any reason this cannot be given, asses' milk is the best substitute. Next to this cow's milk, diluted with an equal proportion of water in which half a teaspoonful of powdered sugar of milk has been dissolved. Cow's milk differs from human milk in its excess of cream and curd. The cream consists almost wholly of oil globules. The addition of a solution of sugar-of-milk reduces it in one direction, and raises it in another, to the level of human milk; thus, sugar-of-milk contains all the saline matters of the milk from which it was made; therefore, by its addition (with water) to cow's milk, while the curd and oil are diluted, the deficiency of the salts is supplied, and thereby its composition is as nearly as possible equalized or assimilated one to the other.

Most infants will thrive well on this hand-feeding, but there are two points of essential importance to its success. One is the giving the food with regularity. For the first two or three weeks the child should be fed every two hours during the day, and once or twice in the course of the night. The interval should gradually be lengthened after the month.

The same rule as to time should be observed, whatever be the food, whether breast-milk or any substitute.

FEEDING-BOTTLES OBJECTIONABLE.—The next point, and one (if possible) more important, is that the feeding-bottle should be most scrupulously cleaned each time immediately after feeding, or small quantities of milk remaining in the tube or teat will become sour. The minutest particle of sour milk taken into the stomach with the other will act after the manner of a ferment, and favor the turning sour of the whole quantity.

It should, however, here be noted, that it does not follow that, because when a child vomits its milk it is found curdled, therefore the whole has been sour at the time of taking it. The first step in the digestion of the milk is that it is curdled by the gastric juice of the stomach, and afterwards dissolved by it. This process, however, is very different from the curdling of milk by its having turned sour out of the stomach, and it has a very different result in the process of digestion.

There is another grave objection to these tubes—they engender and foster idleness on the part of the nurse. It is a common practice to put an infant into its bed or cradle, with the teat in its mouth and the bottle in bed, and there to leave it to suckle itself to sleep; which it generally does, sucking the while even after it has fallen asleep and its bottle is emptied. The child goes on sucking at the tube, but getting no food; the infant, in popular phrase, "sucks in wind." If it does not exactly suck the wind, its fruitless sucking at a piece of india-rubber keeps up secretion of gastric juice in the stomach. This, having no food to act upon, acts abnormally upon the stomach itself, and sets up various disorders of that organ and of the intestines. Such a mode of nursing is little better than the " Gampish " trick of sticking into the child's mouth a raisin in a piece of muslin to "keep it quiet." They are alike occasions to evade the duty of really hand-nursing and carrying the child in arms.

BEEF TEA is the staple of existence in many cases of illness; it is food and physic both in some fevers. It must be most carefully made, on Liebig's principles. The heat employed should not exceed 150°. A thermometer, however, is not commonly at hand, but the meat should be cut up small and

merely covered with water, in a bottle jar, in a sauce pan with
cold water, near a fire, so as not to allow it to boil, but merely
to stew for three or four hours.   The fat may be separated by
allowing it to get cold and then skimming it off.   Mutton-broth
might be made on the same plan, and would be more nourishing than that commonly made.

In the ordinary way of making beef tea, by boiling lumps
of meat, a strong jelly may be formed, and is supposed to show
its strength; but each lump is really case-hardened, and the
most nourishing part locked up in each piece.   The explana-
tion is that flesh consists largely of albumen, which coagulates
at 150° F.; therefore the boiling temperature, 212° F.,
hardens the outer part at once, and slowly the interior.   To
give a culinary illustration, the best way to cook a boiled joint
of meat is to put it into water already boiling, and continue
boiling the requisite time; the outside is at once hardened, and
the gravy is locked up inside.

EGGS.—For the same reason the white of eggs, which consists wholly of albumen, is a most excellent medium of nutriment, where, for any reason, beef tea cannot be given.   The
white of egg stirred into cold or lukewarm milk can often be
given to children or other patients who refuse beef tea.   It is
tasteless and colorless, therefore its presence can be disguised;
whereas the yolk of egg contains fatty matters with albumen,
and is easily recognized by the child both from its color and
its flavor.

WATER, either as an ordinary article of diet or a means of
allaying the thirst in febrile states, requires that great care
shall be taken to ensure that it shall be free from impurities.
The most dangerous impurities to which water is obnoxious
are gaseous matters, and insoluble animal and vegetable matters.   Gaseous matters and vapors are readily absorbed by
water, as seen in the ordinary experience of placing a basin or
tub of water in a newly painted room, whereby the smell of the
paint is quickly removed.   Water, by reason of the same property, should never be drank from a cistern into which there is
a waste pipe having a direct communication with a drain or
reservoir.   The poisonous gases arising from the decomposing
sewage are absorbed by the water, which thus becomes the
vehicle for the conveyance of the poison of malignant fevers.

The decomposing animal and saline matters of sewage also
readily percolate a porous soil; so that if a well and cesspool
be near one another, as is often the case both in town and
country, the water becomes the channel through which deadly
poison is carried.

Rain water received into leaden cisterns, or water in tanks
having leaden pipes leading from them, is often contaminated

by a portion of that metal becoming oxidized and dissolved, **producing** colic and other signs of lead poisoning.

For ordinary domestic purposes, water is classed as hard or soft. The latter is rain water; the former spring or river water. These vary much in their degree of hardness, as may readily be noticed by their behavior with soap. With hard water the soap does not readily make a lather, but curdles on the hand. The source of hardness of water is in the lime and other salts that are dissolved out of the strata of the earth through which it has passed. These may be separated to a considerable extent by boiling, or by the addition of small quantities of bicarbonate of soda. This is the object of some persons who put a small portion of bicarbonate of soda into the teapot when making tea.

Insoluble impurities can be separated by filters, or by any arrangement by which it is made to pass through fine sand or broken charcoal. The charcoal has the property of absorbing gases from water and rendering it sweet and pure.

In the treatment of disease, water is of primary importance, as it allays thirst and fever by diluting the blood and giving the medium by which a poison may be eliminated from the system. In fever and in cholera thirst is often the one great complaint, and the cry is for water ! water ! This indication of nature may safely be followed, and the patient allowed to drink as freely as he will.

Water is the chief of diuretics; it increases the secretion of urine, and promotes thereby the evacuation of effete or irritant matters from the blood.

FARINACEOUS FOODS.—Farinaceous foods should be cautiously given to young infants. Neither the secretion of the saliva in the mouth, nor of the gastric juice in the stomach, is adapted for their digestion. Among the farinaceous foods, suitable for young children, are baked flour, corn flour, biscuit powder, arrowroot, ground root, etc. It is not possible to say in which case each of these may be most suitable; what may be easily digested by one child may not agree with another, or with the same child for long together. After five or six months a crust may be given, but should be carefully watched. When some teeth are cut, the admixture of solids may occasionally be permitted; but, even when all the teeth are cut, it is advisable only to give meat every other or every third day. Soups, beef tea, etc., may be given at other times.

GENERAL DIET.—It is scarcely necessary here to enter upon the diet for adults in health, as this will depend very much upon the pursuits and inclinations of each. It is well known that those who work hard can generally eat well without much regard to what is put before them—"Hunger is their best sauce."

It may suffice to offer a few remarks on the digestibility of some article of food as a guide to invalids, and with reference to the diet recommended under the several headings of disease in the following pages.

It may be stated generally that beef is less digestible than mutton, especially for persons subject to dyspepsia. Beef is more easily digested cold than hot by delicate stomachs. Both these meats will require upwards of three hours for digestion. Salt beef will demand twice the time. Veal, lamb, and young meat generally, is not so easy of digestion as the meat of animals killed at maturer age. Pork in any form is less readily digested than other meats.

FOWLS, POULTRY, GAME, though generally regarded as light and digestible, are not always so in the cases of the invalid or convalescent; they are not wholly digested much under four or five hours.

FISH, especially the white sorts, are easy of digestion, according as they are plainly cooked. Salted fish are more slowly digested fish, as also are those that are fat, such as salmon. Much depends, however, upon the cooking, and of the adjuncts, the sauces, etc.

Melted butter is usually taken with fish, but is better omitted when they are food of the invalid. Butter, when melted, or prepared in any way over fire, readily becomes altered in its composition, and yields various fatty acids, which are the sources of indigestion. This is more especially the case with pastry, such as short pie-crust, etc. For the delicate stomach, fish cannot be too plainly and simply cooked; under these circumstances they form a light and nutritious diet.

SHELL FISH, including under the term oysters, mussels, whelks, lobsters, crabs, are more or less difficult of digestion, and unsuitable for invalids. Oysters are, perhaps, the least open to the objection, but they require three or four hours' digestion, and are not the light nourishment usually supposed, unless very carefully cooked. Sweetbread and tripe are easy of digestion, as also are the brains of animals. Liver and kidneys are the reverse of digestible.

RIPE FRUITS AND VEGETABLES are more easily digested than any of the preceding articles; but then, as they consist of a large proportion of water, they are not so nourishing as animal substances. Vegetarians supplement the deficient nutritive qualities of vegetables by a liberal allowance of animal matter in the shape of eggs and milk.

CHEESE, being almost entirely an albuminous substance, contains a very large amount of nutriment; but, from this element being combined with the fatty acids and some of the oily constituents of milk, it is not easily digested by weak stomachs when taken alone. It nevertheless is often useful in prompting the digestion of other food, to which it sometimes acts after the manner of a ferment when taken in small quantities; for instance, after dinner.

Sausage, when fresh, are not unwholesome, and they contain a large quantity of nourishment in a compact form.

ALCOHOLIC STIMULANTS.—The treatment of disease, and more particularly of convalescence, can scarcely be conducted without the adminstration of stimulants; but it is obvious that it should be accompanied with emphatic caution lest the use grow into the abuse thereof. An occasional dose may soon become the habitual dram, unless self-denial and self-control be exercised.

We are not here called upon to follow in the wake of those who feel it their duty to expose the errors and weaknesses of their neighbors; suffice it that we admit that in all directions we see too free indulgence in alcoholic stimulation. There can be no two opinions upon that point. There is no amount of health or wealth that cannot or will not surely be destroyed by any one who determinedly gives himself up to drink.

The medicinal uses of stimulants are most found in chronic disease, or in acute disease occuring in extremely debilitated states. It is greviously to be lamented that the medical recommendation of stimulants is not always sufficiently guarded and watched. There has been of late a fashion to regard and to teach that all disease proceeds from debility, and therefore that it must be treated with alcoholic stimulants. Allowing (which we do not) that such might be the case, yet the inference that alcohol is the remedy is by no means conclusive. A supply of wholesome nourishment with avoidance of the causes of disease, and bodily and mental rest, will be surer in their present effects and safer in future results. Few medical practitioners can pass many years, or even months, without meeting with the melancholy results of intemperance that began with the medicinal use of brandy and water, champagne, etc. The possibility is here referred to simply as a warning to those who, consulting these pages, may feel justified in advising the use of alcoholic stimulants as a means of combating disease, lest they forget to look also to the discontinuance of their use. As regards the dietic use of alcoholic stimulants, we have only a few words to add to the caution already given.

MALT LIQUORS are, as a general rule, the most wholesome of alcoholic beverages. The alcohol is in them so combined with saccnarine matter and tonic vegetable principles that it can only be separated by a distillation destructive of all other qualities. A small quantity of mild ale or porter, taken with dinner and supper, or luncheon and dinner, supports the strength, and supplies wear and tear.

WINES resemble malt liquors in that, when pure, the alcohol is in a state of chemical combination that can only be superceded by destructive distillation. They have not, however, so much solid matter suspended in them as malt liquors. They are, for this reason, better suited to persons of weak digestive powers. The dietic and the therapeutic uses of wines must depend upon their percentage of alcohol, and upon the development in them of certain acids and spirituous combinations termed ethers, which constitute what judges of wine call the "bouquet." The proportion of unfermented sugar also is a point to be considered in selecting wine for invalids.· Thus, there are sweet and astringent wines, as there are red and white wines, and there are wines in which the fermentations of the sugar is checked, and the sparkling of effervescing wine is produced.

Effervescing wines, champagne and Moselle, are among the most valuable wines for medicinal purposes. The free carbonic acid they contain renders them very serviceable in sickness and vomiting, while the alcohol, being in some peculiar state of combination, is more volatile, acts as a more rapid stimulant, effects passing off more rapidly than those of other and stronger wines.

Astringent wines, such as Burgundy, Hungarian, Bordeaux, etc., are less liable to ferment in the stomach. Port, Madeira, sherry, Marsala, are all stronger wines, and are said to be highly brandied, and therefore less wholesome for ordinary consumption; but they are (if moderately good) more useful for medicinal purposes than the lighter wines, which may be safer for daily use dietically. In this matter, however, as in many others where eating and drinking are concerned, quantity is often a more important element in the question than quality. There is, moreover, so much in fashion that it is almost impossible to say which wines are best. Moderation is the golden rule.

SPIRITS, the type of which may be taken to be brandy, are only of value as medicinal agents, and for these purposes they are sometimes invaluable—e. g., in low fevers, in some inflammations, and in state of debility, in sickness, and generally as indicated under the several headings of diseases in the preceding pages. We have no hesitation in affirming that raw or diluted raw spirits can never be advantageously used merely as ordinary beverages by those who can obtain wholesome malt liquor or wines.

The habit of spirit-drinking (as grog every night) as practiced by many "very respectable people" in the middle classes, is not one whit morally or physically better than the habits of the poor besotted creatures who swarm in and out of the London gin palaces. With the moral aspects of the habit it may be said that we are not concerned, but of the physical aspects we feel morally bound by a solemn responsibility to speak. From our own personal observations we would warn all whom it may concern, that the "night-cap," as it is miscalled, gradually generates disease of the brain, liver, kidneys, with all the horrible train of diseases—delirium, paralysis, dropsy, *cum multis aliis*.

MEDICINES AND THEIR DOSES.

Over and above the physical and psychological agencies which have been referred to in various parts of these remarks, we have now to advise with our readers on the pharmaceutical means of combating disease—means which are commonly regarded as the most direct and indispensible for the purpose of modifying or arresting morbid processes. That the swallowing of drugs, however, is not the whole therapeutics will have been seen throughout these pages; as, nevertheless, their judicious use allays suffering, shortens the course of disease, and promotes restoration to health, we have selected for notice some which we deem most useful, pointing out their most prominent properties, or most common uses.

The appropriate doses are stated under three periods of life—viz.: infancy, childhood, adult age. The doses that are herein advised are quite within the limits of heroic treatment, and may be given with confidence as not unduly large. Where a blank is left, under the head of doses, it is implied that the medicine is not suited for young children. The frequency with which the dose is to be repeated mus be learnt from the instructions given under each disease.

LIST OF MEDICINES.*

Name.	Property.	Doses.			Uses and Mode of] Use.
		Infancy.	Child-hood.	Adult Age.	
Acetate of ammonia, solution of, or Mindererus spirit	†Diuretic, †Diaphoretic	—	2 drms	¼ ounce	In febrile complaints, catarrh, etc.
Aloes	Purgative	—	2 to 5 grains	5 to 10 grains.	As a purge for worms, or for ꞌmmon costiveness.
Aloes, decoction of	Ditto	—	½ ounce	1 ounce	Ditto.

* In preparing or dispensing medicines, weights and measures should be used whenever practicable. They can be purchased of chemists. A graduated wineglass is a safe guide, as it is more definite than the use of spoons in administering medicines. At the same time it is advisable to procure a small glass measure for minims, or drops. It should be observed that the "minim" as measured is equal to two drops from the mouths of many bottles.

† Diuretic, acting on the kidney; Diaphoretic, promoting respiration.

Name.	Property.	Doses.			Uses and Mode of Use.
		Infancy.	Child-hood.	Adult Age.	
Alum	Tonic and astringent	1 to 3 grains	3 to 5 grains	5 to 10 grains	In hæmorrhage,diarrhœa whooping-cough. Dissolved in water. As a gargle. Ten g·ains to the ounce of water. As a lotion for the eyes. Two grains to the ounce of water.
Ammonia, carbonate of	Stimulant	1 grain	2 grains	5 grains	In scarlet fever, dyspepsia, in chronic cough. Dissolved in water.
Ammonia, compound spirit of	Stimulant	5 drops	10 to 20 drops	20 to 60 drops	In debility, spasms, hysteria, fainting. Taken with cold water.
Arsenical solution	Tonic	—		5 drops	Skin diseases and neuralgia. To be taken in water with or after a meal.
Bark, compound tincture of	Tonic	10 to 15 drops	15 to 20 drops	20 to 60 drops	Debility, fevers, ague. Taken in water.
Belladonna, extract of	Sedative	—	—	—	As an external application. To be smeared on the painful part.
Bicarbonate of soda	Antacid	2 to 5 grains	5 to 10 grains	10 to 30 grains	In dyspepsia. Dissolved in water Mixed with citric or tartaric acid, forms effervescing draught.
Bicarbonate of potash	Ditto	2 grains	5 to 10 grains	20 grains	Ditto.
Bismuth, nitrate of	Tonic and astringent	1 to 2 grains	3 to 5 grains	5 to 8 grains	Diarrhœa, dyspepsia.
Bitter sweet (dulcamara)	Tonic	—	—	2 ounces	Skin diseases. The stalks boiled in water, viz.: 1 ounce to a pint and a half boiled to 1 pint.
Borax, powdered	—	—	—	—	Used for thrush; mixed with honey, and applied to the tongue, etc.
Bromide of potass	Tonic and sedative	—	5 grains	15 to 30 grains	Epilepsy and other nervous affections. The dose requires to be gradually increased. Taken dissolved in water
Calomel	Purgative and absorbent	1 grain	2 grains	3 to 5 grains.	Inflammations, biliary disorders, constipation. May be given as a powder or made up into pill.
Camphor spirit or liniment	Stimulant	—	—	—	This medicine is used for external application.
Cantharides or blistering liquid or plaster	Stimulant	—	—	—	For external application only.
Capsicum, tincture	—	—	—	—	Useful as an addition to gargles, in proportion of half a drachm to a six ounce gargle.
Carbolic acid	Stimulant disinfectant	—	—	—	For external application as lotions; and in carbolic acid soap for skin diseases.
Castor oil	Purgative	1 drachm	2 drachm	4 drms to 1 ounce	
Catechu tincture	Astringent	—	20 minims	30 to 60 minims	Diarrhœa — with chalk mixture.

| Name. | Property. | Doses. | | | Uses and Mode of Use. |
		Infancy.	Child-hood.	Adult Age.	
Chalk	Astringent and ant-acid	5 grains	5 grains	10 to 30 grains	Diarrhœa. Made into mixture with sugar water.
Chloral (hy-drate	Narcotic	—	2 to 5 grains	10 to 30 grains	Whooping-cough, sleep-lessness, spasmodic disease. This medicine has more effect in producing sleep than in relieving pain. Dissolve in water. This medicine should be given with great caution.
Chlorate of po-tass	Sedative	1 to 3 grains	3 to 5 grains	5 to 10 grains	In ulceration of the mouth. Dissolved in water.
Chloric ether	Stimulant, antispas-modic	—	5 drops	10 to 30 drops	In painful and spasmodic diseases. Taken with water.
Citric acid	—	—	—	20 grains	To form effervescing draughts with 20 grains of bicarbonate of soda or potash, each dissolved in a separate wine glass of water.
Citrate of iron	Tonic	2 grains	3 grains	5 grains	Debility. Dissolved in water.
Cod liver oil	Tonic and nutritive	½ dram	½ dram	½ to 1 drachm	In debility and wasting diseases. Taken in orange wine or some other simple fluid directly after meals.
Colchicum wine	Purgative and diuretic	—	—	15 to 30 drops	Rheumatism and gout.
Confection of senna (leni-tive electu-ary)	Aperient	—	—	—	In piles or constipation. A teaspoonful for a dose.
Creosote	Astringent	—	1 drop	2 to 5 drops	Vomiting or diarrhœa. In water.
	Stimulant	—	—	—	As a stimulant lotion mixed with water.
Dandelion (tar-axacum), ex-tract of	Aperient	—	—	1 drachm	In bilious disorders. Mixed with water, or the roots boiled in water.
Dover's pow-der	Narcotic, sedative, diapho-retic	—	2 grains	5 to 10 grains	In catarrh, diarrhœa, rheumatism. As this medicine contains opium, it should not be given to infants.
Epsom salts	Aperient	½ dram	2 drms	2 to 8 drachms or 1 oz	In cold water.
Ether	Stimulant antispas-modic	—	10 drops	30 to 40 drops	In hysteria, spasms, fainting. Taken in water.
Friar's balsam	Stimulant	—	—	10 to 30 drops	For chronic coughs. Taken in gum water.
	Styptic	—	—	—	Useful for cuts, applied on lint or rag.
Gallic and tan-ic acids	Astringent	—	3 grains	5 grains	In hæmorrhages. Made into pills, or mixed with gum water.
Gentian, tinc-ture of	Tonic	—	—	1 drachm	Debility and dyspepsia. In water.

Name.	Property.	Doses.			Uses and Mode of Use.
		Infancy.	Child-hood.	Adult Age.	
Goulard's extract and lotion, (*extract of lead*)	—	—	—	—	One drachm added to a pint of rain water, or distilled water, forming a good cooling lotion.
Grey powder (*mercury and chalk*)	Aperient	1 grain]	2 grains	5 grains	In sugar or treacle.
Guaiacum, tincture of	Stimulant and tonic	—	—	1 drachm	In chronic rheumatism. Taken in milk, or water.
Hemlock extract of	Sedative	—	2 grains	5 grains	In spasmodic and neuralgiac or other painful complaints; as pills.
Henbane, extract of	Sedative	—	—	3 to 5 grains	As a pill.
Iodide of potass	Absorbent and tonic	1 grain	2 grains	5 to 10 grains	In chronic rheumatism and glandular disease. Dissolved in water.
Iodine, tincture of	Absorbent and stimulant	—	—	—	For external application in glandular or other chronic enlargments. Apply with a feather or brush.
Iodide of iron, syrup of	Tonic	—	½ dram	1 drachm	In strumous disorders or debility.
Ipecacuanha wine	Emetic	1 drachm	1 drachm	1 drachm	When given as emetic, the dose should be repeated every five or ten minutes until the vomiting begins.
	Expectorant	2 drops	3 to 5 drops	5 to 15 drops	For coughs and colds.
Ipecacuanha powder	Emetic	—	—	20 to 30 grains	In warm water, followed by copious draughts of water to promote vomit
Iron, muriated tincture of	Tonic	2 drops	5 drops	2 to 30 drops	In water, to which sugar is added in the case of children.
Iron or steel wine	Tonic	½ dram	1 drachm	—	
Jalap powder	Purgative	—	5 grains	10 to 30 grains	
James's powder	Diaphoretic	1 grain	2 grains	3 to 5 grains	In catarrh and simple fever.
Laudanum (*tincture of opium*)	Narcotic	—	—	10 to 40 drops	For pains, spasms, or cramps; in water.
Lead, acetate	Astringent	—	1 grain	2 grains	In hæmorrhages. As a pill, made up with moist bread crumbs.
Magnesia, carbonate of	Aperient and antacid	2 to 5 grains	5 grains	½ dram	Dyspepsia and costiveness.
Manna	Aperient	½ dram	1 drachm	—	Mixed with food of an infant.
Matico	Astringent and styptic	—	—	—	Applied on lint or wool, if in form of tincture, or the dry leaf applied on a cut.
Mercurial pill ("*blue pill*")	Aperient	—	—	3 to 5 grains	
Mercury and chalk [*see* Grey powder]					
Morphia, muriate or acetate	Narcotic	—	—	¼ to ½ grain	Only for severe pain. Not to be given to infants or young children.

Name.	Property.	Doses.			Uses and Mode of Use.
		Infancy.	Child-hood.	Adult Age.	
Muriatic acid (*diluted,* 1 *part to* 10 *of water.*)	Tonic	—	15 drops	20 drops	In debility, indigestion, diarrhœa. In two or three tablespoonfuls of water.
	Astringent	—	—	—	As a gargle for sore throat. One part to twenty of water.
Nitre powder	Diuretic	1 grain	2 grains	5 to 10 grains	In febrile disorders and dropsies.
	Stimulant	—	—	1 drachm	As a gargle, dissolved in six ounces of water.
Nitre (*sweet spirit of nitrous ether*)	Diuretic	—	10 to 20 drops	30 to 60 drops	Catarrh and febrile complaints.
Nitric acid (*diluted with* 10 *parts of water*)	Tonic	—	5 drops	15 drops	Debility, sore throat, etc. Same as muriatic acid.
Opodeldoc (*soap liniment*)	—	—	—	—	For external application.
Opium	Narcotic	—	—	½ to 1 gr	In painful disorders; for sickness and diarrhœa.
Oxide of zinc	Tonic and stimulant	—	—	—	Most commonly used in ointment, or dusted on the surface.
Oxymel of squills.	Diuretic, expectorant	—	½ dram	1 drachm	For coughs. Mixed with paregoric or ipecacuanha wine.
Paregoric	Sedative diaphoretic	—	10 drops	20 to 60 drops	Catarrhs and coughs alone, or as above in water.
Potash, solution of	Absorbent and antacid	5 drops	10 drops	10 to 20 drops	Dyspepsia and chronic glandular enlargements Taken in water.
Quinine	Tonic	½ grain	1 grain	2 to 5 grains	Debility, ague—in water, or made into pills.
Rhubarb powder	Aperient	1 grain	2 to 5 grains	5 to 20 grains	
Ditto, tincture	—	—	2 drms	2 drs to 1 oz.	
Salvolatile, spirits of (*see* Ammonia)					
Santonin	Purgative for worms	3 grains	3 to 5 grains	—	Three doses should be given on alternate mornings, in milk or water.
Senna, infusion of	Aperient	2 drms	½ ounce	1 ounce	Infusion made by pouring hot water on the leaves, and let stand until cold.
Sulphuric acid (*diluted with* 10 *parts of water*)	Tonic	—	5 drops	15 drops	In debility and dyspepsia.
	Astringent	—	5 drops	15 drops	Hæmorrhage, diarrhœa, cholera, night sweats. Taken with a wineglass of water.
Tartar emetic	Diaphoretic, depressing	—	—	⅛ to ¼ grain	In febrile and inflammatory disorders. Dissolved in water. Used also in form of ointment.
Turpentine, spirits of	Purgative stimulant	—	—	1 to 2 drachms	For tape-worm. Taken fasting in the morning in milk or water.

| Name. | Property. | Doses. | | | Uses and Mode of Use. |
		Infancy.	Child-hood.	Adult Age.	
Zinc, sulphate of	Astringent	—	—	5 to 20 drops	Hœmorrhage. Taken in water.
	Stimulant	—	—	—	For external use as liniment or stupes.
	Tonic, astringent	—	¼ grain	¼ to ½ grain	In chorea and other nervous affections.
	Emetic	—	—	20 grains	In cases of poisoning. Dissolved in water.

ARTICLES SUITABLE FOR A MEDICINE CHEST

Acetate of ammonia, or Mindererus spirit.
Acetate of lead.
Adhesive plaster.
Aloes.
Alum.
Bark, compound tincture of
Basilicon ointment.
Bicarbonate of soda.
Blistering plaster, or liquid.
Borax.
Calomel.
Carbonate of ammonia.
Carded wool.
Carded oakum. "Stypium."
Castor oil.
Catechu, tincture of
Chalk, prepared.
Cod liver oil.
Compound colocynth pills.
Compound rhubarb pills.

Creasote.
Diluted sulphuric acid.
Dover's powder.
Epsom salts.
Ether.
Forceps of different sizes.
Glass measures.
Grey powder, or mercury with chalk.
Iodide of potassium.
Iodine, tincture of.
Ipecacuanha powder.
Ipecacuanha wine.
Iron, muriated tincture of
Jalap.
James's powder.
Laudanum.
Linseed meal.
Lint.
Lunar caustic.
Magnesia.

Mortars and pestles.
Nitre, powdered.
Nitre, spirits of.
Oil silk, or gutta percha tissue.
Opodeldoc.
Oxide of zinc.
Paregoric.
Peppermint, essence of.
Quinine.
Rhubarb powder.
Scales and weights.
Scissors.
Senna leaves.
Spatulas.
Tartaric acid.
Tincture of benzoin, or Friar's balsam.
Turpentine, spirits of.
Zinc, sulphate of.
Zinc, oxide of.